A Hanging

—— in the ——

Lowcountry

Keith Farrell

A Hanging

——— in the ———

Lowcountry

Keith Farrell

Published by Evening Smoke Publishing, a Conversation Publishing LLC imprint
Charleston, SC

Printed in the United States of America.
First paperback edition August 2022.

Jacket and layout design by G Sharp Design, LLC.
www.gsharpmajor.com

ISBN 979-8-9852879-2-9 (paperback)
ISBN 979-8-9852879-3-6 (ebook)

THE ROPE WAS blue-braided nylon. It was tied around a fallen tree as an anchor and then run up and over the thickest branch of an old willow tree, where it was used to hang a young Black boy. From the ground, he almost seemed to be floating; the thin blue line around his throat was barely visible.

Charleston police and the county sheriff's department had both responded to an anonymous tip that a young Black man had been lynched on a patch of undeveloped land in the plantation district. There, officers had found Devon Grey, stripped naked and hanging at the end of the blue nylon rope. A symbol carved into the tree was identified by one officer as having links to a local white supremacist group. It looked like a weird letter Y inside a triangle. That confirmed everyone's suspicions as to the motive for the horrendous deed.

Everyone could already feel it. Hours before Devon Grey's body would be cut down from that tree, everyone there knew exactly what it meant for Charleston. Recent national events had all but guaranteed it. The city's complicated and unfortunate history would be dragged up once again and thrust into the national spotlight. Twilight was already creeping through the clouds, and by noon, reporters would be pouring in from around the country. Soon protesters would be demonstrating, and then the racist, far-right counter-protesters would crawl out of their holes.

Devon swayed in the trees, stripped of all his humanity; bloated, bloodied, and stiff. The officers below tried not to let the sight bother them. Some even told jokes. When someone asked who was going to get coffee, one quipped that he would because it beat *"hanging around"* there. Some seemed almost hostile—as if it were an inconvenience that would ruin their days and weeks to come. For many, however, there was sadness. How could something like this still happen in this day and age?

The city had prided itself on moving forward but this hanging was a grim reminder of the past that haunted the so-called jewel of the South. Like the fingerprints of the children born into bondage, left indelibly in the bricks that comprised its historic downtown, it seemed hatred had left a lasting mark on Charleston, and no matter how distant and forgotten those marks became, their hold on the city would not fade. All the regal city streets, romantic carriage rides, historic homesteads, and stately manors could never change the story of those bricks.

Now Devon Grey was gone, his story just another chapter in an endless book of Black lives stolen away since the first ship of enslaved men docked at Charleston's ports. A book of men, women, and children whose lives were ended in hatred, often at the end of a rope or a police officer's gun.

Many may have felt the significance of that moment as they gazed upon that heinous scene. However, none could have known just how impactful the hanging of Devon Grey would become for not only the city but the entire country.

1

"YOU'RE YOUNG," REMARKED FBI Assistant Deputy Director Alden Travers. "I mean, younger than expected. Graduated top of your class at Johnson and Wales," he read from the file as he spoke, without so much as a glance at the man sitting on the other side of his desk. "Made quite the name for yourself with that Castile case last year."

"Just doing my job, sir," special agent Daren Renard said plainly. He stared straight ahead, like a prized stallion awaiting judgment. He had dirty blonde hair, blue eyes, and fair skin with a muscular build.

"Cases like that are increasingly important due to the…" Travers put down the file and glanced at the ceiling as if he were searching for the right words. "Political climate."

"Cases of a racial nature," Renard clarified.

"Yes, well, particularly cases of a racial nature that are in the public spotlight. Cases where the narrative can get away from us. The country's come a long way since Jim Crow," Travers said, giving Renard's file one more glance. "We can't let a few incidents drag us backward. It's important that we get the facts and not let social outrage influence our rule of law."

"Of course," Renard nodded affirmatively.

"I think someone like yourself understands the delicate nature of such cases when it comes to the job we have to do."

"I just do what I'm told and close cases, sir."

"Perfect," Travers said with noticeably fake enthusiasm. "I'm sure you've heard what's been going on down in South Carolina."

"The shooting death of the sheriff's deputy, sir?"

"Situation is getting out of control. The whole area has been a goddamn tinder box since that kid was hanged back in January. Devon Grey. The whole thing has inflamed some deep-seated issues for those communities. It's a fucking mess. Protests, counter-protests, accusations of police misconduct. Now, this guy opens fire on a squad car and kills a cop. I don't have to tell you how bad this can get. The Black community is raising hell that eight months later, the police have made no progress on the Grey murder. Our people worked with local investigators, questioned a bunch of Aryans and white supremacists but nothing panned out. Then the damn New York Times ran a story about how quickly we gave up on the case, and it makes us look like shit. That just threw gasoline onto the fire. Ever since there have been anti-police demonstrations. Is it any wonder someone decided to shoot a cop?"

"Why did we pull resources from the Grey case, sir?"

Travers flashed a shit-eating grin and cackled. "Needle in a haystack, Agent. That's what it's like sorting through good ole boys and violent racists down in South Carolina. Plus, the locals got really territorial with us. Best not to give them a heads up that you're coming down."

"What's my assignment?"

"Get down to Charleston and get a handle on what in God's name is happening down there. See if you can figure out what happened to this Grey kid. Maybe we can quell the flames a bit if we can close that case. Or at least a plausible theory. People want answers. Our first report on Grey was filed back in February; I'll be sure you get it. If you need any juice to get things done, let me know."

"I'll leave tonight," Renard said, rising to his feet like a soldier.

"Oh, and Agent Renard…" Travers added. "We're all concerned about how all this is going to land in the press. It's an election year and the president's critics will say these incidents are a reflection of his leadership. Just keep that in mind. If the opportunity comes up… a way for us to put a positive spin on this… I am sure he would be very grateful… and accommodating. And be sure to keep a low profile while you're there. We don't want you to become part of this story."

Renard nodded and then took his leave.

He went straight home following the meeting. His place was located in downtown D.C.; a two-room apartment, completely bare save for a recliner and a flat screen mounted to the wall. Once there, he laid out the items he would bring on his trip: three grey suits, two blue suits, a brown suit, and one pair of jeans. A stack of t-shirts, boxer briefs, shaving kit, socks, a Glock 17 .9mm, and two boxes of ammunition.

The assignment wasn't particularly interesting to him, but at least it would give him a break from the beltway. When he had first moved there, just over a year ago, the idea of living in the nation's capital had seemed exciting and romantic. The patriot in him felt a certain dignity passing iconic American landmarks on his way into the office every day. However, lately, he had begun to grow cynical of the place and the image it prided itself on. Everyone seemed primarily concerned only with their personal advancement. He often wondered if this was the only way to succeed in Washington.

It was a game of favors and pull—it mattered more *who* you knew, not what you knew. And what mattered even more than that was who owed you something. Daren was quite familiar with such transactional relationships. After all, he came from valued, blue-blooded stock. The Renards had quite the family name back home in Connecticut. His old man managed hedge funds in Stamford; another successful chapter in the esteemed family history. The family was old money, and as such, his parents had always held certain expectations of their children. Younger generations were told from an early age that it was their responsibility to carry on the line of Renard greatness. Being in law enforcement wasn't exactly what they'd had in mind. Perhaps, if he was honest with himself, disappointing them made his job all the more enjoyable. He was their eldest son, and he was but a lowly public servant. It was a fact Mavis and Bob never seemed eager to discuss during the holidays.

After packing, Daren booked a seat on the next flight to Charleston. It departed from Reagan a couple of hours later with a stop-over in Atlanta. He was well-traveled but was largely unfamiliar with the South. He'd passed through once or twice, even stopped over in Charleston once. Something about it had always felt alluring as if parts were taken from another time.

In a way, the past offered a romantic tale of the country's origins, forged in rebellion against tyranny, and carved unwillingly from an untamed continent. Daren possessed an affinity for the history of early America that was still reflected in the city's architecture and culture. Yet he knew the romanticism and glorification could not wipe away the shameful, cruel, and bloodied parts of that same history. Perhaps it was easier for people who didn't live in places where that bloody history had forever reshaped the cultural and economic reality to look past those details.

In the South, many people wanted to forget and move past that history. Those who still lived with the legacy and effects of hatred and systemic racism, however, obviously felt differently. And while they couldn't disagree more with the former group, those who saw the Confederacy and the War as their heritage and cultural identity agreed that the past should not be forgotten. Both groups found value in preserving the history of the area, but each had very different ideas on what should be preserved and why. Regardless, the effects of the Civil War and that history of oppression were present in the daily lives of South Carolinians, whether they chose to embrace it, fight against it, or ignore it.

Hours later, Daren was on his way. As he flew over the Palmetto state, he gazed out the window at the vast nothingness below. The majority of South Carolina, aside from the shore and areas around the capital, was sparsely inhabited, undeveloped, and poor. Trailer parks and stretches of wilderness—brackish marshes laced between forests and barely existent towns and cities marred by the rusted remnants of their industrial past. Here a different kind of historic preservation was occurring; the inevitable result of the absence of any progress.

Charleston, however, had not been left behind like the rest of the state. While it had retained some of the elegance and charm of a historic city, economic development and modernity had fueled a period of constant growth for more than two decades. A quaint urban center was surrounded by bustling suburban towns, a thriving shoreline, and beautiful beaches. Charleston was a go-to destination for both tourists and northerners fleeing cold weather and higher taxes.

The plane touched down and Daren was soon making his way through the terminal. Charleston's airport had a very classy and modern feel for its relatively small size. The seating for passengers was quaint and comfy, like a coffee house. It seemed like a place young people might hang out on a weekend. Soft jazz played over the PA speakers. Nothing about it felt particularly southern.

As Daren exited the secured area by the terminals and entered the part of the airport that was open to the public, he noticed a large room with glass walls. Inside, pictures and personal items memorialized the six members of the local African Methodist Episcopal church who had been shot and killed three years earlier when a white supremacist had opened fire on their Sunday service. The brutal and senseless killings shocked the community and the nation. An outpouring of unity and collective grief followed as the city came together in the aftermath of the crisis.

Over the years since, a growingly polarized national climate and a string of highly publicized racial incidents, including several questionable killings of Black men by police, had slowly eroded that unity. The killings of Devon Grey and Sergeant Gregory Noonan had further exacerbated an already volatile social climate, and Charleston was ground zero.

Daren stopped and looked at the pictures of the victims of the AME attack. He could not imagine the hate required to commit such a heinous act—hatred enough to kill someone just because of the color of their skin. When it had happened, Daren had told himself it was just one crazy man—a tragic event but nothing indicative of any larger social issue. Then the marches started; mobs of angry white men with torches shouting racist chants, defending their "heritage." And then the violence started.

He stayed at the memorial for some time, considering what about it bothered him so much. He thought about the Castile case he had worked on—he had done what he was told but still had his doubts.

He considered if that case and these deaths were related. Unsure what exactly was bothering him about it, he left the memorial and headed for baggage claim.

Andrea awoke with dread in her heart. What little rest she had managed was not enough to relieve the exhaustion she always carried. The arrival of a new day only promised more stress, more tragedy, and more pain. She felt the immediate urge to flee. It was here, in her own home, where she was completely safe, that she felt the most uneasy, particularly in the mornings. Each day when she awoke, she found herself full of anxiety; her mind constantly worried and filled with grim thoughts. The expectations she couldn't meet. The relationships she didn't know how to manage. The inescapable sensation that she was always at risk.

"Mommy! Mommy! I have to go soon!" Marcus pleaded from her bedroom doorway. "Get out of bed!"

"Okay, sweetheart. Let Gram get you ready. I'll be out in a minute." She tried her best to sound sweet and motherly. She really wanted to tell the child to leave her alone, and she hated herself for feeling that way. Lately, she always felt so overwhelmed, and her emotional capacity was too low to be the person and the mother she wanted to be.

She threw her robe on and tried not to think about her feelings. Work had always been an escape for her. There she felt like she knew who she was—there she had a purpose and knew what to do. Focus and purpose made the noise fade. It helped her feel normal. It was cathartic and almost therapeutic doing what she did. It felt as if she could heal her wounds by tending to the pain of others.

"He needs lunch money today," Gram told her when she finally showed herself at the breakfast table.

"Why can't he take a lunch?" Andrea asked.

"It's a field trip!" Marcus exclaimed.

"Eat your cereal. Hurry up," Gram instructed him.

"Take the money from the change jar," Andrea grumbled.

She poured herself a cup of coffee and opened the fridge to retrieve the milk.

"We're out of milk," Gram informed her. "You'll have to settle for black."

Andrea sighed and shut the fridge door with frustration. Marcus stared at her with unease.

"Hurry up and eat, child!" Gram chided.

"I have to get dressed," Andrea muttered, taking her black coffee back to her bedroom.

Their North Charleston apartment wasn't much to look at. Uneven walls with sheetrock that failed to meet the floor—ample passage for roaches or even rats. Wiring hung loosely from the ceiling tiles of a poorly installed drop ceiling. The windows were too old to hold back the elements. The drywall was cracked, the countertops worn through, and the linoleum peeled and curled. The complex it was located in was in a similar state of disrepair. Built in the 1980s, it housed low-income families and the elderly.

It was cramped, too. Andrea and Marcus took the bedrooms, while Gram slept on the couch. The three of them made do with a tiny bathroom with unreliable plumbing. On weekends, Andrea would drive their laundry down the block to the North Chuck Wash and Go. That and her late-night trips to the bar were the only times she ever used her car. Most of the time, she left it with Gram, so she could bring Marcus to school and drive him to soccer practice—leave it to her child to want to play the only sport not offered in North Charleston.

In the shower, Andrea closed her eyes and let the hot water embrace her. The heat comforted and soothed her, and she found herself unwilling to get out. Her son would be leaving any minute and would want to say goodbye, and then she would have to catch the bus to work. Begrudgingly, she turned off the water.

Marcus was a sweet boy, still as innocent as an eight-year-old should be. Andrea prided herself on that. Everything she had done, since the moment she had discovered she was pregnant, had been to protect him and enable that innocence. He didn't know about how ugly the world could be, how cruel people were, or how broken they could become. She didn't want him to see the world as a frightening place like she and Gram did—just as her mother had...

Gram did not agree. She saw the world as a dangerous place and felt that sheltering Marcus from that truth was failing to prepare him for the realities he would face. But for Andrea, there was still plenty of time to teach him about all that. For now, he was still young enough that he did not have to worry about it. Andrea had worked hard to ensure he didn't have to encounter it. That included sending him to school in Mount Pleasant, which required her to register him under her cousin's address. It wasn't technically legal, but it gave her son an advantage.

Getting Marcus back and forth to school was a bit of a chore. Gram was more than willing to help, happy to see her great-grandson get advantages she had been unable to provide to his mother. Though, she was skeptical of the white, upper-middle class environment.

"I love you, sweetheart," Andrea told Marcus by the door before he left. She kissed his cheek and wrapped her arms around him tightly. "You have a good day, okay?"

He nodded.

"Do you have your soccer stuff?"

"Yes," he replied, reaching for another hug.

"It's in the car," Gram assured her.

"Bye, mommy," Marcus whispered as they embraced.

Andrea rose to her feet and kissed Gram on the cheek. "Have a good day."

"You too, dear. Be safe," Gram said warily.

Once Gram and Marcus had left, Andrea retrieved a pack of cigarettes and a lighter from under the bathroom sink. She opened the bathroom window, turned on the exhaust fan, and lit a smoke. She sat on the toilet, blowing smoke out the window, and tried not to think about her life.

Her cell rang and she picked it up. "Yeah, what do you want, Paulson?" she asked, exhaling a waft of smoke.

"Good morning to you, too, sunshine," Captain Mitchell Paulson replied.

"I've got ten minutes before I have to leave to catch my bus. You're interrupting my me-time, captain. What is it?"

"Heaven forbid. Alright, listen, you know I don't give a shit about this but...."

"Oh, for Christ's sake."

"It's Deputy Chief Mulholland, Dre. I'm sorry. He says if you don't keep seeing Dr. Leigh, he's going to put you on leave."

Deputy Chief Marshall Mulholland's word was not questioned by those who knew what was good for them. It was rare to see a Black man climb the ranks at North Charleston PD, and Mulholland had done it at a time when it was even harder. He hadn't kissed ass or gotten dirty to get there, either, unlike some others. Marshall Mulholland made rank by working his ass off and slowly earning the respect of everyone in the department. To Andrea and many of the other Black officers, he was a mentor. Had anyone else tried to force her to see a therapist, she would have quit the damn job. But Marshall was different.

"Fine," she sighed. "I'll set something up next week."

"Sounds great to me, but the Deputy Chief says you're grounded till you see the doc."

"Are you fucking kidding me?"

"I know. I set up a 2'o'clock appointment for you. Why don't you stay home and take it easy till then?"

"Mitchell, you're kidding me."

"I'm sorry, Dre. Just go sit down with her and tell her your feelings for a half hour, alright? Can you do that for me?"

She hesitated but knew there was no fight to be had. "Fine."

"Then she'll clear you and we can do the Carson raid when you're done. Okay?"

"It's not like I have a choice."

"Just tell her what they want to hear. You know how this shit works. I'll see you later today."

"Promise you won't move on Carson without me."

"You have my word."

She hung up the phone and slammed her fist into her leg.

When the pain starts, the growth begins. The mantra was his father's by right and his through inheritance; carved into him, chip by chip, over the years. Pain is what separated men. Some avoided it their whole lives, others shouldered it silently. But some men, his father told him, actually thrived in pain. Pain is what had defined his old man and now, after thirty-eight years of life, David Sullivan finally understood his father, because he had finally learned to embrace pain.

Pain is where growth began. To get stronger—to be better—you have to accept the pain. Every day, David reminded himself of this in his garage, lifting weights until his muscles trembled and burned. He accepted it, just as he accepted the soreness that came later; it was proof he was getting stronger.

But the real pain was inside. Within him, there was enough pain to swallow a man whole. No matter how much he lifted, the anger, rage, and resentment remained. That too, he told himself, would make him stronger.

"Hey, love," Marie cooed cautiously from the doorway.

There it was again. The apprehension in her voice. As if he were so horrible, she could barely approach him. The implication angered him. He finished his set of curls and dropped the weights.

"Do you want me to make you breakfast before you go?" she asked softly.

He sighed and grabbed his towel from the bench, slowly wiping his head before turning to face her. "If you're going to make something, sure. But don't go out of your way for me," he replied.

"I'm making Sean pancakes," she said.

"That sounds great."

He came up the steps and met her at the doorway. He kissed her softly and ran his fingers through her hair. "Sorry, baby. It's been rough."

"Maybe you're not ready to go back," Marie suggested.

"You don't want me to go back," he responded defensively. "That's what this attitude I've been picking up on all week is about. Ain't that right?"

"I swear, the shit you get into your head," she scoffed, shaking her head as she walked back to the kitchen.

"Right, I must have imagined that shit the other day, about you not wanting to attend my funeral," he recounted, following her into the house.

"Right, I'm an asshole because I don't want you to get killed," she shot back, the calmness of her tone contrasting the seriousness of the matter. She was well accustomed to and unfazed by his emotional misfires.

"How's that supposed to make me feel?" he asked, speaking sternly but softly so the boy wouldn't hear.

"I'm sorry," she said, placing her hand softly on his chest. "Please, love. Let's not fight. I'm just worried about you. It's dangerous out there, and now your head isn't in the game…"

"I'm fine, baby," he insisted, taking her hand off his chest, grasping it tightly, and pressing it against his lips. "I promise."

"You just buried your partner and best friend; how can you be okay? Skip said you can take time if you need it. I don't know why you're rushing…"

"Everybody's different. I can't sit around the house anymore," he told her. "I feel like I'm going nuts. Better for me to get back into the routine."

"David…"

"*Don't, Marie.* Just don't. Fighting with you is not going to help. That's likely to distract me more than anything else."

The pattering of little feet rushing over the hardwood floor brought an end to the discussion.

"Daddy! Are you going to make it to practice later?" Sean asked, running into the kitchen. He was already wearing his soccer jersey.

"Well, don't I always?" David asked with a laugh, kneeling down and patting his son on the chest. "Still don't know why you didn't want to play football, or baseball even," he said with a slow shake of his head as he rose.

"You wanted your son to go to the best school," Marie reminded him. "The kids at his school like soccer. If you wanted him to play football, we should have stayed in North Charleston or moved to Summerville."

"I wanted him to have a good education. I didn't want him to be a pussy," David sneered.

Sean's excitement turned to shame. His head sank low.

"Oh honey, don't listen to him," his mother reassured him. "You know he's proud of how good you are."

"Damn straight," David replied, fixing his coffee with cream and sugar. "Might not be my idea of a great sport, but you got skills, kid." He could see Sean had taken his words hard and that was okay. The boy needed to be made strong. It sure as hell wasn't going to happen on any soccer team, or at that pansy-ass school he went to where they wanted to get rid of grades.

That was the way the world was now. Everyone and everything was soft and coddled. Everyone wanted to feel good all the time. They avoided pain and thus, they avoided growth. Society had grown weak. Growing up, there had been a certain order to things; socially, politically, and economically. Men were allowed to be men and people knew their place. Feelings were personal; things you shared with your priest, maybe, but that was it. Emotions weren't for public consumption and they certainly didn't earn anyone anything.

Now emotions seemed to run everything. How you felt was more important than what you knew. They wanted to get rid of grades.

Instead of measuring how kids were performing, they wanted to ask, how are the kids *feeling?* They wanted them to follow their aspirations, not prepare for working in the real world. They'd even stopped assigning homework, because heaven forbid, they cause the children any stress. What a joke.

Still, it was better than a public school, especially in a place like North Charleston, where his son would be thrown into an overcrowded classroom full of delinquents—the types of kids he'd be slapping handcuffs on in a few years. There he would have had to learn about the "value of diversity" and other useless politically correct garbage.

David had learned the value of diversity growing up as one of the only white kids in his neighborhood; a privilege that meant daily beatings. It didn't help that his father was a prison guard. The neighborhood boys saw them and the other guard families as a sort of white occupation force brought in to run the new prison.

While David believed the pain of his youth had made him the man he was today, he couldn't help but want better for his son. That was why he worked as hard as he could, doing whatever he could, so he could afford to buy their house in upscale Mount Pleasant; one of Charleston's most affluent areas.

And after all that—after all that he had worked for—they were trying to take it away from him. The city and the damn money-hungry developers continued to push for more housing developments. They wanted to turn his town into another North Charleston. In response, David had joined a group of local homeowners who were opposed to the new developments. They had successfully defeated a plan to build affordable rental properties in their community. However, the new site was just across the street and no more amenable to the local homeowners. Not only would those apartments bring down the market value of their homes, but they would also invite the exact type of people David had worked so hard to move away from. And with *those* people, drugs, crime, and depravity would follow.

David decided to take his bike to the station that morning. Charleston's beauty was never more profound than when the sun was rising over the Atlantic, bathing the city in orange and pink light. The rumble and roar of his Harley felt damn good between his legs—American-made power and strength. He felt like a cowboy riding a steel stead.

Marie hated the bike, of course. She'd bitched like hell when he bought it. Then she'd outright refused to let him take Sean for the ride. After much pestering and fighting, she'd finally relented to a ride down the block and back. Instead, David took the boy all the way to West Ashley and back. The boy had loved it. His mother had been most unamused.

The Arthur Ravenel Jr. was an impressive eight-lane cabled-stayed bridge that crossed the Cooper River, linking downtown Charleston and Mount Pleasant. The bridge had been built to replace its shoddier, uglier predecessors; the John P. Grace Memorial and Silas N. Pearman Bridges. Not that the names mattered. Most locals simply called it the Cooper River bridge, just as they always had, even when it was technically two bridges.

Silas, Ravenel, Bennett—names of supposedly important men. The lowcountry was full of them, the names of rich men who had owned lots of property and even people. Their names adorned buildings and street signs, even neighborhoods and local businesses. Nobody remembered men like David, though. Men who worked the streets. Men who dealt with the filth and kept the boundaries on which the supposedly great men depended. No, men like him were expected to serve and shut up.

He rode over the Ravenel and gazed across the water at downtown Charleston, cupping his cigarette with his left hand to protect it from the wind, while holding the handlebars with his right. He remembered when downtown was dangerous. Now it was a tourist destination—a place for shopping, high-end dining, and exclusive nightclubs. Nobody wanted to think about what went into such a transformation. The city needed men like him, even if nobody knew it—and those who did know it would never acknowledge it.

He was used to being unappreciated. Every day, Marie and the boy seemed to show him that one way or another. Never mind the bosses at work, or his stupid ass partner—that asshole had gone and gotten himself killed.

David peered over the edge and for a moment considered what it would be like to jump, or maybe even drive his bike right into the rail. If he hit it fast enough, he bet he could launch himself right over the fucking top. Though, a bullet would be easier and more his style. Less ambiguous too. He didn't want some assholes thinking he couldn't handle his bike.

He took a pull from the cigarette and thought about his day. Officially, he wasn't back on duty until tomorrow, but he still had some things to attend to first. Checking in with his lieutenant being one. Skip had called and asked him to come into the station. If David didn't know better, he'd be nervous—but Skip was more likely to ask David to cover dirt than to find any himself. After that, it was to the streets for a couple of important meetings. He had to make sure he was seen. When you work the beat, you can't let the thugs think you've stopped coming around.

2

DAREN OPENED THE door to his room, dropped his bag on the floor, and wiped the sweat from his brow with his shirtsleeve. He took a seat on the bed and unbuttoned his shirt. The humidity was awful. D.C. was known as the swamp for many reasons, the least of which was the ungodly weather, but even D.C. was temperate compared to this.

The air was so thick and muggy that it felt as if you could drown in it. One local at the airport had seen him emerge into the heat and had laughed at his reaction. "Down here, we call September second-August," he'd warned.

There was also an awful smell that Daren couldn't place, but it was everywhere. It was a pungent, rotten smell that nearly caused him to gag. He'd asked the woman at the counter of the hotel if there was a trash facility or a factory of some sort nearby, but she just looked at him as if he were crazy.

He decided a shower would help him settle into the new location. Unfortunately, the water pressure was dismal and only further frustrated him. When he emerged from the shower, the sight on the wall above his bed caused him to jump.

"What the fuck is that?!" he muttered to himself. "You have got to be fucking kidding me."

The cockroach was massive. It slowly made its way across the wall, seemingly unbothered, as if it were at home and Daren were the intruder.

For those lucky enough to see, the sight of Daren rushing out of his room with the creature wrapped in a t-shirt, cursing and yelling as he tried to shake it free from the shirt was good for a laugh. The roach clung on tightly in defiance and Daren decided it could keep the shirt, throwing it and the bug into the nearby dumpster.

"Giant cockroach," he told a woman who was watching him with great amusement.

"Oh, sugar, that's just a Palmetto bug," she said with a dismissive wave of her hand.

"I'm sorry?"

"A Palmetto bug. You're in the Palmetto State. They're kind of our unofficial mascot."

"That's... horrifying. Thank you," Daren replied, heading back to his room.

After a thorough inspection to see if any other *Palmetto bugs* were hiding in his room, Daren pulled out his laptop and began to review the Grey case.

The problem with Grey's case was the indiscriminate nature of the violence. Most times, killings are personal; the victim knows their murderer. The ones that don't are typically killed in robberies or rapes—cases where the perpetrator wanted something from the victims. But indiscriminate violence was different.

Assuming that Devon was targeted for his race, which the evidence seemed to suggest, meant that investigators couldn't develop a list of suspects based on his known associates. It meant that in all likelihood, Devon didn't know his killer or killers. There had been little evidence collected at the scene and no witnesses. These were the worst cases; the kind that went cold on day one.

Daren could understand why investigators had had such little luck. He also understood how enraging that must've been for the Black community. No one wanted to tell them that this kind of thing was almost impossible to solve. No one wanted to tell them that they would have to accept it and move on without closure. No one wanted to tell them it would probably happen again.

This killing was put on display like a message was being sent. And the eyes of the nation were watching. It felt like half the country was incensed over the lynching of Devon Grey, and the other half was outraged by the killing of officer Gregory Noonan.

Noonan had been gunned down while waiting for his partner outside a coffee shop in North Charleston, in what was likely another act of indiscriminate violence. Noonan had been the fifth cop in the country to share such a fate in the past fourteen months. The rash of violence had begun as a response to several high-profile police shootings of Black Americans, including the case of Antony Castile, which Daren had been instrumental in closing.

The assassination of a local police officer had rallied conservatives and the far right from around South Carolina and surrounding states. They demanded justice. Nobody wanted to tell them that this kind of thing was nearly impossible to solve. And without a target for their anger, the Black community and their righteous anger became the scapegoat.

Protesters had become a common sight in Charleston. Blue lives versus Black lives. Neo-confederates versus liberals versus conservatives. It was as if the nation's oldest wound had suddenly started to fester, and this was ground zero for the division and polarization taking hold across the country. Daren was sitting on a tinder box.

Letting people in was dangerous. Andrea had learned that lesson when she was young and it had served her well. Everyone wanted to pry, everyone wanted to *talk*, but nobody had much to offer her for solutions.

In second grade, she'd opened up to the school counselor. She'd told him about her father, and how her fears felt like a hurricane; how they'd sweep her up and leave her feeling out of control. She talked about the sense of dread that pervaded her every thought. And what did it get her? More trouble. Child services came by once or twice but that only angered her father and made his wrath all the more fearsome. In school, they would pull her out of class regularly to talk about her problems, which only led to her being stigmatized by her classmates.

After her mother's death, lots of people wanted to *talk* to Andrea. They all wanted her to open up about the way she felt and the things she had seen. She remembered what Gram had told her: "Lots of people in this world want to make you a victim. It's not to help you. They want to make you a victim so they can feel bad for you. So they can make themselves feel special." Though she and Gram avoided most political discussions, she'd always remembered that bit of wisdom.

Andrea had seen it in her personal life, too. If she kept men at a distance and didn't open up to them, they'd eventually leave. If she did confide in them about who she was, what she had been through, and the things she felt, that too would ruin the relationship. At that point, they would get freaked out and leave, or they'd stay, believing a little love and support could erase a lifetime of pain. The latter was worse. Those men would take it personally when their presence in Andrea's life failed to change anything.

After Marcus's father, she'd pretty much given up on dating. There was only one man she trusted. He and her had an understanding. He was the only person she felt she could open up to without fear of judgment. Their relationship was unconventional, to say the least.

"And how is the medication working?" Dr. Leigh asked her.

"It's working well," Andrea answered. Well, it worked as well as it could be, being she'd never taken it.

"That's good," Dr. Leigh continued. "For someone in a high-stress role like yourself, anxiety can be really dangerous."

"I told you, I don't get anxious at work."

"Why do you think that is?"

Andrea looked around the office. Dr. Leigh had tried her best to soften the sterile feeling of the room with decorative pillows, a throw rug, and scented candles. It reminded Andrea of the school counselor's office from second grade. Only she wasn't giving this woman a goddamn thing. She knew all too well that anything she told her could be used against her.

"It's the stimulation. It commands all my focus," Andrea explained. "It's like it absorbs me. All the background noise fades away and I can think clearly. Nothing else seems to matter. It's like… clarity of purpose, I guess."

"Some cops and soldiers can become addicted to what you're describing," Dr. Leigh replied. "The rush of adrenaline. The clarity of purpose, as you put it. That's why so many with PTSD can't wait to get back into the action. It allows them a way to not have to deal with their feelings or process their experiences."

"I could understand that, but that's not me. I just love my job," Andrea replied, defensiveness creeping into her voice.

"But the medication is working?"

"Yes, I feel much less anxious," she lied.

"Good," Dr. Leigh replied, jotting down a few notes on her pad. "I still wish you would talk to me some more, but for now, if you keep coming and keep up on your meds, I will sign off on your remaining in the field."

"Thank you."

Andrea left the office and headed straight to her locker room to suit up. It was time to do what she did best.

Don't ask questions that have answers you wouldn't want to hear. That was Major Skeeter 'Skip' Wilson's motto when it came to his patrolmen. David knew this because Skip had told him as much many times. It was an understanding that Skip formed over his two decades of working in the field. On the street, things weren't always tidy and clean. Rules sometimes had to be broken. Sometimes a good beating might be necessary to prove a point. When you worked a beat, things were more complex than most of the brass would ever admit. Skip, however, understood what cops like David went through. David had always appreciated that. No one could understand that reality unless they had lived it themselves. Law enforcement was a brotherhood forged through that mutual experience. That was why Skip always had his men's backs.

Skip showed David into his office at the Charleston County Sheriff's station and shut the door behind them.

"Thanks for coming down, Dave."

"No problem, Skip. What's up?" David asked, taking a seat.

"Friend of mine in D.C. called me this morning. Seems the FBI has a special agent down here digging around."

"Digging around what?"

"Everything, I assume. He's been tasked with investigating the Grey murder."

"What's that got to do with us?"

"I've been told he's thorough," Skip said. "Now, I don't ask questions about the way you run your beat or the deals you got going with Ellis Bartley and his crew. As long as you keep making arrests, I'm not going to gripe about your methods. But I need you to keep your head down while he's in town and make sure there's no shit lying around for him to find."

"Relax," David said with a laugh. "Everything I'm working on is above board."

"Uh huh," Skip replied skeptically.

"Maybe a few papers weren't filed, or you know, I cut a couple corners here or there—nothing a fucking fed is going to care about."

"And how are you doing with everything else?" Skip asked. "A lot of guys take it hard when they lose a partner."

"I'm good," David assured him. "How are you doing?" He looked at the picture of Skip's late wife, Moira, on the shelf behind his desk. "It was tragic what happened."

"Accidents happen," Skip sighed. "I do miss her terribly."

"We all do, sir," David replied. "She was a lovely woman."

"Anyway," Skip said, never eager to discuss Moira, "I'm assigning you a new partner."

"Look, Skip," David demurred. "I loved working with Greg. He was a brother to me..." He paused, trying to find the right words.

"We're all brothers here," Skip reminded him.

"I would just prefer to ride alone for now, if it's all the same."

"It's not," Skip shrugged. "Sheriff's orders. All patrols are to ride in pairs until the tension dies down and there's less threat out there."

David nodded and smirked.

"Starting tomorrow, you're paired with Deputy Anthony Lane," Skip told him.

"You're sticking me with a rookie?" David asked.

"We were all green once. A veteran like yourself has a lot to offer a new officer," Skip explained. He rose from his seat and shook David's hand, indicating their meeting was over. "Welcome back," he added.

"Thanks, boss." David nodded and took his leave.

3

WILLIAM BARTLEBY CARSON III was wanted in three states. His offenses ranged from evading law enforcement to assault and human trafficking. It was the trafficking of women and children that had landed him on the target list of North Charleston's special victim's unit—Andrea's squad. Despite his notorious reputation, Andrea felt he was their responsibility. Because for all the cities and towns across several states where Carson was wanted, it was North Charleston he called home.

Three years earlier, Andrea and her unit had taken down a safe house being used by Carson and his cousins to kidnap and traffic children. Both of Carson's cousins were killed during the raid, one shot dead by Andrea. In the three years that followed, the unit ran down every lead they could find, but Carson was illusive. He lived under several aliases in Florida for some time, until he ended up wanted for questioning in the kidnapping of a young boy. He next popped up on the radar a year later in Atlanta, where he assaulted an officer and fled the scene of a traffic accident.

Andrea had recently caught word that Carson was operating in the lowcountry again. Sources reported that he was running drugs and trafficking women throughout the region, but any leads they received always seemed to turn cold. A confidential informant of hers alleged that was because Carson had purchased the protection of several local sheriffs. It was information she kept to herself. In her experience, it was more than plausible.

Last week, narcotics had put her unit onto a woman named Sherry Donnell, who was connected to a cocaine distribution ring downtown. They'd been surveilling her home, which included photographing every individual who came and went. Narcotics had taken interest in one individual in particular, whom they determined to be Donnell's source. That man was identified as none other than Billy Carson.

The house was located in Windsor Place, which was a historically Black neighborhood and the poorest section of the city, located in what locals called the neck of the peninsula. The tiny dilapidated home had barred windows, an iron fence, and signs warning off trespassers. A blue tarp was poorly secured to the roof, flapping in the wind and revealing a rotted hole in the shingles. The blue paint was peeling from the siding, leaving the wood vulnerable to mold. While in rough shape, the house was in pretty standard condition for the neighborhood.

Andrea was the first through the door after it was breached, her gun drawn, fire in her eyes. She swept the living room through the doorway to her right, where the female suspect screamed and threw her arms in the air. She then headed for the back of the house as several other officers rushed in behind her and into the living room.

"Down on the ground!" several ordered Donnell.

"Female suspect secured," an officer reported over his radio.

Andrea entered the kitchen cautiously, gripping her gun with both hands and methodically scanning every corner. Slowly, she headed for the bathroom door. "Police! Come out with your hands up!" she commanded, readying her weapon.

The door flew open and a man with long, straggly blonde hair burst out and charged her. Andrea fired, but not before he could grab the gun by its barrel and thrust it downward. The bullet buried itself harmlessly into the floor. He grabbed her by the throat and tried to wrench the gun from her hand. She held on with all her might, knowing her life depended on it, and with her free hand, she grabbed the man squarely by his dick and balls and twisted as hard as she could.

Having secured Donnell, officers Hoyte and Rawls hurried into the kitchen to aid Andrea, only to find her standing over a man writhing on the ground in pain.

"Cuff this piece of shit," she told them, coolly holstering her gun and brushing a few loose strands of hair from her face.

"No sign of Carson," Rawls reported to her.

"Who are you? Where's Billy Carson?" Andrea barked at the man as he was being frisked and cuffed.

"Fuck you! Bitch!" the man exclaimed, then spat on her shoes.

Hoyt responded by punching him squarely in the gut.

"Let's try this again," she said, as Hoyt and Rawls lifted him from the floor.

"Fuck you, dirty fucking coon bitch!"

Another punch in the stomach. The man fell to the ground again, heaved, and vomited.

"Driver's license says his name is Josh McCrory," Rawls noted, rifling through the man's wallet as he groaned.

"Must be connected to the homeowner somehow," Hoyt added.

"We got her in a car outside already," Rawls informed Andrea.

"Fuck! Surveillance said Carson was here. They must have seen this asshole and made the wrong ID," she griped. "Let's get them both down to the station and see what we can find out."

"Wait a minute! I ain't Bill-fuckin'-Carson! I ain't done nothin' wrong!" the McCrory protested. "I don't even look like the man!"

"All y'all look to same to me," Andrea said with a shrug. "Besides, you came at a cop and tried to take my gun. That's prison time right there by itself. I'm willing to bet you wouldn't have done that if there wasn't a warrant out for your arrest already."

The man looked down defeatedly, and Rawls and Hoyt led him out of the house in cuffs.

Nellie's BBQ was one of the few businesses located in downtown North Charleston—or the neck, as it was known to locals. Nellie Brown had grown up downtown, and in 1965, he opened his now locally famous barbeque restaurant in that same community. Nellie believed people leaving the neighborhood was part of the problem. He vowed to stay and that's exactly what he did. The building had some bullet holes, but for the most part, people from the area respected Nellie too much to mess with him or his barbeque place. It certainly didn't hurt that he made the best wings in town.

David respected Nellie. Operating a business in this part of town was a risky enterprise. Nellie had real love for his community. There was something admirable about it, even if David couldn't personally relate. He'd never felt a part of the community he came from, and he never looked back once he left.

Nellie wasn't just a good cook; he also understood the way the streets worked. Like David, he understood that you can't fight the whole community. You had to pick your battles. Both David and Nellie saw Ellis Bartley as a battle not worth fighting. Ellis was too connected and had too much muscle—going up against him would leave bodies littered all over the city.

Instead, David had an arrangement with Ellis's people. He saw to it that anyone other than Ellis's people selling anything in that area wound up in the back of a police car. While this gave Ellis a monopoly, the lack of competition meant less violence. For his part, Ellis agreed to keep any bloodshed out of the public eye.

It wasn't ethical. It wasn't legal. But David had long tired of playing by the rules and cleaning up the mess. For him, any solution that lowered violent crime was worth it. And if it put some extra cash in his pocket, all the better.

David parked his hog outside Nellie's, where Reggie Willis and his crew were hanging. Nellie would allow them to use his corner to run their street crews and hold meets. David found Reggie seated at the only picnic table, eating barbeque pork ribs in the sun. A few of his crew members were seated beside him, while several others hung back by their SUVs.

"Sullivan, my man! Wazzup? Have a seat. You want some ribs, playa?" Reggie welcomed him like an old friend.

"No thanks," David politely declined.

He took a seat at the rusty table, and Reggie motioned for the rest of his crew to leave them in privacy. The three men got up and took a short walk over to the others by the road.

"You mean you're not here for food?" Reggie asked slyly, licking the sauce from his fingertips. He was a man of style and swagger— always dressed well and not afraid to show off his wealth.

"I missed payday last week. You knew I'd be around," David replied, looking around. He never dropped his guard.

"No doubt," Reggie said, pulling an envelope from his back pocket and sliding it across the table.

"Just didn't want you to think our arrangement was not withstanding," David said as he counted the money.

"Nah, I told Ellis you'd be around. After all we've done for you. Shit…"

"That's just it. Had to lay low for a bit."

"No doubt."

David stared across the table, unsure if was comfortable with the new dynamic of their relationship. "And that other thing?" he asked.

"Yo, it's tragic. My man walked down this ally in Atlanta, and… Nobody ever saw that G again. Shit be crazy on these streets; you know how it is."

"Yeah," David said with a nod, rising to his feet. "I know how it is."

"Listen, that crew of youngins is still working too close to our turf in West Ashley."

"Alright. I'll take care of it," David said.

"A bunch of young Gs, ya know? Better you run them off. Otherwise, Ellis will have to…"

"Yeah, yeah. Keep your pants on." David mounted his bike, kicked down on the clutch, and started the engine. The beast roared to life. He revved the 1200 cc engine loudly, then took off, leaving a nice strip of rubber on the road.

The police station wasn't far from the airport, which was practically next to Daren's hotel. Everything in North Charleston seemed to be located in the northern part of the city. Riding through it on his way to the city's police department, Daren found his expectations of the city surprisingly off base. Everything was much more developed and newer than he had expected. Upscale, commercial shopping centers and restaurants lined both sides of the street.

"Is this still *North* Charleston?" he asked his Uber driver.

"Yes, it is," replied his driver. She was a middle-aged Black woman with kind eyes and a warm smile. She drove a Dodge minivan, which was kept meticulously clean.

"I was told it… Well, I was expecting it to be little rougher," he confessed.

"Don't let all this fool you, baby. This area's all been gentrified."

"Oh," he replied. "Economic development and growth, I guess."

"Mm-hm, so they say. Funny, it don't seem to be working that way for many folks."

"But it's good to see development and growth, right? Better than cities staying poor."

"I ain't an economist. Just seems to me, a lot of people who aren't from here, making a lot of money by moving people with more money in. Like they're replacing us. Pushing us out. We get to live in the poor areas; they get new condos."

"It brings jobs, though, right? And opportunity for poorer communities?"

"So they say. That is if you're lucky enough to get one of those jobs. Even then, most don't pay shit."

"There's always a way, though, right? If you're willing to work. You drive an Uber, for example."

She heard it before and was unamused. "I'm a full-time nurse, mister, and I can't afford my daughter's medication. I don't want to be doing this."

"I'm sorry," Daren said, suddenly embarrassed. "I shouldn't presume."

"Well, at least you realize it," she said warmly with the slightest hint of snark.

She pulled the car into the NCPD parking lot and smiled at Daren in the rearview.

"Here you are, baby," she beamed.

"Thanks," Daren said, opening the door to exit the car. "And I'm sorry if I offended you in any way."

She laughed. "I hear worse every day. You're fine," she assured him.

He shut the car door and headed for the front steps of the police station. Inside, he identified himself to the duty desk officer, then took a seat in the waiting area, where he read some more about Devon Grey on his phone.

Shortly after, an older Black man adorned with brass came into the waiting area to greet him. Daren stood and shook the man's hand.

"Special Agent Renard? I'm Deputy Chief Marshall Mulholland," he said.

"It's great to meet you, Deputy Chief," Daren replied.

"Please, just call me Marshall."

"Well, I suppose you should call me Daren then."

"Right this way, Daren. We can discuss this in my office."

Daren followed Mulholland through the secured door and into the heart of the precinct. The noisy, chaotic, and often crass sounds of an inner-city police department almost had a rhythm to it; like a song of justice that, just as the Institution itself, was disjointed, broken, and out of time.

In the back corner, they entered Mulholland's office. The Deputy Chief shut the door and invited Daren to sit. "So, you're looking to sit down with Detective Watts," Mulholland remarked.

"That's right," said Daren.

"Regarding the SVU, or is this about something else?"

"She had a C.I. whose death I'm looking into."

"You must mean Devon Grey," the deputy chief said, rubbing his eyes as if the subject caused him personal grief. "It hurts to think about what happened to that boy."

Daren wanted to keep his cards close to his chest. He didn't understand the politics between departments or the two cities down here. "I'm really not at liberty to say," he replied.

"Right, well, I am glad to see the FBI hasn't forgotten. God knows nobody around here is trying too hard to solve it."

"Why would that be?"

"I'm sorry?" He didn't understand Daren's confusion.

"Why wouldn't people be trying to solve a case like Grey's?"

Mulholland took a breath and searched for the right words. "I took over this job for a man who was caught reclassifying complaints filed against officers," he explained. "He was juking the stats and playing with the language—protecting crooked and abusive cops. In my time here, I've seen officers arrested for dealing drugs, Black men gunned down without justification at traffic stops, cops caught in bed with fourteen-year-old girls. There's no trust in the police in this community, and can you blame them? So, the cops that do want to solve cases, where they gonna turn? Nobody will talk to them. Nobody trusts them. Then you got the damn politics. Wealthy families, Southern heritage, and all that. Everybody's got skeletons in their closets and dirt on their shoes. Something like this happens. Nobody wants to start turning over rocks. People are afraid what they might find. People afraid, maybe their closet is the next to get combed through."

"Well, I don't mind kicking over rocks, Marshall."

"That's good. Of course, that means you won't be around here for long." Mulholland smiled wryly. He looked at Daren as if he were trying to size him up. Daren wasn't going to give him much to go on, but he thought the deputy chief could be an ally.

"Detective Watts is just returning from a raid," Mulholland informed him. "How much of her time will you be needing?"

"That depends."

"On?"

"Mostly whether or not I like her," Daren said plainly.

Mulholland nodded. "Y'all can use my office," he said, rising to his feet. "She'll be with you in just a few minutes."

4

"AGENT RENARD?" ANDREA asked, greeting the man in Mulholland's office with a firm handshake.

"Yes," he replied.

She took a seat behind Mulholland's desk with the confidence of someone who expected it to one day be hers. "I'm Detective Andrea Watts, Special Victims Unit. What can I do for you?"

"Devon Grey was a C.I. of yours."

"Yes," she looked down at the desk and sighed. "It's tragic what happened to him. He informed on a pretty simple case three, four years back. I saw him around after that, but he wasn't a regular source."

"Has anyone gone over possible connections between that case and Grey's death?"

"Not that I know of," she replied. "But that was years ago, and nothing that would have come back on him like this."

"Who was he informing on?"

"Devon was a good kid," Andrea recalled. "He witnessed a shooting when he was 12-years-old. But it was a domestic issue with multiple witnesses. A drunken husband shot his wife's lover. The confidential status was given to him to protect his identity but the suspect pled guilty at trial. Trust me, there is nobody out for revenge in that case."

"I suppose that would have been too easy," Daren remarked.

"I don't know too much about Occam's razor, Agent Renard, but I do know Occam wasn't a detective," she quipped.

Daren smiled. "How would you like to solve a mystery with me?"

"Excuse me?" she laughed. "Why me? No, no. I am far too busy." She didn't have time to entertain this guy—she had Sherry Donnell waiting in interrogation.

"You're a detective, and you're not from the department working the case. You can maneuver without getting in anyone's way. And, I would assume you know your way around down here, and I don't mean on a map."

"I don't have jurisdiction—"

"I do."

"There are other people who can help you. Not me," she insisted.

"You knew the victim. You know where he's from. You find me another person like that," Daren countered. "Plus, someone who—"

"Someone who's Black," she said, finishing his thought. She raised her eyebrow and tilted her head.

"No—I mean, well… Okay, yeah. Fine. I'm white and I'm a yankee," he confessed. "I don't know much about how things run down here, but I'm going to go ahead and assume that's not going to help me."

"How would it even work?" Andrea asked with a sigh.

"I'd deputize you," Daren answered.

"You can do that?" she asked skeptically.

"*Technically*, I can do it whether you volunteer or not."

"So, you're forcing me?"

"No," Daren said after a pause. "I'm not. I do hope you will at least consider it."

"I'm sorry, Agent Renard," Andrea said, rising to leave. "I don't have the time. I have important cases of my own I'm working. They may not make national headlines, but they're still important."

Daren nodded, shook her hand, and gave her his card. "Just think about it. I'll be around," he told her before leaving.

Andrea then headed to interrogation, where she found Mulholland talking to Hoyt and Rawls.

"What's happening?" she asked.

"Donnell is in 1, McCrory's in 2. Neither will say shit," Hoyt reported.

"You were right about McCrory," said Rawls. "Warrants out for domestic battery, skipping bail, and petty theft."

"We can add attempted murder of a police officer to that if he doesn't want to cooperate," she said. "Let me have a crack at Donnell," she added.

The room stank of sweat and body odor. Andrea recognized the smell. As an investigator interrogating a suspect, she knew it well. It was the smell of fear. She could see it on Sherry Donnell's face as she stared at the floor, searching among the dust for the answers to how her life had led to that point.

"I'd be afraid, too," Andrea told her. There was a hint of empathy in her voice. She never came at a suspect the way they were expecting. Shake up their expectations. Keep them guessing. Break the script they're playing through in their heads.

She sat down across from Donnell who was cuffed to the table and shook her head sympathetically.

"Whatchu mean? I ain't scared," Donnell scoffed. "Been here before. Ain't no thing."

"Oh, okay," said Andrea. "Can I ask you one thing?"

Donnell didn't answer.

"I just can't help but wonder, why a Black woman like yourself is working for a racist piece of shit like Bill Carson. I mean, I get why people sell drugs—it's a way to make money. I get it."

Sherry looked at her with surprise.

"I don't give a shit about drugs. None of the men who brought you here do either. We're SVU, Sherry. Do you know what that is?"

Sherry thought about it for a moment before asking, "Like the TV show?"

Andrea nodded. "Yeah, pretty much. We're the special victim's unit. We deal with heinous crimes involving women and children. We go after child molesters, human traffickers, rapists, and really awful, depraved people, Sherry." Andrea waited a moment for her words to sink in and then continued. "So, that's why I ask? How did a sister like yourself get tied up with someone who's on our list?"

"What'd Billy do?" Sherry asked timidly.

Andrea shook her head slowly, stood up from her chair, and began to slowly pace around the room. "Your friend Billy doesn't just traffic drugs, Sherry."

"You mean… people?" she asked, ashamed.

"Little girls even," Andrea told her.

"*No!*" Sherry gasped. She shook her head in disbelief.

"I'll get the photos if you want to see," Andrea offered. Sherry shook her head to decline. Andrea glanced up at the camera hanging in the corner of the interrogation room. "Listen," she whispered, leaning over the table close to Sherry's ear. "Tell me where he is, and I can make this all go away."

Sherry looked up at her, tears in her eyes. "He said he'd kill me."

"I won't give him the chance," Andrea assured her, keeping her voice low.

"He'll know…"

"Not if you tell me and *only me.* Tell me how to find him, and after I take him in, I'll make sure my boss and everyone else knows it was your information."

Sherry hesitated, her eyes darting around as she considered her options. Then she leaned forward and whispered an address to Andrea. Andrea stood up and shook her head. "If you change your mind and want to cooperate, let us know. It will go easier for you," she said loudly enough for others to hear.

"What was that?" Marshall asked Andrea as she left the box.

"Just getting in her head a little," she explained. "She wants a lawyer."

"Did she give you anything?"

Andrea shook her head but could tell Marshall was skeptical. "Let me know if something changes?" she asked, brushing past him to enter the break room.

She fixed herself a cup of coffee and checked her phone. There was a text message from her son. *"A- on my history test!"*

Andrea smiled and tried to find the words to respond. She typed a couple of messages about how proud she was but deleted them. Why was this so hard for her? The truth was, she hadn't known that he had a test that morning, and that made her feel like a failure. That was one of the recurring feelings that pushed her to drown herself in work. It was easier than dealing with the way she felt.

"I'm so proud of you," she finally messaged in reply. It was the truth, regardless of how hard it was for her to show it.

Andrea shoved her phone and her feelings back into her pocket. She pulled out the card that the FBI agent had given her and looked at it hesitantly. Maybe this was a bad idea. For a moment, she considered telling Marshall what she'd learned from Donnell but decided against it. She had been after Carson for years—she wasn't going to chance losing him now.

West Ashley was a rapidly developing suburb located, as the name implied, West of the Ashley River. Most of the town was developed along two major thoroughfares: routes 17 and 61. These multi-lane highways served as arteries to the residential neighborhoods that hung off them like lollipops. As the area grew and transplants continued to move in, the setup was becoming untenable. Traffic congestion was unbearable during certain times of the day. On a bad day, it could take you close to an hour to get downtown, which was less than ten miles away. Though the traffic wasn't yet as bad as Mount Pleasant, where David lived.

West Ashley was actually the birthplace of Charleston. The place where English colonists first settled in 1670 was now a historic site on the river called Charlestown Landing. Ten years later, the settlement moved to the peninsula, and the area west of the Ashley would come to be used primarily for agriculture, eventually becoming home to several slave plantations before the Civil War. To this day, the suburb maintained a large Black population.

Like many major cities, Charleston began developing sprawling suburban subdivisions during the latter half of the twentieth century. Downtown had lost its exclusivity, and white folks with money were lured out to the suburbs with nice, new homes and green yards. Initially, development in West Ashley had been an outgrowth of downtown Charleston, but eventually, construction had connected it to North Charleston via Sam Rittenberg Avenue and highway route 526.

David didn't care for any of it. The never-ending development was too much. Not only was it reshaping the city in ways he did not like, but it was also upsetting the boundaries that had historically kept crime across the river in North Charleston. Upper-middle class developments in the West Ashley plantation district were constantly being burglarized. Cars were routinely stolen or ransacked. Car jackings and muggings would occur in broad daylight, and drugs were being sold openly in residential areas.

Drugs were an ongoing reality of life on the street. No amount of police work, school programs, or federal tax dollars was ever going to change that. David saw the war on drugs as futile and believed it caused more harm than it did good. When it came to drugs, David's strategy was containment. Tell crews where they could and could not operate. Keep the shit away from decent people. Keep the crews from killing each other over turf.

That was the way to get real results, just as he had taught his partner Greg. It was all about keeping things under control. Of course, he took a little off the top and made the dealers pay him rent. That's all these thugs understood. That's how it worked on the street. If he wasn't bleeding them, they wouldn't respect him.

David pulled into the Ashley Hall Apartments complex and made a beeline for the group of Black teens hanging near the basketball courts. The crew recognized him on his motorcycle and started to scatter. *"Twelve, yo! Twelve!"* the kids yelled as they ran. The code raised the alarm to anyone around that cops were nearby.

David pointed his finger at Chris, their leader, commanding him to stay like he was an animal. He parked his bike and made his way over.

Chris shook his head. He already knew what this was about.

"You know, I almost expected better from you, kid," David scolded. "I almost thought you were smart. I should have known better. Your kind never learns easy."

"Shit ain't no thang," Chris replied. "We just chillin'. No crime there, man."

"Sure," David nodded. "And your boys running off, they're not holding anything, right?"

"Look man, we moved out of Windsor like you asked. *I fucking live here, man!* We just chillin'."

"Alright, run your pockets," David ordered.

Chris sighed and turned his pant pockets inside out, removing a pack of cigarettes and a lighter in the process. David gestured for him to turn around, and he obliged so David could check his back pockets and frisk him. David pulled a stack of small bills out of his back pocket.

"Y'all just chillin', huh?" David asked dubiously, waving the bills in Chris's face.

Chris just shrugged. "Gotta earn that cheese, yo."

"People pay you to just stand around a basketball court, huh?" David asked coyly. "Man, I gotta get a job like that." He counted the money, took a hundred for himself, and handed the stack back to Chris. "Listen, kid," he advised. "I'm done asking. This is how it's going to be from now on. And the tax is going to be the least of your worries if Ellis gets wind. You feel me?"

"Where y'all want us then? Shit..."

"Go work down by the mall. Make a deal with those Armenians who run that convenience store, like the crack dealers do."

"Man, they'll fuckin' tax us more than y'all do," Chris complained.

"I don't care. I'm not your fucking agent. Work it out. These apartments and North Charleston are off limits to your crew. Don't make me tell you again."

Tequila Sunrise was the kind of place you went for cheap taco specials and margaritas. The kind of place where the food had no real business being as good or as cheap as it was. Andrea had told Daren to meet her there after to discuss his offer more. He didn't know she had a proposition for him.

He was already sitting at the bar when she arrived. She took a seat beside him and helped herself to a chip from his basket. "Whatcha drinking?" she asked, summoning the bartender.

"A beer is fine," Daren replied, scooping a large quantity of guacamole onto a chip and shoveling it into his mouth.

"Two beers, please," Andrea requested of the bartender. "Whatever's local and on tap."

"I was surprised you called," he told her.

"Why is that?"

"You seemed pretty put off by my asking for your help."

"Well," she said, pausing to find the right words.

"I get it," he interjected. "Who the fuck am I? You got important shit you're into. Just makes me wonder…" He smiled and popped a chip into his mouth. "What is it you need from me that made you change your mind?"

She smiled and shook her head, amused by his directness. "There's a federal fugitive held up about forty-five minutes north of here. Right outside my jurisdiction. A real nasty son of a bitch. Call your FBI buddies and grab his ass. But I want to be there when they take him down," she said.

The bartender brought their beers and Andrea slapped a ten-dollar bill down on the bar. "I got it," she asserted.

Daren shook his head and laughed. "So, what's this guy's deal? Why you want him so bad?" he asked.

"He's scum. Trafficked children. Now he mostly moves drugs. Doesn't sit right with me that he's gotten away with it."

"Okay, but why me? Is there no law enforcement where he is?"

She could hear in his tone that he was not taking the proposition seriously. "I've had multiple sources tell me that he has several local sheriffs in his pocket," she explained. "I happen to have a tip where he's at. I'm not going to risk letting him slip away by tipping off some crooked, redneck sheriff."

"So, you want this dirtbag bad enough to change your mind about helping me out?"

"Pretty much," she admitted. He didn't need to know that she'd thought about Carson every day for years; the images of his victims burned into her mind, particularly the children—taken away from their homes, sold as property, abused, and discarded. She would do whatever was in her power to put that man away. If he were in another state, she'd have to make her peace with it. But there was no fucking way she was going to sit back and let him operate forty-five minutes away. "Carson's wanted in multiple states. Call your boys. Do your thing," she said.

"Yeah…" Daren sipped his beer. "That's not going to happen."

"Why not? He's wanted."

"How do I put this?" Daren asked himself. He rubbed his hand over his lips and searched for the right words. "I'm someone who mostly works alone. They expect me to work alone."

"I don't follow."

"I have a very narrow purview, and I try to keep a low profile. Now, there are a lot of things I can get as it relates to that purview. Unfortunately, I sure as hell can't go summoning federal agents to the lowcountry based on a tip concerning a completely unrelated case."

"So, tell them you have to do this to get my help."

"They'd tell me to find someone else," he laughed. "Or to help you myself."

"Alright then," Andrea replied, satisfied.

"Alright, what?"

"You help me get the bastard," she suggested.

"*What? The two of us?*" he asked incredulously.

"C'mon," she prodded. "You're a special agent from the FBI, right? And I takedown scum like Carson all the time."

Daren sighed. "Okay, so if we take a ride out to the sticks and bring this guy in, you'll help me work the Grey case?"

"That's right."

"Well, alright then," he agreed, shaking his head.

Daren flagged the bartender and ordered a couple of tacos. Andrea insisted beer was the only lunch she needed. As she drank, she looked him over and made her assumptions. His clothing was tailored; his shirt sleeves were fastened with cufflinks, not buttons. His shoes were shined. Another white, upper-class, northerner. Locals didn't care for such types, likening them to the carpet baggers who came down during Reconstruction to buy up land and fleece southerners. To

Andrea, though, his type represented a different kind of predation. The self-righteous men who would roll into town promising to help lift up all the poor peoples of color. White saviors, eager to televise the problems of Black communities, pose for pictures with their children or throw money at the symptoms of poverty.

Why was he there? Why had this white bread, country-club-looking suit come to North Charleston fixing to solve a hate crime? Why had the FBI picked him? Something about it didn't feel right to her. Still, if it meant getting Carson, she'd help him. After all, she had known Devon Grey, and of course, she wanted to know what happened to him—it was working with Daren that made her uneasy.

"What if this guy doesn't come quietly?" Daren asked.

"What's the matter?" she asked, baiting him. "Can't handle it? It's just one guy, mister *Special Agent*."

Daren sipped his beer and shook his head with a laugh. "Alright, fuck it. First thing tomorrow, we'll go get your man."

Andrea smiled, satisfied. "So," she said, moments later. "You're going to deputize me?"

"That's right," Daren said, wiping his mouth with a napkin.

"Is there an oath or something I need to take?"

"Oh, absolutely," said Daren. He grabbed a menu off the bar and held it out before her. "Place your right hand on this near-holy bible of southern-fried, Tex-Mex goodness, and repeat after me."

Andrea laughed and looked at the greasy, stained menu with a raised eyebrow.

"C'mon now. This is serious shit," Daren insisted.

"Alright," she said in acquiescence. She placed her hand on the menu and smiled.

"I, state your name," Daren started.

"I, state your name," she repeated verbatim. They both laughed.

"Do solemnly swear on my love of tacos and corn bread."

"Do solemnly swear on my love of *chicken wings* and corn bread."

"Not a fan of tacos, huh?"

"Not as much as chicken wings," she teased.

"Alright, alright," he continued. "To uphold the Constitution of the United States."

"To uphold the Constitution of the United States."

"And enforce the laws of the United States government thereunder."

"And to enforce the laws of the United States thereunder."

"Close enough," he proclaimed.

He reached over the bar and grabbed a plastic knife. He touched the knife to each of her shoulders as if she were being knighted, and then raised his glass. She grabbed her glass and clanked it against his in celebration.

"Congratulations," Daren said. "I hereby declare you a bonified, deputized federal agent."

"Fancy," she replied, taking a drink. "I can't wait to abuse my power like all y'all mother fuckers do."

They both laughed.

"But seriously," he added, somewhat concernedly, "there's like paperwork and shit that has to be filed. So, don't try to stop any terrorists or anything until I talk to my boss tomorrow."

She laughed, promised to do her best, and ordered them two shots of whiskey. Maybe, if she worked him right, she could figure out what he was up to.

5

DAVID FOUND MARIE sitting in the front row of the bleachers at the Francis Marion Youth Soccer Field. She sipped a bottle of water and watched Sean intently through wide-framed sunglasses. David joined her, kissing her on the head while taking a seat beside her.

"Hello, beautiful," he said.

"Hey, mister," she replied affectionately. "I didn't hear the bike?"

"I took an Uber so I could ride back with y'all," he replied. "How's our little guy doing?" he asked, grabbing a piece of gum from his pocket and sticking it in his mouth. There was no smoking allowed on the bleachers.

"He's gotten much better at controlling the ball," she informed him.

David watched as Sean took his turn dribbling the ball down the field, around a series of orange cones. "You're right. He is getting better."

David had never cared for soccer—Europeans had the weirdest sports. Regardless, he wanted his son to do well at it, and it pleased him to see him improving. "*Good job, Sean!*" he shouted supportively.

Marie beamed at him and placed her hand lovingly on his thigh, happy to see him supporting their boy. "You talk to Skip?" she asked.

"Yup. Just some paperwork and bullshit before I start back tomorrow."

"You're off on Sunday, though?"

"Yeah, that's right."

"Good. You can come to church with us."

"Yeah, great," he said with no attempt to hide his disdain.

"You haven't been in weeks." She tried to keep her voice low in public. "At a time when you need guidance and faith more than ever."

"Have you read the news lately?" he asked indignantly.

Marie furrowed her brow, puzzled as to what he was talking about.

"The fucking church is a disgrace, Marie," he chided, his voice getting louder. "I should drag my ass in there on a Sunday morning so some pedo priest can ask me to confess *my sins*? What a joke."

"David!" she exclaimed. "The sins of a few individuals do not illegitimatize the whole church." She looked around, concerned others would overhear.

"A few?" he asked in disbelief. "It's more than a few. The whole institution is rotten. The ones who aren't guilty are complicit."

"Why do you say that?"

"They all know. Trust me. In institutions like that, you know when it's rotten. They defend the church because that's their team, and they will never hold themselves accountable because that would mean relinquishing power. That's all institutions are, Marie. Power."

"It's important we teach our son to love God and respect the church," she countered.

He knew this was not a question for her. She and David had both been raised Roman Catholic, but David had a much more complicated relationship with his faith. There were a few things he planned on saying to Peter when it was his turn at those gates, that was for damn sure.

On the field, the team had begun drills. One player would dribble around a set of cones, while another attempted to play defense.

David frowned. His son had been paired up with a boy named Marcus, who was the only Black boy on the team. Sean dribbled the ball around the cones and Marcus defended him closely. As Sean rounded one of the cones, the boys' legs crossed and they both took a tumble. The coach made sure they were alright, encouraged them both before sending them to the back of the line, and then continued with drills.

David scoffed and shook his head. "You see that?"

"It's sports, David," Marie said, rolling her eyes. "He's going to fall down sometime."

Later, driving home from practice later, David couldn't help but remark on the incident. "You've got to be more aggressive," he told Sean, who was seated in the backseat of the truck cab.

"Huh?" Sean asked, confused as to what his father was talking about.

"In drills. When you're up against kids like that—"

"David!" Marie scolded him.

"It's just the truth, Marie," David said sternly. "I see it every day at work with these people."

"It's just practice," Sean demurred.

"Practice or not," David insisted. "It's about dominance and establishing yourself as a man. That Marcus kid—his kind don't feel pain the same as you do. They're naturally stronger. So, when you come up against them, you gotta push harder than normal. You have to play a little rougher."

Marie looked out the passenger window and sighed in disapproval.

"Don't even start with that passive bullshit," David told her. "You ever see a man take four bullets, two Tasers, and keep coming? I have." He pulled the truck into T. Jimmy's, the boy's favorite restaurant.

Sean's face lit up with excitement. *"Yes!"* he exclaimed with joy.

David smiled and laughed. Marie took a moment to soften her anger, then joined in the fun. "Are you going to get a giant sundae?" she asked Sean with a wide smile.

"Yeah!" he shouted, jumping out of the truck.

In the parking lot, Sean ran ahead, David and Marie following behind. David took her hand and gave it a little squeeze. She looked at him with that look he knew all too well—the look that said she was not happy with him, but still couldn't help but love him. It wasn't exactly the look he wanted but he'd take it.

Dixie Rex's Saloon was the kind of place where a man could get just about anything he desired—booze, women, or drugs. Daren had been informed that it was the closest local haunt for neo-Confederates and white nationalists.

The honkytonk was located in a small town called Givhans, about forty minutes north of Charleston. Judging from the parking lot, one might have assumed owning a pickup truck was a requirement for entry. Many of the trucks were adorned with the Confederate battle flag and various far-right bumper stickers.

"BETTER TO BE JUDGED BY 12 THAN CARRIED BY 8," one bumper sticker read. Daren snickered at the message. It was a proud declaration of Southern gun culture: shoot first and think later.

He parked his rented Dodge Charger across the street and tucked his Glock under the seat. He exited the car wearing jeans and an Alice In Chains t-shirt—it was the most blue-collar shirt he owned. He had considered picking up a Lynyrd Skynyrd or Ford t-shirt, but he was afraid a brand-new shirt would stand out too much. Nothing spells cop like a guy with an out-of-town accent in a brand-new t-shirt asking questions.

He pulled a dirty, old Jägermeister hat from his back pocket and put it on, adjusting the brim as he approached the bar. His hands were black with brake dust and grease—an authentic addition to his look, which he'd accomplished by taking the front tire off the Dodge and rubbing his hands around the inside of the wheel before replacing it.

Daren opened the door to Dixie Rex's and was immediately hit with the smell of weed, beer, and stale cigarettes. Dixie memorabilia and commemorative regalia of the Confederacy decorated the walls. The floor was covered in peanut shells and spit from chewing tobacco. Country rock blared from the jukebox. The place had several pool tables, two of which had games going, while one had a young woman upon it, stripping for a crowd of eager men waving cash and hollering.

At the bar, Daren saw three men doing shots. Two of them wore plaid, while the third wore a Confederate t-shirt and a Ford hat. They slammed their shots, cheered, and ordered another round.

"I'll get that round," Daren told the old man tending the bar. The three men looked at him suspiciously. "I'm new to town," he said, extending his hand to the group. "Name's Earl."

The three men exchanged unsure looks, then the burliest of them spit at Daren's feet. "Piss off, yankee!" he grumbled.

Daren raised his hands in a gesture of peace and stepped back. The men took the shots the bartender had poured and tossed them back. The bartender looked to Daren for payment. Daren muttered under his breath and handed the man a twenty. When the bartender gave him his change, he ordered a beer and took a seat at the far end of the bar.

"Transplant?" a man asked from a couple of seats over.

"Yeah, I guess I stick out a bit," Daren chuckled, taking his beer from the bartender with a nod.

"Me too," the man replied. He was heavyset with long, brown hair tucked under a camouflage baseball cap, and a scruffy beard. His skin was pale, but the back of his neck was badly sunburnt and had a calloused, leathery look to it from being burned many times. Daren had only seen necks like that before on roofers and knew the man had to work outside.

"You don't sound like you're from out of town," Daren noted.

"That's right, and that's why they're nicer to me than they'll ever be to you. That's my Southern privilege," the man said proudly. "Moved here from Georgia fifteen years ago. I reckon I adopted that lowcountry drawl a bit, too."

"Name's Earl," Daren said, offering the man his hand.

"Ted. Folks 'round here call me Smokey."

"Oh, yeah? Why is that?"

"I'm usually smokin' on somethin'."

"It's great, to be here in Dixie," Daren said, moving over to the seat next to Smokey. "All the history and heritage."

Smokey nodded and sipped his beer. "Confederacy was born in Charleston," he replied. "Whole lot of history in these parts."

"The rest of the country doesn't seem to understand," Daren stated, trying to get a feeling for ole Smokey and whether or not he was wasting his time.

"What's that now?"

"All this Black versus blue bullshit. The crime. I mean, they want to take our guns, but we're not the ones killing each other like it's a fucking war zone. You know what I mean…"

"My friend," Smokey said in a very serious tone. "You got that exactly right."

"History is just one chapter after another about how certain people don't seem to... fit."

"I hear that. It's biological. Some people just don't mix with others. Too primitive. You know what I mean."

"They're hiring people down at the plant," Daren noted. "I'm sure you can imagine the quality of people they're bringing in. It's sad."

"I'm no racist," Smokey said flatly. Daren furrowed his brow and was about to apologize when Smokey concluded, "I hate all people equally!" He let out a boisterous laugh. "Black, brown, yellow, and shit, I even hate plenty of white people."

Daren shook his head with a laugh and raised his glass. Smokey did the same, clanking his beer against Daren's. They both took a long drink.

"Don't get me started on goddamn immigrants," Daren countered. "Fucking sad what's becoming of this country. Though, I'm surprised, to be honest, with what's become of the South."

"What's that now?"

"Just seems like people have forgotten their heritage down here. This is the only bar I could find that even celebrates proper Southern heritage. Where's the pride? Where are the people like us?"

"Keeping their heads down, mostly," Smokey grumbled. "It's a different world now. Everyone is perpetually offended. Charleston is a damn tourist trap. Everything has to be *politically correct.*"

"I just thought, once I moved here, I would be able to do something. Stop sitting around and bitching at the TV news, you know?"

"Whatcha lookin' to do?" Smokey asked cautiously.

"Nothin' much... You know... Rustle some feathers. Piss off some of those politically correct people. Maybe more. Help the cause. I just see those *animals* shutting down freeways on TV—destroying their own neighborhoods. It's downright anti-American. We need to do something."

"You lookin' for a political group?"

"Yeah, you know… Political. Social. Whatever. As long as it's properly Southern if you know what I mean."

"There's the South Carolina Secessionist Party, but they're just a bunch of trolls with badly made signs."

"Yeah, I'm looking for more… *active* groups."

"There's the League of Southern Heritage. They're based in Charleston. It's more of a gentleman's club for people who know people."

"Sounds like Klan for rich people."

"Basically. There's the… European Defense Force—or something like that, anyway. But they mostly cook and sell meth."

"That's not exactly what I had in mind," said Daren.

Smokey nodded and sipped his beer. "Aryan Brotherhood is mostly active in the clink, so probably not what you're looking for. Of course, there's always the Klan. But these days, it's underground. You have to be invited."

"Any of these people from these other groups connected to this Klan?"

"Probably. That shit is all kept hush, hush, though."

"And this League of Southern Heritage doesn't sound like the type of place that accepts membership applications, either," Daren replied.

Smokey nodded. "No, they're not exactly an open group. Of course, the most elite and secretive group is rumored to be the Order of the Southern Cross."

"What's their deal?" Daren asked.

"Who knows? Mostly a conspiracy theory. Folks like to blame them for things ain't nobody can figure out. Heinous acts. They say it was started by Klansmen who were tired of burning crosses. Real fire and brimstone type shit, ya know?"

"You think it's bullshit?"

"I think it's something I don't ask a lot of questions about. But that's just me minded my own. 'Spose if I were to give my pennies on the matter, sounds like a rural legend."

"A rural legend? I've heard of *urban* legends."

"Well, yankee, down here we got our own tall tales," Smokey said with a laugh. "The swamp monsters are my favorite, personally."

The bar was suddenly crowded with men seeking drinks. The woman dancing on the pool table had finished her show. Daren could tell Smokey wasn't comfortable talking around so many people. "Thanks, Smokey," he said with a nod.

"Welcome to the lowcountry, Earl," Smokey replied.

Daren finished his beer and motioned to the bartender for another.

Their sex was almost a competitive sport. They would push each other, dominate, and consume one another. It was relentless and desperate—two bodies coming together in dire need of each other's touch. It was frantic and fiery but also intimate and safe. Together they could express what they each felt afraid to feel. It was passion and lust to wash over the contempt they each held for life. They had an unspoken understanding of each other's needs. Sometimes, it was rough and expressive of anger or grief. Other times it could be focused and slow, comforting and intimate. It was never dull or rote.

Andrea interlocked her fingers with his, holding tightly as she rode him in the back seat of his pickup. She moaned and gasped, her body tensing up before releasing an internal wave of euphoria, then collapsing onto his chest.

It was a much-needed release for them both. For Andrea, it was one of the only things outside of work that made her feel normal—it quieted the noise and anxiety. She wasn't sure exactly what he got out of their regular meetups. She suspected it was, in some way, the same for him. Whatever *this* was, it wasn't something they talked about much.

Tonight's match had been held in the backseat of his truck, which was roomier than her Ford Focus. Andrea climbed off him and retrieved her panties from the floor. She slipped them on then grabbed her pack of smokes from the front seat, lighting two and handing one to him. She stared out the back window of the cab, which was completely covered in a large Blue Lives Matter American flag decal—a black and white flag with one solid blue bar running through the middle.

"Thanks," David replied, taking a long drag from the cigarette and exhaling with a satisfied sigh. "Damn, Dre... You are good..."

"Not so bad yourself," Andrea replied with a crooked grin. She found a t-shirt of his on the floor, gave it a smell check, and then used it to wipe the sex from her body. He smiled and gazed at her with admiration.

They had never made much sense but neither of them cared. They were both cops and they were both a little fucked up. That was all the common ground they needed. He was married to a mouse of a woman, and they both had sons. However, Andrea and David didn't speak of their families. Their relationship was purely physical. It served its purpose without the entanglement and emotional complications that dating always brought. It grounded her. She always felt calmer and more able to cope with life after seeing him.

David smoked, flicking his ashes into an empty beer can. The truck was parked under an overpass in a grass lot used for event parking near Patriots Point—a battleship and military museum located in Mount Pleasant. This had been a frequent spot of theirs. It was where they had first hooked up, just over four years earlier, the night of the city's Fourth of July fireworks show. After watching the fireworks over the river from the deck of the battleship, she and David had run to beat the crowd back to the parking lot and slipped quickly into the back seat of his pickup. Now, whenever they didn't have the time to make getting a room worth it, they would meet here. Unless an event was going on, in which case, David would usually have her meet him at his boat.

The boat was where David would stay when he was fighting with his wife. It was a small, rusted, and moldy fishing boat with a small cabin. The vessel hadn't seen much time on the water since he'd owned it and was in a constant state of repair. She liked their meetups on the boat because it was cozy and rustic, but sometimes he wanted her to sleep there and she didn't care for that. There was something too real about it. She was always assessing this thing between them—always worried he was getting too close. The emotional distance was what made it all work.

However, sitting there with him in his truck, soaked in each other's sweat, smoking without a word, she couldn't help but feel comfortable and even happy. The thought crept through her mind where it sounded an alarm, sending its emissaries through her limbs in tingling sensations—the all too familiar waves of anxiety. The very notion of feeling comfortable with someone made her feel immediately vulnerable and scared. The urge to leave and never call him again took hold of her mind. Despite the inclination, she took a breath and told herself to stop worrying. Something inside her wanted to feel safe with him.

"So, your back to work tomorrow?" she asked, eager to shift her mind's focus.

"That's right," he replied.

"How do you feel about that?" She was always careful not to get personal, but couldn't help but wonder how he was feeling after everything he had been through.

"Okay, I guess. It's going to be weird without him for sure."

Andrea ran her fingertips over his stomach and traced the Celtic cross tattooed on his left breast. "This job takes pieces of us sometimes," she said.

David nodded and pulled her closer. She rested her head on his chest and allowed him to twist the curly strands of her hair around his fingers. "Life is just one thing after another taking pieces of you till there's nothing left," he said. "That's what my father always told me."

Andrea looked up, expecting him to kiss her, but he just stared out the window into the distance. "My father always told me that you start with nothing and you have to take whatever you can," she countered.

"Could be both," he considered. "It's a race to get what you can, and people will take whatever they can from you."

They smoked and laid in silence for a bit, Andrea's thoughts wandering to Carson and the federal agent she'd made a deal with to get him. "I should probably head home soon," she said, breaking the silence.

"Oh? No round two?" he asked playfully.

"I've got this fed I'm meeting downtown early tomorrow," she replied as she pulled her jeans up over her hips.

"*A fed?* What's that all about?" David asked.

"Just some shit," she said, looking around to make sure she had all her things. She didn't want to leave an earring or something for the wifey to find.

"What kind of shit?"

She stopped and laughed. "Since when do you care what I'm doing?"

"Well, you're not usually meeting a fed," he laughed. "Sounds interesting. What's going on?"

"Just helping him out with a little something," she replied.

He looked at her as if he was trying to read her face. "Being a little closed lip, huh?" he teased. "What, you don't trust me?"

"We never talk shop," she said in her defense. "It's about Devon Grey mostly."

"Shit," said David, his tone shifting from playful to grim. "They having any luck with that?"

"Doesn't look that way."

"I would have thought you'd mentioned it to me, being I was one of the units that responded that night," David said defensively.

"Like I said, we don't talk shop." She leaned over and kissed him, then opened the backdoor, and climbed out of the cab.

"See you soon?" he asked.

"Always," she replied with a wink.

Daren stumbled into his room sometime around midnight. His pursuit of information had perhaps led him to consume a few too many drinks. He certainly hadn't intended to drink so much that he'd be forced to leave the rental in Givhans and Uber back to the hotel. Nonetheless, he was now drunk and carless.

He sat on the edge of the bed and fumbled with the lamp, unable to find the switch. After what seemed like an interminable battle, he was able to make the damn thing emit light. Victorious, he sat the light down upon the table and immediately gasped.

"*You dirty son of a bitch*," he muttered, staring wide-eyed at the wall above his bed. He tried to remove his right shoe but lost his balance and fell backward onto the bed. He regained his balance and sat up, looking at the wall in horror. This cockroach was even bigger than the last, and Daren felt like it was watching him. He was not one to be afraid of bugs, but this thing freaked him out. He rose to his feet, and looked around for an object he might squash the invader with but found nothing suitable.

"Fuck this," he said, grabbing his phone and exiting the room.

As soon as he walked out into the thick night air, that foul smell nobody else seemed to notice greeted him and burned his nostrils. It was acidic and overpowering, and after a night of drinking, it was the last thing Daren wanted to smell.

Irritated and inebriated, Daren marched around the corner and into the front office. Bad instrumental jazz filled a poorly lit lobby. The smell of stale coffee had a sobering effect as he approached the counter.

"Hello?!" he called out to the room behind the counter, looking around and seeing no one.

A few moments later, an older Black woman emerged. She was short and looked up at him like she was already tired of his bullshit. "Mm-hm, yessir?" she asked. "What can I do ya for?"

"Yes, hello…" he paused to read her name tag. "Candace. Hi. There is, well, there is a giant cockroach in my room, Candace." He looked her straight in the eyes to impress the legitimacy of his claim.

She held his gaze without batting an eye and replied, "Mm-hmm..." An awkward moment of silence passed, each looking at the other with confusion. "And what is it that you want, sir?" she asked.

"Well, as I said, Candace. There is a rather large bug in my room. In fact, I've already removed one, so at this point, I am left to conclude there's probably more where they came from."

"Did you want another room, sir?" she asked, unfazed by his report.

"Well, are those rooms also housing giant roaches?"

"This is South Carolina, sir," Candace flatly replied.

"So, most likely," Daren concluded. She turned and walked away without saying a word. "Uh… *Hello?*" he called after her.

A moment later she returned. She placed a can of Raid Roach Killer on the counter. "Will there be anything else?" she asked.

Daren took the insecticide and sighed. "Can you at least tell me what that awful smell is outside?" he asked.

"All I smell is the beer on your breath," she said dismissively.

Daren nodded and exited the lobby.

When he reentered his room, he held the bug spray ready like it was a weapon, ready to battle the beast, but it was nowhere to be found. He checked around his bed and under the furniture to no avail. Finally, unable to find the intruder, he sat on his bed, the bug spray close by on the bedside table, and pulled his laptop out from his carry-on bag.

Daren rubbed his eyes and tried to clear the fog. He did a web search for the League of Southern Heritage. The group was led by a man named Avery Dylan. They'd stirred the pot quite a bit years back, sinking big bucks into the political campaigns of racial extremists and anti-immigration initiatives. For the last ten years or so, they'd been relatively quiet.

Further searches revealed the group had taken legal action against another local group that had tried to use its name to imply an association with the League. It was called the Southern Defense League and was started by Avery Dylan's son, Josh, as a more grassroots, activist, arm of the League. But Josh had never cleared the idea with daddy, and the League did not like having any associations with the types of folks Josh was recruiting. The League viewed itself as members of the forgotten Tidewater class—guardians of *true* Southern heritage. It was about class and elegance as much as it was about racial purity. Josh Dylan's spinoff was more the stuff of angry men in chewing tobacco-stained t-shirts screaming at women outside of abortion clinics or intimidating Black voters in line at the polls.

After the legal action, the Southern Defense League was forced to change its name to the European Defense League. It was relatively short-lived, though, as Josh Dylan and several of his associates were soon thereafter busted manufacturing methamphetamine in the Charleston suburb of John's Island. Dylan ratted on his suppliers and friends and was sentenced to time-served after three months in holding. His release had enraged many in the community, with the local paper authoring an op-ed blasting the judge for falling prey to Avery Dylan's influence and wealth. All this had transpired the previous summer.

This was all pertinent because the European Defense League's insignia was the same symbol that had been carved into the tree from which Devon Grey was hanged. The problem was the symbol, a Norse rune referred to the as the life rune or sometimes an algiz, while not as well-known as symbols like the swastika, had a long history of association with white supremacists, and thus could not be definitively linked to one group. Investigators had questioned members of the EDL, but interestingly enough, not Josh Dylan himself, who had a corroborated alibi putting him in North Carolina the day of Grey's murder.

Josh Dylan, his quarreling with his father, and the EDL were all logical places to start. The way he saw it, if he wanted to solve a hate crime, he might as well start with the most notorious local racists.

Daren read some more about the Dylans and their family history until he found himself nodding off. Groggily, he went to shut his laptop but stopped. Remembering what Smokey had told him, he decided to do one last search on the Order of the Southern Cross. He found that the group was allegedly named for the original pact that had formed the KKK in New Orleans in 1865. Most modern references were from conspiracy sites and far-left blogs that alleged members of the police force and local politicians were all associated with the Southern Cross. While it was intriguing, it was also likely baseless. He shut his laptop, laid back on the bed, closed his eyes, and waited for sleep to come. He was meeting Watts in downtown Charleston in the morning. Maybe she could recommend a better place to stay.

6

HISTORIC DOWNTOWN CHARLESTON wasn't very large. At one point the city had been entirely located on the small peninsula now referred to as downtown. Like many U.S. cities, Charleston's boundaries had been extended numerous times to accommodate suburban sprawl. From the 1960s through the turn of the century, money and people poured into Charleston's many suburbs, resulting in an abandoned and increasingly blighted downtown. Then, in the past fifteen years or so, the wealthy started pouring money into preserving and revitalizing downtown. Suddenly, everyone wanted to live in the historic sections, which caused real estate prices to skyrocket.

Charleston's historic charm and Southern aesthetic had helped transform it into a bustling tourist destination. It was a go-to location for vacations and one of the hottest cities to get married in on the east coast. It was a beautiful city; stately looking, pastel colored homes were built close to the curb, beside roads lined with beautiful oak trees that above formed leafy canopies. Historic church steeples stood out as the tallest structures on the peninsula. Horse-drawn carriages brought tourists past all the must-see locations: Rainbow Row, the battery, the market, and various homes that once belonged to wealthy, well-known names.

Andrea walked along the top of the seawall that lined the battery located at the tip of the peninsula. From there she could see Fort Sumter, the infamous site of the first shots of the Civil War. She looked out over the rough sea at a ferry bringing tourists back from the fort. Then she gazed over her shoulder toward the battery, where a monument consisting of two allegorical statues stood. One of the statues, the woman, adorned in a long dress, represented the city of Charleston. In front of her, a male figure stands nude, a sword in one hand, and a shield in the other. Upon the shield was the state seal. The engraving on the monument read, "To the Confederate Defenders of Charleston." It had been erected in the 30s, to memorialize a generation of veterans who fought to keep her ancestors enslaved. Now, some eighty years later, it still stood there at the base of the city. She wondered if the city could ever reconcile its desire to leave its history in the past with its attempts to romanticize and profit from it.

It had rained overnight and the seas were high. Hightide frequently flooded downtown, and when the city got enough rain, many roads would become impassable. That was a part of life here, as much as the traffic and the institutionalized racism. Sometimes, it felt as if mother nature were trying to swallow the city.

Daren emerged from the back of an Uber, looking a bit rough. She smiled and waved from atop the seawall to catch his attention. He crossed the street and climbed the stone steps to join her.

"Wow, it's beautiful here," he said, taking in the sight. The wind whipped and howled, forcing them to speak loudly to be heard over it.

"It really is," she replied. "I wanted to show you this because if you're going to be here, investigating a murder, and asking questions about race, you need to understand what this city is all about."

"I'm a student of history," he insisted. "I know all about the South."

"Mm, I'm sure you think you do," Andrea replied, shaking her head. "But studying and living are very different things. How much time you spent in the South?"

"Before yesterday?" he asked with a laugh that seemed to acknowledge her point. "Alright, Watts. Show me what I need to see."

"The first of them are just starting to show up," she said, pointing across to the Confederate monument. A few men had begun to gather there with signs. One read: "*You Can't Tear Down History.*" Another read: "*Censorship is the tool of tirants,*" with tyrants misspelled.

"The Secessionist Party started the tradition. Now we get people from all types of hate groups. They all come here to defend the Confederate statues and scream about being replaced."

"That's fantastic!" Daren said. Andrea looked at him, confused. "Tell me local PD has been identifying them. Keeping plate numbers? Pictures?" he asked.

Andrea laughed and shook her head.

"They're exercising their First Amendment rights, Agent Renard," she said, disdain dripping from her voice. "That would be profiling these people for their political beliefs."

"Come on," he gasped. "Local PD wants to solve a hate crime, but they're not looking into open racial extremists?"

Andrea could only shrug. "Guess there's too many to keep track of down here. We leave that to y'all."

Daren nodded, pulled out his phone, and was soon on the line with someone in D.C. "I need local uniforms to set up down here and take information on anyone coming to these protests," Daren said into the phone. "Now. The protest is just starting now. Do whatever you got to do, just make it happen... Uh-huh... Has my paperwork for Watts been filed with the Marshal's Office? Okay. Great."

"Wow," Andrea said. "I guess that's what it's like to have some actual pull."

"I got you deputized in under twelve hours, too," he bragged.

"In my world, there's red tape everywhere. I can barely do my job."

"I'm the guy they send in when they want to cut through the tape," he replied.

Andrea was impressed but all the more skeptical. A man with that kind of pull could easily screw over anyone he wanted to. Did he really need her, or was she there to lend him legitimacy, or even cover? Her instincts told her to proceed carefully. She didn't want to find herself in a situation she couldn't control. For now, she was in control, and she could always back out of their arrangement if she needed to.

She directed his attention to ferries on the water, heading to Fort Sumter in the distance. "Do you know what that is, mister history buff?"

"I'm assuming that must be Fort Sumter," Daren replied.

"And do you know who's on those boats?" Andrea asked with a raised eyebrow.

"Tourists?"

"And if you had to guess, what color do you think most of those tourists are?"

"I would wager they're mostly white," he said.

She nodded and then he nodded slowly as if he were slowly dissecting and processing what she was telling him.

"Now look around you," she continued. "Look at these beautiful historic homes."

"It's picturesque. Beautiful. Historic," Daren remarked.

"But what does it represent?" she asked.

"History?"

"When specifically?"

"Early America."

"*Antebellum* America," she corrected him. "Pre-Civil War."

"Well, that's part of the city's history, right?" he asked.

"We were a British colony, at one time. Do you see statues to the king or the Union Jack flying anywhere in South Carolina?"

"I hadn't considered that," he admitted.

"Now look at these all these homes. All that wealth in the Antebellum South—where did it come from?"

"A lot of it came from slavery," he answered with an understanding nod.

"*All* of these wealthy families benefited either directly or indirectly from slavery. These homes stand today as supposed monuments to Southern elegance and class. People tour them and take pictures of them. But they were built through blood and oppression."

"Isn't this true of all of history, though? It's all ugly and it's all uncivilized," Daren argued.

"We don't romanticize, sanitize, and sell every chapter of history like this city does its Antebellum history."

"I'm still not sure what you're trying to tell me. I mean, I get the gist of your points, but what does this have to do with the case?"

"You're here digging into racism in a city where race touches everything. Our entire image is based on a whitewashed version of history that marginalizes Black Americans."

"Maybe what the situation needs is an impartial outsider, who's not concerned with history or local socio-economics. I'm here to find out who murdered Devon Grey. That's it."

"And just how do you think you're going to find the truth if you don't understand the context of what happened?"

"What context?" Daren scoffed. "Some racist hillbillies lynched a Black kid. That's the end of the story."

"Racist hillbillies are a dime a dozen down here," Andrea laughed. "That's why nobody is making lists of people like that," she said, pointing to the group of protesters. "Because the difference between them and half these people's relatives and friends is pretty much just a damn sign."

"What are you trying to say?" Daren asked. "You think there's a cover-up or something?"

"No, I'm just saying there's a lot of reasons why folks might not go looking too hard around here. And I'm saying that these kinds of things get folks nervous. There's a lot of secrets buried; a lot of people and families with unsavory histories or associations."

Andrea gazed across the water. The morning sun was rising and breaking through the clouds. It danced across the ripples and bathed the city in light. "This city wants so badly to move forward," she said. "But it's stuck in the past."

"And what about North Charleston?" he asked.

"*That* city has moved forward quite a bit," she replied. "But there's a lot of barriers and not everyone is moving with it."

"What kind of barriers?"

Their conversation was cut short when a sheriff's cruiser pulled up to the battery, and the driver looked around, noticeably unsure.

"More on that another day," Andrea said, walking down the steps and crossing the road to the cruiser.

"Wait, Watts," Daren said, catching up to her and putting his hand out to stop her. "What was all this about?"

"Like I said, I just thought you should know," she told him. "And maybe I wanted to see how you reacted to it."

"Like a litmus test or something?"

"More or less."

"How'd I do?" he asked.

Andrea rolled her eyes and continued across the street. Daren followed.

"That bad?" He laughed uncomfortably.

"Could've been worse."

"How so?"

"You could have been *explicitly* racist," she said. "Or you could have patronized me more." She could tell her remarks puzzled Daren, which made her smile. They reached the cruiser, and Andrea knocked on the driver's window. "Is this CCSO's idea of undercover?" she asked the deputy.

"I'm sorry?" the deputy replied.

"You're here because the Agent Renard's call, right?" she inquired.

"Well, yes, but no," the deputy tried to explain. "We've got a unit in an unmarked car on the other side of the battery to watch the protest. Sheriff wanted me to come down here and ask you two a favor."

"*Us?*" Andrea asked, confused.

"What's he need?" asked Daren.

"There's... Well, let's just say it's an unusual situation," said the deputy. "Weird even... Sheriff thought, since we have a federal asking for our help on the same day, well... figured it just might be proper to ask if y'all could come take a look see."

He was a young kid, white with short, buzz-cut, brown hair. Andrea had met many like him. Farmhands and jocks who, after realizing they'd never make it in the pros, hung up their jockstraps and became cops. They still chased cheerleaders and pounded beers with their bros on the weekends, only now they had authority over others and a license to use deadly force. "What's this concerning, deputy?" she asked him.

"Dead pigs, ma'am," the deputy replied.

"I'm sorry, did you say *dead pigs?* Like farm animals?" Andrea asked in disbelief. "I'm sorry, but we're a little busy today."

"Where?" Daren interjected.

"Summerville, sir," the deputy replied.

"Great, can you bring us to my car in Givhans after?" Daren requested. Andrea blinked twice, unsure of what was happening.

"Yes sir, not a problem," answered the deputy.

"Fantastic," Daren said, grabbing the handle to the car's back door. He looked at Andrea, who stood stiff, scowling at him. "Relax. It's on the way to my car," he reassured her. "We'll go see what's going on with these dead pigs, and then we'll go catch this human trafficker of yours. We'll make a whole day out of it," he said with a smile.

"Didn't I just warn you about patronizing me?"

"Sorry," Daren replied with a smirk.

"You really want to see what's up with these pigs?" she asked.

"Don't you?" he asked eagerly. "A Southern sheriff wants us to take a look at dead pigs. *This is some real local color!*" She sighed and he opened the back door. "You want to sit in the cage with me?" he asked.

Andrea was annoyed but decided it was better to placate him, at least until they caught Carson. She climbed into the back of the cruiser and Daren slid in behind her.

"How'd your car end up Givhans?" she asked Daren as they pulled away from the battery. Daren ignored the question and stared out the window at the racist protesters, now numbering near a dozen.

He noticed another group was coming together on the other side of the park, led by a few Black women.

"Counter-protesters?" he asked.

"Yup," Andrea said, rolling her eyes. "Yelling at the racists in the park. Making a real difference…" She could see her sarcasm surprised Daren. She raised a hand, as if telling him not to ask.

As the cruiser drove past the counter-protesters, she stared at one woman in particular. The woman had long braided hair and a face of steely determination. Andrea could not help but admire her—she was purpose personified. The woman caught her looking and stared back with a look of disappointment. Andrea knew the look as well as she knew the woman. It was her sister, Mikayla.

Vultures feed off the dead. The dead sow's bloody corpse called to them like a hot lunch special. The sheriff and another officer were shooing them away when Daren, Andrea, and their driver, Deputy Gibbs arrived. Gibbs put his emergency lights on and parked alongside the sheriff's SUV. But the sheriff took issue with this and ran up to Gibbs's window to object.

"You gotta pull onto the grass, son," the sheriff instructed. "This road's too narrow."

Gibbs did as he was told, and the three exited the car.

"Sorry, about that," the sheriff explained. "This road is a damn hazard. We want to widen it, but it'll never happen. Can't cut down the precious trees and ruin the scenic drive by our goddamn plantations, you see?" He was a gruff man with a thick, blonde beard, and was considerably younger than Daren had expected.

Cars sped by in both directions at speeds of fifty, sixty miles an hour. "Does seem a little narrow," Daren remarked.

"Anyway," the sheriff said, extending his hand to Daren. "You must be Special Agent Renard. I'm Sheriff Mark Greenly"

Daren shook his hand and looked him squarely in the eyes. It was something he liked to do when meeting people. He found it made some people uncomfortable, and he tended not to trust those people. Greenly returned the look and smiled confidently.

"Please to meet you," Daren replied. "This is Detective Andrea Watts with North Charleston's Special Victims Unit. I've deputized her to assist me with my investigation."

"Detective," Greenly said with a courteous tip of his hat. He and Andrea shook hands. "And this is Sergeant Kelly," Greenly said, introducing them to the man to his right. "He's with the animal control unit."

Daren shook Kelly's hand and smiled. "So, tell me about these dead pigs," he said.

"Started happening about a month ago," Kelly replied. "We got a call that someone had hit a pig. Now, we got a lot of boars in these parts. So, that's not all too unusual. But it wasn't no boar—it was a pig from someone's farm. Even stranger, this pig wasn't hit, it was shot. Someone just left it there by the side of the road."

Sheriff Greenly and Sergeant Kelly led the group over to the pig. Daren slapped on a pair of latex gloves he got from Kelly and knelt beside it. He swatted away flies and tried not to gag. The smell was already quite bad.

"Then we found three others within the next two days. All shot with high caliber rifles and ditched on the side of the road," Kelly continued.

"Come to find out," Greenly added. "Dorchester county has been finding them, too."

"That's the next county over," Andrea told Daren.

Daren poked and prodded the bullet holes with his finger. "No bullets," he remarked. That concerned him. "Sheriff," he said, rising quickly to his feet. "I'm afraid you have a real problem here."

"I ain't no fool, Agent Renard," Greenly replied. "I know something ain't right here. That's why I wanted to talk to you. What is it you think we're dealing with here?"

"Well, the good news is that Sergeant Kelly here can go home," Daren replied.

"I'm sorry?" Kelly scoffed.

"I mean unless you're worried about pressing animal cruelty charges. But I would say there are bigger concerns here," Daren concluded, removing his gloves and handing them to Kelly to dispose. "You guys got a terrorism unit, right?" he asked Greenly.

"Threat prevention, yes sir. They work with all y'all at the FBI." Greenly answered.

"Have they been made aware of any of this?" Daren asked.

"As of now, they have not," said Greenly.

"You're going to want to call them."

"Just what is it you think is happening here, Agent Renard?" Greenly asked, the concern rising in his voice.

"Sheriff, you have a pattern of violence here that indicates a larger threat," Daren tried to explain.

"This is absurd," Kelly protested. "I told you, Sheriff—he's a hammer, so everything looks like a nail. Terrorism threat?! C'mon, y'all. It's dead pigs! Probably just some kids being kids."

"Look, he's right," Daren retorted. "I'm not from around here. I'm not familiar with the culture or the customs. So, for all I know, maybe redneck teens do shoot pigs with high caliber rifles, remove the led, and ditch them on the side of the road for fun."

Kelly rolled his eyes.

"I'll tell you three things I see," Daren continued. "One: you have recurring incidents where pigs are being executed. Two: these pigs are being ditched on the side of the road, which means somebody doesn't want the owners to know they're shooting their pigs. And finally, three: they're removing the rounds before they discard the pigs."

"Why would they do all that?" Gibbs asked.

"What you have here is someone practicing killing. Now, I don't want to be an alarmist, but what kind of person do you suppose would practice killing multiple targets and then ditch the evidence?"

The group fell silent, including Kelly. A collective chill washed over them.

"I'm going to assume the other pigs have been destroyed?" Daren asked.

Greenly looked to Kelly who nodded. "I knew something wasn't right here," Greenly said to Daren. "I'm sure as shit glad you were here today to confirm it."

"Something about this is very unsettling," Daren agreed. "Whoever is doing this is practicing for something."

Greenly removed his brimmed hat and ran his fingers through his hair in exacerbation. Andrea stood back from the group a bit, observing. Daren could tell she was more interested in assessing him than whatever had happened to the pig.

"Of course, you'll want to save the pigs from now on," Daren told them. "Check them for any brands or tags. Find out where the pigs are coming from and you'll be closer to finding whoever is doing this. I'll make a note of this in my report, but you'll want to notify your threat prevention unit immediately."

Greenly nodded understandingly. Vultures circled overhead and perched in the oaks above, waiting for a chance to swoop back in for their lunch. The scene gave Daren an eerie feeling.

"Gibbs will bring you back to town," said Greenly, as he walked them back to the cruiser.

"He's actually going to bring us up to the rental car I left in Givhans. Watts and I got a predator to catch," Daren told Greenly.

"And a stop over to North Charleston PD for some equipment," Andrea added.

"Oh, well, then… happy hunting," said Greenly with a firm nod.

Sheriff Greenly shook hands with Daren and Andrea before they parted. As they pulled away in Gibbs's cruiser, Daren saw the sheriff standing over the dead sow with a look of disbelief. "You seem unconcerned about all that," he said, turning to Andrea. "You think I'm wrong?"

Andrea pierced her lips and shook her head slowly. "No, I don't think you're wrong. This is America, there's a mass shooting every day. We just don't care about them all," she said.

"Terrorism is still a serious threat," Daren argued. "It's not really the same issue if we're talking about inner city violence."

"And why is that?" she asked.

Daren almost started to explain that one issue was driven by hatred, the other by socio-economic factors but he stopped. Considering her perspective, he suddenly understood that the varying causes didn't matter so much as the lives lost, and in the end, the distinction seemed blurry at best. "I guess I don't know," he admitted.

7

THE TRAILER WAS barely visible from the road. Thick oaks covered in Spanish moss provided shade to the property and privacy from any passersby. The trailer, once white, was slowly being reclaimed by nature and was now discolored with mold, and covered in moss and vines. A dirty, old mattress was laid conspicuously in the front yard, the sight of which gave Daren uneasy feelings.

The property, which contained the only residence in sight, bordered a marshy creek. Every rock, tree, and discarded household item was covered in a thick, leafy vine. The creek appeared to be entirely consumed in one tightly-knit knot of vines.

"What is all that shit covering everything?" Daren asked Andrea.

"Kudzu," Andrea replied. She lit a smoke and offered one to Daren. He grimaced, declined, and cracked his driver-side window for fresh air.

"This is a rental, you know?" he remarked. She raised an eyebrow in consideration then continued to smoke. "So that's the vine they say is strangling the South," he said. "It's almost pretty."

"This time of year," said Andrea. "In the winter it just looks like death strangling the living."

"Sounds lovely…"

"The kudzu is a curse. At least that's what my gram always says."

"How's that?"

"In the Antebellum South, this was the land of plantations. The South's whole economy was dependent on the plantations, and the plantations were dependent on slave labor. The whole system was unnatural. Native Americans taught the pilgrims how to rotate crops to keep the soil fertile, but the plantation masters didn't care about any of that. Cotton was the cash crop and that's all they wanted to grow. Didn't matter none that the soil was being sucked dry—just like the men and women working those fields. They drove their slaves to death working that land, and at the same time, they killed the land," Andrea explained.

"So, where does the kudzu come in?"

"The Kudzu was supposed to replenish the soil," she explained. "The land owners imported it from Europe and began planting it everywhere. But it didn't belong here. It had no predators in this environment. It just spread and spread, covering everything, and killing off other species. So, Gram says the Kudzu is a curse. A reminder from God that the crimes of slavery and colonization cannot be simply covered and forgotten."

Daren stared at the Kudzu vines. "Amazing how something can change the environment like that."

They were parked just down the road from the trailer, the nose of Daren's rental car peeking out from a field of overgrown grass. Daren had wanted to drive right up and knock on the front door. Andrea had laughed at the notion and told him that's not how it's done. "He's a fugitive. He won't go quietly," she'd told him.

Daren didn't want to come across as out of his depth, but he was, and he knew Andrea could tell.

"You've never done this before, have you?" she asked, concerned.

"Not exactly," he admitted.

Andrea sighed and shook her head. "Really? Special Agent with the FBI and you've never apprehended a suspect?"

"I'm an investigator!" Daren exclaimed defensively. "I solve crimes and close cases. I don't storm buildings and take down bad guys."

"Have you ever even fired your weapon?" she asked.

"In the field?"

Andrea sighed and rolled her eyes.

He stiffened up; his ego bruised. "I'm a federal agent," he asserted confidently. "I've been trained to do this. Relax." He wasn't going to sweat about some redneck. He didn't need the fourth degree from her about it, either.

"Listen," she said. "Carson is in that trailer. He's hurt a lot of people—a lot of children. I'm not letting him get away. Now chances are, we wait for the right moment, we can go in and I'll have the son of a bitch in cuffs before he can blink. But if shit goes down, I can't be worried about you. I need to know you can handle yourself."

Daren reassured her. "Like I said: I'm good." She was starting to irritate him.

Andrea raised her eyebrow then nodded slowly. "*Like I said*, shouldn't be a big thing. When the time comes, just follow my directions. If we catch him off guard, he won't be able to put up a fight."

"You sure we don't want to call in the locals? Do we know for sure he's got them in his pocket?" he asked. The trailer gave him a bad feeling. He wasn't going to admit it, but he was scared.

"I don't know which sheriffs he has on the take but if he's living here…"

"There's probably a reason," Daren concluded.

"Ain't too hard for a trafficker to buy a hillbilly sheriff only making thirty-five-K-a-year," she noted.

They sat there for some time, watching the property. Daren gazed at the oaks as their leaves danced in the wind, sweat dripping down his face. He started the car and welcomed the rush of cold air from the vents. Andrea saw him sweating and smiled amusedly.

"How long do we sit here for? What are we watching for?" he asked impatiently.

"I told you to buy snacks and drinks," she said, grabbing a small plastic bag from under her feet and handing him a bottle of water.

Daren took the water with a grateful nod. "I didn't think we'd be sitting here all day," he countered.

Another hour passed. Daren finished his water and soon thereafter exited the car to urinate. When he returned, Andrea nudged him with excitement. "Look what we have here," she said, pointing down the road.

A man with long, greasy, blonde hair and a straggly beard was staggering down the road toward the trailer. He wore overalls with no shirt underneath. His shoes were tattered and torn.

"That Carson?" Daren asked.

"No," Andrea replied. "Probably a customer. Here to by some of that blow Carson's slinging."

"So, we wait till he comes out, scoop him up, and squeeze him?"

Andrea smiled. "Wow, you actually *are* a cop!"

Daren couldn't help but laugh.

The man crossed onto Carson's property and approached the trailer door. He knocked, was quickly let inside, and emerged less than five minutes later. The man briskly crossed the lawn and began to walk down the road towards Daren and Andrea's location. They waited until he'd passed before pulling out.

Daren slowly pulled the car up beside the man, and Andrea flashed him her badge.

"*Oh, fuckin' come on!*" the man yelled in frustration, instantly aware he was busted.

"There's still a chance for you to walk away from here without charges," Andrea told him.

"We don't even care about the coke in your pocket," Daren added.

Confused, the man waited for instructions.

"Get in the back," Andrea commanded. The man shook his head in disbelief before complying. "What's your name?" she asked him as Daren drove slowly down the road away from Carson's trailer.

"Squid," the man answered.

"Squid?" Daren asked with a chuckle. "That's what your birth certificate says?"

"Y'all charging me or what? Didn't know you needed my fucking social security number, mother's maiden name and shit," Squid shot back.

Daren examined the man through the rearview. He smelled awful and spat when he spoke. His front teeth were rotten and Black.

"What kind of information you got?" Andrea asked, turning in her seat to face him.

"Shit," Squid laughed. "Y'all be surprised what I know. I'm like a squirrel. Runnin' 'round gathering up everyone else's nuts. I know where everybody's dirt is buried."

"Squid is like a squirrel, and you dig up dirt," Daren repeated in disbelief. "Makes perfect sense. How much blow did you snort in there?"

"Fuck off, pig. I know the drill. Y'all wanna roll me. That's fine by me, but can we hurry this the hell up, please? I got places to be."

Daren shot Andrea a look of doubt and shook his head.

"Who's in the trailer?" Andrea asked Squid.

"Y'all looking for Billy or Trip?"

"Bill Carson is in the trailer?" Andrea asked.

"That's what I just said, sweetheart."

"Who's Trip?" Daren asked.

"He's fuckin' Trip, man," Squid said with a defiant shrug. "What the fuck else is there to say?"

"Anyone else in there?" Andrea asked.

"Nope, just Billy and Trip."

"Are they armed?" asked Daren.

Squid laughed, shook his head, then pinched his nose and snorted. "Do y'all know who you're even fuckin' with? Yeah, they're probably fuckin' armed, man!" He cackled in disbelief.

"Did you see any weapons?" Andrea asked.

"Just a knife on the table. But I know Billy's got a gun somewhere."

Daren caught Andrea's concerned glance. He could tell she was unsure if she could count on him. It was true that he had never been in a fire fight, but he had spent countless hours on the range. He reassured himself—he was a capable shooter with quick reflexes.

"Billy and Trip are fuckin' crazy, though, y'all. I don't even like dealing with them," Squid added.

"Then why ya here?" Andrea asked.

"Gotta score somewhere," Squid said with a shrug.

"What else can you tell us?" asked Daren.

"I don't know, man. What do you want to know?"

"When would be the best time for us to pay him a visit?" Andrea asked.

"Well," Squid began, taking a moment to ponder the question. "Trip is out cold, man. He's been partying for three days. And Billy… Well, if I were y'all, I'd wait till Jeopardy."

"With Alex Tribec?" Daren asked in confusion.

"Fuck yeah, man! Billy always watches on Saturday."

"Jeopardy airs Monday through Friday," Daren corrected him.

Andrea looked at him and shook her head. "Must be a white people thing," she said.

"Nah, man," Squid insisted. "Saturday is, like, the greatest hits or whatever. It's like the best of Jeopardy or some shit. Starts at 6:30. Billy loves that shit for some reason. He's always yelling out the answers— ain't never get 'em right, but still…"

Andrea gave Squid a smoke for his troubles before they cut him loose. Once he was gone, Daren gave Andrea a worried look.

"There's only two of them and one is incapacitated," Andrea reassured him. "Don't worry, if they try to hurt you, I'll just kill them."

Simple enough. Daren looked at his watch. It was going to be a very slow afternoon.

There were few things worse than breaking in a new partner. The trust that David had with Greg was not something that two people could establish overnight. It took years of working together. He knew it wasn't rational, but he resented his new partner. This kind of uncertainty put him on edge.

Deputy Anthony Lane, a baby-faced Black man fresh out of the academy, returned to their CCSO-issued SUV with two coffees. He took his seat—the position where Greg had once sat—and handed David one of the coffees.

"Thanks, rook," David replied. He sipped his coffee and examined Lane. He didn't have anything against Black cops per se, but the politically incorrect truth of the matter was that sometimes it was harder for them to do the job. They had to learn they were first and foremost *blue*.

Lane tried to make small talk, but David was not interested.

"I like to sit here," David told him. "This part of the peninsula is where a lot of the crime from North Charleston spills over."

"It's hard to keep track of where our jurisdiction is," Lane replied.

"County has pockets on the peninsula and throughout North Charleston. Areas that haven't been incorporated into either city. You'll get to know where they are, but there's a map in the glove box if you want to take a look."

Lane pulled out the paper map and unfolded it, laying it out on his lap. It was a street map of Charleston, North Charleston, and the surrounding areas. The areas that fell under either Charleston PD's or North Charleston PD's jurisdiction were grayed out in pencil.

"Dispatch mostly knows what addresses go to who, but learn it anyway. It can be a bit confusing," David told him. Lane nodded and studied the map. "The good part of it is," David continued, "These other departments don't know the boundaries all that great, either. We operate within their cities. They pretty much defer to us when push comes to shove. We can push those boundaries a little if we need to."

Lane nodded again and continued to study the map. David could tell he was nervous. At least he wasn't cocky.

Just up the road, a car containing two Black males rolled through a stop sign and continued toward the highway. A perfect test. David dropped the shifter into drive and punched the gas.

Lane was taken by surprise and quickly stuffed the map back into the glove box. "What's up?" he asked.

"They rolled through that stop. Let's see what you got," David replied, hitting the switch and turning on their emergency lights. He sounded the siren a couple of times and quickly rode up on the vehicle's rear. The car, an older white Honda, pulled over immediately.

"Let me see what you got," David said again. "Approach passenger-side. I'll back you up from the rear."

Lane nodded and exited the SUV. David opened his door and slowly emerged. Lane walked alongside the curb to the passenger window, identified himself to the two teen passengers, and asked for the driver's license and registration. David positioned himself at the rear of the vehicle on its driver-side. He unclipped his holster and rested his right hand on the grip of his service firearm.

Lane smiled and handed the papers back to the driver. David shook his head with a tsk and approached the driver-side window.

"What's the story here, Deputy?" David asked Lane as he leered into the vehicle, his hand still resting on his gun.

"Everything is fine, Sergeant. I was just telling them they can be on their way," Lane replied.

David glanced around the car suspiciously. The kids were nervous as hell. A good sign they were hiding something. He motioned for Lane to join him and walked to the rear of the vehicle.

"Just some kids out cruising," Lane explained. "I gave them a warning."

"You gave them a written warning?" David asked, feigning surprise.

"No," Lane said, confused. "Obviously, not. I didn't see the point…"

"Oh, you didn't see the point," David repeated snidely. "Why am I not surprised?" he asked himself.

"What's that supposed to mean?" Lane asked defensively. "They just rolled a stop sign, man."

"Have they been drinking or using drugs? I sure as hell smelled marijuana, did you ask either of them about that?"

Lane stammered, unable to find words.

"Did you know we've had a pair of kids doing B-and-Es in West Ashley?"

"Sergeant, these are just some kids out cruising. The driver said it's his birthday. I thought we cut people breaks?"

"Not kids who fit the description of suspects."

"What description is that?" Lane asked defiantly. "*Black?*" David stared at him and shook his head in disbelief. "Well, is there anything else?" Lane pressed. "Or is every Black kid out here a B-and-E suspect?"

"I told you," David said sternly, stepping closer to Lane and lowering his voice. "I smelled marijuana. That's probable cause."

Lane shook his head and sighed, but David was not discussing the matter any further. His hand still firmly on his gun, he ordered the driver out of the car.

"Do it slowly!" David instructed him. "Deputy Lane! Please remove, search, and secure the male passenger in the front seat! I've got Coolio here," he sneered, remarking on the driver's cornrows.

The driver did as he told, as David ordered him to place his hands on the hood of the car. David positioned himself authoritatively behind the man, kicked his feet apart, and then pressed his head down firmly onto the hood. The man trembled as he searched him. David pushed harder against the back of his head and tears started to leak from his eyes. "Why you so nervous?" David asked sternly.

The driver didn't speak, he just shook with fear.

"This is bullshit," the passenger remarked as Lane searched him.

"Just calm down and be cool," Lane urged him.

David finished searching the driver and cuffed him. Lane did the same with the passenger.

"What the fuck did we do?" the passenger yelled.

"You're not under arrest," David told them as they sat them on the curb. "We're just securing you so we can finish safely searching the vehicle."

David could see their fear. He instructed Lane to search the vehicle while he kept an eye on the two suspects. It wasn't long before Lane emerged from the front seat with a tiny plastic bag of bright green pot. He reluctantly handed the baggie to David.

"What's left of a gram bag," said Lane.

"Okay, thug life," David said to the driver. "We found it under your seat? You coping to it, or we gotta drag you and your buddy downtown and make him roll on you?" The driver sobbed. "C'mon now, sunshine," David said with a laugh. "Be a man and own it!"

"It's mine," the driver muttered.

"That a boy," said David, grabbing the driver by his arms, which were still cuffed behind his back, and lifting him to his feet. "Deputy Lane, you may release the passenger, but he'll have to find a ride. The car will be impounded."

Lane muttered something under his breath before complying. David shook his head disapprovingly and proceeded to place the driver into the back of the SUV.

8

DAREN WASN'T SURE how tight the bullet-proof vest was supposed to be around his torso. He kept pulling at it, loosening it, and then tightening it. He could tell Andrea was amused. "Can I get a little help?" he finally asked.

"Didn't learn this in training?" Andrea quipped, condescension dripping from her voice. She made him lift his arms and tightened his vest. "You want it snug, just not so snug you can't breathe," she told him.

Daren watched her as she adjusted the vest and found himself admiring her dark brown eyes—they had such purpose behind them. He looked away, not wanting his gaze to linger or his mind to fully articulate how attractive she was.

Andrea finished adjusting his vest and then checked her gun. She racked a round into the chamber and tucked it into the holster in the back of her jeans. Daren checked that his gun was secure on his hip, a preference she had, for some reason, found amusing. She peered over the car, through the tall grass, and down the road toward the trailer.

Daren checked the time on his phone. 6:32 PM. The cicadas had begun to make their awful sound, and that smell was back. "You smell that?" he asked.

"Smell what?" Andrea replied.

Daren shook his head. "Nothing. Are we ready?"

Andrea placed her hand on his vest, looked him in the eye, and said, "Listen. This isn't a big deal." She spoke with a calming and assured tone. "Just stay by my side and back me up. I do this all the time."

"Hey, I'm cool as a cucumber," he said, trying his best to keep his voice level.

She nodded and pointed across the street. "We'll approach tight to the tree line until we get to that palm, then we'll cut into the woods so we can approach the trailer from the side and avoid any windows."

Her confidence calmed his nerves. He nodded and followed her, both darting across the road.

Daren had certainly not anticipated doing anything like this on this assignment, but he needed a good detective with knowledge of the area, and frankly, almost everyone else from her department seemed like a piece of shit. An assumption that was backed up by the department's reputation for scandal and brutality, never mind what Deputy Chief Mulholland had told him. Daren was due to give his first progress report tomorrow and he hadn't even begun to investigate. Truth was, without Andrea, he wouldn't know where to start.

He followed Andrea down the road, along the tree line, and into the woods. They crouched down low and moved slowly to avoid making noise. Not far into their advance, Daren noticed how loudly he was breathing. He stopped, crouched against a tree, and tried to focus on slowing his breath.

Andrea saw him and shook her head. "*Stay close to me!*" she whispered emphatically.

Daren nodded and continued, crouching low, and trying to move as silently as possible. As they reached the end of the wood line near the side of the trailer, Andrea paused and quickly raised her hand, signaling for him to freeze. She was looking ahead, concerned. Slowly, she turned her head and shifted herself around just enough so he could see her face.

"*Move right!*" she whispered sharply.

They swiftly ducked behind a large oak tree to their right. Pressing against the trunk, they hunkered close together. Andrea nudged him and nodded toward the yard, behind the trailer, where a shirtless man in torn jeans was standing, pissing into the creek.

"That's not Carson," Andrea whispered. "Too big."

"So, Trip isn't passed out," noted Daren. He suddenly felt less than great about their odds. He leaned in close to her and whispered, "Let's pull back and stake the place out. Wait till he's alone."

Andrea furrowed her brow and shook her head.

"*Come on!*" Daren urged. "Two on two in a trailer... That's dicey."

Andrea sighed and nodded reluctantly. She was pissed off, but he could tell she knew he was right. The man had finished pissing and was heading back inside. "Fine," she conceded. "Fall back."

Daren sighed with relief. He turned around to head back toward the road, but on his next step, he felt his foot catch on something. "What the hell?" he asked, maybe too loudly.

"What? What's wrong?" Andrea asked, stepping closely behind him.

Daren felt down around his foot and discovered a piece of fishing line running across the ground.

"*It's a trip sensor!*" Andrea exclaimed.

Daren was stunned and unsure what to do. Andrea grabbed him by the back of his vest and pulled him so hard that he fell back onto his ass. Before he knew what had happened, she was dragging him back behind the oak tree. He laid there with his back against her, and her back pressed firmly against the oak. He lifted his head to look back at her, and she held a finger to her lips to keep him silent.

Then the shots started. The first whipped through the leaves to their left. A moment later, the second buried itself into the ground to their right. The sounds of the gunfire were confusing. Daren could hear the supersonic whizzing sound of the bullets flying by and the *thud* they made when they impacted the ground before the reports coming from the trailer. He froze in fear, totally unsure of what to do.

"Get on your feet!" Andrea yelled, nudging him forward.

Daren lurched forward, rose to his feet, and pulled his gun from his holster. Andrea already had hers drawn. She knelt on the ground, leaned around the oak's trunk, and fired several rounds at the trailer. He leaned left to do the same, but a round struck the tree close to his head, and he reflexively jerked back.

That's when the small caliber rounds turned into a hailstorm of automatic fire from a military-grade assault weapon.

They dove to the ground, the rounds cutting through the brush around them and boring deeply into the trunk of the oak that shielded them. The fire rained relentlessly for what seemed like an eternity but was only about thirty seconds. Then it stopped. Daren leaned against the tree, his ears ringing loudly, gasping for breath. Was he going to die here?

Andrea rose to her feet, grabbed him by the vest, and pulled him close. *"You feel that fear? Do you feel that energy surging through your veins?"* she asked him as she shook him. "It's telling you to freeze right now because you can't flee, right?"

Daren nodded, trembling.

The gunfire started again, this time the automatic fire and the small rounds came together, both aimed at the tree. Daren instinctively tried to dive toward the ground, but Andrea held him up and shook him.

"Listen to me!" Andrea yelled to him over the chaos. She placed her hand on his chest as she had earlier. "Focus on that energy! You can use it!"

Daren didn't want to use it. All he wanted to do was to get the hell out of there before they both got killed.

"You can use it!" she urged him again. *"You can use that energy you feel right now! Focus it! Use it to fight or we're dead!"*

Scared but with no other options, Daren tried to do what she was telling him. He focused on the panic and felt the energy pulsing through his veins. Somehow, her words had seeped through his confusion and triggered a switch. He took a breath, and everything seemed to slow down. His vision and hearing sharpened. His gun once again felt steady in his hand. A rush of adrenaline replaced his fear. He took another breath and nodded.

"That's it," Andrea told him, noticing the change in his demeanor. The gun fire ceased again. "Next time they stop to reload," she said, "you cover me."

Daren nodded. He knelt down and readied his weapon. Moments later the hailstorm started yet again. When it stopped, Daren leaned out from the tree and aimed his gun. He could see one man by the front window, reloading an assault rifle, and another by the door with a pistol. He recognized the man by the door as the pisser from outback—Trip. That meant the man in the window must've been Carson. Daren nodded at Andrea, then fired three rounds at Carson followed by two more at Trip. Carson and Trip both took cover as Andrea sprinted through the woods toward a group of trees in the front yard.

Daren ducked back behind the oak and waited for the men to return fire. The hostile fire started a moment later followed immediately by three shots fired from his right that must have been from Andrea. The rifle fire began again, but this time the rounds weren't being directed toward Daren. He leaned out from the tree and saw Carson firing from inside the trailer toward Andrea's position in front of the property. Daren fired three rounds at Carson, who ducked down out of sight of the window. Trip, however, wasn't going anywhere. He had been shot once in the chest and again through the head. His dead body was slumped down, pistol still in his hand, propping the blood-smeared trailer door open.

Andrea emerged from the brush moments later and hustled over to Daren's side. "Got one," she reported.

"I saw," said Daren. "Nice shot."

Andrea motioned behind him. He turned just in time to see Carson sprinting across the backyard and into the creek, a pistol in hand. Andrea brushed a few curls of hair from her face, coolly cocked her head side to side, raised her gun, and set off toward the creek like a cat stalking its prey. Thoroughly impressed and now coursing with adrenaline, Daren readied his weapon and followed her out of the woods, past the trailer.

They came to the edge of the creek, which was covered in a thick maze of kudzu. Andrea looked at him and shook her head, then began wading in. Daren cursed under his breath and followed. The cicadas, crickets, and the sound of the water created a living cacophony that made him shudder. He felt the warm water rise to his crotch as he attempted to step through the kudzu. Further, they waded, until the water was nearly up to his chest. Andrea, who was at least four inches shorter, held her gun high, outright, and ready as she navigated the water.

They came to a tiny island that had been all but swallowed by kudzu. The vine bridged both sides of the island with the creek flowing beneath. Andrea signaled for Daren to go left as she headed right.

Daren could feel his heart pounding as he made his way through the water toward the island. He lowered himself down as far as he could without going underwater to get under the vines. As he passed beneath the kudzu, a large, bright yellow spider dropped down onto his face. He swatted at it and tried to back away, losing his footing and plunging beneath the water. When he came up and regained his footing on the other side of the kudzu, the spider was nowhere to be found—nor was his gun.

He dove under and attempted to sweep the bed of the river with his hands, frantically feeling for his gun amongst the mossy rocks and mud. Unsuccessful, he came back up for air. He moved closer to the kudzu and tried again.

Daren didn't see Carson wading through the water towards him. As he fished for his weapon, Carson came upon him, grabbed him by the back of his head, and pushed him down into the water. Surprised and disorientated, Daren tried to push back, but Carson grabbed the back of his vest and pushed him down even further. Daren felt the air escape his lunges as he panicked and tried to fight. He tried to find his footing, but the rocks of the creek bed just slid beneath his feet. He tried to fight the instinctive urge to inhale, as doing so would fill his lungs with water. He tried to kick and thrash his way free one more time, but it was useless. He stopped fighting. His panic melted away. He accepted that we would die there.

9

PAIN: THE ONE thing most people spent their entire lives avoiding. But pain could not be avoided. It was as regular as it was integral. Pain was always a part of life, no matter how much people wanted to lie to themselves about it. It was necessary, too. Without pain, men would be soft, and soft men were incapable of doing what had to be done. It was the burden they carried. Feeling pain. Bearing pain. Becoming stronger.

Most people didn't understand this. Marie reminded David every day that women in particular didn't get it. How could they? Men had shielded them from the unpleasant and painful for all of existence. They killed the tigers and the savages, charged the beaches, and went into the foxholes. Men built Western Society through pain. Every step of the way men laid down their bodies like bricks in a wall. Nobody appreciated that anymore.

It was always the same. Marie pleaded on and on every night at the dinner table, prodding him, asking him questions she didn't want the answers to—questions with answers she and her fragile sensibility couldn't handle. It just wasn't in her nature to understand pain or the things men have to do.

"Are you even listening to me?" an irritated Marie asked as he chewed his steak. The boy had gone to a friend's house for the evening, and she had been talking at him endlessly. David gave her a withering look, ignored her question, and continued to read from his phone.

David spent much of his downtime in the local NIMBY (Not in My Back Yard) groups on social media. There he had found people who were likewise concerned about the overdevelopment of the area and housing policies that threatened their property value and the quality of their neighborhoods. There were thousands of homeowners in the Mount Pleasant area alone who felt the way he did. Like David, they had worked hard and bought a piece of the American Dream in a safe neighborhood away from all the crime and the shit. But greedy developers were changing all of that. First, they increased the housing supply, which impacted the value of their homes. Then the new homes brought more traffic, and worse, more transplants—more northerners without proper Southern values who wanted to change the South. If that wasn't bad enough, developers wanted to build apartment buildings and affordable housing in affluent areas. David had tried so hard to give his family a home in a safe area, away from the urban environment. Now the urban element was being brought into their communities. It infuriated him—yet another assault on his way of life.

Drake's Court was the latest development the NIMBYs had targeted for opposition. Its developer, Grant Newton, was a familiar foe of local NIMBYs. They'd clash with him over several projects in the past. Two years earlier, the group had successfully blocked a mixed-use apartment complex and shopping center Newton had wanted to build in downtown Mount Pleasant. Newton was an ideological developer—the worst kind. He actually believed that there was some virtue to what he did.

Stirring up opposition to development was pretty easy. Such opposition often bridged conventional political lines. It was a goal that united homeowners of various ages and beliefs. Some wanted to stop development for environmental reasons. Others believed that it was changing the beauty and the culture of the lowcountry. They all worried that their property values would be negatively affected and that the exclusivity they had managed to purchase would be stripped away from them. Most local NIMBYs didn't like transplants, either, but they were welcomed to join and help stop development in Mount Pleasant.

Marie again interrupted David's train of thought to say something about her mother coming to visit for Christmas. David muttered a thoughtless reply and continued to stare at his phone.

The city had placed a hold on the development of Drake's Court after the opposition had argued that there was not enough parking in the plan to accommodate the demand the development would bring, and therefore the development would adversely impact neighboring residences. The opposition had turned the city council against the development over just two parking spaces.

David read through the comments under the article about the news in his NIMBY group. Everyone agreed it was a big victory, even if the argument about parking was not objectively sound. The city had been looking for a way to cave to public pressure, and the opposition had provided them with one.

He went to the original post on The Courier Post's page and read the comments. The pro-development crowd was pissed, and that delighted him.

"Great victory for the city," he wrote. *"Fuck the YIMBYs and greedy developers."*

He read over his comment before posting it, then reread the comment with joy several times. It was tame but likely enough to bait some fuckfaced loser into coming at him.

Marie said something else, but he missed it entirely. She sighed loudly. David dropped his fork onto the plate and sighed with disgust. It was always some passive-aggressive bullshit with her. "Well, dinner is obviously ruined," he said, rising to his feet and throwing his napkin onto the table.

"I just want to know that you're listening to me," Marie said timidly.

There it was— *she always did this.* She would start a fight and then get defensive and act wounded when he reacted. It was this kind of bullshit that really pissed him off.

"Listen, Marie," he said, his voice rising. "I got enough shit on my mind already. *You wanna fucking fight?* Do you think that will help me acclimate to work, or whatever you fucking called it?"

Marie looked down at her plate and slowly shook her head. "No. I'm sorry."

"You know what I'm dealing with and yet you still insist on breaking my fucking balls!"

"David, please," she said softly. "Don't." Her eyes pleaded with him for calm.

"*David, please!*" he mocked her. "God-fucking-forbid that I have a little time to decompress after my first day back at work. God forbid I be able to read the news while I eat and not be fucking hounded. I have told you time and time again, and you just don't get it. I don't know if it's because you just don't care, or if you're actually a fucking idiot."

"I'm sorry if I upset you, but I should not feel ignored by my own husband," Marie argued. "Please don't call me names."

"So, you're not sorry. You're just excusing it and not listening to a fucking word I said, yet again!"

David could feel his blood boiling. She always fucking did this! She would get him worked up to the point where all he could feel was the rage boiling inside of him. Then there was nowhere to put it—nothing to do with it. She caused the storm and then always wept about the damage. He was tired of it.

He stormed out of the kitchen, away from the source of his fury. Into the bathroom he went, the door slammed shut behind him. His anger clouded his thoughts and made everything around him seem to fade into the background. The thought of punching the door was never consciously decided upon, but the sound it made and the rush of pain on his first gave him some release.

Bath water—the colder, the better. Diffuse the bomb before it blows up again. He didn't want to deal with the fallout, or the self-loathing that would inevitably come after. He opened the bathroom window and retrieved a joint from his stash behind the medicine cabinet. He lit the joint and inhaled deeply, trying to calm himself down.

That dumb, stupid bitch. She always did this. She always pushed and pushed until the ugliness and the rage poured out. Then somehow, *he* would feel guilty after. That would lead to familiar territory—more self-loathing. That's why he resented this shit. Because it ultimately led to him hating himself and feeling like shit, even when he felt he was completely justified. She always wanted to talk about everything—to ask him questions about how he felt. She didn't seem to grasp that from the time he was a boy, he had been training himself to *not* examine his feelings. There was nothing there to find except excuses and shame.

Marie told him that wasn't healthy—as if she were an expert. She'd dropped out of school before she'd gotten her degree. Telling him what was wrong with him and critiquing his every thought and feeling gave her some sort of sense of superiority over him. Maybe it was just to make up for her failures. Whatever the reason, David resented her for it. Always needling and asking questions. Even now, as he tried to move on from the death of his partner, she continually dragged it up. She mentioned Greg's name at least once a day. She would ask about the investigation into his death. She would talk about his wife, or bring up memories of him. He couldn't get away from it.

He rested the joint on the counter, stripped naked, and plunged himself into the cold bath water. The shock instantly reset his nervous system and quelled the rage. He settled into the cold and let it embrace him.

David smoked the rest of his joint and checked his comment on the Drake's Court post. One individual had taken the bait, but David no longer felt like trolling. He left a half-hearted comment calling the man a cuck and dropped his phone onto the ground.

The emptiness always followed the rage. Sometimes he thought of death and how nice it would be—the only release men get from the pain they carry. He often thought about the different ways he could kill himself. However, even as his mind tried to convince him otherwise, David did not want to die. It was more of a recurring fantasy—like flipping off your boss and quitting your job, only a little more extreme. Still, it was the same sort of ideation—imagining over and over again what it would be like, or how he would do it. He hated himself for feeling that way, too. Suicide was for cowards and weaklings. Real men used the pain to make them stronger.

10

SOME PEOPLE PANIC in high-stress situations. Not Andrea. She lived for them. The higher the stakes, the more focus she was able to tap into. It was there, in the place where all the other noise stopped—the place where she was not a mother, nor a granddaughter, nor a woman of color but just a cop with a singular purpose—that she felt released from all her pain.

That focus could be all-consuming. To the point where nothing else in life had much room. Bill Carson had lived in her head, renting space, invading her thoughts and her private moments for too long. Maybe it was an obsession—she didn't care. All she cared about was making sure that Carson paid for what he had done.

However, sometimes her dogged determination, relentless focus, and obsessive nature led her to make bad decisions. She would become so singularly focused on a case that she would begin to lose sight of anything else. This obsession had led her to disregard her safety on several occasions. Now, she realized, it had led her to disregard the safety of another.

Somehow, seeing the fear on Daren's face broke that obsession's spell long enough for common sense to take hold. She had used this man as a means to getting to Carson, and she'd broken protocol several times in doing so. Now she was about to lead this poor boy into a situation she knew damn well he wasn't prepared to handle. *The man didn't even know how to put a vest on.*

"*Come on!*" Daren urged. "Two on two in a trailer... That's dicey." As the two crouched low in the woods outside of Carson's trailer, he was urging her to turn back.

Andrea reluctantly agreed. This situation was not what she had expected and despite every impulse she had, she didn't want to get Daren killed. Nor did she want to depend on his ass to back her up if shit went south.

She motioned for Daren to head back through the woods toward their car, but as soon as he tried to step forward, he stopped.

"What the hell?" he muttered.

"What's wrong?" she asked, stepping closely behind him. Her heart stopped. In an instant, she recognized that Daren had tripped either a boobytrap or a sensor. She closed her eyes and waited for the explosion that would kill them. When it didn't come, she grabbed Daren by the back of his vest. "It's a trip sensor!" she yelled, pulling him back as hard as she could.

They both fell to the ground. Moving as quickly as she could, Andrea kicked her boots into the ground to push herself back against the large oak, pulling Daren with her. She planted her back against the tree trunk and pulled Daren back between her legs. He looked up at her with confusion and panic. She motioned for him to stay silent. Then the gunfire started.

"Get on your feet!" Andrea ordered him. She needed to be able to move. He lunged forward and slowly got up.

Andrea knelt down, leaned around the base of the tree, and fired three shots at the trailer to suppress the fire. She ducked back behind the tree just before the barrage of hellfire began. She and Daren instinctively hit the ground. Bullets tore into the tree trunk, sending wood chunks flying past them overhead, and into the ground around them, kicking up dirt and dust.

Andrea didn't panic. The fire didn't even make her flinch. Instead, she remained calmed and counted rounds. She listened to the reports and determined one man was firing a small caliber handgun, likely a revolver that carried only six rounds. The other man was firing an AR-15 or a similar style assault rifle that had been modified to fire fully automatic.

When the fire stopped about thirty seconds later, Andrea stood up and lifted Daren to his feet. She grabbed him by the vest and pulled him close. She had to try and get him to turn off that fear and focus or they were both going to die. *"You feel that fear? Do you feel that energy surging through your veins?"* she asked him. "It's telling you to freeze right now because you can't flee, right?"

He was trembling. He seemed to hear what she was saying but was still looking around wildly, like an animal searching for the nearest hiding place. The barrage of gunfire began again. Daren tried to dive to the ground, but Andrea held him. She shook him again and locked eyes with him. *"Listen to me!"* she yelled, placing her hand over his chest. "Focus on that energy! You can use it!"

Shit—she didn't know how to hack this man's mind. She didn't know if he even could tap into the panic and use it like she did. She wasn't a guru or a mentor; she didn't know how to instill confidence and abilities in others. She only knew what worked for her and her admittedly fucked up mind. Nonetheless, she barked her truth at him like it was universal—a matter as simple and commonly understood as tying shoes.

"You can use it!" she shouted. *"You can use that energy you feel right now! Focus it! Use it to fight or we're dead!"*

Remarkably, this seemed to have some effect. Daren seemed to loosen up, his eyes stopped darting around in contemplation of escape. He took a breath and nodded at her.

"That's it," she said, somewhat surprised.

She told him to cover her the next time the shooters stopped to reload. He nodded and readied his gun. When the fire ceased, Daren leaned around the tree and began suppressive fire.

Andrea leapt from behind the tree and darted for another about thirty yards away near the front yard. She ducked and rolled behind some nearby brush and then crawled to the tree. She heard Daren's cover fire stop, and Carson and Trip were soon firing at the oak he was pinned behind.

Andrea took a step out from behind the tree, knowing they had not seen her reposition herself. She raised her weapon, took a breath, and squeezed the trigger twice. She watched one round hit Trip in the chest and the other explode out the back of his skull. Carson immediately turned his fire in her direction, and she dove back behind the tree for cover. When Carson stopped shooting, Daren began firing at the trailer again from his position. Andrea took that opportunity to sprint back to Daren.

"Got one," she said, unable to contain her cocky smirk.

"Nice shot," he replied.

That's when she saw Carson running from the back of the trailer toward the creek. He carried a small revolver—having likely run out of ammunition for the rifle. She was no longer concerned with caution. Carson was right there, and she wasn't going to let him slip away. She rolled her head to crack her neck, then went after her target. Daren followed closely behind her.

They came to the edge of the creek, which had been nearly overtaken by kudzu. Andrea looked at Daren, a northern boy from the suburbs, and shook her head—he was not going to enjoy this. She waded into the creek, the chorus of crickets, cicadas, and frogs growing louder as they approached its center. She scanned every corner of the creek with her weapon ready.

Side by side, they came to a small island. Downed trees on both sides had allowed the kudzu to bridge the creek and completely cover the island. Andrea inspected the area for a moment and then reluctantly motioned for Daren and her to split up. He went left as she headed right.

Andrea dropped down low, bringing the water up to her chin, and carefully ducked under the kudzu, keeping her gun raised next to her head, safe from the water. She came up on the other side and spotted an overturned Jon boat to her right. Cautiously, she approached the boat, both hands gripping her gun. Reaching the boat, she kicked it lightly then stepped back and prepared to shoot whatever might emerge. Nothing. She kicked the boat again, sending it a considerable distance across the water. Carson didn't emerge from the boat, but a deadly Water Moccasin did.

Andrea jumped back, but the snake had spotted her and was pissed off about being disturbed. It came across the water toward her aggressively. She held her breath and focused on the snake and its path toward her. As it neared her, it crossed over a broken ore laying against some jagged rocks. She waited till the snake was about halfway over the ore and then lifted her leg. The cottonmouth bared its fangs and opened its jaw to lunge just as her foot came down on the ore, launching the snake through the air and into the trees beyond the creek. She sighed with relief, but then immediately heard a commotion on the other side of the island. *Daren!*

She quickly made her way around the island, splashing loudly as she did. As she rounded to the other side, she saw Carson holding Daren down, face-first, under the water. Without hesitation, she planted her feet and fired three shots; a double tap to Carson's back followed by a final shot to the head. It was over in seconds. His body collapsed into the water. The mist of blood and brain matter that left Carson's head hung in the air for longer than it took her to kill the man. After years of obsession, Carson was dead.

Daren emerged from the water a moment later, shaking and gasping for breath. He rose to his feet, looked at Carson's body floating beside him, his brains leaking from his head, and vomited.

"Easy there, Renard," Andrea said, holstering her weapon. She helped Daren up and led him past the body and out of the creek, his arm around her for support. He continued to cough, gag, and tremble uncontrollably. "You alright?" she asked as they crossed the lawn near the trailer.

"Yeah. I'm good," he replied, trying his best to sound believable. She couldn't help but laugh.

"Is something about this funny?" he asked.

Andrea looked at him and smiled. He smiled back and laughed himself. "Just happy you're alive," she said.

"You're fucking crazy, aren't you?" he asked.

"A little." She smirked. "Come on," she said. "Let's get you back to the car and call this in. Then we'll find you some dry clothes."

Silence was a weapon when used correctly, and David knew how to wield it with expert precision. He knew Marie's insecurities and how to use her attachment to him against her. He knew how to turn the tables when she had angered him, how to leave her upset and pleading with him. No words were needed. Maybe a curt door shut in her face while she was pleading. A sarcastic laugh, or a scoff when the moment was right. Finally, he would withdraw all affection and regard, and that would cause her to panic every time.

Marie's father had left her and her mother when she was six years old. He knew her well enough to know that behind her façade of confidence was that scared little girl still unsure why her daddy had left. She had grown up wanting his love and approval, and feeling rejected because of it. Rationally, of course, she knew that her father was a drug abuser and a fuck up and that it was not her that caused him to leave. But somewhere inside, that little girl still believed she was the reason, and she was deathly afraid of being abandoned again.

David found her weakness somewhat endearing, as pathetic as it was. She needed him, and that made him feel good. It made him secure in the fact that she would always be there. That was why silence was indeed the best weapon. It allowed him to get what he wanted without losing his temper. In this state, he still had control. When he used his words, when he would fight with her, it would drive his anger to rage. That's when he became something he was not proud of—that's when the beast awoke.

He ignored her knocks on his office door and focused instead on trolling people online. The YIMBYs, the Black Lives Matter rabble, the Social Justice Warriors, the libtards—he hated them all. They were all different variations of the same social disease. Everybody wanted something for free. Nobody wanted to work. Everyone had someone to blame for their situation. Slavery had been over for a hundred and fifty-fucking-years, and people still wouldn't stop talking about it. He was unfazed and felt no guilt about it. His family had come from Ireland and had never owned slaves. He'd be damned if he was going to pay reparations or feel guilty about being white.

"Paul seems to have lost his balls," David wrote in one comment, replying to an SJW. *"It's probably for the best. That way when his she-beast wife wants to fuck, Paul can honestly tell her he can't get it up."*

"Nicole just wants to spread her legs freely without consequence," he wrote in response to a feminist on a post about abortion restrictions in the South. *"I guess scrambling babies like eggs is a small price to pay for being an unrepented whore."*

In the comments of an article about Black Lives Matter groups shutting down freeways to protest police violence, he commented: *"These animals kill their own every day. They loot their own businesses. Now they're shutting down freeways? Hope they try it in my city."*

David fantasized for a moment about running his car through a group of protesters and smiled. The entitled fucks would be so shocked. He sipped his beer and sighed, becoming bored with idiots online. Nobody had responded with sufficient anger to engage him. He thought about sending some messages to some liberal news sites—typically a good way to vent out some of his frustrations, but even that didn't seem appealing.

He took out his phone and looked at his message log with Andrea. He'd text messaged her four times in the past two hours and she had not replied. She was probably out fucking that federal agent. The thought made him angry.

Andrea was the only woman he'd ever felt understood him. She, like him, had an empty hole inside her that she tried to fill with the job and anything else she could find. Plus, the sex was amazing. He'd never been with a white woman who could fuck like that. The stamina, the relentless energy—she fucked him like a woman who had been waiting for years to see him. Every time. And she would let him do pretty much *anything*. Marie was a prude by comparison; she always wanted to caress him and look him in the eyes while they were fucking. It was a major turnoff.

However, Andrea was clear that she was not his. She didn't date but reserved the right to, and whenever David brought up her sex life, she shut down the conversation. She was an independent woman, she would say, and she would fuck whoever she wanted to fuck. David's imagination took this to wild conclusions, and he often ruminated about who she might be fucking and when.

Marie entered his office, despite his ignoring her knocks, interrupting his thoughts. David put down his phone and looked at her, ready to hear her out.

"I'm sorry," she said, her head hanging low. "Please, David... Please don't shut me out like this." He stared at her, waiting for more. "I shouldn't have pushed. I shouldn't have prodded. I know how hard all this has been for you."

"You keep expecting me to feel things like you think I should, and to act like you expect me to, Marie. You know that's not me, baby. You know I gotta do it my way," he said, his tone offering concession. He didn't want to fight anymore, either. His anger had faded, and he had punished her enough.

"I know," she said. "I'm sorry."

"I might not process things like you do, but I'm not a rock," he replied. "I have feelings. I just handle them myself. Internally. It's a process. One that keeps me on the job and out of my head. I can't have you trying to rattle things around. If I open up those flood gates, I'll be useless." It was his truth, as much as he hated to reveal it. He had to keep his feelings about Greg, and even his feelings about himself locked away. It was the only way to keep being a cop. It was probably the only way to keep himself from eating a bullet.

She came around his desk and straddled his legs, sat on his lap, and parted her sheer, silk nightgown invitingly, offering herself to him. He ran his hands up and down her back and over her thighs while she placed her hand over his crouch and squeezed gently. Aroused and engorged, he brought her lips to his, kissing her passionately. She pulled back, looking at him with surprise—it'd been so long since he'd kissed her like that.

David saw the passion in her eyes and rose abruptly to his feet. He forcefully turned her around, kicked her feet apart, and bent her over his desk like a perp. She gasped in pleasant surprise. In a moment, his pants were down and he was inside her. She moaned loudly. He held her by her shoulders, then by the back of the neck, pushing her down into the desk as he took her from behind. The position made him feel powerful and that turned him on even more. Harder and harder he thrust until the desk started to move.

He soon finished. She laid still against the desk for a moment, her legs quivering. Slowly, she rose and looked at him with curiosity and a hint of embarrassment. He kissed her, told her he loved her and promised he'd go to church with her and the boy in the morning. He then led her out of his office.

Church wasn't something he looked forward to, but he knew she wanted him there. Besides, he needed all the points he could get with the big guy upstairs. David knew he was an asshole—he knew the darkness inside of him all too well. He tried to use it for good the best he could—that's why he became a cop. Though, he still had plenty for which to repent.

And Marie, well, she was a good woman, and for all he put her through, he could oblige her for a couple of hours on Sundays. Even if he did resent the Church for its corruption and hypocrisy.

11

LOCAL LAW ENFORCEMENT wasn't too amused when they arrived at the scene. Daren quickly surmised that they'd rather not be there, or at work at all for that matter. The way they saw it, an out-of-towner and a fed came into their jurisdiction and killed a couple of rednecks on a Saturday night without so much as a courtesy call. None of them gave a damn what had gone down, either. A sheriff's deputy had scratched down only a few notes as Andrea had recalled the story. That and Daren's name and title were all they needed to dismiss whatever else had happened. They did some preliminary work on the scene and called the state police to the scene per protocol. SLED—the state's law enforcement division—showed up to provide logistical support. They fished Carson's body out of the creek, bagged both corpses, collected brass, and went about reconstructing the shooting with Andrea. Daren flashed them his identification but mostly kept quiet and let Andrea handle things.

He'd had enough of their laughs, anyway. Yes, he'd nearly been drowned by a scrawny redneck and saved by a woman. He could see them snickering about it. Probably didn't help that he was in swim trunks and a neon green t-shirt—the only clothes the nearest Dollar

Mart had. Nor did it help that they had to retrieve his firearm out of the creek for him.

Daren watched Andrea in awe. She had just killed two men and she seemed completely unnerved. Calmly and levelly, she recalled the details to the state investigators, slightly bending the truth on the details that had brought them there. She told them a CI had tipped her off to Carson's location.

After what felt like an eternity, Andrea drove Daren in his rental car back to his hotel. She wanted to get drinks. He could tell she was still amped up. He took a rain check and told her they had a lot of work to do tomorrow. She left him with his rental and took an Uber back to the station.

Alone in his hotel room, the roaches didn't seem very intimidating anymore. He thought about everything he had just experienced. It felt unreal—as if he'd dreamed it. The gravity of the situation wasn't lost on him; he knew he'd nearly died that night. Yet he felt nothing.

For some reason, it reminded him of when his grandfather had died. His mother and father had cried. His brothers had cried. But Daren, who had been closer to his grandfather than any of his siblings, did not. He'd felt nothing, and that had made him wonder what was wrong with him.

He opened his laptop and began to write a report for the Deputy Director. The report detailed Andrea and Daren's arrangement, and briefly recounted the firefight in Givhans. He closed by promising more details on the Grey case as soon as possible, then sent the report in an email. The Deputy Director would have his ass if he heard about the shootout anywhere else first.

He changed out of the Dollar Mart ensemble and into a pair of boxers and an undershirt, then crawled into bed. While he waited for sleep to find him, he thought of Andrea. She was a damn impressive cop. She had sure as hell saved his ass. Often, people like her made Daren feel bad about himself. She'd spent her life working the streets—she knew how to survive. Daren was just a brain in a suit. He was good at piecing puzzles together, but more importantly for his career, he was good at following orders. He knew he wouldn't have his job without his education, and he wouldn't have had that without his parent's connections. The real kicker was that Andrea probably made half the salary he did.

The thought of how close he'd come to having his existence snuffed out crept back into his mind. It almost made him want to laugh—it just felt so unreal and absurd. Then he recalled Carson's limp body floating face-first in the creek, his brain exposed and leaking out his skull. It was the first fresh body he'd encountered up-close in the field. It was an unpleasant image, and he tried to push it from his mind.

Instead, he turned his thoughts to the morning. He would feel a bit more in his element chasing down leads, questioning witnesses, and piecing together facts. He drifted to sleep thinking about Devon Grey's case. If Grey had been the target of a hate crime, why had he been singled out by his killers? And why hadn't other victims turned up? And how many suspects were they looking for? One man could have conceivably strung Grey up, but it would have been quite the task. It was likely two men or more. But why would a group of rednecks lynch just one man and then not commit further violence? He began to consider the possibility that Grey had known his killers. Perhaps there was something about Grey that investigators had missed.

It was hardest when she was alone. Andrea tried to keep her thoughts, her fears, and her guilt at bay. It was the comedown that followed whenever she wrapped a big case, and she dreaded it. The energy from the firefight and the urge to avoid that comedown led her to the station's gym for a late-night workout—better than drinking alone.

The skeleton crew was on, and the building was nearly empty. It was the only time she could use the workout facilities without being bothered by muscle-headed dude-bros. She warmed up by doing a half-mile on the treadmill, then hit the rack for some squats. She fired off some sets on the leg extension machine, then worked the punching bag for a bit before hitting the showers.

In the shower, she let the hot water embrace her and closed her eyes. She replayed the moment she'd shot Carson over and over again. So many years and so much energy had led to that moment, and then it was over so fast. She'd almost expected to feel relief, but instead, she only felt dread.

Showered and dressed, Andrea headed out to the parking lot to wait for her Uber. She was surprised to see Marshall Mulholland waiting for her on the bench outside the door. Andrea sighed. In her impulsiveness to catch Carson, she had lied to him, disobeyed him, and broken protocol.

"Have a seat," he told her.

Andrea sat beside him and tied back her wet hair. Then she looked at him expectedly, like a child waiting to hear it from a disappointed parent. "Well?" she asked, her anxiety building.

"Well, I suppose I should say congratulations," Marshall replied. He pulled out a pack of filterless Camels, lit one, and handed the pack and a lighter to Andrea. It wasn't her brand, but she didn't care.

"You gonna report me?" Andrea asked, lighting her smoke and then handing the pack and the lighter back.

"I should. Runnin' around, getting into gunfights in other jurisdictions. Keeping witness tips from me. Why? So, you could kill him
yourself? No, I know—you don't trust the other departments. As if
ours is so clean…"

"Marshall—"

"No, I know," he stopped her. His voice was stern, but he
was clearly disappointed. "It's Andrea Watts versus the world.
Right? Not even those of us who have your back get to know what
you're doing."

They sat in silence for a few moments, smoking. She didn't know
what to say.

"No," Marshall finally said, breaking the silence. "I'm not going
to write you up. I should. But then I'd just be running one of the few
cops I trust out off the job. How am I ever going to right this ship if
the good ones don't stick around?"

She didn't say anything. She felt terrible for putting him in
this position.

"But can I?" he asked.

"I'm sorry?" she replied, unsure of what he was asking.

"Can I trust you? You lied to me. You put a man's life in danger.
Have you considered that?"

"I saved his life," she said defensively.

"He wouldn't have been there if not for you, Watts" Marshall
reminded her.

"He's just some paper pusher with a white savior complex,"
Andrea scoffed. "He comes down here, acting like he's got all the
answers, swinging that dick around. One Black boy who made the
papers. That's all those assholes in Washington care about. One
Black boy. How many Black boys were killed in this city since? How

many will be killed in the months that follow? None of them get the headlines. They don't get a special agent from Washington."

"Does Devon Grey's life not count?" Marshall asked.

The question rattled her. She didn't know what to say.

"You've grown cold," Marshall added. "I see it happen. Especially to our men and women of color. The system seems so indifferent to the suffering of our communities. That's because the suffering of Black Americans has *always* been a part of our nation's history. It's constant. So, it becomes normalized. It stops shocking us. Gang violence, domestic violence, police violence, drug overdoses…We see it all so damn much, anyone would become indifferent to it. Then you meet someone like this Agent—someone who doesn't see it all the time. In fact, like most people, I'm sure he's probably real good at turning his head and pretending these problems don't exist.

"But every once in a while, something happens that permeates their white bubble. What happened to Devon Grey is something that shakes the fundamental perceptions and values many Americans hold. A lynching, in this day and age. Well, sure—you and I ain't think nothing of that. Ain't called a lynching when a cop shoots down an unarmed Black man in this country, but you and I know it's all the same. For most people, though, that kind of horrific event shakes the very core of what they believe to be true about this country. It makes them angry. They want to find who is responsible and lock them in a cage, like Rufus Luschenant. Because when we identify the monster and lock them away, then all is well. People can sleep at night thinking all is right with the world again. They need that monster—he's their scapegoat. It allows them to say, *'It's not us, it's not our culture, it's this one man—this monster.'*

"That's what I resent," said Andrea. "It's like I'm playing their game or something."

"Let me ask you something," Marshall interjected. "Does Devon Grey's life matter less because of all this bullshit? Do the media circus and the white people lining up to save us mean that finding the truth isn't important?"

"No, of course not."

"They want to make him out to be a special case. Some would say, to make his murder matter more than the hundreds of other racially motivated murders that happen in this country every year. It's like they think it absolves them—the media, the politicians— all of them. Because this *one* incident is so overt, so naked, and it happened in a place with a history of racial oppression and violence. It fits a narrative that allows everyone else to remain ignorant of their culpability."

"Shit. My Uber," Andrea exclaimed. The driver had arrived, grown tired of waiting, and left without her noticing.

She was about to use her phone to call for another when Marshall placed his hand over the screen. "Leave it," he told her, seemingly annoyed at her distraction. "I'll give you a ride home."

"Sorry," she replied, sticking the phone into her back pocket.

"My point is that those people's perspectives don't matter. It doesn't matter one bit to Devon Grey's family, that's for sure. It doesn't matter to his community. Why do you think Black activists around here are so pissed about it?"

"Because, like you said, it's naked and overt. It's reminiscent of dark times for our people and cities."

"And no answers. Even when the whole world sees it for what it is—when there's no denying it's a crime committed because of race—even when the whole world is shocked and the act is universally condemned, justice eludes us."

Andrea nodded understandingly.

"You can reject the idea that Devon's death is more important than the others without making it less important. Don't do that to him. Who cares what narrative it feeds, or the politics of it all? Who gives a damn what this agent is all about? You have an opportunity to bring justice to that boy's family."

He rose from the bench and motioned for her to follow. As they walked to his Buick Regal, a light mist of rain fell upon them. "You've been deputized as a federal agent?" he asked her.

"So I'm told," she said.

He nodded, curling his bottom lip as he pondered the situation. "Suppose that means you won't have to wait to be cleared on the shootings today."

"I assume not."

"What's it like?" he asked with a chuckle and a shake of his head.

"What's that?"

"Being able to do whatever you want under the color of the law?"

She rolled her eyes. They both got into the car, and she asked for another smoke. Marshall was silent for most of the ride. When he neared her complex, he sighed, as if he were trying not to say anything more but was about to give up and let her have it.

"What is it?" she asked, expecting the worse. "Don't bite your tongue now."

"I just wonder," he said, his voice pained. "What you're going to do when you run out of fires to put out. When you can't keep the commotion going and those things you're running from finally catch you."

Andrea looked down, not wanting him to see how much his words hurt. Then she gathered her composure and looked him in the eye. She didn't say anything—what could she say? He knew her better than she cared to admit. "Thanks for the ride," she finally said before quickly exiting the car.

Marcus had been asleep for hours by the time she came in. She ran her fingertips through his thick hair, lightly scratching his scalp. He made a little sound of delight. She smiled and then carefully curled up beside him on his little bed. She gently propped his head up and slid her arm underneath. He snuggled up closer to her instinctively.

She laid there for some time, watching her son sleep, and gently caressing him. Then she tucked him in, kissed him on the forehead, and quietly left his room.

"You know that don't count for much," Gram snarked from the kitchen table. She had been sitting there in her robe, waiting to talk to Andrea.

"I'm sorry, what?" Andrea asked tiredly.

"You can't make up for never being around by loving him while he sleeps," Gram replied.

The remark angered Andrea. She wanted to yell but didn't want to wake her son and she was too exhausted to fight. "I've had an incredibly long and trying day," she replied, raising her hand as if to tell Gram to stop. "I don't need this right now."

"Of course, you have. Isn't that the point? You make sure every day is as demanding as possible."

"Because what I do isn't important?" Andrea snapped back.

"Just like your sister," Gram remarked, shaking her head.

"That's actually funny," Andrea said. "How the hell am I anything like Mikayla? I think you need to get some sleep."

"You're exactly the same. You're both on missions with no time for yourselves or those around you. Both two hurt little girls turned into women angry at the world."

"Is that what you think?" Andrea asked, tears welling up in her eyes. "That I'm just raging? I do what I do to help people. Because nobody was there when I was a kid to help us."

"But you can't heal yourself by punishing people who hurt others, child. You know that, right?"

"Yes, I know that!" Andrea exclaimed, struggling to keep her voice down. "I know that. I'm not trying to heal myself. I'm just trying to help—"

"You're trying to punish, Andrea. It's about making people pay, isn't it? Isn't that what it's really about?"

Tears were now streaming down Andrea's face. "So, what if that is true?" she sobbed. "Somebody needs to do it. Somebody needs to make men like my father pay."

"And what about your son? While you're off punishing the world, you're missing his life. What's worse—you're not giving him the love and support he needs to be a good man."

"Marcus is a *good boy*," Andrea insisted.

"For now," Gram warmed. "What do you think it is that makes good boys into bad men? When there's not enough love in their hearts, baby. That's when the hate gets in."

Andrea retrieved her smokes from the bathroom in a huff and retreated to her bedroom. She didn't care what Gram thought or said about it. She closed the door, lit a smoke, and sat on the floor by her window. The overwhelming thought of how disappointing she was to everyone in her life made her cry. She considered that she had killed two men that night and felt no remorse or conflict. That too made her feel like shit. It was like her emotions were broken, all she could feel was dread, sorrow, shame, and anger. Anything else was fleeting.

Her first kill had not been so easy. A disgruntled old man had refused to drop his pistol during a domestic violence call. When he pointed the gun in her direction, she'd had no choice. The following weeks were hard. She'd replayed the incident over and over again, and she'd felt incredibly guilty. Ultimately, she had required therapy to get over the event.

Her second kill was easier. The monster had been pimping children out of his rat-infested apartment. When they raided the place, the son of a bitch tried to grab a little girl as a hostage. Andrea reacted quicker than he could grab the child, shooting him once through the head. Some trauma had resulted—maybe a few restless nights. But in the end, she just didn't have any compassion for the man and felt no qualms about ending his life.

Now, several kills later, the act seemed to barely resonate. Thinking of herself as a killer wasn't new. If she was honest with herself, it wasn't so much the lack of remorse that bothered her but the pride and satisfaction she felt when she recalled shooting Carson. That crooked toothed motherfucker would never hurt another child. He'd never sell another woman as property. His brain was fish food, and that was probably the best use it had ever been put to. And yet, she wondered what these feelings said about her.

Unable to sleep and thinking about what Gram had said, Andrea's thoughts turned to her sister. She pulled up Mikayla's website on her phone. Always outspoken, her sister had amassed quite the following. She was a regular guest on several local news outlets, an author, and host of a popular podcast, *Black Charleston*.

Andrea noticed that Devon Grey was one of the topics of Mikayla's most recent podcast, and downloaded the episode. She retrieved a pair of headphones from her bedside table and plugged them into her phone.

She laid down on her bed and listened to Mikayla introduce herself in her typical prideful fashion. Attitude and self-assurance dripped from her voice, something Andrea had always admired. Mikayla then spent some time covering local news as it related to the Black community before getting to Devon Grey.

"We are coming up on eight months, y'all," Mikayla said. "Nearly one year without justice—without any suspects. In fact, when you ask Charleston PD if they have a working theory of what happened to Devon Grey, they say that he was hanged in—and I quote—an 'apparent crime of racial animist.' A-fucking-*apparent* crime of racial animist. *Apparent?!* Are you kidding me? Y'all, this is America—this is Charleston. We've got a Black boy, stripped naked and hung from a tree. A racist symbol was carved into a tree nearby. I mean, my God people. This boy could have had a sign hanging around his neck, *'Killed for being a nigger!'* and people would still be acting like they weren't sure if it was racial.

We know. We all know because we live it. We've experienced the hatred. Many of us have experienced the violence. Whether it be from a redneck with a white supremacist flag flying from his pickup truck, or from the very people who are supposed to protect us—the police. We see how we are targeted again and again. They can't gaslight us. We know the world we live in. We see it. But it's all politics and exonerative language when we're talking about white people committing crimes. When it's Black people, boys are called men, and guilt is presumed.

That's why I'm calling for action. Next week, Black Lives Matter and all our sisters and brothers from other ally groups will unite in Charleston. We will be taking action to highlight the city's refusal to call Devon Grey's murder what it was: a lynching. And to demand that they put more resources into investigating his death. This city has made zero progress on this case. It's almost like they don't want to find the truth."

Andrea stopped the playback and frowned. She thought of messaging Mikayla and urging her to not inflame the situation, but she knew her sister wouldn't hear any of it. Mikayla would scoff and remind Andrea that she had chosen the *other side*.

Mikayla had always viewed Andrea's decision to become a cop as a betrayal. To Andrea, raging against the system on a street corner wasn't an effective way to change anything. She felt she could do more to help people from within the system. It was a disagreement that eventually fractured their relationship.

As she drifted to sleep, Andrea thought about what Marshall had told her. If she could help solve Devon's murder, maybe it could help to quell the anger she felt swelling within the community. Or was she simply looking for another obsession again to keep her busy—another fire to fight? The question didn't matter too much. She only knew how to be herself, regardless of what her motivations were.

12

FAIRFAX - FALL 1989

NINE-YEAR-OLD DAVID BURST through the doors of Fairfax Elementary School, jumped over the flight of concrete steps, and bolted down 14th street, clutching the straps of his book bag tightly as he ran. His teacher, Mrs. Hamilton, had taken pity on him and allowed him to leave school five minutes early. It was enough of a head start on the other kids to get home safely. Unfortunately, the kids from his school were just one of the groups that loved to beat on David. The kids who didn't go to school at all were even worse. They would throw rocks at him, flash weapons, and even threaten to kill him.

The animosity wasn't merely racial. Yes, David was a scrawny, pale white boy living in a town that was eighty-five percent Black, but what made his life particularly rough was the fact that his father worked at the new Allendale Correctional Facility. The prison had just opened that year, and white men like his father had moved to town to take jobs as guards at a facility with an almost entirely Black inmate population. The townspeople viewed them as oppressors and spoke of the prison guards as slave drivers.

David ran past the Tiger Mart where the dropouts he was so scared of usually hung out and was relieved to see they weren't there. He ran down the street of newly built houses and up the driveway past his father's Oldsmobile, then into the kitchen, shutting the door quickly behind him. He felt safe again. Of course, there was one more obstacle for him to dodge: his father.

David's father was a raging asshole, and David lived in constant fear of angering him, or worse, disappointing him. The things David saw and heard were enough for him to understand why the locals hated his father and anyone else who worked at the prison. Though he could not articulate it, at eight years old, David understood his father was part of an unjust system.

The other guards were over the house often, drinking with his father. David never minded, as it distracted the old man and kept him off his ass. They'd drink and play cards, and David would crouch low at his bedroom door, listening to their stories about work—stories about men killing other men, about beating men with clubs, about drugs and rape, and all sorts of sordid details that both shocked and fascinated him. He'd even once heard his old man and another guard bragging about beating a prisoner to death. "Beat him so bad his heart stopped!" they laughed.

On this day, however, David discovered his old man was alone. His father was talking on the phone when David came running into the house. The old man frowned and motioned for him to wait. He grumbled a few words into the receiver, and then hung up the phone. "What's all this?" his father asked him sternly.

"What?" David asked, playing dumb.

"You're home early."

"Teacher let us out early," David replied, heading for his bedroom.

"Just a minute now," the old man warned. "I was speakin' to you, boy."

"Sorry, father," said David, his eyes falling to the floor.

"You come runnin' through here like you terrified of somthin'. Tell me you ain't runnin' from them boys that beat your ass."

David looked down, ashamed and unsure of what to say.

"That's what I thought," his father said, laughing at him. "You just a little pussy, huh? My own son. Whatcha think I should do 'bout that now?"

"I don't want to be a pussy, sir. There's too many of them boys and they're all older and bigger than me."

"Yeah, and there's more prisoners than guards where I work. You think we let those animals run the show? Maybe if I beat your ass every goddamn day, it'll toughen ya up some. Maybe that's what you need—some pain."

The beatings he'd handed out so far certainly hadn't made David feel any tougher. They'd just made him hate the old man. *You can't have growth without pain,"* the old man would always tell him after beating his ass. *"I'm doing this for your own good,"* he'd say. Then it was usually, *"Look what you made me do,"* when bandaging the boy's wounds afterward.

"What do ya think 'bout that?" his father asked.

"I'll be tougher, sir," was the only thing David could think to say that wouldn't illicit an ass kicking.

But that wasn't enough for his father. He pulled him out to the backyard and told him to wait while he fetched two three-gallon tin buckets. He instructed David to hold the buckets while he filled them with the hose. He tried to fill them to the brim, but David could not hold them up.

"You really are a pussy," his father muttered disappointedly as he dumped half the water out onto the lawn. "Start with this," he instructed. "Hold them buckets up. Arms out wide. Don't put let me catch you without those buckets in your hands."

"For how long?" David asked, his face strained. His arms were already tired.

"Does it hurt?" his father asked.

"Yes, sir," David answered, hoping for mercy.

"Good," the old man barked with a nod. "That's what getting stronger feels like."

He went inside. David struggled. His arms screamed for him to drop the buckets but he held on. Desperate to be anywhere but in his body at that moment, David thought of his mother and their time together on his seventh birthday. She had taken him out of school without his father knowing. They'd gone to McDonald's and the mall. She bought him a cupcake and sang to him.

David missed his mother but tried not to think of her. When he did, he became angry and resentful at her for leaving. This was a happy memory, though, and at that moment when his arms burned and his shoulders ached, it was an escape. He remembered how her perfume smelled, how the chicken nuggets tasted, and the songs that played at the mall. He remembered her smile. He thought of her and that moment so deeply and so intensely, that he stopped feeling his arms—he stopped feeling anything. In his mind, he was back with his mother, reliving that day.

His mind in another place, David didn't realize it had started raining. When the old man shook him, David snapped back to reality. He had no idea how long he had been standing. His hands tingled, his arms were numb, and he was soaking wet. His arms were shaking and the buckets were overflowing. His father had to grab him to bring him back to reality. The old man cursed at him for not listening and told him to put the buckets down and go clean up for supper.

The next day David could not lift his arms, which made defending himself against the neighborhood kids impossible. Four of them jumped him and tore apart his school books. They told him his father was a Nazi and a slave master, on account of his position overseeing the prison labor crew. David wished they knew that he hated his father too.

The old man was not amused when David came home the next day with a busted lip, swollen eye, and a book bag stuffed full of torn-up book pages. Luckily for David, the drunken fuck was too preoccupied with his friends. They were preparing for what appeared to be some sort of party in the backyard. "Pathetic," was the only thing his dad said to him before ordering him to stay in his room for the night.

Later that night, David snuck into his father's room and peeked through the window. He learned that the party was a night of inmate fights organized by the guards. A paddy wagon came with ten inmates, and two at a time they were brought to a roped-off, makeshift ring in the backyard. Then guards would place bets and drink while the prisoners fought.

The event was the first of regular bi-weekly fights organized by his father and the night crew at the prison. The fights were brutally violent, often lasting until one man was completely incapacitated. At first, the violence frightened David, but soon he became enthralled by what he saw. On those nights, he would pretend to be asleep, only to later sneak into his father's room and watch the fights from the bedroom window. A few months later, he got braver and started sneaking out into the kitchen for a better view.

One night, about four months after the first fights, David's father ran to the kitchen to grab a bottle of whiskey and discovered the boy watching. David was sure he was going to get a beating, but instead, his father laughed. He looked at the boy with pride in his eyes.

"You watching the fights?" his father asked, surprised.

"Yes, sir," David answered meekly.

The old man seemed to deliberate on how best to handle the situation before grabbing his whiskey and turning to head back outside. "You can watch from the back porch, but keep to yourself," his father told him before exiting. David felt a rush of pride. His father didn't hand out approval very often.

Out to the porch, he went, finding a comfortable corner to sit in—close enough to see the fights through the porch lattice but far enough away to still feel safe. The next fight was a big, burly, bald man versus a muscly, lean man with large bushy hair. The smaller man had a lot of confidence. He moved around quickly, firing sharp jabs, and shuffling his feet. He smiled as he landed blow after blow on the big man.

But the bald man just stood there, taking each shot without even flinching. He stared at the smaller man and waited for him to tire out from all that movement. David saw the confidence slip from the smaller man's face as he realized that his blows weren't having an effect. He spun around and kicked the bald man directly in the abdomen with all his might. The bald man simply grabbed his foot and tossed the smaller man back like a sack of potatoes. The smaller man tried to get up, but the big man rushed him and came down upon him with all his might. The first punch was probably all it took. David gasped. Blood sprayed from the smaller man's mouth as his head bounced off the ground. The big man then grabbed him by his hair, lifted his head, and delivered another devastating blow.

David saw the guards climbing over the rope to end the fight. However, before they could get to him, the big guy lifted his foot and stomped down on the other man's head with all his weight. David heard the man's skull break and gasped. The guards grabbed the big man and pulled him back, but it was too late to help his opponent. As blood poured from the man's split and caved-in skull, his body shook and convulsed, his limbs twitching and jerking uncontrollably. David looked on in horror, his hand clasped tightly over his mouth to keep from screaming.

"Fuck, man, somebody put that dog down," one of the guards said as the inmate convulsed in the mud.

Another guard stepped toward the injured man and drew a gun from his waistband. David's father looked back at him, as if considering what his son was about to see, then turned away with disregard. The guard fired one shot into the man's head and his body immediately went limp. An eerie silence fell over the crowd.

"Bring him back with the others," his father instructed the other guards. "We'll say he tried to escape."

That night, David could not sleep, haunted by images of what he had seen. He lay awake for hours, replaying the man's death. Whenever he would shut his eyes, he would see that enormous inmate crushing that man's skull.

His father tried to speak to him about it the next morning. "These men are animals," the old man explained. "They're locked up because they're dangerous. If they don't kill each other, they'll die in prison, or get the chair. Don't matter, either way, you see? They're practically dead already. It's like dog fighting."

13

THE MORRIS STREET Baptist Church stood at the center of Charleston's historic downtown. Located just a couple blocks from King Street, the church had long been described as the mother church for all Black Baptists in the lowcountry. An elegant brick edifice with heavenly white pillars framing its entranceway, the Morris Street Baptist Church had first been organized by a group of Christians with African descent, some of whom were former slaves, all the way back in 1865. The church had major significance to the Black faithful ever since.

There were plenty of other Black churches, many of which were a lot closer to where they lived. But Gram had been going to the Morris Street Baptist Church since she was a child—back when more Black people could still afford to live on the peninsula. As such, she made the journey downtown nearly every Sunday.

Andrea parked her car across the street. She leaned over the backseat and kissed Marcus on the head.

"Come to church," Gram insisted. "All this can wait. It's the lord's day."

Andrea tried not to roll her eyes. "You sure Miss Ana can give you two a ride home after?" she asked, ignoring her grandmother's invitation.

"Mm-hm. We'll be fine, child," Gram replied. "Come on, Marcus," she called to her great grandson as she climbed out of the car.

Andrea said goodbye to her son one more time as he bounded after Gram. The downtown sidewalks were bustling with parishioners and worshipers of all types and ages, making their way to their preferred houses of worship. Sundays were for sacred things in the Holy City—church, family, and in the fall, football.

Andrea drove away and headed back to North Charleston to meet Daren at his hotel. She wondered how he was holding up after nearly being drowned. She almost expected him to be having some trouble processing what had happened, but when Daren answered the door to his room, coffee in hand, he seemed fine.

"Good morning," he greeted her.

"You seem in a good mood," she replied.

"Yes," he exclaimed. "Because today we aren't chasing rednecks through swamps. Today, we are investigators working a case."

"You like being an investigator?"

"I do," he replied. "It's like solving a puzzle. Only you gotta find your own pieces."

"So, what's the plan?" she asked.

Daren motioned to the miniature coffee maker on the dresser. "We need to get some more coffee," he informed her. "Then we need to go through all of this." He slapped a stack of paper on the bed. "That's everything Charleston PD faxed over from the Grey case, and everything I have from the FBI."

"Have you gone through it?" She started thumbing through the file. The images of Devon Grey's body were unsettling. She'd never worked a case where she'd known the victim.

"Yeah, and let me be the first to say, they haven't found shit."

"That bad?" she asked.

Daren sat on the edge of the bed and sipped his coffee before answering. "Doesn't seem like they did much. They checked around for witnesses. Established a call line for tips. Talked to his mother and known associates… The usual bullshit when they don't have a fucking clue." Daren stood up and began to pace. "So, how do you investigate an act of indiscriminate violence?"

"I honestly have no idea," Andrea admitted. Her specialty was in crimes involving the exploitation of women and children. She'd never worked a hate crime.

"Because it's damn hard, if not impossible to do," Daren concluded. "You can't start with the victim, which is where detectives always start, because the victim likely didn't know his assailant."

"So, where do we start?"

"We have to look at the possible motives for indiscriminate violence. Then we have to find suspects in the area that might have such motives," he said. "People associated with hate groups and extremist ideologies for one."

"That's a lot of people in South Carolina," she countered.

"That's why the FBI didn't bother putting much time into the case," he told her. "Too many suspects and no solid leads."

"That's encouraging," Andrea said with a sigh. She sat on the foot of his bed and read through the file. "Is there anything useful in here at all, or you just making me read it all for fun?"

"Well, I'm good, Watts, but I'm not perfect," he said with a laugh. "Need you to see if I'm missing something."

She sighed again and dropped the papers onto the bed. "You think we got a chance in hell in solving this thing?" she asked.

"I don't know, honestly." He leaned over her shoulder and pointed to a picture of the life rune. "This is where we should start, though. That's the symbol that was carved into the tree Devon Grey was hanged from. It's called a life rune. It's got a long history of being used by awful people for hateful purposes. Our killer signed his work," he noted.

Daren opened his laptop and propped it up on the dresser.

"You need a bigger room," Andrea remarked.

"You should meet my roommates," Daren replied as he punched keys on the laptop.

Andrea saw the can of insecticide and understood. "You need a new hotel."

"Oh, are the roaches not standard in the lowcountry?" he asked, completely deadpan.

Andrea laughed. She waited for him to pull up what he was looking for on the laptop, her eyes scanning the room for clues about the man with whom she'd partnered. She noticed his wet clothes from the shootout at Carson's in the sink and what appeared to be vomit in the trash can near the bed. "Well, your hotel sucks, but how are *you* doing?" she asked.

"Fine... What do you mean?" he asked, confused.

Before she could reply, Daren had plunked the laptop down onto the bed beside her. "The investigation linked the symbol this group—the European Defense League," he said.

"Josh Dylan's group," Andrea said knowingly. "Avery Dylan's son."

She was well aware of *Avery Dylan*, the elitist worm. Her sister had personally clashed with him several times. He was old money, descendent of the planter class—which was a fancy term for folks who made their fortunes off slavery. Dylan was a professional

148

demagogue and racist who sold hate as intellectualism. He fancied himself a historian, although he had no formal degrees and preached disproven romanticist bullshit. Dylan's views may have been less popular than they were forty years ago, but he hadn't noticed. He hob-knobbed with mayors, councilmen, congressmen, and senators, and that was because he financed them all. As long as they were right-wing and willing to legitimize him and his League, they would get a nice check.

"So, you're familiar."

"Yeah, I know all about Avery Dylan," she said. "But he and his circle are a bunch of weak wristed old men. They didn't do this."

"You've heard of the League," Daren said, opening a new tab on the web browser to reveal a newspaper article from 2010. "Are you aware Josh Dylan's split with his father and the Heritage League was because Josh wanted to foment a race war?"

Andrea read the article, recalling bits of it from what she'd read at the time. "Yeah, I remember this. Then Josh and his crew just started cooking meth."

"Yup. That was shortly after daddy made Josh change the name of his group to the European Defense League. Of course, once the law came down, Dylan ratted on all his people and got off with time served."

"So, they were all locked up when Devon was killed," she concluded.

"That's right. Except for Dylan himself, but he has an alibi putting him out of state," Daren added.

"We sure that checks out?"

Daren retrieved the copy of Grey's case file he'd printed for Watts and thumbed through it to double check. "His mother and several locals place him at a restaurant in Charlotte that night. I guess he went to stay with her after the fallout here."

"Probably banished by daddy," Andrea surmised.

"Wouldn't surprise me."

"Well, Charlotte is, what, three hours' drive? What time was he supposedly at this restaurant?"

"Till close, which is midnight," said Daren, shutting the file and handing it back to Andrea.

"Is it possible Dylan ordered the killing?" she asked. "Or if not, he may know who did it." She looked in the file and shook her head. "Nobody's talked to him?"

"No," said Daren. "But we should." He paced around and rubbed his chin while he thought. "Still, we ought to check into the other possibility, too. Either Devon Grey was the target of indiscriminate violence, or he was murdered by someone he knew—regardless of the reason."

Andrea nodded and rose to her feet. "So, we run down these scumbags, make a list with all their racist-ass hick names on it," she said. "Then we talk to the family, friends, classmates, and anyone who knew Devon. Find out if anyone had any reason to harm him."

"And we might as well cross-check associations from the two lists and see if anyone pops out," he added, closing his laptop. "So, let's go see the mother."

"What?" Andrea balked, confused and concerned. "Why would we start with the mother?"

"I've got to wait on the warrants for the white supremacist groups, and she's local. I figured, start where the kid lived."

"It's Sunday," Andrea informed him with one eyebrow raised. This man had clearly never been in the South on a Sunday.

"What? Who cares?" Daren asked. "We'll go after church or whatever."

"No, we ain't bothering this grieving mother on the lord's day. Un-uh. Sorry, but it's rude, and she won't tell us a damn thing if we start like that."

Daren nodded and curled his bottom lip as if he hadn't considered this. "Alright, Watts. It's your city. You know the customs. You tell me where we're starting today."

Andrea thought about it for a moment and the answer came to her. She knew exactly where they needed to begin.

14

THE STELLA MARIS Roman Catholic Church was one of many historic structures on the quaint and affluent Sullivan's Island, located just over the drawbridge from Mount Pleasant. Lavish beachfront properties lined the island's few streets, interspaced with buildings dating back to the 18th century. It was the location of Ft. Moultrie— the other, smaller fort near Ft. Sumter that nobody ever talked about—and at one time or another, Edgar Allan Poe had lived there. But now it was mostly an exclusive sub-suburb of an already exclusive suburb and a go-to location for destination weddings. Aside from church, David rarely came there.

Stella Maris was one of the oldest churches in the area. Its stone edifice invited curiosity, while its tower evoked the feeling of a more chivalrous time when both power and faith were sacred and ordained. Inside, the walls and ceiling of the nave were made of beautiful hardwood. At the head of the nave, a shrine to the Virgin Mary stood under a domed ceiling painted blue with gold stars.

David stared at the Virgin Mary and then at the painted stars above. The church had been built by Irish immigrants in the early 19th century. Even if he never listened to the sermons, and found the institution of the Church to be hollow and corrupt, he'd always appreciated the building. More importantly, the right kind of people came to church here, and that was why David had chosen it.

The way he saw it, religion wasn't really about what God you prayed to as much as it was about identifying which tribe you belonged to. This was as true in the lowcountry as it had been throughout the history of worship. It was tribal, political, and often racial. It wasn't that you worshipped, it was a matter of *where*, and with *whom*, you chose to worship that said it all. It was a statement about your cultural outlook, your family background, and your social class membership. Do you worship in a shack with people who live on the street, or do you worship in a grand cathedral with politicians and police?

The Roman Catholic Church had long stood as an example of this distinction. Men with golden scepters sitting in lavish palaces demanding others be selfless and give what they can. That money was fed into an endless pool of wealth of resources which fueled private financial endeavors around the world and an endless bureaucracy of church officials. That kind of wealth and influence was real power.

David had grown up in the Church. His mother had insisted upon their regular attendance. That had ended, of course, when his mother left and his father moved them to Fairfax. Ever the devote Catholic if asked, the old man would never set foot in another church as long as he lived. David wasn't sure if it was the old man's unwillingness to face his sins or the fact that church reminded him of the wife he'd lost.

When David returned to Charleston to become a police officer, he was told it was important to be seen at church. Being Irish, Catholic, and a cop, Stella Marris was the logical choice. Several of his fellow men in blue went there. It's where Greg had gone to church.

The Church disillusioned David in more ways than one. It all seemed like a sham to him. Splash some magical water on yourself, pretend to sing some songs, and confess your sins to some anonymous pederast. He never let his son participate in church events. He didn't trust a single one of the so-called holy people. Anyone associated with the church was suspect to him. How could they continue to be a part of such a corrupt institution?

Marie didn't share in his skepticism of the Church. He probably would have stopped going by now if it hadn't been for her. Ten years ago, when they had first started dating, she told him that his being Catholic was practically a requirement as far as her mother was concerned. That pressure her parents put on her to be a good Catholic was now the pressure she put onto him and the boy. David couldn't help but resent her for it. Like she was trying to save his soul—*as if it needed saving.*

Marie nudged him gently, breaking his daze. It was time to accept communion. At least the service was nearly over.

David stood and shuffled out of the pews and into line. Sean stood in front of him. He clapped his hands firmly over the boy's shoulders and squeezed them just hard enough to make him wince and squirm. "Stand up straight," he teased as the boy wormed and laughed.

"Stop it, Dad!" Sean cackled.

"Knock it off, both of you!" Marie scolded under her breath. "Be a better example, please," she whispered into David's ear.

David rolled his eyes. "Don't, Marie," he whispered back. "Don't fucking press my buttons. Not here."

"Sorry," she replied woundedly, looking ahead. "Just please be respectful."

Sure, she said she was sorry, but she didn't mean it. She was still mad and it was obvious. As if he had embarrassed her. David took a breath and tried to let it go—he had too much to deal with today to let her bait him into a fight. Still, he felt wounded.

They stood in line with several of David's fellow officers and their families. All waiting for a little piece of the body of Christ and a shot of grape juice. This allegedly made them one with Christ, or paid homage to his sacrifice or some shit. David couldn't remember and he never listened to the sermon. Most of the time he would zone out, lose himself in his thoughts, and the time would fly.

The boy went first, and he was always happy about this part. It was a snack to him with absolutely zero spiritual relevance. Marie went next, closing her eyes as Father Shaughnessy placed the flavorless, cardboard-like wafer on her tongue—undoubtedly imagining some divine connection as she sipped from her plastic cup of juice.

"When was your last confession, David?" Father Shaughnessy asked when it was his turn.

Who the fuck did this guy think he was? This was the kind of shit David didn't need. "A few months or so, I don't know," he replied with a chuckle. "I didn't know you were keeping track."

"I am your spiritual father, David. Like all the officers in my flock, I worry about you. I know the burden our men and women in blue carry. I urge you, my child, to let the Church and Jesus take those conflicts from your heart."

"Thank you, father. I will. It's just been rough since Greg died. I haven't talked to anyone about much of anything."

Shaughnessy nodded understandingly and placed his hand on David's shoulder. With the other hand, he took a wafer off a gold plate and held it out for David to take.

"Then let this body of Christ absolve you of your sins until you are ready to share them before God."

David took the sacrament and rejoined his family. If there was a God, he had some things to say to him when they finally met. This entire fucking game was rigged. Humanity was a wasteland of sin, moral turpitude, and misery. Men like him did their best in a shitty world, and yet that prick was sitting on high judging everybody for their faults when he was the one who set the board. If this was his grand plan, he must be an idiot or a sociopath—and here they were, made in his fucked-up image.

Before freeing them from their weekly torment, Father Shaughnessy brought the congregation together to pray for the protection of the men and women of law enforcement. Marie smiled and squeezed David's hand as the priest lauded the virtues of law enforcement and those who serve the lord by wearing the badge.

"And a special guest is with us here, today," Shaughnessy said. "Miranda Wright, please rise."

A young woman with olive skin and long curly brown hair rose. She'd been crying and her makeup had run all over her face. David knew who she was, though they'd never met. He'd seen pictures and heard all about her.

"Miranda was engaged to marry officer Greggory Noonan. As many of you know, last month, this city and all of us lost Greggory. Struck down in the line of duty by a man with hatred in his heart. And though Greggory is with the Lord now, we here on Earth have all mourned him. For some, that has been a more private affair. So, today we welcome Miranda back to the congregation to continue her healing with us. Please join me in praying for Miranda and Greggory's family."

David sighed, irritated. "Let's go," he instructed Marie. "I don't want to think about this shit."

She recoiled just a bit, her mouth agape as if shocked by his decision. He scoffed at her judgment, took Sean by the hand, and headed for the doors. Marie reluctantly followed.

The reverberations of joyous worship could be felt and heard for blocks surrounding the Morris Street Baptist Church.

"That's coming from a church?" Daren asked incredulously.

Andrea smiled slyly and raised an eyebrow at him in response. They walked from where she had parked four blocks away to the nexus of the ruckus and entered the church.

Inside, the congregation sang and swayed, clapping their hands in rhythm as they nodded affirmatively. A woman played the organ with fire and the choir led the song. Some worshippers raised their hands high as if embracing the lord's love from above. Others nodded along slowly and tried to fan themselves with paper fans or their hats. A tired old air conditioner in the corner pumped as hard as it could, but could not abate the heat and humidity. Sweat poured from the parishioners as they moved and sang.

Daren had never seen anything like it. Growing up, church had meant boring lectures, disinterested people, and the occasional monotone song. The environment of the Morris Street Church was more like a party than any church he'd ever been to. These people were legitimately having a good time.

"Okay, this is quite the sight, but I'm still not sure why we're here!" Daren called over the celebration to Andrea.

She leaned in and raised herself on her toes so her mouth was closer to his ear. "A good investigator should understand the people he's talking to," she said.

He felt her breath on his neck as she spoke and stepped back reflexively. Andrea shot him a confused look, then motioned for him to follow her. She led him around to the side of the building and down the pews, bumping into people and apologizing along the way. She came to an older woman and little boy who were singing and swaying near the front. They both stopped in surprise when they saw Andrea. She embraced them both with big smiles, and nodded to Daren, assuring him it was okay to join her family. He smiled and nodded hello to the older woman and the boy. Unsure of what to do, he stood with his hands clasped at his waist and awkwardly bobbed his head to the rhythm. To his relief, the song soon ended.

Andrea hugged the boy again and asked him how he was doing. "Marcus, Gram, this is Agent Daren Renard," she said. "I'm helping him with a case." She then introduced him to her family. "Daren, this is my Gramma, Angela, and my son, Marcus."

"It's nice to meet you," Daren said warmly. The boy smiled but shyly ducked behind his mother. Andrea's grandmother smiled and extended her hand. He took it and shook it gently.

"It's lovely to meet you," Gram said. "Y'all missed the service, I'm afraid. But happy to see you here nonetheless!"

"Actually, I wanted Daren to meet Reverend Abney," Andrea replied.

Her grandmother scoffed and waved her hand dismissively. "What's this? About a case? Andrea, not on the lord's day."

"Gram, I still gotta work, lord's day or not." The old woman grumbled something under her breath. "I love you too, Gram,"

Andrea replied with a smile. She then bent down and kissed her son. "And I love you, baby. You be good now."

The boy nodded but didn't speak. Daren noticed that he continued to watch his mother after they'd walked away.

Daren followed Andrea to the pulpit, where she introduced him to the reverend. He was an older Black man with a gentle air about him and a bushy gray beard. He asked them to have a seat by the pulpit and promised that he would be with them as soon as he said goodbye to and blessed everyone. Nearly an hour later, after he'd done just that, the reverend returned and sat beside them. "Andrea, my child, it's been a long time," he said to her. His voice had an almost soothing rasp to it.

"I'm usually working on Sundays," she lied.

"Doing the lord's work in your own way," Reverend Abney said with a firm, understanding nod. He then extended his hand to Daren. When Daren shook it, the reverend warmly placed his other hand over top, wrapping Daren's hand in an embrace.

"It's a pleasure to meet any friend of Andrea's," Abney beamed.

"The pleasure is mine," Daren insisted. "That was something else, I gotta say. I don't think I've ever seen church done like that."

"We love the lord and we love one another," Abney declared. "So, when we come together, it's not out of some sense of duty or obligation. We come together out of love. It's a celebration! There's nowhere else I'd rather be."

"Well, that's certainly different than what I've experienced," Daren replied with a laugh.

"Now you're welcome to come join us any Sunday," the reverend said.

"Hold on now, you can't just let *anyone* in," Andrea teased.

The three laughed and Abney placed his hand on Daren's shoulder. "You better watch out for her," he warned with a smile.

"She's keeping me honest, that's for sure," Daren teased.

"Reverend," Andrea said, her tone becoming more serious. "Daren is in town trying to take another look at what happened to Devon Grey. I've agreed to help him."

The reverend shook his head and furrowed his brow. "Awful shame what happened to that boy. An awful shame," he said with a heavy sigh. "What can do y'all for?"

"Well, to start, what's the community saying about it off the record, when nobody's around?" she asked.

Abney tilted his head back and forth and smacked his lips together as if debating what to say. "You know talk is talk, Andrea," he demurred. "I ain't never been one for rumors."

"So, people are talking?" she asked.

"It's just conjecture is all, but yeah, they talkin'. People look at this town, its history, these racist organizations, neo-confederates, police violence."

"What's police violence got to with this?" Daren asked.

"Suppose folks don't think cops around here care much about what happens to Black folks. What happened to Devon Grey was an awful tragedy, but it's nothing new. The people of Charleston love to stand in groups with candles and act shocked whenever something like this happens, but it's not new. Look at Rufus Luschenant. It was only three years ago and it's barely mentioned anymore."

Daren nodded and recalled the memorial he had visited at the airport. He remembered the horrible day when Rufus Luschenant had walked into a Black church and executed six of its members. The act of racial terrorism had reverberated across the nation. The event stood out in Daren's mind as one of several that had ignited a rash of violence and division across the country.

The climate of division eventually led to Daren's assignment in Michigan last year, where he'd investigated the officer-involved shooting death of a middle-aged Black man named Anthony Castile. The bureau had been given a strong mandate to take cases of a racially sensitive nature and put them to bed as quickly as possible to quell any further escalation of violence. In a sense, Daren's journey to the low-country had begun there with the heinous actions of Rufus Luschenant.

"That's where you should be," Abney told Andrea. "Bring him to talk to Pastor Mosley." Abney saw Andrea's reaction and shook his head. "He needs to see it," he said, referring to Daren.

"I don't want to bother Pastor Mosley," Andrea replied. "They've dealt with enough."

"From the moment our ancestors were brought here in chains, it's been constant pain and suffering," Abney replied, rising to his feet. "Curtis Mosley knows that better than anyone. You want insight into hate groups? He's the man to ask."

The reverend apologized to them and told them he had to take his leave. "I've got medication to take and a wife who will be awful sore if I'm late," he said as he walked them to the door. "God bless both of you for what you're doing," he added as they left. "I'll pray the truth finds you."

Andrea and Daren both thanked the man for his time and his prayers, then walked back to her car.

"I don't think we need to go to the AME Church," Daren remarked.

"Well, I don't feel great about it, either, but Abney is right. Pastor Mosley may have some valuable insight. And it's Sunday—we can't do much else."

Daren rolled his eyes. "I'd rather be drinking if we can't work," he remarked. He suddenly felt very out of place and uncomfortable. The thought of going to the AME church where Luschenant's attack had taken place filled him with anxiety.

"Maybe later," Andrea replied with a smile.

"I'm just not sure if it's a place where I should be," he admitted reluctantly.

"Funny that thought never crossed your mind before coming here and taking this case in the first place," Andrea countered, irritation creeping into her voice. "A white man who knows *nothing* about Southern culture, let alone Black culture. Yet here you are."

They stopped at the car, Andrea waiting for a response, Daren at loss for words.

"You don't get to do this," she said, pointing at him. "You don't get to come here and pretend to care, and then turn your eyes away when it gets uncomfortable. Does the color of your skin make you feel uncomfortable all of a sudden? Welcome to my fucking world."

Andrea got behind the wheel and slammed the car door in frustration. Daren stood outside for a moment, considering what had just happened. He felt embarrassed and slightly defensive. He wasn't sure whether to argue with her or apologize.

After a few moments, he got into the car, still unsure of what to say.

"You know," Andrea remarked as she drove. "If there's something about this that makes you uncomfortable, you might want to spend some time with yourself and figure out what that is. Because it ain't just the color of your skin. It's deeper than that. Why is it that you feel you shouldn't be at a place like the AME church?"

Daren honestly didn't know the answer, but the question bothered him. "I don't have to spend time with anything, and I don't have to explain shit," he scoffed. "I'm an outsider, a lawman, and yeah, I'm white. Heaven-fucking-forbid I have some respect and consideration before I go into a Black church where a white supremacist murdered a bunch of people. I'm just trying to be a little sensitive, and I honestly resent the implication," he added. His voice was tense and strained.

"Is that it?" she asked skeptically.

"That's it," Daren stated sharply. "I honestly don't even see the point in half this shit. We're here to investigate a murder. Why are we touring churches and meeting at historical sites? I don't need a fucking history lesson, Watts. I need to figure out who killed this damn kid, so I can file a report and move the fuck on from this goddamn, roach-infested, smelly fucking state."

"Smelly?" she asked, confused.

"Yes, I keep asking you and everyone, *what the fuck is that smell?*"

She laughed. "You must mean the pluff mud."

"Pluff mud?"

"Mm-hm. All the seawater, sea life, and dead organisms mix with the mud. Creates kind of an acidic, fishy smell. None of us really notice it much anymore," she replied.

"Reminds me of visiting my aunt and uncle in Northwest Connecticut," Daren recalled. "Come spring, all the farmers would spread cow shit all over their fields. Fertilizer. The whole town smelled so goddamn bad. But my aunt and uncle couldn't smell it. They were always surprised when I said I could, even in the house."

"You get used to shit," Andrea remarked. "Then you don't notice it anymore."

Daren nodded his head and sighed. "Yeah, I suppose you do."

"Listen," Andrea said, shifting her tone. "I don't know you or what you're about, but you're down here trying to understand race politics and social dynamics on the fly. You think I want to drag your white ass around, explaining shit to you, telling you what fucking *pluff mud* is? But you helped me with Carson, and I nearly got your ass killed. So, I owe it to you to help you. That means you're going to have to trust me, even if it makes you uncomfortable sometimes."

Daren nodded and gazed out the window. The memories of struggling underwater came back to him. He felt his heart pounding in his chest. The image of Carson's dead body floating face down in the creek, his brain oozing from his skull, was stuck in his mind. He pushed the thoughts from his head and tried to focus on what Andrea had said. "Alright, Watts. You lead, I'll follow," he replied.

He had a sudden urge to be alone and to be good and fucking drunk. He had too much on his mind, and he didn't know where to begin sorting through it. All he wanted to do was turn it all off, retreat from the world, and drink until he forgot everything he'd been through and learned in the past seventy-two hours. Instead, he was going to visit the site of a terrorist attack.

15

DAVID COULD NEVER understand how half the bangers he saw on the street dressed. It was as if they had no respect for themselves. Not Reggie, though—he always rolled in style. His Black Escalade sported platinum rims, tinted windows, and likely armored doors. He wore stylish clothing and jewelry. David always appreciated class, even if Reggie's style was a bit flashy for his taste. He watched Reggie's driver park the Escalade and sipped his vanilla milkshake.

Reggie emerged from the passenger seat, shaking his head as he looked around. "Can't believe you made me come all the *white* the fuck out here," he said with a tsk. He shook hands with David and leaned in for a half-hearted bro-hug—the kind where you quickly lean into each other and punch each other on the back.

Reggie's driver stood close by, arms folded, silently scanning the families eating dinner for threats.

"I sure as shit wasn't coming to the ghetto on a Sunday," David retorted. "You wanted to meet—here we are."

Taster's Shake Shack was a diner-style drive-in that served all manner of grilled and fried food along with an extensive line of milkshakes. David loved their milkshakes and so did his son. He liked to surprise the boy by bringing him home a shake once in a while. David's father had never done stuff like that for him.

A waitress approached them with an iPad in hand. She was probably about nineteen, and despite her best attempts to appear chipper, the despair she held for her job seeped through her every step. "Can I get you anything, sir?" she asked Reggie.

Reggie looked her up and down with a twisted smile then politely declined.

"So, what is it?" David asked once the waitress had left.

"Big D Roy."

"Excuse me?" David said. He knew the name, but it was so ridiculous, that he couldn't help but ask Reggie to repeat it.

"Big D Roy," Reggie replied. "He run them West Ashley boys and some other crews down John's Island."

"Yeah, I've heard the name," said David, sipping his milkshake. "What about him?"

"Ellis wants him out the game," Reggie explained.

David shook his head and scoffed. "I told him I was done with all that," he said. "I've got a new partner. Makes that kind of thing pretty hard. Tell him to get one of his other guys to do it."

"Ellis wants *you* to do it. He said, 'Have Sullivan do it. He owes us.'"

David finished his milkshake and tossed it into the nearby trash receptacle. "So, it's like that?" he asked, rising to his feet and staring Reggie down. "He thinks he's got some leverage on me or something?"

Reggie's driver stepped closer, but Reggie held his hand up to calm him. "Ain't like *that*," he told David. "Ellis just wants someone he can trust. Says he'll double the rate of last time."

David wanted to punch Reggie square in the nose. The driver would most likely draw on him if he did, but David was pretty sure he could grab the .338 holstered to his ankle, under his jeans, and light that fat fuck up before he had a chance to aim whatever bulky arm cannon he was carrying. Guys like that *always* carried impractical sidearms. Of course, then he'd have to kill Reggie, too, and he needed him to keep Ellis in check.

"Alright fine, but I need his name and a location of where I can find him," David said reluctantly.

"I already told you his name," said Reggie.

"Big D isn't a fucking name. What's his mother call him?"

"Oh, his name Michael, I think," said Reggie, looking to his driver for confirmation. The driver nodded.

"Michael Roy, got it," said David. "And where do I find Mr. Roy?"

"He lives in Park Circle. I'll send you the details."

"Alright. Tell Ellis I'll be by to settle up after it's done," David said.

Reggie nodded and returned to the Escalade with his driver. David found the waitress and ordered a chocolate milkshake for his son.

There's something deeply unsettling about visiting the site of a terror attack. The tragic loss of life. The unfathomable mindset of those who seek to indiscriminately harm others. The anxiety that no one is ever really safe anywhere—that evil could strike at any time without warning.

Andrea thought of Marcus and the world he had to grow up in. A world where he could be the target of violence for the color of his skin. A world where even going to church came with risk. He was barely old enough to understand it, and yet he would carry it with him for the rest of his life.

She thought of her mother, may her soul rest in peace. How her life was taken from her by a man who felt he owned every inch of her body and therefore had the right to kill her. She remembered the indifference of the white officers who came to their apartment afterward. To them, it was just another case of Black-on-Black violence—another day, another dead Black woman.

She thought of Gram, a woman who grew up during Jim Crow. A proud woman who was perhaps too accepting of the status quo but refused to allow anyone or anything to prevent her from living her life. Gram had gone directly to church after the attack on AME, to pray for those that had been lost, as well as the soul of the man who had killed them. "Any man with such hatred in his heart is a man in great pain," Gram had told her that day.

Andrea didn't care about the monster's pain. Plenty of people had pain—she carried hers with her every moment of every day. She could never use that pain as an excuse to hurt someone who didn't deserve it, and she rejected the notion that Christianity demanded she forgive such a man.

She had barely been to church since. It felt hollow and almost like self-subjugation to her. If there was a God, why would good, faithful people be made to suffer so much for so long? How could an entire country rise to prominence while enslaving its fellow man? How could that country be allowed to cover its sins with the cross? Where was God's judgment? And how long would he allow their people to be raped, murdered, and strung up like animals? How could he allow a terrorist to walk into a house of worship and slay innocents gathered in his name? He could keep that lion from eating ole Daniel, but he couldn't make Rufus Luschenant's gun jam? Were Black Americans experiencing a never-ending test of their faith? Were they Job, being purposely slighted by God in some sick contest with Satan himself?

Truth was, Andrea didn't hold much faith in a higher power, and she felt that religion itself was just another institution tainted with inequality. For white Americans, religion had always been about maintaining tradition and that meant reinforcing cultural dominance. For Black Americans, it was a spiritual bonding of individuals joined together in common suffering. That's what made the attack on the AME church so particularly egregious and awful: church was the place where their communities had always sought refuge and peace.

Pastor Mosely led Andrea and Daren through the AME church, showing them where the shooter's first victim had fallen on the steps outside, then down the pews, pointing out the exact spots where worshippers had been killed. For each, he took a moment to talk about who they were, the things they had done in life, and to share a personal memory about them. He had known them all before their deaths, but now their names were forever etched into his memory. His careful recalling of their careers, dreams, and loved ones was his way of keeping their memory alive.

Mosley finished the tour by explaining that the church would soon be demolished, and the congregation moving to a new building. "There's too much pain and grief here," he explained.

The pastor hung his head low, noticeably shaken from the tour. Andrea placed her hand on his shoulder. "I'm sorry to make you relive that again," she said.

"It's alright," Mosely replied. "It's important that people know what happened here."

Andrea looked at Daren. He'd been sheepish the entire tour. She could see he was struggling with something. The three took a seat on a bench at the front of the pews. Aside from them, the building was empty.

"Pastor Mosely, as I mentioned before, Daren and I are working the Devon Grey case," Andrea told him.

"That boy died nearly eight months ago. Y'all still fishing?" he asked, indignantly.

"We're looking into local hate groups or individuals who might be radicalized enough to do something violent."

"Hold on now," the pastor replied, rising to his feet and walking off toward the back of the church. Andrea and Daren exchanged puzzled looks.

"Where's he going?' Daren asked.

"No idea," said Andrea. "You doing alright?" she asked him.

"Yeah, I'm fine."

Andrea looked at him a moment longer, trying to read his reaction.

"Here ya go," Mosely exclaimed upon his return. He handed them a shoe box containing stacks of handwritten and typed notes and letters. Andrea took the box in disbelief and began thumbing through it. "Of course, most are anonymous or use aliases," he added. "But that's every hateful message we've received since the attack. Except for the online messages, of course."

"Those may actually be more helpful," Daren explained. "We might be able to link the email addresses or social media accounts. I don't suppose you kept any log of those online messages as well?"

"We got them all," Mosely said with a grim nod. "There's a lot of them, sadly."

"How about social media comments?" Andrea asked.

"There's unfortunately quite a lot of those. We haven't bothered to keep track," Mosely admitted.

Andrea looked at Daren, knowing they had the same thought. "Pastor, would you be able to have someone go through all the social media posts from the past couple of years and screenshot all the hateful or bigoted comments?" she asked.

Mosely gave her a side-eyed glance and sighed. "I don't quite think you understand how much content you're talking about," he retorted in mild protest. "You'll have thousands of comments to sort through."

"It's a place to start," Andrea said. "You mind if we keep these?" she asked, shutting the box of hate. She was not looking forward to reading through it all.

Mosely shook his head and raised his hand to indicate he did not want the box back. "I only held onto them all because I had a feeling one day, I would have to hand them over to someone like yourself," he replied. "And I will get to gathering those online messages and comments."

Andrea and Daren thanked the pastor for his time, and he promised to be in touch. They left and decided they would go review the physical evidence from the Grey case at the County Sheriff's office. They were both silent the entire ride there.

16

DAVID NEEDED COKE.

The small-time dealers on the south end were easy to roll on, but you could never be sure how much they were holding. David needed at least half a key to make sure the charges wouldn't get pled down, and lifting a brick from the evidence room was easier than it should be. So, that's what he did.

Michael 'Big D' Roy lived in a redeveloped and largely gentrified area of North Charleston called Park Circle. The neighborhood was literally a large circle of interconnecting streets surrounding a public park. Most of the lots were half-acre or larger, all with relatively new housing. Some relics still stood from before redevelopment, but most of them were on the market and soon to be redone.

Big D's house was a small single-story brick ranch with a built-in car port on the corner bordering the park. David parked his pickup on the opposite end of the park and peered through the tinted windows with a small pair of binoculars. He watched an old, rusted airline van with the words "Ice Cream" plastered to the side with faded lettering make its way toward the park. The speaker precariously mounted to the top of the van blared the lyric-less audio files for Christmas karaoke songs.

What kind of sick fuck plays *Here Comes Santa Claus* in this heat?

That's when David spotted Big D. The man was indeed quite big. He was at least six-foot-four and must've been three hundred pounds. Not somebody David would ever want to try and restrain. When the cops came, they'd better bring backup.

David watched as Big D strutted out of his house, two young kids beside him, and flagged down the ice cream man. The van stopped right at the foot of his driveway, sending all the nearby kids flocking to his yard. Big D smiled and greeted them all. David was surprised by what he watched next. Big D reached into his shirt pocket, pulled out a large wad of cash, peeled off several bills, and told all the kids that the ice cream was on him. They cheered and thanked him, and he smiled, taking a popsicle from the man in the van, and then retreating back into his house, sweat pouring from his face. The children got their ice creams one by one and disappeared back into the neighborhood.

David was impressed. For a moment, he even felt bad about what he was about to do. Then he remembered who Big D was. All the ice cream sandwiches in the world could never change that, what he did, or the harm he'd caused. Guys like him used pain and suffering for profit and power. That's why David didn't mind doing anything in his power to take people like that down. He knew Big D was responsible for hard drugs flooding the streets, and using kids to move his product, too. He knew he was responsible for murders and gang shootings where innocent people had been hit. All of it came with the territory.

Guys like Big D never had to face consequences for any of it. They never touched the dope. They never did the hits. They never got near the dirt. The only way they ever got taken down was when the state or the feds cared enough to help get it done. It required lots of resources, wire taps, and the works—everything needed to build a RICO case.

David saw things a little differently. The drugs would always be around so long as there was a demand, and there was *always* going to be demand. Once he came to terms with that, he realized the real goal should be a reduction in violence, particularly violence that harmed innocent people. Drugs would always be in demand, so drug dealers would always be around. It wasn't drug dealers themselves that were the problem—it was the competition. Competing factions led to violence.

Ellis, for all his faults, was a pragmatic man who saw bloodshed as costly. David would rather he be in control of the downtown drug trade, and as long as David helped keep the competition away, the violence was kept to a minimum. David enforced the boundaries Ellis had agreed to with various other factions. But sometimes, an asshole like Big D would just refuse to play by the rules.

This was a win-win, even if David hated to admit it. It allowed him to get scum like Roy off the streets and maintained Ellis's control of the market. Better this than shootouts and gang wars. David wasn't always proud of the things he had to do—sometimes he was downright ashamed. The greater good was never easy to serve.

He sat back and lit a cigarette. He would wait for dark before making his move.

The rope was missing. Each of them had gone through what little evidence there was in the plastic bin marked "GREY, DEVON", and each had double-checked the list of the evidence that was supposed to be in the box. The rope used to hang Devon Grey was missing.

"Uh, I'm not sure," Deputy Hereford stammered.

Daren looked at him contemptuously then turned to Andrea in disbelief. "Are you telling me you've lost the murder weapon?" he asked the deputy incredulously.

"I—uh—Well, you see, everything was in this box and…"

"Uh-huh," said Andrea. She put her hand on her hip, rolled her eyes, and took a deep breath. Hereford had not made a great impression so far. When he had brought them to the evidence locker, he had discovered it was unlocked, which had both embarrassed and perplexed the young man. "Well, we've seen how locked tight y'all keep your shit," she said. "I need you to get me the log for this evidence. I want everything from the moment it came through."

Hereford gave her a quick, "yes ma'am," and was on his way.

Daren sorted through the piles of photos. "No autopsy," he remarked.

"Coroner says the cause of death was asphyxiation, which is consistent with the crushed larynx and broken neck," she remarked.

Daren pushed the coroner's report aside with a nod. "How many men you think it would take to hang a boy that size?" he asked, examining the pictures of Devon's swollen and broken neck.

"A strong man could do it alone," she said. "But I'd bet there were two… Maybe three."

"This is all we got?' Daren asked in disbelief. "Some photos, a coroner's report, and a missing fucking rope?"

"There was nothing at the scene. No clothes—he was hanged naked. No cell phone. Not even any useful pieces of trash or anything nearby."

"He was brought out there. Somebody abducted him and brought him out there to hang him," Daren concluded. "So, the question becomes *where* did they grab him from?"

"And were there witnesses?" Andrea added. "The mother says Devon left the house around 8 PM the night before, and she has no idea where he was going or who he was with."

"How about the cell company? We get a warrant, they can trace the locations," Daren suggested.

"Unfortunately, his phone was a prepaid."

"What's that now?" Daren asked.

"Prepaid phones. Burners. They sell them cheap—you buy prepaid cards with minutes on them to use them."

"So, there's no contract."

"Or identifying information," Andrea informed him. "I know you all fancy, but we know about cell phone tracking down here," she added with a nudge.

Deputy Hereford returned to the room with a printout in hand. He handed the paper to Andrea and shrugged. "Evidence was checked in from CPD. The officer who brought it said everything was there—"

"Who signed off on it?" Andrea asked, examining the paper.

"I did…" Hereford admitted, sheepishly.

"Un-fucking-believable," Andrea exclaimed.

"Wait a minute," Daren interjected. "CPD? Charleston Police? What was it doing there?"

"Jurisdiction is a bit of a mess around here," Andrea explained.

"CPD originally took point on the case," Hereford explained. "It was later decided that the Sheriff's Office would take the case."

"So, the evidence was transferred," Andrea chimed in. "I've seen this before. The rope is probably still at CPD."

"So much for the chain of custody," Daren smirked. "So why did the case change departments?"

Hereford shrugged, unaware of the answer.

"Probably a matter of where the body was found," Andrea explained. "I'll explain on the way." She then turned to Hereford and added, "If you're lucky and the rope *is* at CPD, maybe I'll be nice and not tell your CO about this."

The deputy's head dropped.

Sunset rays of orange and gold set the Ashley River ablaze. The colors of the sky reflected vividly from the water, painting everything in its vibrant hue. In the distance, yachts, ferries, fishing boats, and shipping vessels cut across the fiery scene like tiny voyagers carving their paths through an endless sky.

Daren stared out the window at the beauty as they drove down the highway and across the river. Behind them, North Charleston; ahead of them, West Ashley. Just a river between them, and yet on the far side Daren could see the mansions lining the water, each with a private peer stretching from its yard over the marshy banks to a private dock. Some had small yachts anchored.

The beauty of the scene was tainted by Daren's observation. It made him feel uneasy, as many things had since his arrival in the lowcountry. He thought about what it had felt like to be held under water—how it had felt to accept that he was going to die. He thought about what it must have been like for the victims of the AME church attack to have faced their deaths so unexpectantly. He thought about the children. *Why had he been so lucky?*

"You alright?" Andrea asked, breaking his train of thought.

"Yeah. Just a peaceful sunset," he remarked.

She'd asked him that a few too many times for his liking. It was getting annoying. She was always parsing her concern with inspection.

Sometimes he felt like he was on trial around her. Other times there was almost a comradery of sorts, but his inability to get a feeling of how she felt about him made him uncomfortable. He wondered what she knew about his record.

"So, the jurisdictions here are such a mess," Andrea explained as she drove. "Each city has set areas it patrols, but there are all these pockets where the sheriff's office is responsible," she said. "A lot of times there's confusion about who has to respond where. Dispatch is pretty good at sorting it out but…"

"But not always," he concluded.

"It doesn't make too much of a difference, because the departments all cooperate," she added. "But shit like this can sometimes happen."

"You've got North Charleston PD, Charleston PD, and the Charleston County Sheriff's office all covering the same areas?"

"Don't forget Dorchester County Sheriff's Office, the Hanahan County Sheriff's, the Mount Pleasant PD, Folly Beach PD, and probably some other assholes too, all operating in the same greater Charleston area."

"Holy shit," Daren remarked. "The bureaucracy and bullshit are bad enough when there's one department in a city."

"And as I'm sure you can imagine," she added, steering the vehicle down the exit ramp. "The sheriffs' departments around these parts have quite the sordid history."

"I did spend a lot of the time reading about your department," Daren noted. He watched her closely to see her reaction.

She smiled and nodded. "Oh yeah, there's some real pieces of shit there."

"What are we doing in West Ashley?" he asked, changing the subject.

"Can't bother the mother, but we can scope out his neighborhood. Then we'll head downtown and see if they have our rope."

Daren nodded and thought about the kind of people who would abduct a child off the street. It seemed quite brazen. Was it premeditated? The event itself, most likely, but not the victim. Devon Grey was probably just in the wrong place at the wrong time. The most likely explanation in Daren's mind was a small group of men looking to impress a hate group—maybe even as part of an initiation.

What bothered him about that theory was the apparent randomness of the event. There hadn't been any other killings like Grey's anywhere else in the country, thankfully. And from what he could find, there was no recent history in the area of lynchings or even unsolved murders of people of color that fit that narrative. If it was an organized killing in any way, it would stand to reason that more blood would be shed.

Perhaps it was just a couple of young kids acting out murderous fantasies—riled up by their fathers' tales of the "good ole days" when they'd string up Black folks for fun. Even that didn't make sense, however. The scene was too careful.

Daren hated to admit it, but none of their theories really made sense to him. Something was off about the whole case.

Andrea drove them to the neighborhood where Devon Grey had lived with his mother. It was a historically Black neighborhood named Sherwood Forest after the legend of Robin Hood. The houses were small and in various states of disrepair. Some were surrounded by chain-link fences and had barred windows.

They drove through the neighborhood, suspicious faces glaring at them. "Have a hard time thinking somebody would try something in here," said Andrea. "Too many eyes." She drove back across the main road and into the parking lot of a gas station.

"What are you thinking?" Daren asked her.

"Going to see if they got tapes we can pull," she replied, nodding to the gas station. "Maybe he came in that night." She pulled her car up to the pumps and parked. "Fill her up for me?" she asked with a smile. "I'll talk to the attendant about security tapes."

Daren couldn't help but smirk at how she had managed to get him to fill her tank. It was no concern to him—the Bureau would cover the expenses. She had been driving them around all day, after all. He inserted his credit card into the card reader and selected 87-octane. While he waited for the tank to fill, he read the news on his phone. There had been another suspicious police shooting involving a Black man. This time in Toledo.

He thought of Anthony Castile, a father working three jobs to provide for his kids, who was shot and killed during a traffic stop. Daren's report had cleared the officer involved.

"Tapes only go back a week," Andrea informed him when she returned.

"Figures." Nothing about this case was going to be easy.

The Charleston Police Department was a stately building located on the west end of the peninsula overlooking the Ashley River. The building also housed municipal offices, a DMV, and a courthouse.

It was early in the afternoon when they arrived. Inside, folks were easygoing and friendly until Andrea and Daren explained who they were and why they were there. It took some cajoling, but they were able to get access to the evidence room to check for the rope. A duty officer named O'Brien escorted them down the stairs and through the locked steel doors.

"Let's see…" O'Brien said, leading them down a narrow aisle of shelving stocked full of boxes and bins. "DB1222," he read from his clipboard. "So, it would have been stored in this bin." He pulled out the bin with a 'DB1222' tag from an old label gun and opened it up. "Nothing here," he remarked, combing through the bin. "Just some evidence from the bridge jumper last week."

Daren was disappointed, but then he noticed something on the back of the shelf where the bin had been. There, wedged between the shelf and the wall, he could see an evidence bag that had nearly fallen behind the shelving unit. He reached behind the shelf and grabbed the bag. "Found it!" he declared, relieved to see a blue rope inside.

O'Brien checked the number on the bag as if another blue rope might have been there from some other case. "I'll be damned," he replied. "I have no idea how it got wedged back there…"

"Biggest murder case this city has seen in years, and y'all almost lost the murder weapon," Andrea snarked.

"Probably useless anyways," O'Brien said in defense of his department. "The lab didn't find shit on that rope."

Daren and Andrea exchanged a look of disbelief. It was no wonder that such a difficult case had grown cold so quickly. The disregard on display was baffling.

17

NORTH CHARLESTON - SPRING 1996

ANDREA WAS ALREADY awake when her bedroom door cracked open and Mikayla, seven years old, hurried inside and shut the door behind her. She then climbed right into bed with Andrea. At the age of ten, Andrea was already well accustomed to providing care and comfort to her sister.

Mikayla would always come to her room when she was scared of the weather or *him*. That night, was twice as bad because the storms were as angry and scary as their father. She pulled Mikayla close as their father screamed and the thunder clapped.

Andrea always tried to be strong for her sister, even though she too was often afraid. She felt a responsibility to shield and protect her little sister. She would reassure her that everything would be fine, and sometimes, she would read her a story to distract her. Other times she would hold her and sing softly to her while their parents fought angrily below, or as the thunder raged above.

That night it was both. Doors slammed, glass broke, and curses were screamed while thunder rattled their house. Mikayla cried, wanting the chaos to stop—wanting to feel safe enough to sleep.

Andrea held her tight and ran her fingers through her hair affectionately. She sang *Colors of the Wind*, Vanessa Williams's hit song from Mikayla's favorite movie, Pocahontas, urging Mikayla to help when she couldn't remember the lyrics. They sang softly together, and Andrea held her with all her love. She tried to impart love with touch, almost believing that if she loved her really hard, she could shield her from the world around them.

A loud crash of something being smashed into the wall caused her to jump, and Mikayla began bawling again. "WHORE!" their father roared like a beast. More smashing followed by his booming voice shouting at their mother. The thunder crashed loudly outside.

"Remember Folly Beach last year?" Andrea whispered to Mikayla.

"Yeah," Mikayla replied through sniffles.

"Remember how warm the water was?" she asked, gently rubbing her back.

"It was like a bath," her sister replied.

"Remember how awesome it looked when the sun set?" Andrea asked.

"It looked like a painting," Mikayla replied.

Andrea had a secret. She had learned that if she really thought deeply about another place or time; if she thought about how it felt, looked, smelled, or tasted, she could transport herself there and almost escape whatever was happening around her. She often walked the shores of Folly Beach in her mind to escape the reality of her life. She spent a lot of time in her head or buried in books, whatever she could do to take her mind away from that house and her father's wrath.

Her mother insisted her father wasn't a bad man. He was a veteran of the Vietnam War who had not fared well after the war and turned to drugs for relief. That wound up getting him arrested and imprisoned for six years. According to her mother, those years behind bars had changed her father. He came out more haunted and burdened than before, and became quick to violence. "They destroy men in prison," her mom had explained. "Your father needs all our love to help him get back from that." Yet, for all her mother's defense of him and his actions, she took the brunt of his abuse. He was a drinker and drug abuser who came and went as he pleased. She would complain he smelled like whores, and he would accuse her of being paranoid. She would berate him for not coming home for days at a time, and he would smack her around and tell her that he would do as he pleased.

Andrea's mother had always been a prideful woman, which was why it was so confusing for Andrea to watch her suffer her father's anger and abuse. Then one day, Andrea saw her father grab her mother and throw her against the wall like a ragdoll. At that moment, Andrea understood something she had not quite been able to articulate: that it was dangerous for a woman to stand up for herself against a man.

That night, however, her mother seemed to be done taking his shit. As Andrea held Mikayla, she could hear her mother rebuking her father, telling him she would call the police if he ever laid a finger on her again. Then her mother said something else that caught Andrea's attention. "And you ain't hittin' my girls ever again, either!" she yelled. "Or I swear to God, I will put your ass back in prison!"

Andrea thought of her father's spankings, and the times he would grab her by the arm hard enough to leave marks. She thought about all those smacks on the back of her head. Once, he had even spanked Mikayla so hard that the poor girl was unable to sit comfortably for days.

The apartment fell silent soon after her mother's threat. Whatever she had said and done had diffused the situation. Andrea heard her father leave not long after. Soon after that, the storms passed and Mikayla fell asleep. Peace was rare in their household, and when it came, Andrea was always anxious about what would come next.

She snuggled up to her sister and held her tightly. Closing her eyes, she wondered if maybe the fighting and the violence would end now that her mother had stood up for herself and them. Maybe now her father would be forced to treat them better. If he couldn't, perhaps her mother would make him leave. She fantasized about what it would be like to have a normal family where everyone felt safe. She thought about what life would be like if her father changed. Finding that hard to imagine, she thought about what it would be like if he were gone—for her and Mikayla to live alone with their mother. She imagined waking up every day without fear and anxiety. She imagined watching movies with her mother or helping her cook dinner, all in peace. Maybe someday, the three of them could be happy. Maybe someday they could all have peace.

Three days later, Andrea's father returned home and brutally murdered her mother while the girls listened from under the covers in Andrea's bed.

18

THE SUN WAS now down, and the lights inside Big D's house were now on, radiating out through iron-barred windows. David walked briskly but quietly along the curb, approaching Big D's house on his right. He looked at his truck, which he'd left parked up ahead before walking around the block. He wanted to be able to leave quickly once he was done.

He palmed the brick of coke tucked inside his hooded sweatshirt and quickly turned up the driveway. Spotting a camera, he crouched low and to the side of an SUV parked in the drive. Covertly, he made his way up the driveway, past the camera, and into the carport. Once inside the carport, he squeezed himself between the wall and the old Pontiac that was parked there, and slowly made his way to the front end of the car. There he dropped to the ground and scooched under the car's front end.

He pulled the brick and a roll of duct tape out from his sweater and proceeded to tape the brick to the backside of the front bumper, making sure it was secure. Carefully rising to his feet, he went to leave, but accidentally brushed against a set of jumper cables that were hanging on the wall. The cables fell to the ground, knocking over a case of empty beer cans on their way, and causing a dog inside the house to bark. David cursed under his breath and hustled out of the garage.

The door that led to the house from the carport swung open just as David ducked around the corner and pressed himself against the outside wall. He could hear Big D moving around inside the carport, his cautious steps coming closer. There was nowhere for David to go and no way for him to move without being seen. He was stuck and it was only a matter of seconds before he would be discovered.

David took a deep breath and drew his Smith and Wesson 45 from the back of his waistband. He readied the weapon, stepped out from behind the wall, and pointed it at Big D, who was holding a pistol himself.

"Police! Drop it!" David yelled.

Big D furrowed his brow and looked at David with skepticism.

"I said fucking drop it, big boy!" David barked, his finger pressing against the trigger ever so gently, ready to pull it back in an instant. "Do it, or I'll light you up with your kids watching," he threatened.

Big D looked at his two boys staring out the window and dropped the gun. "This is some bullshit. You one of Ellis's cops, huh?" Big D charged. "Out here by yourself in a hoodie in the dark."

"Shut the fuck up," David ordered. "Hands on the trunk of the car, legs spread, now!"

"Go ahead, I ain't got shit on me," Big D taunted as David searched him.

"Don't move or I swear to fucking God I'll paint that Pontiac with your brains," David warned him as he stepped back and pulled out his phone. He hit the icon to call dispatch and informed them that he needed immediate assistance.

"Assistance for what?!" Big D asked in anger. *"Assistance in framing my ass?!"*

"You're a drug dealer, don't cry victim," David replied, his gun still aimed at the man's back.

"Good luck proving it," Big D scoffed.

"My CI says you got a half-key of cocaine somewhere on the property."

"Uh-huh," said Big D. "And I'm sure you weren't out here planting exactly that on my shit. Look at your ass, dressed like a mother fuckin' burglar! Out here sneaking around by yourself and shit. This is some fucked up shit. This is just white cops setting up another Black man."

"Shut the fuck up," David commanded. "I'll fucking shoot you just to shut you up, and nobody would give a damn about it either. Just another dead hood rat drug dealer."

"Fuck you, racist pig!"

"Let me ask you something," said David. "I see you buying ice cream for the kids, acting like mister fuckin' Rogers. But you use kids to move product. Your own kind, too. How do you live with yourself?"

"What the fuck you talkin' about?"

"How many kids you kill? How many dead from your drugs?" David asked. "I just want to know how many ice cream cones does it take to make up for something like that? Is that how you sleep at night?"

"It's all part of the game. Those kids are valued customers! If I don't sell to them, somebody else will. Like Ellis LaMarche! I ain't never hurt a kid, man! I love kids! Shit—you're worried about morality and you work for Ellis?!"

"Yeah," David conceded. "He's a piece of shit, too. But you stick with the devil you know."

"You got the balls to ruin my life but not to kill me?" Big D asked him, rising from the back of the car, his arms wide. "You going to send me away, you might as well just fucking kill me now, pig. What do you think will happen to me in the big house? Ellis's people won't let me walk out of there alive. You're sending me to my death, so just fucking kill me now!"

Big D stepped toward him aggressively and David took two steps back. "Don't do it," David warned. He motioned to the window, where Big D's kids were watching in fear. "Don't make them see that," he urged. "Personally, I don't give a shit what happens to you. You're right, your life is as good as over, either way. I would hate to have those kids see their daddy get shot in their driveway."

Big D looked at his boys and saw they were frozen in terror. He sighed, turned around, and placed his hands back on the trunk of the Pontiac.

Backup arrived about five minutes later, and the responding officers immediately took Big D into custody while they waited for additional units to search the domicile.

"My source said the half key is somewhere in the Pontiac," David told the detectives from Narcotics when they arrived. When they recovered the brick, David congratulated them on a fine job, and then flashed a wide smile at Big D, who was watching from the back of a squad car.

"Congrats to you," a detective replied. "I don't quite understand why he taped his drugs to a car that doesn't have an engine in it."

"What's that?" David asked, confused.

"The Pontiac—it's got no engine. Why tape the drugs to an immobile vehicle?" the detective wondered.

"Probably just a hiding spot," David suggested.

"Yeah, probably." The detective looked at David's clothes and pursed his lips. "Sergeant, forgive me, but what, exactly, were you doing out here again?"

"Checking on my CI's tip," David responded defensively. "What the fuck do you think I was doing?"

"You were out here by yourself, without anyone knowing?" the detective asked, his brow furrowed.

"I just wanted to make sure there was actually an old Pontiac at this address before I called the cavalry in." David patted the detective firmly on the shoulder. "Make sure I'm not sending y'all on a wild goose chase."

The detective looked at Big D in the back of the patrol car and then back at David. He seemed to visibly shrug off his concerns with a little shake of his head, then extended his hand to David. "We appreciate the due diligence," he said.

David shook his hand firmly and nodded. "True blue, baby," he replied. "We gotta watch out for each other."

"We're going to tear apart the house, see what else we find," the detective told him. "Kids will go with social services," he added. "That's always a shame."

"Life's pain. They'll get used to it," David muttered.

The detective nodded.

19

THE MARINER SUPPLY store in West Ashley smelled like rubber and fresh paint. After some searching, Daren and Andrea finally found an employee taking stock of trailer parts in an aisle near the back of the store. The kid barely looked old enough to have a job.

"Alex," Daren said, reading the kid's name tag. "Fella down at the hardware store said you guys might sell rope like this." He opened the evidence bag and pulled the rope out far enough for Alex to examine.

"Yeah. Blue nylon rope. Aisle four," the kid informed them, turning back to his task at hand.

"Do you sell this *exact* rope, though?" Andrea asked.

"More or less," Alex replied without looking up.

"What the hell does that mean?" Daren asked. *"More or less?"*

"It's blue nylon rope. Aisle four," Alex repeated.

"Well, this rope right here," Andrea said, taking the evidence bag from Daren and holding it close to Alex's face. "This rope was used to lynch Devon Grey. You heard about that?"

Alex's face dropped, then turned red. "Oh, I'm—I'm sorry," he stammered.

"Can you maybe take us to aisle four and help us see if *this rope* was purchased here?" she asked.

Alex took the bag from her and gave the rope a close look. "Yeah, this is standard blue nylon rope. You can buy it here," he informed them.

"Really?" Andrea asked, hopeful that they had their first lead.

"And probably about three dozen other places around here," Alex added, handing her back the rope and shaking his head. "Sorry, but there's no way to tell where it was bought."

It was what Andrea had expected when Daren suggested tracking down the source of the rope. But she'd figured it was worth a shot.

Slightly deterred, they left the store and headed back to her car.

"Well, all in all," Daren said with a deep breath. "We got nothing."

"We'll start with the mother tomorrow, begin working relationships. Cross reference that with the white supremacist groups you talked about, and whoever Pastor Mosley comes up with. See if any names make multiple lists."

"Why do I have a sudden fear that that list might be longer than a name or two?" Daren asked as they climbed into her car.

"You're finally starting to understand where you are," Andrea replied as she started the car.

She drove Daren back to his room and told him again to get a different hotel. He assured he that he would, and invited her inside for drinks. "We could talk over the case a bit," he suggested.

"I have to get home to my kid," she said. "I'll be here first thing in the morning."

He nodded, said goodnight, and went inside. Andrea grabbed her phone from the center console and immediately texted David: *"Hey, where you want to meet?"*

Roaches always died on their backs. Daren sat alone in his room with his thoughts, watching one such unlucky Palmetto bug as it laid on its back, kicking its legs about. Initially, he had believed the insect to be dead, however, upon kneeling down to dispose of it with a paper towel, he noticed it was still kicking.

He read online that roaches that have encountered poison will become unable to control their nervous systems, which results in their flipping onto their backs. Another site said that roaches were a bit like turtles, insomuch as getting knocked onto their backs could be a fatal occurrence. Daren wasn't sure which was right, but he found himself fixated on the bug.

He sat and watched the bug for some time, sipping on the twelve pack of microbrew beer he'd picked up at the gas station across the way. Now on his third beer, he was surprised that the bug was still alive. How long would it take to die? An even better question was: Why did he care?

Something about the bug bothered him. There was the fact that, for some inexplicable reason, Daren hated the creature. The unsightly and ugly form of its prickly exoskeleton and those large, shiny wings made him cringe. But then, part of him felt bad for the bug. It had no concept of the larger world around it, nor why humans wanted it dead. At one point, it had been in its element—just another bug in a land of a million bugs. At some point, however, civilization had come and its environment had changed. Now it was a pest.

The roach kicked its legs again, a vain attempt to buck off death, and Daren remembered kicking and thrashing beneath the water, trying with fading strength to fend off death. He remembered what it was like to feel the panicked urge to breathe but knowing that taking a breath would fill his lungs with water and seal his fate. He remembered what Carson's hand had felt like on the back of his neck, and could still hear the man's muffled laughter.

Daren tried to shake the memories from his head but they were too strong. He could feel his heart rate rising. He grabbed his beer and headed outside for some air.

The night air was thick, heavy, and moist. He missed Connecticut, where the summer nights were almost always cool enough to provide some relief from the heat. He thought back to when he had first moved to DC, and how he had hated the summers. But the thickness of that lowcountry air was something else. He could feel the moisture sticking to his skin. Everything felt wet and smelled awful.

Daren leaned on the railing, sipped his beer, and watched the traffic go by. He'd seen a sign on the highway earlier which read, "TARGET ZERO: 203 Traffic Deaths This Year." It made him think about the hundreds of people who died every year in that state while driving home, heading to the store, or commuting to work. A grim verdict on the quality of drivers in the state, perhaps, but the reality was the same everywhere to varying degrees. Driving a car was dangerous. Probably one of the riskiest things people did on a daily basis and yet, nobody thought twice about getting behind the wheel. They never consider that their trip to the store might be their last. The frivolousness of when and how people died gave him anxiety.

He gazed at the construction site across the road. A new restaurant was being built. For now, the site was an eyesore. Heavy equipment had torn into the earth and left thick tracks in deep mud. Piles of debris were dumped into grungy-looking dumpsters. That was life: tearing things down to make them anew. Making things ugly so they could be made better. There was something almost poetic about it, and at the same time, unsettling. Daren considered all the men and women who were connected to the restaurant project. The architects, engineers, interior designers, plumbers, HVAC specialists, zoning officials, entrepreneurs, and the would-be restaurant staff. All these people and more whom he probably couldn't even imagine were connected to this project. How many, he wondered, would perish in a car crash before it was brought to fruition? How many would die in their sleep unexpectedly? How many would wake up one day and find themselves diagnosed with a terminal illness? And what would their legacy be? *A goddamn Italian bistro?* A chain restaurant that charges twenty dollars for a plate of spaghetti?

Maybe that was too judgmental. Surely, not every person could do something meaningful in their lifetimes. Time on this planet was limited for everyone, and you had to find some way to spend it between birth and death—some way to give yourself a purpose, even if it was ultimately meaningless. Even if it was just to erect chain restaurants in already overdeveloped cities.

Perhaps this was more about him. What was he doing with *his* time? Was there really any meaning, or was he just keeping himself busy until the curtain dropped? He retired back to his room, deciding the matter was too deep for his drunken mind to contemplate.

He did know one thing: If he had died in that creek two days earlier, his legacy would have been significantly less impressive than an Italian bistro. The bistro would provide jobs, it would feed people, and bring them together. If Daren had died, his work would have amounted to little more than a signature on a report that had exonerated a cop that should probably be in prison. The higher-ups he strived to satisfy and impress would forget him in a second. The thoughts troubled Daren, so he tried his best to shut them out.

Back in his room, he discovered the roach was still twitching—still kicking its legs and struggling against the inevitable. Daren sighed, feeling cruel for letting it suffer, and took mercy on the creature, stepping down on it and firmly twisting his foot.

The sex was angry that night. Andrea could feel David's frustration being expressed through the force with which he fucked her. She didn't mind. This was what they had together—a release for whatever feelings they were carrying. Sometimes it was angry, sometimes it needy, and sometimes it was raw and nasty. The passion and the feeling of being wanted made her feel good, but the wave of euphoria that washed over her when he made her cum was the real payoff. It was one of the only times she felt relaxed. It never lasted long, but those moments after sex were such a reprieve from the constant anxiety that governed her mind.

David sat up, his body glistening with sweat, and slid his underwear back on. The back of his truck cab was filled with smoke and undoubtedly reeked of sex, thanks to the rain, which had forced them to keep the windows up. "So, how's that case you're helping the fed with going?" he asked, lighting a smoke.

"The Grey case? Just getting started really," Andrea replied, taking his smoke from him with a smile, and forcing him to light another.

"Heard you two went all cowboy on some rednecks up in Givhans," said David. "That part of all this?"

Andrea smoked and listened to the rain. "No, not really." She trusted him, but she never talked about the details of her cases.

"So, what's this fed like?" he inquired. She could tell he was curious and fishing for details.

"I don't know," she said, contemplating how best to describe Daren. "He's sharp but kind of ignorant at the same time. Typical northeastern white collar, arrogant, dickwad. Acts like he's the only one who *truly* understands the world."

"So, you're getting along great," David teased, chuckling.

"Well, he's not bad. Just a little naïve about… well, about everything. He's got good instincts, though."

"What's his name?"

"Renard. Daren Renard." She could tell he was jealous. He always asked about other guys.

"Spending a lot of time with Daren, huh?" David asked. His tone was jocular, but she knew better.

"It's just work," she said dismissively.

"And how about the case? No leads?"

"I mean, we got a bunch of white supremacist groups we're looking into."

"But nothing solid?" he asked, and sensing she was being tight-lipped added, "Come on. I'm interested. You know I was one of the responding units that night."

Andrea hadn't stopped to consider that he might care about the case. "I know," she said. "I just don't like talking shop. *We* don't talk shop. But, no, I don't have anything solid yet."

"Damn shame what happened to that kid. It was an awful thing to see." He sighed and shook his head.

Andrea felt bad she had iced him out and realized he may be of some help to their investigation. "Maybe tomorrow you could meet us there?" she asked. "Walk us through the scene as you remember?"

"I don't know, Dre. I'm off tomorrow."

"That's perfect," she said, hopeful. "C'mon, do me the favor. It's better to have someone who was there than to walk through the scene based on pictures."

"My wife likes to keep me busy," he replied, but she knew better.

"C'mon," Andrea persisted. "You can meet Daren, size him up," she added with a smile.

"Oh, well, if I get to meet *the* esteemed Daren of House Renard," he said in his best fake British accent. They laughed and kissed. "Alright," he conceded. "Let me know what time, and I'll meet y'all there."

20

DOWNTOWN CHARLESTON WAS flooded again. Ocean water from the morning tide sat stagnate on streets, making many roads impassable. Some drivers dared their way through water high enough to flood their engines. Daren watched one car hesitate and stall out while trying to traverse the flood waters. The man's engine seized, and Daren knew the car was instantly totaled.

Andrea had told him the peninsula often flooded at high tide, especially when it rained. It had rained all morning, and Daren was amazed at how much it interrupted life in the city. As he walked from his new hotel to a nearby diner, he saw roads closed, deadlocked traffic, students on foot trying to find a way to class, and businesses closing down for the day.

"Won't it subside with the tide?" he'd asked the deskman at his hotel.

"Some. But if it keeps raining, the streets will flood worse this afternoon, and nobody will be able to get home." Back in New England, they were accustomed to snow shutting things down, but seeing rain paralyze a city was a new one for Daren.

He had checked into the Courtyard Hotel located downtown late the night after being unable to sleep and discovering yet another giant cockroach in his room. He figured that after slumming it with the bugs for a few nights, the Bureau owed him. His new hotel was beyond classy at $320 a night. To his delight, the room was clean, and he had found no bugs.

Still, he'd been unable to sleep. The thoughts of that roach twitching and kicking on its back kept popping into his head for some reason. When it came to mind, it reminded him of being face down in the creek, struggling for life. The thoughts left him feeling unsettled and on edge.

He bought an umbrella from the shop in the hotel lobby and went for a walk. He stopped when he reached the Bear Patch, a quintessential upscale breakfast café. The kind of place that served food and drinks Daren had never heard of and would never dare try. Luckily, they also had coffee and eggs and bacon. After waiting about fifteen minutes for a seat at the bar, he ordered his breakfast and read the news from his phone in silence, the night still weighing heavy on his eyes.

When the bartender brought his coffee, Daren asked the man sitting beside him to pass the saucer of cream to his right. The man obliged.

"Rough night?" the man asked.

"Something like that," Daren muttered, splashing the cream into his coffee.

"This flooding is something else," the man continued, not sensing Daren's desire to be left alone. "Ended up calling out of work because I can't get off the peninsula. I work over on James Island. Cable repair guy. You know, we're the assholes who make you wait around at your house all day, only to tell you we can't fix the problem."

Daren gave the man a sideways glance and sipped his coffee. He was in no mood to entertain conversation. "Well, enjoy your day off," he remarked, politely nodding his head and raising his mug to the man.

"What about you, fella? What do you do for a living?" the man asked.

"Oh," Daren replied, now fully annoyed. "I'm an FBI agent. You know, the assholes you don't ever want showing up at your house."

"FBI?" the man asked, oblivious to Daren's attitude. "Whatcha doin' in town?"

"Working," Daren said tersely. Then, after the man looked at him with disappointment and confusion, he added: "I'm sorry, I can't really talk about it."

The man nodded and smiled, satisfied. "Well, let me buy your breakfast," he offered.

"No, sir. It's fine," Daren protested.

"Sir, whatever you're doin' here, I'm sure it's somethin' I'd appreciate. My daddy was a lawman, and well, I can tell you've had a rough night. You're probably far from home, down here, serving our country. I'd be honored to buy your meal, sir."

Daren looked up from his cup, and for the first time turned to face the man. He was a bigger gentleman, with bushy brown hair. He had a pack of smokes rolled into his shirt sleeve. Daren had initially judged him to be another dumb redneck. He had been annoyed by the man's insistence on speaking with him. But in the end, the man was offering simple kindness, expressing gratitude, and attempting to extend him respect. Daren was humbled and slightly displeased with himself. "My name's Daren," he said, shaking the man's hand.

"Thank you for your kindness. I'm afraid it's not what I'm used to where I'm from."

"Name's Chuck," the man replied. "Pleased to meet you, Daren." He shook Daren's hand with pride. The bartender brought Daren's breakfast over, and Chuck informed him that he would be picking up Daren's tab.

"Really, you don't have to do that," Daren said, still feeling guilty for his attitude.

"No, sir. It's my pleasure," Chuck insisted.

Daren thanked the man and started in on his food. The man settled up with the bartender and left soon after, leaving a $10 bill on the bar for a tip.

"Stay dry!" Chuck said in parting.

"You too!" Daren called back. He finished his breakfast just before Andrea walked through the door. "Hope you weren't hungry," he said, wiping his mouth with a napkin.

"Have you seen me eat yet?" she joked, taking a seat beside him.

"No, but I heard tell you like chicken wings."

"Swore an oath on them once," she said with a grin.

"City's a goddamn mess today with all this rain, huh?"

"Just another thing this place refuses to admit is a problem." She flagged down the bartender and order a coffee. "I've got us an escort for the crime scene. A sergeant with the sheriff's office who was there the morning of."

"Great." He stared out the window at the falling rain, his mind flashing again to the creek, his fight for life beneath the water, and then that damn dying cockroach for some reason. "Good work," he said.

"You alright?" she asked, stirring cream and sugar into her coffee.

"You think about the other day at all? Carson's?" he asked.

"Sure," she replied hesitantly. "Hard not to. But I try not to let myself linger on it too much."

He nodded, understanding she didn't want to talk about it. He paid for her coffee against her protest, explaining that he'd gotten a free breakfast.

"Southern hospitality," she remarked after hearing about his encounter with Chuck.

They left the Bear Patch and drove to meet the sergeant at the scene. In West Ashley, they passed a Southern Baptist church, and Daren remarked, "That's twelve—*twelve* churches on this drive so far." Then they passed an Episcopal church, then a First Baptist church, and then soon after, one of those corporate mega churches. "Fifteen!" he exclaimed with a laugh. "Jesus Christ! How many goddamn churches do they need in one place?"

"Charleston *is* the Holy City," Andrea replied.

Devon Grey's body had been discovered in a clearing beyond the woods just off the road of an incomplete development called Ashley Circle in the plantation district. The development was compromised of four large curved sections of roads that together formed a circle.

"What the hell is this?" Daren asked. "It's a road to nowhere." The road was wide and lined with parking spots but there were no cars.

"Large commercial development," explained Andrea. "They built a Walmart on the other side, but then a local group of NIMBYs sued the developers."

"A nimby?"

"Not In My Backyard. Local activist groups opposed to new development," she said.

"Looks like they lost," Daren noted, nodding to a large sign displaying the name of a local real estate agency.

"Yeah, but they managed to stall the project so long, all the companies that were going to build pulled out. Then the investors pulled out. Land's back on the market, but the project is essentially dead."

Daren drove through an intersection and onto the next section of the undeveloped circle.

"There," Andrea instructed, pointing ahead. "Park behind that black truck with the Blue Lives Matter sticker."

A man with short dark hair and an unshaven face was there waiting for them. He wore a Sheriff's Office t-shirt with the sleeves cut off and a pair of torn jeans.

"David Sullivan," David introduced himself curtly. He looked Daren slowly up and down before extending his hand to him. When Daren shook his hand, David squeezed it unnecessarily hard.

Daren squeezed back and pretended to be fine with the male machismo on display. "Special Agent Daren Renard."

"It's great to finally meet you," David said, releasing Daren's hand from his grip, then stepping over to Andrea. "Dre's told me a lot about you," he added, lightly placing his hand on her back for just a moment.

Message received. Daren knew the type all too well. The performative masculinity was a response to a perceived threat. This man wanted him to know he had a personal relationship with Andrea.

"I got called in early that morning," David said as he led them through the brush. "Watch out for snakes," he called back to Daren with a laugh before continuing. "I got here about dawn, which meant the circus was already here." He pushed aside tree branches and stepped carefully as he proceeded through the thicket.

"Were these branches checked for fibers? Clothing?" Daren asked, awkwardly pushing aside a branch. His sneakers were covered in mud.

"Yeah, of course," David huffed. "But they didn't find shit." He motioned ahead. "It's right up here. This is where they found him."

"If it weren't for the tip, how long do you think it would have taken till somebody found him?" Andrea asked.

"Who knows. Weeks. Months. He could still be missing. Nobody comes out here," David answered with a sigh.

"Yet the anonymous tip came in the night he was killed," Daren remarked. "It had to have been one of the involved parties."

"Guilty conscience?" Andrea suggested.

"Either that or they wanted him to be found. What good is a hate crime if nobody knows it happened?" Daren countered.

They came to a small clearing. Loose strands of yellow police tape still hung on nearby trees.

David pointed to a large tree. "That's the one he was hanging from." Then he pointed to a large fallen tree to their left. "And the rope was anchored here to this tree. Right next to the carving."

Daren crouched down and examined the symbol that had been carved into the tree.

"You think this is like some secret society shit?" David asked.

"I don't know," Andrea said, shaking her head slowly. "Maybe."

"Or an underground chapter of some organization... Perhaps some assholes trying to start their own group," Daren suggested.

"So, y'all just out here fishing in the dark?" David cackled. "Dre, I know you care about what happened to this kid, but this case went cold on day one."

"No surprise given the police work I've seen done here," countered Daren.

"Is that right?" David asked before spitting at the ground. Another message received.

"Alright, alright, easy, fellas," said Andrea. "Let's not start beating our chests now."

Looking around the area, Daren was quickly disappointed. While seeing the scene in person had given him a better picture of where Devon was hanged, it had provided little else. There was nothing to see out there. He swatted the mosquitos away and grumbled about the bugs in the South. David shot him a funny look as if he were amused by his fragility.

Men like David were always hostile toward him. Daren suspected that something about him made them insecure or uncomfortable, and made them feel the need to assert their male dominance. Sometimes it was subtle—a tone of voice, maybe a casual smirk. Other times it was more overt, like an excessive handshake or shoulder slap.

"This is a waste of our time," Daren concluded. "Was there anything about the scene you can tell us that wasn't in the report?" he asked the sergeant.

"Hey, I didn't have to come out here on my day off for some fucking cold case. She asked me to be here," David griped.

"I appreciate your taking us out here," Daren said to assuage his irritation. "I was just wondering if you had anything else to tell us before we leave. We've gotta go interview the mother."

"No." David shook his head and looked to the ground for a moment like he was stewing. "But if I think of anything, I will be sure to let y'all now."

They walked back to the road, and Daren waited in the Charger while Andrea walked David to his truck.

"Is that your boyfriend?" Daren asked her once they were driving away.

"I don't see how that's any of your business," said Andrea.

"Just curious," he said. "I noticed he was wearing a wedding ring."

She looked at him, her eyes narrowing. "Let's get one thing straight," she said. "My life is not up for discussion. Working this case with you doesn't entitle you to shit."

Daren nodded, feeling slightly embarrassed. "Sorry I asked," he said sincerely. "It's none of my business."

Satisfied, she turned her head and stared out the passenger window. She didn't speak for the remainder of the ride.

21

"KENNY, MY MAN, what's happening?" David sat behind the wheel of his truck, parked outside a large colonial-era mansion with large white pillars and a giant front door. A yacht, a beamer, and several Escalades were parked along the estate's long, winding driveway. "I need you to do me a favor," he said into his phone. "I need a little background on a fellow agent. Nothing fancy, just the basics: ya know, who he is, what he's been up to... Nah, he's just down here poking around and I'm trying to see what he's up to... Yeah, his name is Renard. Daren Renard... Okay. Thanks, buddy. Yeah, tell Beth I said hello..."

David ended the call and tucked the phone into his pocket before retrieving his gun from the center console. He knew that Ellis's people would take it from him at the door, but he'd look weak and foolish to come without it. Times like these he missed Greg—it was always good to have a man waiting for you outside.

Ellis's property was formerly part of a plantation—something the North Charleston kingpin took great pride in. David had first thought the man must have a morbid sense of humor—a Black man living in the master's house of a plantation—and he did, but that wasn't his reason for living there. Ellis had told him one night over drinks that it was a statement about what was owed. He said his ancestors had worked on a plantation, but now he owned one. "All these mansions ought to be owned by Black Americans," he had told David. "It was our ancestors that built them. Our sweat and blood that made their wealth." Ellis loved to ramble on about his world views, race and politics, and why he was wrongly cast as a villain in society.

David was greeted at the front porch by two armed guards, which was typical. They frisked him, took his gun as he had expected, and led him inside. The entrance led to a large foyer with a grand staircase leading to the second floor. The men directed him to his left, to a large parlor room with plush couches and an elegant stone fireplace.

He sat on one of the couches and examined the room. The walls had ornate, hand-painted wallpaper—Ellis had mentioned it several times. Over the fireplace was a painting of Black men, presumably slaves, working the fields.

From around the corner, somewhere down the hall, David could hear Ellis telling someone: "I don't care what they say. That wasn't the negotiated price... I have to go, one of my piggies is here."

David snarled and shook his head. Hearing Ellis's Oxfords approaching from down the hallway, he shifted his glance back to the painting.

Ellis entered the room. "Classic Antebellum romanticism," he said of the painting. "Really complements the overall theme of this place, I think."

"Which is?" David asked, genuinely curious.

"Isn't self-evident?" Ellis asked, taking a seat on the couch across from David. He crossed his legs and set his glasses down on the coffee table. As always, he was impeccably dressed. "Reclamation!" he said with the timbre and bravado of a minister. "Taking back what is ours."

David couldn't help but laugh. "You always struck me as too damn smart for this life," he said. "One of the smartest people I know, no doubt."

"Flattery won't get you a bonus, Sergeant Sullivan," Ellis grinned. Nearing the end of his sixth decade on Earth, he was a man of sophistication and refinement who carried with him an air of experience and wisdom.

Ellis raised his eyebrows and snapped his fingers. Reggie appeared immediately from the hallway. "Go and get our boy in blue his pile of green," Ellis instructed. Reggie nodded and quickly left the room. "Reggie tells me we may have miscommunicated our request to you yesterday," he said to David with concern. "I explicitly instructed him to offer you the job for cash. He tells me you may have interpreted this as me exerting leverage over you."

"He said you said I owed you," said David. "That sounds like leverage."

"That is a very unfortunate understanding. I appreciate our relationship, David. I appreciate your dependability."

"Then why mention me owing you anything?"

"Well, because you do. And if you couldn't tell from our many talks, I am a stickler for what is owed."

Reggie returned with two stacks of banded bills and handed them to Ellis. "I trust an extra fifteen thousand will ameliorate the misunderstanding and restore our relationship to its former condition," Ellis said, gently tossing the stacks of bills to David.

David caught one and quickly retrieved the other from the floor. He flipped through the bills to give the appearance of due diligence. "I think that's more than fair," he replied, tucking the stacks of money into the waist line of his jeans. "I want to make something clear, right here, right now," he added, rising to take his leave

Ellis looked at him amusedly. "Go on then, son. Out with it."

"I don't work for you," David insisted. "We have an arrangement."

"Arrangements, partnerships, employees," Ellis said with a wave of his hand. "It's immaterial. In the end," he added, his voice growing stern. "This is still America. The only thing that matters is who has the money."

David laughed and shook his head. "See, I can see why you think that," he smirked. "Because everyone around here kisses your ass. But the reality of the situation is that you are allowed to operate and live freely because it's beneficial to me. Money might buy you a big house, but real power comes from authority." He flashed his badge. "This is power. This gives me power to decide who gets to do what—who gets to operate, who gets to live…"

"I'd watch your tone, *boy*," Ellis scolded.

"I'd watch yours, old man," David shot back. "I ain't your employee or your pig. See, you can sit here on your plantation and pretend, but the truth is *I own your ass*." He stepped closer and two of Ellis's men entered the room. "Truth is that men like me still own you. We always will."

Ellis raised his hand to relax his men. "It's okay, boys. He's just venting some steam," he laughed.

David laughed, amused at Ellis's hubris. "If it wasn't for me, those Dixie Mafia boys would have killed you years ago," he sneered.

"Oh, I think we more than made that up to you," Ellis reminded him. "That was no small price, either. Now *you* owe *us*."

"No," David insisted. "No, that's not how this works. Push me and see what happens," he warned. "You'll see what happens." He went to leave but stopped. He put his hand out and waited for the guard to return his gun.

The guard looked at Ellis, who nodded and waved his hand. "Let him go," Ellis said.

The guard gave David his gun. "That's right," David scoffed on his way out.

There is something foreboding about neighborhoods where homes have barred windows and doors. It broadcasts a message to passersby that they are not safe or welcomed there. Daren couldn't imagine growing up in such an environment, and not feeling safe in your home.

Andrea had explained that the neighborhood was a historically Black development. She told him that West Ashley had traditionally been Charleston's Blackest suburb. Of course, she added, that led to many avoiding and disparaging the suburb for decades. That was before the population boom and suburban sprawl had turned West Ashley into a very white, upper-middle class town. Even still, the bias persisted, she told him, as some people still referred to the town as *West Trashley*.

"It's just jarring," Daren remarked as he slowly drove the twisting roads of Sherwood Forest. "To see this kind of poverty *right here*. You're telling me the only shitty neighborhoods in West Ashley are Black neighborhoods?"

Andrea nodded. "This isn't poverty, though. These are working-class families. And don't call it shitty when you're speaking to these folks, either," she added sternly. "They work hard to own these homes. Shit, you should see where I live…"

"Point taken. How does this happen, though?" he asked. "This kind of segregation—let alone the disparity of wealth?"

Andrea shot off a list of causes like she had prepared them for a school report: "Federal housing policies. Local zoning. Discriminatory lending. Social attitudes. Racism." Daren nodded introspectively.

He pulled the car up to the curb outside 364 Nottingham Row. He noticed nervous eyes upon him as he emerged from the Dodge; neighbors peering out timidly through barred windows, and the cautious leers of people on their porches. Something about a white man in pressed clothes pulling up in a new car spelled trouble. He was thankful he'd had the foresight to recruit Andrea.

They walked up a broken stone path overgrown with grass to the front door. Rusted bars with peeling white paint covered the screen door, which hung crooked and loose. Andrea pressed the doorbell. They waited for a minute, the sun beating on their backs. Daren wiped the sweat from his forehead and wondered how long his shirt would hold back the swamp beneath it. They rang the doorbell again and waited. It was several moments before the door cracked open, revealing a middle-aged Black woman in a wheelchair.

"Can I help you?" the woman asked cautiously through the crack in the door.

"Ms. Grey? I'm detective Watts with the North Charleston Police Department." Andrea held out her badge for the woman to inspect. "And this is Special Agent Renard with the FBI."

"Is this about Devon?" she asked, clutching her chest. She looked at them, her eyes welling up with tears, hoping to hear some news. "Have y'all found some answers?"

"Yes, ma'am, it is," Andrea replied. "And sadly, no we haven't. But we're hoping to."

"None a y'all spent much time on it before," Ms. Grey scoffed.

"Ma'am, I completely agree," Daren interjected. "That's why I've come down here from Washington. To see what's going on with your son's case. Do you mind if we come in and ask you some questions?"

"I answered all the questions," said Ms. Grey. "I did it for the local police, for the sheriffs, for the F-B-I. You think you gonna ask me somethin' they ain't already?" She laughed skeptically and opened the door wide. "You're welcome to try."

Ms. Grey's home was like most of the houses in the area: a small, single-story ranch with an attached garage. At one time, the house was probably fairly nice. But the outside was now weathered and worn, and the inside unkept—not just the clutter and the mess, but the old, peeling wallpaper and discolored patches on the ceiling where water had seeped in. The house had an almost sweet smell that Daren recognized yet couldn't place.

"Excuse the mess," Ms. Grey said, wheeling toward the kitchen. "It's been hard to manage with Devon gone."

"I'm so sorry to hear that," Andrea replied. "Do you mind if I ask what…" She paused, searching for the right words.

"Arthritis, dear," said Ms. Grey. "Worst case my doc has seen in thirty years of practice. I was still hobblin' around when Devon died. Doc says the stress and grief worsened the condition. It's just so bad in my knees. I can't stand most days." She offered them seats at her kitchen table. "I'd offer you something to drink," she said. "But then I'd have to ask you to get yourselves."

"We're fine, thank you," said Daren, taking a seat.

"Ms. Grey, would you mind telling us about the last time you saw Devon? About the night he went missing?" asked Andrea.

"As I said a hundred times. I was watching TV. It was dark, probably about 8 o'clock or so. Devon told me he was going out. He'd be back a little later."

"Did he give you any indication where he was going?" Daren asked.

"No, and I'm sorry to say I never asked. Devon was a good boy. He'd come and go as he pleased. I never could keep up with him if I tried. I trusted him."

"Did he have any friends or relatives nearby that he may have gone to hang out with?" Andrea asked.

"I honestly don't know, dear," Ms. Grey replied.

"Did he ever mention any fights he might have had or incidents with people who might not have liked him?" Andrea inquired.

"Not that I can recall."

"Ms. Grey, it says in the file that your son hadn't been to school in quite a while," noted Daren. "When exactly did he stop going?"

"Probably about a year or so before he was killed." Ms. Grey looked down with shame. "I know you probably think I shoulda forced him. Maybe I shoulda, but he was a stubborn boy."

It was clear to Daren that this woman had no clue what her son had been up to on a day-to-day basis. Every answer she gave to questions about his personal life, girlfriends, friends, or associations was vague and unhelpful.

Before they left, Ms. Grey was kind enough to show them Devon's room. Hip hop posters and swimsuit models were plastered all over the walls. The floor was covered in dirty laundry. She allowed them to poke around, but they found nothing of interest. They left her Daren's card and told her to call if she thought of anything else, then thanked her for her time.

"It's just a random crime," Daren said as they drove away. "In all likelihood, it's just some random racist fucks indiscriminately targeting a Black kid. That's the only thing that makes sense. And how the hell do you solve that?"

"When hating Black people is too wide a net…" Andrea sighed, trailing off in thought. "There are thousands of shallow graves around this state. Little mounds and depressions in the earth where God-knows-how-many slaves are buried in unmarked graves. Nobody cared about their lives enough to mark the spots where they were buried. Like dogs. And nobody cared enough to ask why they died, either. They were slaves—used up and then buried out back like an animal. Oh, *'We've come so far,'* they say. *'That was another time.'* Yet a Black boy gets lynched and we can't even begin to compile a goddamn list of suspects because racism is too common in the year twenty-fucking-eighteen!"

Daren didn't know what to say. He could hear the pain in her voice, and it made him feel ashamed.

They drove to the burger shop where Devon had worked and talked to his former manager. This too was a fruitless outing. Devon kept to himself at work, always showed up for his shift, and had no confrontations or beef with anyone else on staff. The restaurant had no record of racist threats or incidents.

"All his former classmates were questioned too," Andrea remarked, browsing over Grey's file on her phone as Daren drove. "We can follow up, but until school starts back up in a couple weeks, it'll be hard to track some of these kids down."

"I think we're wasting our time," Daren remarked. "This was a hate crime. It was probably random. It's very unlikely that he knew his attackers."

"What's the plan then?" she asked.

"Let's grab some lunch, and I will check on our warrant for those white supremacist groups. See if we can start building a list of names."

Andrea nodded while reading from her phone. Suddenly, she gasped and stiffened. *"Oh shit!"*

"What?!"

"Pull over!" she yelled.

Daren took a quick right and pulled into the parking lot of a shopping center. "What's wrong," he asked, bringing the car to a quick stop.

"I have to go!" Andrea exclaimed. "My sister... I..." she was flustered and unable to find the words. "Something is happening downtown. I need to go," she managed to explain.

"I'll drive you," Daren suggested as she climbed out of the car.

"No," she replied. "It's fine. I'll Uber. Go check on the white supremacist stuff. I'll be in touch." She shut the car door and hurried to the sidewalk, her thumbs furiously tapping against the screen of her phone.

Daren pulled out his phone and did a web search for downtown Charleston. A breaking news story was the top result—the headline: *Black Lives Matter Protesters Shut Down Highway in Charleston.* The subhead read: *Protesters Prepare for Standoff with Police.*

22

CHARLESTON'S BEAUTIFUL, HISTORIC downtown was framed by two majestic rivers that met at the Atlantic Ocean. The Ashley and Cooper Rivers had once served as the city's boundaries, but that was long ago, before the era of white flight and suburban sprawl. The city's iconic Ravenel Bridge now linked the peninsula to Mount Pleasant on the other side of the Cooper River. On the west side of the peninsula, residents coming from West Ashley would cross over the Ashley River via an extension of Interstate 526 known as the West Ashley connector. Coming over the connector, one could see the city marina below to their right and boats of all types on the water. The downtown skyline was low enough that the Ravenel was also visible from the connector; building restrictions helped keep it that way.

It was there, on the connector, that protesters had implemented their plan. Just before the extension split off between an exit that led to the marina and the main off-ramp that fed traffic to Calhoun Street and downtown, they had formed a human blockade and brought traffic to a halt. Soon after, the police had shown up, followed by the media.

Andrea thanked her Uber driver for getting her as close as he could on the connector, then took off running down the freeway. She ran past cars full of angry commuters and vehicles that had been abandoned so their owners could see what was happening. She pushed through a mob of angry commuters and made it to the police line, where she found the ranking officer.

The police were lined up in riot gear across from the protesters, blocking them from the motorists. From behind the police line, the angry motorists yelled swears and slurs at the protesters. A glass bottle launched by the protesters at the police shattered against one of the officer's tactical shields not far from Andrea's head.

The protesters carried a banner that read: "BLACK LIVES MATTER: JUSTICE FOR DEVON GREY." Other signs read: "Stop the 526 Expansion!" and "Black Neighborhoods Matter!" One woman stood at the front with a bullhorn, shouting at the police, and leading the protesters in chants. It was Mikayla.

"Excuse me, sir," Andrea attempted to get the commanding officer's attention. "*Excuse me, officer!*"

"*Yes, what?!*" the man barked.

"Detective Watts!" Andrea shouted to be heard over the commotion. "North Charleston PD!" She showed him her badge.

"*What can I do for you, Detective?!*"

"*That's my sister!*" Andrea yelled, pointing across the line to Mikayla. "If you let me talk to her, I might be able to end this!"

The officer looked at Mikayla, then to the line of officers in riot gear. "You got about five minutes till we get backup on the scene!" he told her. "Once they're here, we're breaking this up one way or another!"

Andrea nodded to signify her understanding, and he motioned for her to go ahead. She made her way through the police and toward the protesters, bottles, rocks, and various objects flew overhead, first from the angry motorists at the protesters but then in both directions. She held her hand up in an attempt to shield her head.

As she got closer, Andrea could hear what Mikayla was saying into the bullhorn. "The highway has always been a tool to segregate us! To wall off our communities! To displace our homes! To ensure that white people don't have to see us! Don't have to interact with us! They tore through our communities to build them! Now they tell us they're going to expand this highway, demolishing more Black homes! So that white people who commute through our neighborhoods can get home to their plush plantation developments quicker! We keep moving, and moving, as they keep building and building! Pushing us out of our homes! Out of our communities! None of it is for us! We're just in their way! We are not their equals! When a Black boy is lynched in a wealthy white suburban area, the city shrugs! But when a police is killed, they spend unlimited money and man hours trying to find his killer! We are not disposable! Let me hear it!"

"WE ARE NOT DISPOSABLE!" the crowd chanted. *"WE ARE NOT DISPOSABLE!"*

Andrea reached her sister and tried to get her attention. But Mikayla was too focused on the crowd. "A Black boy is lynched in Charleston and nothing happens!" she cried into the bullhorn. "One white man gets killed during a robbery, and the city holds a goddamn town hall meeting on violence in the community! One officer gets shot, and the city rallies to protect *'blue lives.'* There are no blue lives, Charleston! People are not blue!"

Andrea tugged at her shirt, and Mikayla pulled back in shock.

"What are you doing here?!" Mikayla yelled over the chants and noise. "Get out of here before you get hurt! Or worse, you're forced to choose a side!"

"I can take care of myself! You're the one that needs help! You're going to get these people hurt!" Andrea shouted.

The chants grew louder as a bus full of officers in riot gear pulled up the off-ramp and started to unload. The protesters were now surrounded by cops on both sides.

Mikayla looked behind her at the officers lining up, and then to her right, down the exit ramp that led to the marina. There, on the ramp, the press was amassed, both local stations and affiliates of the big national networks. "We're right where we need to be!" she exclaimed. "Whatever happens will be broadcast all over the world!"

The riot police, now in full formation on both sides of the protesters, started to beat their shields with their batons in unison. This, like the drummer boys who marched so vulnerably alongside armies in the Civil War, was a way to keep the officers coordinated and even in their advance.

"Mikayla, please!" Andrea shouted. She tried to think of anything to dissuade her baby sister from the decision she'd already committed to. "I'm working with the feds on Devon Grey's case! This isn't going to help!"

Mikayla looked at her with confusion. For a moment, Andrea thought she might have at least intrigued her sister, but the thought was disrupted when a canister of tear gas was shot into the crowd. It hit a young man in the head about forty feet from where Andrea and Mikayla were stood, splitting his head open over his eye and knocking him to the ground. Screams followed as the can began spewing gas. Two more cans were fired nearby.

Mikayla quickly swung her bag off her shoulder and retrieved two gas masks with face shields. "You're one lucky bitch," she said, shoving the mask at Andrea.

Andrea stood in shock for a moment, watching as people attempted to carry the injured man to the side of the road, as the gas choked them and burned their eyes. People, some only teenagers, coughed and gagged, and some fell to the ground. Many were prepared, however, and donned gas masks of various types and quality. The mask Mikayla had given her was military grade. Andrea quickly pulled it over her head, adjusting the straps so quickly, that she accidentally pulled out some of her hair.

The cops halted their advance about twenty feet from the protesters, at which point they began to douse the crowd with pepper spray. This worked fairly well on the east side of the protest, where police had advanced up the off-ramp from downtown because the wind was to their backs. On the west side of the stand-off, however, where motorists were still gathered, watching and yelling in anger, the wind carried the tear gas and pepper spray back at the police and motorists. While the police wore protective gear and gas masks, the motorists were exposed. Most were able to retreat to their cars unharmed, but those who had been in the front hurling bottles and slurs at the protesters were caught in the foul wind. Men gasped and heaved, leaning against the hood of their cars. Others fell to the ground, coughing and struggling to breathe.

Mikayla grabbed Andrea and lifted her mask enough for her voice to escape. "Go!" she shouted. "Hold your badge up! Tell them you're a cop!"

Andrea nodded, pretending to agree, but when Mikayla turned to address a fellow protester, Andrea grabbed her arm, twisted it behind her back, and handcuff her. "*The fuck are you doing?!*" her sister yelled in protest.

Several protesters started in on them to protect Mikayla, forcing Andrea to draw her firearm. "*Back up!*" she yelled, waving the gun around as she marched Mikayla through the protest. "Back the fuck up!"

The protesters looked determined—like they were about to try and rush her and free Mikayla, but before they could, the police line crashed violently into them. Batons struck heads and limbs, and protesters fought back using their hands or whatever they could find on the ground. Andrea pulled her sister close and held her badge out like a shield, hoping it would be enough to protect them as they made their way toward the exit ramp. The first riot cop they encountered saw her badge and held back from swinging his baton. Two more did the same, as Andrea slowly led them out of the crowd. But just as she thought they had made it, a baton struck her on the back of her head.

Andrea fell to the ground. She could hear a man yelling, "She's a cop!" and her sister calling her name, the pain was so intense she felt unable to open her eyes. After a few moments, she slowly rose to her feet, wincing with pain. A couple of riot police helped her and her sister away from the commotion.

They reached the concrete divider by the exit ramp, where they stood in silence and watched as the police brutalized, handcuffed, and rounded up the protesters. Mikayla shook her head in anger. "What exactly do you think you're doing?!"

"Saving your ass!" Andrea snapped, fumbling in anger for her keys to unlock Mikayla's cuffs.

"Nobody asked you!" Mikayla yelled. "Saving me from your brothers in blue?! Please..." Mikayla rolled her eyes.

"You're going to get yourself killed—"

"It's my life! My right! My decision!" Mikayla's rebuke was sharp. "This is *my* choice! This is how *we* fight," she motioned to the crowd being rounded up and dispersed. "This is how it's always been. You can't change that. Just because they gave you a badge... It doesn't mean the rest of us don't still have to fight. You'd rather shut down the protest to protect me, but Dre, don't you see? Don't see there's no neutrality here? That when you shut us down, you pick a side?" Mikayla's anger was turning to sadness. Tears leaked from her eyes.

"You're right," Andrea said, uncuffing her sister and rubbing her head. "It's not my place. I'll admit that much. But when I heard what was happening—I don't know. I just had to protect my baby sister. I'm sorry. I was wrong."

"It's a start," Mikayla muttered. "Always was stubborn." She scowled, rubbed her wrists, and shook her head.

"I miss you," Andrea said disarmingly. "Can I buy you lunch?"

"Suppose it's the least you can fucking do," said Mikayla. "But I gotta make sure all these folks have access to their lawyers and shit."

"And who would've done that if you had been arrested with the rest of them?"

"We got people seeing to it," Mikayla countered quickly before realizing she'd outed herself. "Alright, fine. I suppose an hour won't kill me."

The warrants had come down and several groups had already complied by providing their membership lists.

Hatred was more common than many like to think. That was the inescapable conclusion when you were forced to look at it. And for most, it required being forced, because most were happy to avoid it. The national narrative—the story Americans told themselves every day—was one of righteous infallibility.

As Daren combed through the longer-than-expected list of people associated with the various white supremacist or neo-Confederate groups in the area, he thought about that conclusion. It bothered him. He'd been raised to believe that racism was mostly a thing of the past. He found himself recalling his cab ride from the airport when he'd been so certain that redevelopment was good for everyone. From the moment he'd arrived in Charleston, nothing had been what he'd assumed.

He ate fried chicken from a take-out place for lunch, while parked at a nearby grocery store, and tried in vain to keep his greasy fingerprints off the list he'd picked up from the print shop. The list was overwhelming him. It was shit. The whole case was shit, and his failure seemed inevitable.

The liquor store across the street called to him. Something about this case, something about *this place* made him want to drink until he passed out. He thought of that cockroach again, kicking its legs and waiting for death. Then he thought of being held underwater and trying to fight against the urge to breathe. He thought of Carson's brains leaking out of his skull.

Maybe just a six pack...

23

"YOU JUST GONNA eat and not say anything to me?" Andrea asked.

"Figured I finish my bagel before we fight," Mikayla replied.

She had a point. "Well finish up then."

Colonial Lake was located in downtown's historic Harleston Village. The man-made rectangular, tidal lake was fed from the ocean through underground channels and surrounded by a beautiful walkway and historic houses. It was a common destination for locals to fish, jog, or just enjoy the view.

There, on a bench overlooking the water on the lake's east end, Andrea sat waiting to have her first conversation with her sister in nearly six years. They had stopped to grab bagels at a nearby café, but Andrea felt too anxious to eat. She wrapped hers in a napkin, placed it on the bench beside her, and patiently waited for her sister to finish. "It's nice down here," she remarked.

"It's beautiful. Such a lovely city. It's shame that rather than share it with us, white people built suburbs to get away. As soon as Black people weren't in chains anymore, they built lavish communities as far away as they could from people like us. They made laws to ensure we were kept in our place. Then after decades of erecting barriers to people and wealth around those urban centers and watching the property values crash, white people decided, 'Actually, we *do* want to live in our quaint historic downtown.' So, they started buying up the property—fixing up what they had left to fall into disrepair. Now, how many Black people do you see in Harleston Village? How many Black people in Charleston do you think even live on the peninsula? Can't afford to. So, we started moving into the suburbs. And they segregated us there too. Everywhere we go, anywhere we want to live, an invisible wall is put up around us. One peninsula—two cities. One predominantly white; one predominantly Black, as it's been since it was nothing but slave camps. They've always needed us—to pick their cotton, to till their fields, to man their machines, to flip their burgers—but they never want to share anything with us. That's the history of these two cities and this country. We built what they enjoy, and now, when we try to stand up and demand an equal piece, the country descends into chaos."

"I know the history," Andrea said with a sigh. "I wanted to talk about *us*."

"This is about us," Mikayla told her. "You've been so busy proving to the world that you're strong, it's like you don't want to admit reality."

"What reality is that?"

"That you're not strong. You're scared. So, you joined a terrorist organization that gave you a gun and gives you the feeling of safety. You became blue so you didn't have to be Black."

"I became a cop to help people, Mikayla. Why can't you understand that?" Andrea asked pleadingly.

"Because cops hurt people, Dre. Because when Black boys and girls see a cop coming, they're afraid."

"All the more reason for me to be one! We can't change it if we just leave it to white people, right?"

"Oh, you changing it?" Mikayla scoffed.

"Yeah."

"You changing it?" she asked again in disbelief.

"Yeah, I'm trying…"

"How?"

"*How?*" Andrea couldn't believe the question.

"How the fuck are you changing anything? What have you changed?" Mikayla demanded.

Andrea was frozen, her hands trembled, and her mind raced. She felt unable to function, unsure of what to say or do. She wanted so badly for her sister to understand her, love her, and see her as a hero like she used to. But instead, everything she did to try and do something positive with the hurt she carried inside seemed to drive Mikayla further away.

"I'm trying," Andrea said in a slow, measured voice, "to change it one interaction at a time. Every person I encounter on this job. When people need us, it's not some asshole with rage issues coming through that door, *it's me.* Can't you see the value in that—in reforming institutions from within?"

"And how many times did you have to accept what shouldn't be accepted?" Mikayla asked. "How many times have you had to advert your eyes or bite your tongue? How many times have you had to let casual racism slide? Sexism? Tell me you haven't had to let shit slide. For every interaction you change, how many are you helping to reinforce?"

Andrea didn't know what to say. She took a deep breath and fought back the tears. "I have rescued women and children from traffickers. I have helped women escape abusive relationships. I have put child abusers in prison and in the ground. I am helping vulnerable people, Kay. You're too blinded by your political biases and your hatred of the police—"

"*Biases*?!" Mikayla stood from her seat and shook an angry finger at her sister. "You're just a pawn! A foot soldier for white supremacy and the patriarchy. Let's talk about *your* biases. Gram says you even got a white fuck boy." She shook her head in disgust. "What more do I need to say? Blue by choice, white by injection."

Andrea rose to her feet too, matching her sister's volume and anger. "You think they see me as one of them? Do you think my badge makes me immune to racism? You think I don't have to deal with it every day?" she insisted. "Shit, you surround yourself with Black activists—I bet I deal with more racism on a day-to-day basis than you do. I get called a coon or shit-skinned or worse so often at work it doesn't even phase me anymore!" She could see her sister had softened her stance, surprised at what she was hearing. "None of it is going to change until we have Black lawmakers, Black cops, Black lawyers, and Black judges. *You* said that to me, Kayla. *You* said that to me my first year of community college."

"Bitch, I wanted you to go to law school," Mikayla said, tears flooding her eyes, but laughter finding its way through. "Didn't think you'd latch onto that cop part. Thought you'd go become a civil rights attorney. You were always so damn smart."

Andrea laughed too, and they both wiped the tears from their eyes.

"C'mere," Mikayla said, holding her arms out.

Andrea's heart soared. She wrapped her arms around Mikayla and sank her face into her chest—her little sister was four inches taller than her. The hug felt like home and reminded Andrea of the love and bond they shared. She had missed her so badly.

He was four beers deep when the big boss himself called.
Daren attempted, to the best of his ability, to sound sober.

"Have you been drinking?" Assistant Deputy Director Alden Travers asked.

"Couple of beers with the local detective, sir... Watts." Daren cleared his throat. "You know, you gotta show these locals you can hang with them before they trust you."

"This is the woman you had us expedite a deputization through the U.S. Marshalls for?"

"Yes, sir."

"The woman with whom you proceeded to get into a gun fight with?"

"Yes, sir... That's correct."

"And those two men you two killed, are they a part of the Grey case?"

"No, sir." The line went silent for a moment. "Sir?" Daren asked.

"Agent," said Travers. "I'm going to be blunt. Are you fucking this woman?"

"Um, I'm sorry, sir?" The question baffled Daren.

"Are you fucking her, or trying to fuck her?" asked Travers. "Because I'm at a lost as to what the fuck you're doing down there."

"As I said in my report, sir, I need her. There's like ten goddamn police departments with overlapping jurisdictions down here, sir. The politics are too much for an outsider to navigate or understand. She knows the culture, too. The people."

"Is she biased?"

Daren paused and furrowed his brow. "What do you mean?"

"Don't get P.C. on me, Agent. This detective is Black, I take it. So, is she biased?"

"I'm not sure I understand, sir."

"I'm sure you saw what happened on the freeway today," Travers told him. "Now these goddamn white nationalist and far-right groups are organizing a response rally."

"I hadn't seen that," Daren replied, still unsure what Travers was getting at.

"The point is this situation is getting worse. Your orders were to take a second look at the Devon Grey murder, not to chase some chocolate pussy all over the lowcountry. It's due diligence since we've been raked over the coals in the press for not putting enough resources toward the case. You're window dressing. I mean, I thought I was clear, and you were bright enough that I didn't have to spell it out for you, but Jesus Christ—if there's no evidence, then there's no real motivation. That's only a hate crime if someone wants it to be a hate crime. Do you understand me?"

"I'm sorry, sir, maybe I've had a few too many," said Daren. "Are you telling me to bury this case?"

"Holy Christ, don't be so dramatic, Agent. I'm telling you that saying we don't know doesn't look good, and it's certainly not helping the country right now. Nobody wants to see violence. Nobody wants to see cops getting shot or—"

"Or protesters being beaten?" Daren interjected.

"Nobody wants to see anyone else getting hurt, Agent. Now, do you have any leads?"

Daren stared at the list of names of white supremacists. "I'm working on a few," he said.

"Work them if you got them, but by the end of the week, if you don't have something solid, then we need to think about other ways to conclude our report on this case."

"It's clearly a hate crime, sir. People won't go for that."

"It is what we say it. Just like with Castile and that cop—what's his name, there—Andreoni?" Travers asked. Daren sighed. The name had already been on his mind. "You did a good job with that," Travers told him.

"I just went with the facts," Daren said defensively.

"You picked the facts, Agent," Travers said sternly. "I've seen the reports, the ballistics—the firing pattern doesn't fit with Andreoni's story."

"Castile's fingerprints were on the gun, sir."

"Sure. But how'd they get there?"

Daren didn't know what to say. He knew Travers was right.

"You can deny it to yourself if it helps you sleep at night," said Travers. "But you shouldn't have to. You did a *good* thing. I know it doesn't seem like it, but this country is teetering on the edge right now. We need trust in public institutions. We need trust in law enforcement. We need less racial outrage and division. We have to keep order. One case—*one life* doesn't matter in the grand scheme."

Daren remained silent.

"Figure out what happened to Devon Grey if you can. If we solve the case and catch an evil racist, everyone is happy. Justice is done and public trust creeps back up. But if you can't, I want a report suggesting it was a gang hit or something."

"Sir, with all due respect, I don't think—"

"If you won't do it, I'll send someone down who will," Travers interrupted.

Daren paused but then agreed. "Yes, sir," he said.

"Are we clear?"

"Yes, sir." Daren ended the call, and sat in silence for several moments, stewing, before throwing his phone at the mirror hanging over the desk in his room, smashing it. He grabbed the chair from under the desk, which was now covered in glass, and threw it across the room into the wall. Then he threw his beer bottle at the wall, exploding tempered glass back with such velocity, that a piece struck him and cut his forehead.

He sank to the floor and began to sob. The feelings he'd been fighting off for more than a day overwhelmed him. The reality he had been avoiding about himself, was now spelled out in no uncertain terms. He was a lackey. Promoted young and naïve—a useful tool. Just dumb enough to believe he was actually a good agent. He *had* ignored the ballistics in the Castile case because his superiors had strongly insinuated what conclusion he should come to. And he was all too willing to do it. Nothing had ever been difficult for Daren Renard, and he was always apt to take shortcuts or bend the rules. He'd been taught his whole life that the world worked with winks and nods.

It's not that he wanted to exonerate a guilty cop. It's that he was told the truth would be too damning to the department, the city, and the country. There had already been several incidents that year of police violence against individuals of color, and Bureau had told him that they needed a way to change the narrative. They assured him his report would not be the last on the case, but that it would be best for everyone if, at that time, they had an official report that at least suggested the plausibility that Andreoni was justified in shooting Castile. Daren did exactly that, using the fingerprints on Andreoni's firearm to corroborate his story that Castile had resisted arrest. He did include a footnote that the ballistics suggested that Castile was not as close as Andreoni claimed when he was shot, but the footnote was not included in the final report.

The Bureau was so impressed by Daren's argument, that they closed the book on the matter. They never disclosed the ballistics results, only telling the press they were "inconclusive." Sergeant Robert Andreoni was exonerated and continued to serve as a law enforcement officer to that day. Daren had been surprised by how it was handled, but he was assured Andreoni was telling the truth. They told him the ballistics didn't matter—that confrontations like that were traumatic events, and Andreoni's memory was probably flawed. It wasn't his fault if the details didn't line up. He was a *good* man, with a family. Castile? He was just some street hustler and weed dealer. He'd even been busted for armed robbery once. *Which of those two men did he think was telling the truth?* Andreoni was a law enforcement officer—he was one of them. A good guy. Part of the thin blue line. Castile was a thug.

Daren had tried to live with it, to accept what he was told, and to tell himself he had no control over how it all went down, but he always had doubts. Sometimes he would awaken in the middle of the night, and find himself thinking about it. He'd lay awake for hours, feeling guilty, wondering if he helped a man get away with murder.

When Andreoni was cleared, Black Americans took to the streets across the country. Daren remembered thinking they didn't understand the full context—that they were making the matter far too simple. Now, sadly, he realized it was he who hadn't understood. Not only that, but he had wanted to dismiss their anger and their rage, simply because he felt guilty. Then the police killings started. That put cops everywhere on edge and further increased incidents of police violence and abuse of power, which led to more pushback from groups like Black Lives Matter.

After the case, Daren had poured himself into his work to block it out, drinking whenever the guilt would find him. Most of the time that meant he was behind a desk, buried in paperwork. Despite doing what he had been told, those above him kept him at arm's length for a while. Finally, just over a year later, he was called to Travers' office and given his current assignment. He'd thought it could be a chance to redeem himself in a way. To do right by someone who was clearly the victim of a hate crime. But the case had always seemed too thin, and somewhere in the back of his mind, he had always been afraid that this was exactly what would happen. He had feared that he would be used once again to take "control of the narrative"—to once again manufacture a lie.

But he had managed to lie to himself enough to believe it could be different. Then he was nearly killed by some coked-up, hick trafficker. Ever since it was like he was trying to escape something. Now, having the truth spelled out for him, he realized it was the feeling of shame—shame for who he was—shame for the life he had lived and even more for the life he'd failed to live. His had been a life of self-aggrandizement, arrogance, and self-delusion—an empty shell of a life that amounted to nothing more than a fuck-you to his miserable parents. He'd climbed so high on nothing but his goddamn ego, and in that position, he took the power he'd been given and started a goddamn wildfire. A fire that now threatened to consume the entire nation.

Daren thought again about that roach kicking its ugly, skeletal legs, trying its best to fight against death. In some ways, he was like that roach: worthless and yet so convinced of its need to live despite its unwillingness to adapt. Maybe he should have taken a nice big gulp when Carson had him under the water. Maybe he should have died then. Maybe that's what he deserved.

Alcohol had a way of stimulating conversation.

The County Store at the Marina was a local secret that had some of the best, affordable food on the water. The building bore the signs of age, tropical storms, and hurricanes—its floors were as warped and crooked as its ceilings were stained from water damage. But the food was delicious, and the view wasn't bad either. It was a place locals could go and not have to deal with hordes of tourists.

After many tears and apologies at the lake, Andrea confessed that she was starving and that a bagel was not going to cut it. Mikayla said she could always eat, so the two had walked over to the County Store. Once they got there, Andrea felt great. It was as if her anxiety had been turned off for the first time in years. So she ate, and then she ate some more. She ordered hot wings, fried shrimp, coleslaw, cornbread, collard greens, and a little dish of ice cream. She ate it all, to her sister's amazement.

"I have never seen you eat like that," Mikayla remarked. "You pregnant or something?" she teased.

"I usually have trouble eating," Andrea confessed. "It's like my brain is always finding something to worry about. It can't settle down long enough to enjoy anything. Plus, my stomach is always in knots." She sipped her beer and tossed her last fry into her mouth. "It's like I know I have to eat, but getting the food in is a battle."

"I guess that's how you stay so thin." Mikayla finished her second martini and looked for the waitress. "I think I'll have another," she told her.

"I think I'm just relieved. I thought you hated me," Andrea admitted.

Mikayla smacked her lips together. "C'mon, Dre. *You're* my big sis. I love you, and you should know that."

"We ain't spoke in years. You don't call."

"Phone goes both ways, don't it?"

"I guess I didn't feel right calling if I'm being honest. Not after all that shit came out about my department back in 2013. I was ashamed. The stories were so horrible…"

"It's still hard to understand how you can work at a place like that," Mikayla admitted.

"If people like me won't," said Andrea, "then all that's left is people like them."

Mikayla nodded reluctantly and sighed. "Well, I'm glad you don't work a beat," she said. "At least I know after today, you'll never be the one showing up to arrest me." She laughed.

"Do you remember when Gram used to take us out to eat?" Andrea asked, excited to share memories with her sister again.

"You always wanted to get pizza," said Mikayla. "But I always wanted chicken."

"We always got chicken, too," Andrea noted.

"Because Gram wanted chicken, too," her sister insisted.

"No, we just didn't want to hear you bitch," Andrea teased. "Do you remember, after we got dinner, she'd bring us by the video store?"

"One movie or one game. That's all we were allowed."

"But whenever we asked for more…"

"She always caved."

"Do you remember what she would say if we picked up a movie that didn't represent Black folks well?"

"*Oh no, child! I ain't havin' that on my television.,*" said Mikayla in her best impersonation of Gram.

"I remember watching The Green Mile with her!" Andrea roared before trying her own impersonation of Gram: '*What? This Magic Negro is going to heal all the white men and they gonna kill him anyway?*'" They both laughed. "She wasn't wrong," Andrea added with a shake of her head.

"It's just funny. She acts like she has no idea where either of us gets it from," Mikayla said, shaking her head. "Like we caught dissent and wokeness in the wind."

"She's a proud woman." Andrea nodded firmly to emphasize the point. "Damn proud. She just wants to be left alone and be unbothered by anyone. She has seen more racism and prejudice than either of us could probably imagine, but she doesn't talk about it. She's happy with what she has and the way things are."

"That's fine," Mikayla replied, her voice tensing up a bit. "She can be happy with that. But she shouldn't tell me what to do with my life, or act like she doesn't get it."

"I know," Andrea sympathized. "She doesn't get what I do either."

"She says we're both running from what happened to us," Mikayla scoffed.

Andrea looked out the window of the County Store at the boats docked at the marina. "Maybe we are," she said after a moment.

"Well, call it what you will. There ain't nothing in the past worth carrying. Especially if it hurts you," her sister countered.

Andrea nodded. She agreed with her on that much. "I've missed you," she beamed.

"Oh, girl, you know I missed you, too. Get over here and hug me again!"

Andrea crossed over to the other side of the booth and embraced her sister. Then she excused herself to use the bathroom. When she returned, Mikayla was shaking her head and looking at her phone. "What's the matter?" Andrea asked.

"Ut-uh, this city is not going to do this," Mikayla remarked in disbelief.

"What is it?" Andrea asked, taking her seat.

"I've gotta go," Mikayla said, pulling a twenty from her back pocket and tossing it on the table. "This group, Right-Unite, they're holding a rally downtown on Thursday to—and you're going to love this— *preserve their heritage* and send a message to BLM."

Andrea shook her head. "They're tossing a can of gas onto the fire…"

"I've gotta go. We have to plan our response." Mikayla rose from the seat.

"Wait!" Andrea exclaimed. "Kayla, don't. I've got a bad feeling about this. People might get hurt."

Mikayla leaned over the table and stared at her older sister with resilience in her eyes. "People always gettin' hurt, it's just nobody cares when their skin ain't white. You can't change that." Mikayla turned and left.

Passion, anger, and booze had roused their disagreeable feelings, and their reconciliation suddenly felt uncertain. Andrea ordered another drink, and stared out the window over the water. More rain was on the horizon.

24

DAVID FINISHED HIS workout and went straight to his home office to be alone. The past couple of days had left him stressed and withdrawn. He didn't want to hear Marie's questions or deal with the boy's constant need for validation.

He sat in his desk chair, behind a large computer monitor, and watched the rain beat against the bay window. Sometimes he wondered how long he'd have to continue to suffer existence. Maybe some thug would ventilate his skull on a traffic stop one day and it would be all over. Sudden—no seeing it coming. That's all he really cared about was that it happened quickly. The idea of dying slowly as a decrypted old man didn't feel very appealing. He'd seen his old man go through that, and he'd sooner put eat a bullet.

He lit a joint—a habit that was becoming too frequent—and tried to not think about anything. He didn't want to think about Greg, or Marie, or Dre, or Devin-fucking-Grey. He just wanted to get stoned and be a little numb to all the bullshit for a while. He wondered when the next time he'd have to piss in a cup for work would be. No matter—Skip would take care of him.

One thought David couldn't push from his mind was about Ellis. The power dynamic was now imbalanced, and Ellis was testing him.

He told himself it would be fine, but perhaps he needed to correct the man. His kind was like dogs; only obedient through fear.

What really pissed him off was the way Ellis had spoken to and about him. Calling him a pig, and talking to him like he was hired help. He had forgotten who held the power.

David's thoughts were interrupted when his phone vibrated and lit up on his desk. He checked who was calling and then answered. "What's up, Kenny?"

"I got some information on your federal agent," the voice on the line told him.

"Oh, yeah? What's his story?"

"He's a lackey. An errand boy for the suits in Washington."

"What's that mean?" David asked.

"I see it all the time. They pick young, brown-nosing, self-assured little pricks with no experience, blow some smoke up their ass, and basically pull their strings whenever they need to. Of course, that means he's connected, too. Not someone to fuck with—catch my drift?"

David sat up in his chair, perplexed. "So, what's he doing down here?"

"My guess is he's there to downplay or cover up whatever happened to that Black kid last winter."

"What makes you say that?"

"His only other case was the Antony Castile shooting last year up in Michigan. Let's just say, between me and you, that cop belongs in an orange jumpsuit. But your boy here, he wrote a song and dance about the case that ignored a bunch of evidence."

"You send me the file?" David asked.

"I'm sending it now, along with the stuff about the Castile case. But David…"

"Yeah?"

"This is classified information. I can get in major trouble."

"Don't worry about it. I ain't gonna say anything to no one," David reassured him.

He hung up the phone and waited for the email. When it came, he reviewed Daren Renard's file as well as the files on the Castile shooting. He took a hit from his joint and contemplated whether or not to send the documents directly to Dre. It wasn't too difficult of a decision.

He forwarded her the email with a short message: "Just a heads up… We should talk. Don't trust this guy. He's got an agenda and it ain't good."

Self-loathing is only amplified by the intoxicants it demands, yet it requires them nonetheless like a fire needs fuel. Sometimes, you want the fire to die out. Other times, you want it to burn the whole damn world.

Daren was good and deep in a hole of self-loathing when Andrea knocked on his door. He flung the door open wide and invited her in.

"You're a mess," she said, looking around the room at the various empties.

"You don't look so hot yourself," he replied. "So, what's up? Your sister—that shit all good, or…?"

Andrea looked at him, anger burning in her eyes, and shook her head. She held a stack of papers tightly in her hands.

"What's that?" asked Daren. "You got a clue?"

"Oh, I got a fucking clue," Andrea said. She threw the papers at him, scattering them across the room. "A fucking clue who you really are."

Daren sighed and then nodded. "That's good," he said. "You should know who I am."

"You already know what I'm talking about, don't you?" she charged.

"Well, I'm assuming that's my file, so… Yeah. I mean, I was hoping you wouldn't figure it out, but I knew you would." Daren sipped his beer and sat, defeated, on a couch that was situated near the door to the balcony. "I just figured it out, myself, believe it or not," he stammered.

She shook her head again, tears welling up in her eyes. "How do you live with yourself?"

Daren raised his beer to her in response. "I drink."

"You really had me fooled. I thought you cared," she told him.

"I did," he replied, glancing at some of the pieces of his file strewn about the room. "I did. And I wanted to do good. I really did. For Devon and for you. But I'm just an errand boy," he said with a shrug. "I fooled myself into thinking maybe I was more but…"

"I shoulda fuckin' known." Andrea put her hands over her face and let out a little scream of frustration. "That's a lie," she admitted in frustration. "I *did know*, but I wanted to use you to get Carson."

"What did you know?" Daren asked.

"That you were a fraud. An inept man with a white savior complex, and that I should stay the fuck away from you!"

"I'm sorry," Daren said after failing to find any other words to offer. "I'm truly sorry."

Andrea was crying now, which he could see made her angrier. "Fuck you! Fucking piece of shit, drunk-ass, racist mother fucker! Go back north where you fucking belong." She slammed the door as she left the room.

Daren stared into the broken mirror. He didn't blame her for hating him. He thought about his career, his life, and his near-death experience. He stared at the shards of glass on the floor, inspecting himself, and thought about the man he'd become.

Fear and anxiety can do strange things to a person. Until you wake up one day and you're estranged from the only people you love. That's where Andrea now found herself, and following her emotional reunion with Mikayla, she longed for personal connection. She wanted to love and be loved so badly, but this need caused her great distress. Every relationship she had formed as a child had been shattered or strained so badly, that she now instinctively viewed personal connection as an emotional risk.

Even her own son, whom she loved more than anyone in the world, was a risk. Was she fucking him up? Would he hold her mistakes against her? Even the thought of him one day leaving home hurt, and made her want to withdraw from him. But he was just a boy who needed his momma. *Why was she so fucking broken?*

Andrea had a couple of cups of coffee to sober up before heading home to face her fears. She realized as she thought about it, that her entire adult life had been spent running away from anyone and anything that made her feel. The only adult connection she had was with David, and he was safely married, which meant he came with no obligations or expectations. Even Gram made her feel emotionally unsafe—one day she would pass on and leave this world. Nothing was permanent, and Andrea feared she would always be abandoned in one way or another by everyone.

The Grey case had been a convenient distraction—another case to obsess over so she could avoid her family and her feelings. Now that distraction was gone, her reconciliation with Mikayla, no matter how tenuous, had forced her to face what she was hoping to avoid. For the first time, she found herself wondering if she wanted to be a cop. She was only sure of one thing at that moment: she wanted to hold Marcus and tell him she loved him.

Gram and Marcus were watching television when she got home. They were pleasantly surprised to see her home so early. Marcus greeted her at the door with a hug. She rubbed the back of his head and embraced him tenderly.

Gram, being Gram, seemed to recognize just what Andrea needed, and joined the hug at the door. "Didn't expect you this early," she said as they embraced. "We already ate, but lemme fix you something, baby."

"That's okay, Gram," Andrea replied. She kissed Gram on the cheek and then Marcus on the head. "Whatch y'all watching?"

"His cartoons just ended. We were going to pick a movie," said Gram.

"You want to watch with us, mommy?" Marcus asked her, still clinging to her tightly.

"Sure, baby." Andrea smiled and rubbed his head affectionately.

They sat on the couch and Marcus put on his favorite movie, *The Black Panther*. Andrea teased that she never would have pictured Gram watching a superhero movie. Gram simply shrugged her shoulders and replied, "It's pretty good."

25

"**YOU WANTED TO** see me, Skip?" David had just arrived at work. He hadn't even had a chance to change before he was told to see the boss.

"Good morning, Sullivan," Skip replied from behind his desk. "I just wanted you to know you'll be riding solo for a few days."

"Oh?"

"Lane washed out," Skip informed him.

"Really?" David was surprised and somewhat relieved. "He fucking quit?"

"Yeah, unfortunately," Skip confirmed.

"Why—I mean what did he say? Did he give a reason?"

"Said being a cop wasn't for him," Skip replied. "Sheriff says we can allow solo patrols during the day now, anyway, so you can have your wish. We'll pair you off with someone for your nightshift on Friday."

"Yeah, yeah, sure, whatever," David muttered as he walked away. He couldn't believe Lane had quit. *Had he washed him out? That was all it took?*

He shook his head, pushing open the door that led downstairs to the locker room. To his surprise, there, on the steps, he found Lane, holding a box packed with the contents of his locker. They both stopped and stared at each other in tense silence for a moment.

"Can't believe you fucking quit," David sneered.

"Just like you wanted, right?" Lane replied.

"Oh, what? I'm supposed to feel bad for you? If you couldn't handle it, then I'm glad you're quitting."

"You're a real piece of shit you know that." Lane tried to make his way up the stairs, past David.

"Oh, is that right?" David asked, blocking his way. "Why don't you put the box down and tell me that?"

"Nah," Lane shot back, shoving past. "Save it for the streets. You can beat on all the Black men you want out there."

David was infuriated. He pushed Lane in the back, causing him to trip on the steps and spill the contents of his box. "You got something you want to say to me?!" he barked.

Lane rose to his feet slowly, wincing in pain. He shook his head and sighed. "No. I have absolutely nothing to say to you." He stared David squarely in the eyes, then turned away and began picking up his things.

The move disarmed David. He'd never seen someone back down from a physical confrontation with him. He stormed down the stairs, leaving Lane to gather his things. "Get the fuck outta here, boy! This is a man's job!" he called back up the stairs as he charged through the locker room door.

As David dressed, he thought about it some more and decided he was happy to be riding solo. He didn't need anyone limiting him. Especially with Ellis trying to leverage him. He needed to be able to maneuver freely.

Still, something about Lane's quitting had bothered him. He thought about the way Lane had stared him down and refused to fight him. *Why had he looked at him like that?* Like he was some repugnant piece of shit? Like he was some kind of racist or something. And that remark, about beating Black men—what horseshit. He could go cry a fucking river about it. David understood what it took to survive in the world, and what it took to make a difference on those streets: dominance. Men only understood fear, pain, and dominance. His father had shown him that. Men like Lane who didn't understand that would be eaten alive on the streets. In that way, he'd done the guy a favor by washing him out.

Dominance. That was it, David realized. It all seemed clear to him now. Since Greg's death, he'd been absent and withdrawn. He'd given an inch, and now Ellis was trying to push him a mile. He finished dressing and shut his locker. The badge he wore had more power behind it than any thug on the streets. Perhaps it was time to make sure Ellis understood that.

An increasingly empty mall stood across the street from poor, Black neighborhoods with substandard housing. The mall had once been a glaring example of economic disparity—a commercial center packed with white people shopping in stores that those living in the mall's shadow could never afford. But those days had come and gone, and now both the mall and its surrounding neighborhoods stood as examples of bad zoning decisions.

The National Express Business Center was located on the main road, next to the mall's south entrance. The center offered computer access, packing, printing, and shipping services with National Express.

It was there that the anonymous tip had been placed regarding Devon Grey's hanging.

It was early Tuesday morning when Andrea pulled into the parking lot and shook her head in disbelief. After a long night of smoking cigarettes in the bathroom and thinking about her life, she had decided that she couldn't just give up on Devon Grey's case. She owed it to his mother, to Pastor Mosely, and her sister. She had told them all she was looking into it, and they had all looked at her with hope in their eyes. Daren Renard may have been full of shit, but that wasn't going to stop her from asking around some more. She knew the chances of finding anything were slim, but she needed to try.

She walked past a Charleston PD patrol car parked by the entrance and nodded at the officer behind the wheel. He, of course, ignored her.

Inside, a young white woman with short hair greeted her from behind the counter with a smile. Andrea flashed her badge long enough to get the impression across, but quickly enough so the woman wouldn't notice that she was outside her jurisdiction.

"I'm working with the FBI," Andrea told her, stretching the truth just a little. "I'm wondering if the manager is available?"

The young woman enthusiastically told her to wait while she got the manager from the back.

A tall Black woman with gorgeous, elaborately applied eye shadow and braided hair soon emerged and greeted her. "Hey! My name is Nicolette, what can I do for ya?" she said.

"Hi, Nicolette!" Andrea said, matching her energy and tone. "Can I ask you some questions about your cameras and computer access?"

"You looking into that poor boy's death again?" Nicolette asked, shaking her head. "Sure, sugar. Whatever I can do for you."

"Yes, ma'am, we are," Andrea confirmed. "I'm hoping there's something we overlooked here. Some way we could figure out who used your computers to leave that anonymous tip."

"I wish there was, shug. But like I told the FBI, the sheriff's…, and Charleston PD—our computer automatically deletes the camera footage after 48-hours if we don't manually save it. And whoever used the computer, must have jumped on one that was already logged on, because nobody bought time around then."

"I'm sorry?" Andrea asked, not sure she understood.

"The computer access is sold in minutes. You can buy time in cash from the counter, or by using your card at the computer itself. But we didn't have any sales that late. People will often buy an hour or two, then leave before their time is up. Whoever your tipster is, must've jumped on a machine that was already paid for."

"Figures," Andrea muttered.

As they were talking, the door to the store swung open, sounding a chime to notify employees whenever someone arrived. The officer from the patrol car outside walked in, jabbing his finger at his phone with confusion. "Is the Wi-Fi down?" he asked, continuing to paw at the device in frustration.

"Probably just needs to be reset," Nicolette replied. Then she looked at Andrea and said, "Excuse me for a moment," before walking into the back.

Andrea eyed this specimen of the city's supposed finest while they waited for her to return. "Working hard?" she asked.

He gave her a side-eyed glance and scoffed. "Excuse me?"

She flashed her badge and rolled her eyes. "Save it."

He shook his head and scoffed again. "Figures. All the same."

"And what's that supposed to mean?" Andrea asked, whipping her head around.

"Females with a badge," the officer replied with a dismissive laugh. "Always out to prove something."

"Maybe that's just what real police work looks like from where you're sitting, parked in the shade," she retorted, raising one eyebrow and shaking her head in disapproval.

"You should be all set, shug!" Nicolette cheerfully informed the officer as she returned from the back. He nodded gruffly, stormed out of the store, and was soon driving away with haste. "What did you say to him?" Nicolette asked Andrea with a devilish grin.

"Just asked him how work was going." Andrea smiled and shrugged. "Is there anything else you can think of? Any other way we might be able to figure out who left that tip?"

Nicolette shook her head and sighed. "Sorry, darlin'."

Andrea left her card and told Nicolette to call if she thought of anything. Another dead end—Daren's absence hadn't changed her luck.

Dylan Hall was quite beautiful for a place with such an ugly history. The Daniel Island property, like most of the area's most beautiful historic homes, was formerly a plantation. The Dylan family was old money and old Southern blood, and according to the plaque adorning the gate, they had owned the property since Ashley Avery Dylan III had built it in 1823. Of course, Daren knew enough to know that meant that ole Ashley Dylan's slaves had built the place.

Daren sat on the front porch, sipping sweet tea from a mason jar, waiting to see the owner of the estate—the infamous Avery Dylan. A crew of Hispanic laborers worked the property, and a Black woman in a maid's outfit had shown him to his seat and brought him his drink. It was all a bit much for him to see people of color having to work for a vile white supremacist.

Daren had done some reading on Avery to prepare for his visit. He was a man who, at one time, would have been known in the lowcountry as a Dandy. He dressed exceptionally well, carried himself with great dignity, and was overly concerned himself with formalities. He spoke with the slightest hint of femininity. Dandies in the South, like Avery, never married, many preferring the company of men. However, the culture was rigidly conservative and steeped in Southern traditionalism, so any suggestions of homosexuality were denied.

A man Daren recognized to be Avery Dylan soon emerged from the house wearing pleated slacks and a white collared shirt. His shoes were well shined, like those of a man who never had to step in dirt.

"Oh, heavens, I do apologize, Mister Renard," Avery said as he crossed the porch. "I didn't realize the humidity had gotten quite so dreadful!" He stopped, placed both hands on his hips, and turned around, shaking his head in disapproval. "Sally! You had our guest waiting in this heat?!" He turned back to Daren. "I am so sorry, Mister Renard." He extended his hand and Daren hesitantly shook it. "What can I do for you on this beautiful day in our Holy City?" he asked.

"Well, Mister Dylan, I'm in town trying to solve a murder."

Avery shook his head and smacked his lips together in regret. "That is most terrible to hear. I am quite appalled by the thought of violence." He took a seat across from Daren.

"The murder of Devon Grey."

"Oh, the colored boy that was lynched last year," Avery said dismissively. "Y'all still trying to figure that out, huh? Well, I wish you all the luck."

"We're looking into white supremacist groups," Daren said, placing his tea down on the table between them.

"Oh, would you like a refill? Sally makes *the* best sweet tea if I do say so myself."

"No, thank you, I'm good." Daren cleared his throat as if he could somehow dislodge the uncomfortable lump he felt there. "Listen, Mr. Dylan—"

"Please, call me Avery."

"Okay, Avery… Let's cut the shit. You know why I'm here. You can't look into a racist group in the South without coming across your name."

Avery laughed and waved his hand. "Well, I suppose depending on your definition, that is true to a point. Politics creates such hyperbole, you understand. Now, my son, bless his heart, may be of more interest to you than myself, I am afraid."

"His European Defense League was questioned in connection to the Grey hanging," said Daren. "You got any information about that?"

"No, Mister Renard—"

"Agent," Daren corrected.

"My mistake. *Agent* Renard, my son has a penchant for… acting out, one might say. I loved the boy, but unfortunately, I do not think I was the best father."

"Can't imagine that," Daren replied dryly.

Avery looked off over the porch rails at his property. "I was a busy man. We tell ourselves we're doing it for our children, but… Well, that's just a lie, now isn't it?"

"Avery, you said your son would be of interest to us. Why?"

"The boy hangs with a rather uncivilized sort. Criminals. Drug dealers. Dangerous people without much regard for consequences,"

Avery explained. "But what makes me worry is that Josh thinks he has something to prove."

"To you?"

"Well, yes, I suppose. Me and his motley crew of redneck renegades. I'm sure you saw the legal battle we had?"

"Over the names of your hate groups. Yeah, I saw."

Avery looked at him with arrogant disdain, but cleared his throat and kept his tone warm and hospital. "The League—"

"The Southern Defense League?" Daren asked, evoking the name of his son's former group for no other reason than to frustrate the man.

"There is only *one* league, Agent Renard. The Southern *Heritage* League. It's a respectable organization comprised of the most esteemed gentlemen in the lowcountry. We stand for the preservation of the greatest culture and heritage history has known."

"You're fancy racists. I got it," Daren snarked.

"Yes, well, my son never conducted himself in a manner fitting of the League. He tried to start his own, however. My fellow trustees decided we could not abide such things. We sued and shut down his so-called *Southern Defense League.*"

"Then what happened?" Daren asked, although he already knew the answer.

"My foolish son started another organization, and they decided to manufacture methamphetamine to fund their operation," said Avery.

"Which you helped him out of trouble for," Daren remarked.

"Not exactly, Agent Renard," Avery confessed. "Truth be told, I have a lot of influence around the lowcountry, and my money *has* bought a lot of loyalty. Unfortunately, that judge took it upon himself to presume what I would want in such a situation, and never bothered to even place a call."

"You're saying the judge let him off easy without your say?"

"Mm-hm. It appears ole Judge Clark saw the Dylan name on the docket and thought he could do me a favor," said Avery. "I do wish he had called, though. I would have told him to throw the book at my delinquent son."

Daren's mouth tightened and his brow furrowed. "You wanted your son locked up?"

"God yes," Avery explained. "He's an embarrassment. A disgrace to my name. And, I tell you—this is the God's-honest-truth, Agent Renard—he's dangerous."

"How so?"

"Josh wants to start a race war," Avery said.

"Yeah, I read his manifesto," Daren replied.

"Seems he's almost set on violence, Agent Renard. Now, I sent him to live with his mother in North Carolina—tried to get him away from some of these folks he'd fallen in with, but he just assembled more idiots up there. Things like that colored boy getting hanged—Dylan would call that a *'precipitating incident',*" said Avery. "The kind of thing that gets people on all sides seeing red. The kind of thing they think might start their damned race war."

"You think your son was involved in the lynching of Devon Grey?" Daren asked.

Avery sighed and rose to his feet, then slowly walked over to the corner of his porch. "Sadly, I was convinced as much. Now he's got an alibi, but what about all those men who follow him?"

"We've only got his known associates from the group down here," Daren informed him. "Do you have any way of finding out who he might be running with up there?"

"No, Agent Renard. I'm afraid I do not. I am, after all, the reason he's been exiled from this great city."

"So, I don't understand," Daren said, walking over to join Avery. "Your group *doesn't* want race wars and white supremacy?"

"Race wars?" Avery scoffed. "Heavens no! We are a dignified group that seeks to maintain our heritage, and advance our culture and traditions politically." He pulled a finished wooden tobacco pipe from his pant pocket along with a book of matches. He took a minute to light the pipe before continuing. "There's a dignity and class to what I want to promote. These more… well, shall we say more common nationalist types—they don't really exemplify the best of white culture."

"White culture huh? Like Burger King and NASCAR and shit?"

"Western Civilization, Agent Renard—perhaps you've heard of it. Why is it that we're the only race that's not allowed to be proud of our heritage?" Avery asked him.

"Sorry, but I don't quite buy it," said Daren. "Your whole dignified, classy racism just seems like bullshit. I bet you were happy to see that boy lynched."

"No, I assure you. I find that sort of thing quite distasteful. It's a new era, Agent Renard. It's about understanding where we are as a people—as a movement. America was built on white supremacy—white culture. We don't need to burn crosses and lynch people. It's the twenty-first century for heaven's sake!" Avery laughed again, highly amused at his logic. "No, today protecting white heritage is called *preserving history*. It's about making us great again. It's about conserving what this country has always stood for. That's a message that people can understand—one they can feel in their bones."

"A kinder, gentler racism. Sounds like you prefer to keep your hands clean while others do your dirty work."

"Now, Agent Renard, I have welcomed you into my home, as any decent Southern man would. But I will not abide unfounded mischaracterizations of myself or the League."

"So, if your son is out lynching people, that kind of takes the rosy smell off your shitty group, huh?"

"I wouldn't put it in those terms exactly," Avery demurred. "But more or less."

Daren nodded. "If I find out you're lying to me, I'll be back, and I won't be so polite," he told Avery before leaving.

Avery's nouveau-racism was nauseating, but Daren found the sit-down helpful, nonetheless. It had almost surprised him how quickly the man had thrown his son under the bus. It made sense when he considered the big money around Avery and the League of Southern Heritage. They spent a lot of time and money painting themselves as an organization of class and elegance. Avery's son, on the other hand, was another story. Avery had said so in no uncertain terms. He believed his son was somehow connected to Grey's killing, and Daren believed him.

26

DESPITE THE SHIT he was dealing with at work, David tried his best to enjoy dinner with his family that evening. He even helped Marie to prepare the meal by chopping peppers and onions. She was so surprised to see him helping, and it had put her in a great mood. David had to remember this more often—a little extra effort bought him a lot of emotional leeway. It felt like the first time in months that she wasn't pressing him about his feelings. They were just a happy family, eating dinner, and talking to their son about his upcoming soccer game.

"You bet I'm going to be there!" David exclaimed to Sean. He got up from his seat to grab a beer from the fridge, but upon opening the fridge he frowned. "No more beer?" he asked his wife.

"There should be more in the fridge in the garage," Marie replied. "Sit down, honey. I'll get you one." She wiped her mouth with a napkin and started to get up.

"No, that's alright," David said, holding his hand out for her to stop. "You relax, baby. I'll get it."

She smiled and batted her eyes at him. He smiled back, winked, and then headed for the garage.

In the garage, David retrieved a bottle of beer from the fridge and popped it open on his work bench. He took a sip and was about to head back into the house when he glanced out the garage door window and saw an unfamiliar car parked at the foot of his driveway. He put the beer down and opened the lid of his tool case. He pulled out a snubbed nose .38 revolver and tucked it into the back of his jeans.

David opened the garage door and cautiously started down the driveway toward the car. It was a red, decked-out late-80s Audi. The driver, seeing him coming, waved enthusiastically like he recognized him. David stopped and reached for his gun, but before he could pull, he felt the muzzle of a gun press against his back.

"Easy there, cracker," the assailant told David as he disarmed him.

David raised his hands slowly. "Hey, if this is robbery, you take anything you want."

The assailant laughed. "You wish this was a robbery, piggy! Let's go, get in the car."

David reluctantly walked down his driveway and climbed into the back seat of the Audi. The driver, a young, Black man with a platinum grill flashed him a sparkling smile. "Welcome to my ride. Sorry to say it will be your last!"

The gunman who'd abducted him climbed in beside David, his gun trained and ready. He looked enough like the driver for David to surmise they were related.

"Where to?" the driver asked the gunman.

"We'll take him out to marshes on the Cooper. Leave his ass for gator food."

"Gators don't eat dead bodies," David informed them with a laugh. "Get real."

"Motherfucker, did we ask you?" the driver snapped.

"He right, though. That ain't gonna work," the gunman replied.

The driver pulled away from David's house. "Who fucking cares? The fish and shit will eat him. Or somebody will find his bloated ass floating in the drink. Don't make no difference."

"Could have just shot me in my driveway if y'all were smart," David replied.

"That's what I said," the gunman retorted.

"We were told to make you disappear. So, this is what we doing," the driver said, irritated with the gunman. "Enough debate."

"So, I guess this is Ellis's way of letting me know our arrangement is no longer valid," David remarked, staring out the window. *Was this it? Was this how he was going out?* If so, he was going to take at least one of those pieces of shit with him.

"He told us to tell you that you should've known your role—not have bitten the hand that feeds or some shit," the gunman said.

"I bet he was a bit more eloquent," David replied.

"Bet," the driver confirmed.

The car continued out of David's neighborhood, then onto the highway and away from Mount Pleasant. David thought of Marie. She'd probably figured out he was gone by now. He wondered if she was worried or pissed. Maybe both. He wondered if he would see her again and if he did, how he would explain.

Andrea knew the smell of weed well. She'd smoked her fair share when she was a teenager, and her sister had smoked more. Back then, Andrea had always laughed when Gram would remark while doing laundry that Mikayla's clothes smelled weird. Gram didn't know what that smell was but Andrea did.

Andrea knocked on Ms. Grey's shaky screen door and waited patiently. When Ms. Grey finally answered, she smiled warmly, happy to see Andrea again. "Come on in now," she said invitingly, backing her wheelchair up enough for Andrea to open the door.

"It's lovely to see you again, Ms. Grey," Andrea said, shutting the door behind her as she entered.

"I hope you have good news," said Ms. Grey, her eyes again full of hope.

"I'm sorry, no," Andrea admitted, hanging her head. "But I am still trying to find answers."

"Then what brings you back here?" Ms. Grey asked, her spirit noticeably deflated.

"Ms. Grey, I couldn't help but notice just now, and the last time I was here…" Andrea paused, searching for a way to say it without offending. "The smell."

"If you're saying I'm unsanitary, then I'm sorry, but I do my best," Ms. Grey retorted defensively.

"No, no, Ms. Grey, I mean the marijuana."

Ms. Grey didn't say anything, she just stared down at her lap.

"I'm not here to judge you, or to give you a hard time, Ms. Grey. Really, I'm not," said Andrea. "I didn't say anything before when I was with the man from the FBI because I didn't want to embarrass you, and I didn't think it was relevant."

"But now it's relevant?" Ms. Grey asked.

"I'm hoping it might be." Andrea crouched down so she was at eye level with the woman. "Ms. Grey, did Devon get your pot for you?"

The woman looked away and began to cry.

"Ms. Grey, I promise, nothing is going to happen to you," Andrea assured her. She took the woman's hand and squeezed it lightly. "I don't care if you smoke a little weed for the pain."

"It's not that," Ms. Grey replied through tears.

"Then what is it?" Andrea asked.

"You know what they will say about my son," she cried. "If anyone finds out where he was going… His life wouldn't matter anymore. He'd be just another thug killed buying drugs."

Andrea understood. Sadly, she knew Ms. Grey wasn't wrong. "So, Devon *was* going to get you weed that night?"

Ms. Grey bit her lip and shook her head. "I'm afraid to say."

"I promise you," Andrea told her, gently squeezing her hand, "I will follow up by myself, and I won't say nothing to nobody unless it makes a difference."

Ms. Grey nodded. "He would go and get my smoke for me when I needed it."

"Do you know who he got it from, Ms. Grey?"

She nodded again. "His cousin. Malik."

Andrea went to the kitchen and got Ms. Grey a paper towel to dry her eyes. "Ms. Grey, thank you so much," she said. "I promise, I will keep that between us. Now, can you tell me where I can find Malik?"

The air was thick and rank. Daren swatted away the mosquitoes as he made his way out from the brush. He'd returned to the scene because he wasn't sure what else to do. He thought, perhaps, he'd missed something earlier in his frustration with that sergeant who Andrea was dating. Sadly, he'd come up with nothing.

He climbed into the Charger, and sat behind the wheel, unsure of what to do. He wanted to find Watts and apologize to her, but he knew she wouldn't want to hear it.

He was about to drive away when he looked up at the large Lowcountry Realty sign. He pulled out his phone, dialed the number, and waited. "Yes, hello. Glad I caught you before the end of the day… I was wondering if I might be able to get some information on a property… Mm-hm. Yes, it's on Ashley Circle… Yes, that's right…"

27

ANDREA MADE HER way up and down Ashley River Road and Ashley Hall Road, driving through every apartment complex along the way—and there were a lot. Some of the complexes were like mazes, stretching back far beyond the main road and intertwining with other complexes. She drove slowly through the maze of parking lots and curvy roads with speed bumps every fifty feet, past basketball courts, pools, and laundry rooms, looking for groups of kids.

All Ms. Grey could tell her was that Malik worked with a crew in an apartment complex somewhere off Ashley River. Ms. Grey had explained that she hadn't spoken to that part of the family in years, and wouldn't know how to contact Malik or his mother.

It wasn't much to go on, but it was the strongest lead she had. She now knew exactly who Devon was going to see when he was killed. Maybe he was in the wrong place at the wrong time, and some racist hicks abducted him. It was certainly possible, but could Devon have been killed over drugs? People didn't get killed over weed very often, but weed money was another story. On the street, owing someone money was risky.

Andrea told herself not to jump to conclusions. As a detective, she'd seen it happen before. Investigators will get so locked into a theory or stuck viewing a case in a specific way, they ended up missing what's right in front of them.

She came across a group of teen boys hanging outside a V-Mart gas station and pulled up to them. Being a woman of color in a shitty car, the boys assumed she was looking to score. Two of them approached her immediately.

"What's good, sista, whatcha need?" one of the boys said to her. He was a skinny Black kid sporting a Gamecocks jersey and a black bandana.

"We got that bomb-ass weed, girl. And some snow if you want to ski," the other child informed her. He was also Black but shorter and more muscly than the other and wore a tank top to show it off.

Andrea smiled and shook her head. "Y'all got no creep. What if I was a cop or something?"

The Gamecocks fan laughed and shook his head. "Nah, you're way too fine to be five-oh!"

"For real, though!" the kid in the tank top exclaimed.

Andrea batted her eyes and pretended to blush. "Aw, ya'll think?"

"For sure!" the Gamecock replied.

Andrea batted her eyes again, rolled her window down all the way, and invited the boys closer with her finger. They both came close and leaned on her door, eager to hear what she had to say.

She used her eyes to gesture down at her lap. Convinced she was flirting, both teens leaned in and looked down to see her badge lying on her lap. "Now," Andrea whispered to them. "A dozen cops got eyes on me," she lied. "Try to run and my squad will pounce on all y'all. But you help me out with some information, we can pretend this never happened. You can even lie and tell your crew you got my digits."

The two boys looked at each other, each dumbfounded and scared. "Damn! You cold as ice," the kid in the tank top said.

"Iight—well played. Whatchu wanna know?" the Gamecock asked her.

"I'm lookin' for a player named Malik," she said. "Slings trees around here."

The boys looked at each other and shrugged. "He ain't with our crew," the Gamecock said.

"Nah, never heard of him," the other agreed.

"I was told his crew worked apartments near here," she said.

"Shit, he gotta be with the crew that used to work 'round here," muscles told her. "Big D—," he started to say, but the kid in the jersey shot him a harsh look and he bit his tongue.

"What's that now?" Andrea asked.

"There was this other crew," the Gamecock explained. "They worked the apartments mostly. But they—uh—relocated."

"Y'all run them off?" Andrea asked.

"Nah, nothin' like that," he assured her. "Just a business arrangement, like."

"Where's this crew's new location?" she asked.

"They run some corner by the mall now, I think," said the muscular kid. "But they been having some supply issues if you know what I'm saying—so who knows if they working."

Andrea nodded. "Y'all got five minutes before I call drug enforcement on this spot," she added with a friendly smile before driving away.

Incompetence was far less tolerable than stupidity.
A person's intelligence wasn't necessarily important unless it caused

incompetence. As far as David was concerned, stupid people were a necessary part of society, even if they were insufferable. Somebody needed to flip fries, just like someone had to do brain surgery—and he was no brain surgeon, himself. He, however, had no patience for incompetence. Incompetence resulted when stupid people were placed in roles where they should not be. This being one of his greatest pet peeves, it seemed a fittingly cruel twist of fate that his life could soon end at the hands of two insufferably incompetent hitmen.

"*Then why don't we just take him out into the fucking woods somewhere?!*" the driver yelled, exacerbated with his accomplice.

"Sure, which fucking woods?!" the gunman in the back yelled in response. "*Where, dawg?!*

"Jesus fucking Christ, will you two shut the fuck up!" David barked. "Somebody, please, just fucking shoot me, because I sure as shit don't want to listen to you two bicker for another goddamn second!" His abductors looked at him in stunned silence. "And who the fuck abducts someone from their fucking house without a plan?!" he continued. "Y'all couldn't have at least let me have dessert while you figured this out? *Fucking amateurs!*"

"Hey, nobody asked you!" the gunman snarled, waving his pistol in David's face.

"I don't know," the driver said. "Maybe we should just call Ellis and ask the man."

David started laughing uncontrollably. "Yeah, I'm sure he's going to love to hear about that! I mean, if he didn't kill you for your incompetence, he'd *definitely* kill you for discussing it over the phone."

The driver looked at the gunman in the rearview mirror. Both men were now visibly nervous.

"Are you guys new or something?" David couldn't help but tease them. "I mean, where did he find you guys, Craig's List for thugs? I'm glad Ellis doesn't want to work together anymore because, honestly, if this is the quality of the people he's hiring—" The gunman struck David in the mouth with the butt of his gun. David grabbed his mouth and winced in pain. He could feel the blood running down his chin and into his hand. "Well," he said, his hand covering his mouth, "That's a start." He sat up and wiped his mouth on the sleeve of his T-shirt. "Would you assholes just pick a place to kill me already. I mean, you could drag it out, and beat the shit out of me, but it's just going to get more blood on your upholstery." He wiped his bloody hand on the leather seat and smiled a bloody smile at the driver through the rearview mirror.

"Oh, motherfucker..." the driver muttered. He pulled the car sharply off the road and into a muddy field beyond a row of pines and stopped the car. "Alright, do it here. Hurry up," he told the gunman.

"What?!" the gunman exclaimed, looking around. "That's a main fucking road, like, right fucking there!"

"Yeah, bro, "David laughed. "I think this is someone's front yard," he remarked amusedly.

"I'm done with this shit, just fucking open the door, shoot him, and we'll leave his ass right here!" the driver ordered.

The gunman leaned forward and pointed. "He's right, though. There's a house right fucking there, dawg!" As he was leaning forward and pointing, David noticed the butt of his .38 tucked into the back of the man's jeans. Before either of his abductors knew what was happening, David lunged at the gunman. He kneed him squarely in the back and grabbed the man's left arm with both hands, neutralizing his gun hand. In an instance, David had the man's arm pinned down on top of the front seat, the gun pointing perilously at the driver, who backed away in fear and fumbled for the door handle. The gunman squirmed in shock, as David pinned him against the seat with his knee. David growled as he pushed his full weight down upon the man, then, with his right hand, he retrieved his .38 from the man's waistline.

It was over in seconds. Four shots—two apiece. The gunman got two in the back of the skull. The driver held his hands up, and shouted, *"Please!"* Pathetic—two in the face. The windshield and driver's side window were painted in the blood of David's assailants.

He quickly checked both bodies, lifting a gun off each of them, and a pack of smokes off the driver. He lit a smoke, got out of the car, and hurried to the road.

Motorists and their passengers shot him bewildered, concerned, and frightened looks as he made his way down the road, his shirt and face soaked in blood. His temper was cooling, and it occurred to him he was drawing attention to himself, so he quickly dipped off the road. He took a seat behind an old rock wall, pulled out his phone, and made a call. "Yeah, it's me… Remember that arrangement we discussed? It's time."

It wasn't common to see a sharp-dressed white man around those parts. As such, Daren stood out from down the road.

Andrea parked the Focus in front of her building and emerged shaking her head, a preemptive rejection of anything he had to say. "What the hell are you doing here?" she asked. "You come to my home?" She found herself unable to stop shaking her head.

"I—"

"No," she snapped, raising her hand flat like a stop sign. "You know what? I don't want to know. Because then I'd have to listen to your voice."

"Look, I get that you hate me—" Daren started.

"Hate you?" she laughed mockingly. "I don't even *know* you. You just some suit with an agenda."

"You're right," he conceded. "You're right that that's what they want me to be. I was too stupid and arrogant to see it."

She scoffed and brushed by him. "I ain't got time for white man confessional. It's not up to me to absolve you of your sins, Daren."

"Look," Daren said pleadingly. He stepped in front of her and put his hand over his heart. "I know I'm a piece of shit. I know that this entire mess—everything happening down here... I know that what I did in Michigan played a role in starting all of this. I believed the bullshit they told me—the bullshit I told *myself*—because it allowed me to not have to ask hard questions. But, Watts, ever since I got here, everything I've seen—the things you've shown me—it's like none of it added up based on what I thought I knew. I wanted to believe in this country. I wanted to believe that it really was an exceptional place. I was so desperate to believe that because it made me feel like I had purpose. I shut my eyes to so much because it didn't belong in the picture I wanted to see."

Andrea sighed. She wanted to be angry at him, but his eyes pled with her to hear him. She wanted to hate him—to throw him out as irredeemable, but his epiphany felt real, and for some reason, she wanted to believe him. "Alright, let me go get my smokes if we gonna get all personal and shit," she said.

Daren smiled anxiously. "I'm sorry, Watts. I truly am."

Andrea nodded slowly. "Good."

She hurried up to her apartment and inside to the bathroom, where she retrieved her smokes and a lighter. "Going out for a smoke?" Gram asked her on her way back out— her passive-aggressive way of calling Andrea out. "I'll quit soon," Andrea promised.

Outside, she and Daren sat on the steps that led down to the parking lot and talked. He told her his side of the investigation into Castile's shooting death. "I'm a goddamn fool for believing them, but I swear, I never thought that report would be the final word," he said.

"You ignored evidence because you were told to." Andrea recounted, sighing. "Well, you did wrong," she said. "But you ain't the cause of all this shit happening here. You're just not that important. This is a fire that's been raging for centuries."

"Feels like I'm waking from a dream," Daren replied. "Everything—*everything* looks different. I don't even know who I am now... Am I just a pawn? All I've done is perpetuate a system of injustice."

"Slow down, now. You getting' *too woke,* too fast," Andrea said with a laugh. "You'll give yourself whiplash."

"What do I do, though, Watts? How do I fix it, or even try to undo some of the damage?"

"You can't," she told him. "Just do better. Listen to the experiences of others. Don't go around thinking you already understand everyone and everything."

Daren nodded. "I keep thinking about the other day— about Carson's..."

"Thought that might have fucked you up," she admitted.

"I don't think it was ever clearer to me in those moments before you saved my ass, that I've spent my life trying to be someone I'm not. I think some part of me has spent my life trying to prove who I'm *not* to my parents, but I never really thought about who I *was*... Or who I wanted to become."

Andrea smoked and listened to the wind blow. It rustled the palms in the parking lot and felt cool against her skin. She looked at Daren. "It's okay. It's normal to be a little overwhelmed after something like that."

"I was ashamed of who I was in that moment—ashamed that if I died, nothing good would have come from my life. Just some *yes-man*—a pathetic, self-absorbed, entitled shell of a man. All that power and wealth I was born into, I could have done whatever I wanted to, and all I did was carry water for some racist cop."

"Listen, Daren," said Andrea. "We all like to think that we are in control, doing whatever our free will wants, but we're mostly products of our circumstances. That's the truth society doesn't want to hear, because it's easier to blame individuals. We are who we are—there's biology and all that, sure—but at the end of the day, it's circumstances and experiences that shape us. We don't choose where we're born, who are parents are, or any of it. We're just thrown into it. We think we have a choice, but the truth is we're all on tracks, and those tracks were shaped by factors larger than us before we were even born."

"That sounds grim," Daren remarked. "Like we're trapped and nothing we can do will change what lies ahead for us."

"Change is hard but not impossible," she countered. "But first, you have to understand what shaped your track."

"And what circumstances made yours?" Daren asked.

"My father was an angry man," she confessed through puffs of smoke. "He used to beat on my mother when he was mad, and that was just about every day. My sister and I did our best to avoid his wrath, but my mother—well she had to put herself between him and us, so she got it bad. Anyway, my sister used to come running into my room when it got bad. We would lie in bed together, and I'd try my best to calm her down. One night, I heard my mother actually stand up for herself. My father left, and I remember thinking that things would be different." She took a deep breath and tried not to cry. "A few days later, he came back and beat her to death with a roofing hammer while we listened from my room."

"Jesus Christ…" Daren gasped. "I'm… sorry…"

"That night it happened… my sister was in my bed again, scared to death, and my mother's screams were so bad. I'd never heard her scream like that… and then all of a sudden, she stopped, and it was just silent. I knew something bad had happened," Andrea recalled. "I heard my father coming down the hall, and I told Mikayla to close her eyes and pretend to be asleep. I shut my eyes and tried to slow my breath. I remember hearing the door to my bedroom open, and…" Andrea paused; the memory was as vivid, terrifying, and felt as real then as it had at the moment. "I could feel him staring at us. I heard him step close to the bed… He just stood there, hovering over us for so long." Andrea could not hold back the tears any longer. "I kept thinking he had just killed my mother, and now… now he was going to kill us."

"Watts—I—" Daren stammered shaking his head. He didn't know what to do or say, so he put his hand on her shoulder. "I'm sorry."

"After what felt like an eternity, he left my room, went downstairs, and called 9-1-1 to turn himself in," she said, wiping the tears from her cheeks. She couldn't believe she was sharing this with him. "Are we bonding?" she asked, the slightest hint of laughter breaking through her tears.

"I guess so," he said.

Andrea leaned into him, and he put his arm around her and squeezed lightly for just a moment, then she sat up. "I guess all this has made me think about who I am, too," she admitted. "I saw my sister yesterday. It was the first time we'd spoken in years. Somehow, despite being from the same damn home, we turned out so different. Somehow, despite having the same wounds and the same goals, we wound up on opposite ends of things."

Daren nodded. "Feels like a lot of people are divided right now."

"A lot of pain in the world," Andrea agreed. "I think most people are incapable of understanding their own pain, never mind the pain of others."

Daren nodded again and sighed. "My boss wants me to write another bullshit report on all this if we can't figure out what happened," he confessed.

"What's he saying?" she asked.

"Wants me to just write it up as a gang hit or something."

"Well, I hate to make him happy, but turns out, it may have been drug-related."

"What?" Daren asked, confused.

"I circled back with the mother. She smokes weed to cope with the pain of her arthritis. Turns out she *did* know where Devon was headed when he left that night."

"Out to score her some grass," Daren guessed.

"Exactly. He's got a cousin named Malik, rolls with a crew that used to work the Ashley River Apartments."

"Used to?"

"Yeah, according to the crew that I talked to nearby, they came to some sort of business arrangement and relocated."

"Uh-huh," he replied skeptically. "They made an arrangement, huh?"

"Right, sounds like a turf battle. Maybe Devon got caught up in all that," she theorized.

"So, where's Malik?"

"I got a lead on him," she said. "I'm going to try and find him tomorrow."

"Alright, you do that," Daren said, rising to leave. "I'm talking with the owner of the property where Devon was found. He's some infamous developer. Seems like a lot of people don't care for him or his projects too much."

"Good idea," said Andrea. "Maybe there's a reason that location was picked."

"My thoughts exactly. And I want to keep looking into these white supremacist groups too," said Daren. "I talked to Avery Dylan."

"Oh? No shit."

"Yeah, he was surprised his son had an alibi. Thinks him or one of his dirtbags are who we're looking for," he reported.

"Well, now that's interesting," Andrea mused. "Let's keep working that angle, but I think it's looking more like this has to do with drug sales."

"Perhaps," he replied before he walked away. "But if there's one thing I've learned down here, it's that everything is about race one way or another."

"You are learning some things!" she replied, stomping out her cigarette butt. She followed Daren over to his car. "So, we split up then tomorrow?" she asked.

"Yeah, but keep in touch," he told her.

"Oh, I almost forgot," Andrea added as Daren got into his Charger. "Sheriff Greenly was looking for us. They found three more dead pigs."

Daren shook his head. "Three more?! Did they report it with anti-terrorism?" he asked.

"Supposedly, they're doing that today," she said, shaking her head.

"I don't like the feeling this is giving me, Watts," Daren said with a heavy sigh.

"I don't either," she agreed. "Do you think that they could be related? Could whoever killed Devon be connected to these pig killings?"

"I don't know… Maybe, but it's doubtful," he said as he started his engine. "You don't go from killing people to animals. It's usually a one-way street in the other direction."

"Maybe something to keep an eye on though, either way," she suggested.

"Yeah, I agree with that," he said. "Tell the Sheriff's office to keep us in the loop, but they need to contact anti-terrorism."

Daren drove away, and Andrea decided to have one last cigarette before heading inside.

Ellis Bartley was a man of habit. He liked to retire early, usually with a woman or two. But by 11 pm at the latest, they would be asked to leave. It was then customary for him to have a joint on the sunporch before heading to bed. For a man with so many enemies, Ellis Bartley was very comfortable at home and slept very soundly. He paid people well to ensure as much. But there were two things Ellis had not considered: the greed that power creates, and the power that greed holds over others.

Greed and power were two things Ellis should've been well aware of, having built his empire shot by shot, body by body. Ellis had killed anyone who stood in his way, including his mentor and partner, Duke LaSalle. But power can make people blind to what's around them, and if Ellis had thought about it, he wouldn't have been surprised by what was about to befall him.

After all, Reggie had been at the same level without advancement or additional compensation for so long, and he'd done so much of Ellis's dirty work. Sure, he had money and a nice car, but all that was just a sliver of the pie. Reggie put his ass on the line every day, enforcing for Ellis, collecting for Ellis, driving around for Ellis. It really hadn't taken much for David to convince him. Once the idea was in Reggie's head, David had to repeatedly pump the brakes—always telling the kid that the time wasn't right yet. That was because Ellis had still been useful to David. Now, however, that had changed.

It was ten minutes to eleven when Ellis made it out to his back porch and lit his joint. "I have a piece in my robe," he calmly warned when he heard someone breathing in the dark.

"You'll never get it out in time," David said, emerging from the corner, his gun trained on Ellis.

"I'm disappointed, but not entirely surprised you got away from my nephews," Ellis said, hitting the joint. "They were new applicants, and I figured this was a simple task. I should thank you, really—they clearly weren't cut out for the job."

"Consider it a parting gift."

"But how did you get past my guards?" Ellis asked, unfazed as he stared down death.

"I sent them home," Reggie replied, emerging from the house. He walked right up to his boss and took the joint from his hand. "You never offer me any of your weed, either," he said, taking a puff from the joint. "Why you gotta be such a cheap motherfucker?"

"We could still work something out, gentlemen," Ellis assured them, raising his arms wide in a gesture of peace.

"It's too late for that," David replied.

"You should've seen this coming, old man," Reggie said, grabbing Ellis by the back of his hair, and pulling a switchblade from his pocket. He yanked Ellis's head back, and whispered, "You always told me business was cutthroat."

Reggie dragged the blade quickly and firmly across Ellis's throat from ear to ear. Ellis gasped and tried to scream but his vocal cords were cut.

David holstered his gun and watched Ellis grasping at his throat and squirming as he bled out.

"You look like shit," Reggie said to David, wiping his blade clean on Ellis's robe while the man was still writhing.

"It's been a rough day," said David. Ellis was still now, but his blood continued to spill. David stepped back to avoid getting any on his shoes.

"Looks like everything worked out," Reggie replied, hitting the joint he'd stolen from Ellis. "You want some of this?"

"Eh, what the hell," David answered after a moment of consideration, taking the joint and inhaling deeply. "We good here?" he asked Reggie, passing it back to him.

"Take me a day or two to smooth out the transition, but yeah…" Reggie paused and looked at Ellis's bloody body slumped over in the chair. "We good."

"Remember this," David told him before leaving. "Because that could be you one day." He motioned to Ellis. "At the end of the day, there will always be someone in your crew, or another crew, who's eager to take your place, and no matter how much money you have, you will never have a badge."

Reggie nodded. "No doubt. I think we'll have a long and prosperous relationship."

"And any debts that Ellis thought I owed him are done. Agreed?"

"You the king maker," Reggie said, extending his fist for David to bump. "I got it."

"That's right," David replied, pounding Reggie's fist with his own. "Enjoy your kingdom, Reggie. Keep the violence to a minimum, no shootings on the streets, and keep that shit out of the schools. Got it?"

"Yeah, I know the rules," Reggie said.

"Who's gonna help you clean this up? Someone you can trust?" David asked, looking at the bloody mess.

"Lot of hungry people out there," Reggie said with a smile.

David nodded, relieved that he wouldn't have to deal with any of it. Now, all he had to worry about was what he was going to tell his wife.

28

VINCENT WAS A newly built residential neighborhood developed by Grant Newton in Mount Pleasant. Like most of Newton's developments, Vincent had been the source of considerable controversy from its initial conception and was a continued source of contention. Depending on which website Daren read, Newton was either an innovator challenging the status quo or a greedy developer that would destroy the town if not stopped. Daren was interested to talk to him because he was the owner of the property where Devon Grey was hanged.

After reaching out, Newton had invited Daren to Vincent, so he could see his work for himself. They'd agreed to meet at the Irish pub located near the main entrance of the neighborhood.

"I have to admit. I don't think I've seen a residential suburban neighborhood with its own pub," Daren remarked, sipping his beer.

"That's right, Daren," Newton replied. "After you've finished your beer, we'll take a little drive, and I'll show you what I mean when I talk about how mine's a different approach to building."

Newton was a middle-aged man with gray hair and an Irishman's pale complexion. He spoke with a smooth, almost elegant, low-country accent that made everything he said sound charming. Despite his wealth, Newton drove an old pickup truck and dressed rather casually. Daren found him interesting, particularly the way he spoke about developing—like he had his own philosophy on the matter.

After lunch, they climbed into Newton's Chevy, and he proceeded to give Daren a tour. The neighborhood was large but had narrow, windy roads. There were no speed bumps or traffic singles. The homes were quite beautiful, too.

"We wanted them to look like classic lowcountry colonial era homes but new," Newton said. "It's about taking what's good from history—the beautiful architecture, the big porches, the gas-powered lanterns—and combining it with the modern. The feeling of historic charm without the rats and the electrical problems."

"It's a very distinctive neighbor," Daren admitted, looking around.

"We wanted the front porches right up close to the road. Today, everything is built based on exclusion. In the old days, people wanted to be near the road. They wanted to hang out on their porches and talk with their neighbors. And that creates these beautiful walls for each street."

"Yeah, I noticed there were no front yards," said Daren.

"The entire concept of a front yard is wasteful, and a perfect example of how we build everything wrong today."

"What's wrong with a front yard?"

"It's taking space for no reason. Then you have to use water to keep them green and expend time and energy to cut and maintain. What a ridiculous concept." Newton maneuvered the truck down the windy streets and came to a stop next to a lake. "We got two manmade lakes here, and some really picturesque canals. Not to mention several parks throughout. Those are functional, community spaces that add value for everyone, and we were able to build them because each lot is only a half-acre, with no lawns."

"It's really beautiful," Daren said.

"Let's walk out to the pier," Newton suggested.

Daren agreed and followed the builder out to the water. At the end of the pier, they sat on the bench and took in the view. It was a breathtaking neighborhood.

"It's like a paradise," said Daren. "But you have to be a millionaire to live here, right? What's the average home go for?"

"Now we're starting to get at your line of questioning on the phone," Newton replied. "Why some people don't like me or my work." He sighed and looked off across the lake. "The average home, to answer your question, Daren, goes for just over a million dollars. So, yes, I am afraid this neighborhood has become a wealthy enclave of sorts. But it wasn't supposed to be," he explained.

"We come back to my philosophy about building," Newton continued. "I am sorry to keep boring you with this kind of stuff, but I think it's important to understand if you want to understand the types of disputes I'm involved in."

"It's fine," Daren assured him. "Please, go on."

"I think we need to build neighborhoods and cities like we did before the modern era—before suburban sprawl. Before we decided that building should be a way to keep people apart, it used to be more organic and practical. Development used to bring people together.

"Then after the Civil War, white people began building outside urban centers, away from the populations they could no longer own. They passed segregation and zoning laws to enforce barriers based on race and class. Things changed and people didn't want to live beside one another anymore; they wanted to protect the value of their property. That meant exclusion. The more exclusive a place was, the more valuable it was on the market. So, the incentive to build exclusive, suburban neighborhoods was there, and entire industries arose and became dependent on this new model: oil companies, automobile companies, construction companies, and endless lobbyists.

"Of course, the feds said they couldn't red line anymore in the seventies. But white suburbia found a way. Developments of carefully planned market value price out entire demographics out of cities.

"Then they built all these poorly designed, cookie-cutter neighborhoods along one or two main strips, like lollipops—thousands of homes, all with multiple vehicles, all full of people who have to commute to work on the same roadways. So, what happens? Everything gets congested, so we build *more roads* or we widen the roads that are already there. Only we're not going to tear up our new suburban McMansions, right? So, we tear up poor neighborhoods—we tear up Black neighborhoods. Now those people have nowhere to live. Why? Because nobody around here wants to build affordable housing when the profit margins are so much better on high-end real estate."

"Wow," said Daren. "This is a lot to take in."

"Vincent has residential, commercial, and public zoning all in one neighborhood," Newton explained. "That in and of itself was almost impossible to achieve. But it was also supposed to have housing of varying values, including *affordable apartment housing* and mid-market homes. My goal was to build a truly inclusive neighborhood, where people of all backgrounds and classes could live, work, and play without having to drive anywhere."

"Seems like a great idea," said Daren. "I don't understand why people would be opposed to that."

"The surrounding neighborhoods were convinced the development would bring the value of their neighborhoods down. Every aspect of this design was criticized. I was told none of it would work:

the street layout, the plot sizes, the lack of uniformity in housing design, and particularly the commercial real estate. But it's larger than that," Newton tried to explain. "This threatens the current model. There's a lot of money in keeping things the way that they are—powerful lobbies." Do you think oil companies or Detroit want us to build walkable neighborhoods? They want us to need cars for everything."

"Tell me about the property on Ashley Circle," Daren prompted.

"Not much to tell. We had a great plan to put a mixed-use development—"

"Mixed-use?"

"Residential, commercial, and civic use all in one place. Like Vincent but with apartments and more commercial space. Of course, the NIMBY groups got together and sued, like they always seem to do."

"The 'Not In My Backyard' people?"

"Yeah, that's right. This one got blocked because of environmental impact, but they always find some reason. My favorite is when they say the commercial properties and affordable homes will bring 'the *wrong kind* of people.'"

Daren raised his eyebrows and shook his head in disbelief. "You ultimately won the lawsuit, though, right?" he asked.

"Yes, but it all took some time and our investment partners and the companies that were committed all pulled out. Nobody wants to keep their money tied up in a project that might never move forward. So, it's on the market now, and I lost a good chunk of change. The murder you're investigating obviously didn't help the situation," Newton added.

Daren looked around at the lovely homes lining the lake. Two children sat on the far shore, playing with a little remote-controlled boat. "Do you think you've made some real enemies doing what you do?" he asked the developer.

"Oh, I suppose," Newton acknowledged. "But you know, any man who stands for something is bound to."

"I guess I'm wondering if someone could have chosen that spot to lynch Devon Grey as a way to fuck you over," Daren mused.

"I'm sorry, I just don't see it," said Newton. "It's just not logical. The properties and the investors had already pulled out. I don't see what it would have accomplished."

"Have you had much interest from prospective buyers?"

"Well, no," Newton admitted. "I suppose not."

"You think racist groups would take issue with the way you build?" Daren asked.

"Well, sure. Like I said, the way we build now is about exclusion and segregation. I would imagine that people who don't want to live near specific groups of people probably don't like the idea of getting rid of zoning much." But when pressed on whether he could think of a specific group that might have threatened him or given him trouble, Newton demurred. "I'm sorry, I don't think so."

Daren toured the rest of the neighborhood with Newton. It really was wonderfully designed. It felt elegant yet down to earth. The homes were a lot like those he'd seen in the historic areas of downtown Charleston. But those homes were reminders of the troubling history from which they came. The new houses here in Vincent stood for something else. They were beacons of a possible future, not monuments to the past.

After the tour, Daren thanked Newton for his time. "I'm sorry I couldn't be of more help," Newton told him. "I wish you the best of luck in your investigation."

It was another lead that seemed to go nowhere. Frustrated, Daren headed back to his hotel. Maybe Watts would have better luck with Devon Grey's cousin.

The drug game in any major city is too much for police to handle. Between elected leaders exerting pressure, and the media reporting about it all the time, the cops had to do something. That just meant busting street-level dealers, which were usually just children and small-time dealers. The real movers never touched the drugs and rarely saw consequences. For that reason, among others, Andrea never cared for narcotics work. She'd become a cop to help protect people, not to ruin people's lives. If it were up to her, drugs would be decriminalized. Prohibition is what created the environment where crime and violence were commonplace.

That being the case, Andrea didn't have any informants or connections in the drug world. She had driven around all morning, asking groups of teens around the mall if they knew where she could find Malik. Nobody wanted to talk.

It was nearly noon when she found a group of six boys standing outside of a small corner store. Andrea parked her car and got out to approach them. One wore an Atlanta Braves hat and a bright red tank top. He flashed her a smile. "Got your skies on, shorty? We got mad snow," he said. He couldn't have been a day over sixteen.

"Nah, I ain't about that," Andrea declined.

"Some trees then," the boy suggested. "We got that sour diesel! Bomb-ass-shit!"

"I'm looking for a player named Malik," she said, flashing her badge.

All the boys scattered except for the one she was talking to, he just smiled and laughed. "So, you the twelve that's been asking around for me all day," he laughed. "What, you one of Ellis's cops?"

"I'm sorry, what?" Andrea asked, unsure of his implication.

"Ain't no thing," Malik dismissed. "Whatchu need?"

"My name is Detective Watts," said Andrea. "I wanted to talk to you about your cousin."

"Which one? Jamie? I told y'all I didn't take his damn scooter. He got drunk and left it somewhere or some shit," Malik explained.

"No," said Andrea. "I mean your cousin Devon."

"Oh, word," said Malik. "Fucked up what happened to him."

"Yeah, it is." Andrea paused, searching for the right way to ask. "Malik, did you see Devon the night he was killed?" Malik looked at her skeptically. "I'm not a narcotics officer, Malik," she assured him. "I don't give a damn how you make your money."

"Sure, but if I end up in one of your reports, someone who is gonna come lookin' into me," he argued. "Facts."

"I can't say for sure that won't happen," Andrea admitted. "But it might help us figure out who killed your cousin. Nobody else knows where he was that night at any point. You can be a big help. Don't you want that?"

"I don't want to go to jail," Malik replied. "Devon's already dead. I'm still fighting out here."

"I'll do everything I can to keep your name out of this," she told him.

"But you can't promise."

"No, I can't promise," she conceded.

"Sorry, I can't help you," he replied.

Andrea sighed, weighing her options, and hating herself for what she was about to do. "You already tried to sell me drugs," she said. "Tell me what I want to know and live free another day, or turn around and put your hands against the wall. The choice is yours."

"Damn! You cold as hell!" Malik complained.

"I'm fighting out here, just like you," she shot back.

"Yeah, Devon came around for some smoke that evening," he begrudgingly admitted. "But it wasn't no thing. Like nothin' happened."

"Where did you meet him?" she asked.

"He came 'round to my place. Ashley River Apartments."

"Your crew have any beefs that day, or at all in the days before?"

"Nah," Malik replied, but he seemed to be holding back.

"Any beefs at all?" Andrea pried.

"Not really," he demurred.

"Tell me about the arrangement that brought your crew here," she prodded. "Why aren't y'all working the area by your crib anymore?"

"Because we ain't stupid."

"Who runs that territory?" she asked.

"Like, I said, I ain't stupid," Malik grumbled.

"So, somebody you're afraid of," Andrea noted. Who's Ellis? Is it possible that Devon got mixed up in some of that?"

Malik laughed. "You must be trippin'. Devon was lynched! If some brothas wanted to send me a message or something, they'd come at us straight. Nah, ain't no homies lynching people. Besides, ain't nobody have any reason to fuck with me, let alone my cousin for buying a fucking dub!"

"Tell me about Ellis," she repeated.

"Ellis Bartley runs the area where we used to work, iight?" Malik snapped. "But you didn't hear that shit from me—last thing I need," he muttered.

"And Ellis has cops on his take?"

"You heard what I said," Malik replied, shaking his head.

"Alright," she said. "What time did you see your cousin that night?"

"I don't know, maybe 'round 8-9 o'clock."

Andrea nodded and handed the boy her card. "If you think of anything else, give me a call."

Malik laughed and dropped her card on the pavement. "Nah, can't be having that shit on me," he said. She turned to leave but he called after her. "I hope you catch them racist ass motherfuckers who killed my cousin!"

Andrea nodded her understanding, got into her car, and drove away. She checked her phone—Pastor Mosley had called to tell her he had the printouts of all the hateful comments the church had received on social media, and that she was welcome to come by and pick them up. She texted Daren to tell him she was going to do so and would meet him at his hotel after.

29

WEST ASHLEY - SUMMER 2015

DAVID KNOCKED ON the door and waited nervously for an answer. His partner, Greg, stood behind him, shining his flashlight on the stoop. David knocked again, but there was no answer.

"I say we just leave," Greg suggested, shining his light around the property. "Honestly, we'll just tell dispatch we showed up and no one answered. Must be a false report."

"Yeah, except we have to make sure no one is in danger," David replied, pounding his leather-gloved fist firmly against the door. "Charleston County Sheriff's Office, open up!" he yelled.

"It's the *Lieutenant's house*, for fuck sakes, bro!" Greg chastised him. "If he's in there, he's going to have a fucking shit…"

"Yeah, well, somebody fucking called us, so…" David knocked again. "I don't know what else we're supposed to do."

Skip's department-issued SUV sat in the driveway outside of the attached two-car garage. Greg cast his light over the vehicle. He walked over to the garage and shined his light through the windows of the garage door. "I don't see shit," he said. "Let's just say it was a false report. Somebody's probably just trying to get Skip swatted or something."

David sighed and looked around. It was nearly 3 AM and none of the neighbors appeared to be awake. Perhaps, it had been a false report. "Alright, maybe we can call him or something."

Just as they were about to leave, the door cracked open. Skip peered out from the darkness, looking drunk and disheveled. "Hey, boss, y'all good in there?" David asked, trying to see into the house. It was a nice home—it looked a lot like his.

"Hey, boys," Skip grumbled. "Yeah, everything is fine. Did the Smiths call?" He leaned outside and leered at the house next door. *"They should mind their fucking business!"*

"Having a rough night, I see, sir," David remarked.

"But everything is fine, right, sir?" Greg was quick to add.

"Everything is fine, boys," Skip said, stepping forward enough for David to see the blood on his shirt.

"Sir, are you hurt?" David asked.

"It's nothing," Skip insisted.

Inside, David could hear Skip's wife sobbing. "Sir, is Moira okay in there?" he asked.

Skip looked back into the house nervously. "I—I—didn't even mean to do it, Sullivan. *It was an accident!*"

"It's okay, sir," David assured him. "How is Moira? Is she alright?"

Skip nodded slowly. "Just a little banged up."

"Can I see her, sir?" David asked.

"We just want to make sure everyone is alright," Greg reassured him.

"Hey," David said in a hushed tone. "I can help you, Skip. But I need to know Moira is okay." Skip nodded and opened the door to let them in.

David found Moira in the kitchen, holding a bag of ice up to her swollen, bloody lip. She also had an ugly bruised lump on her forehead.

David took a seat beside her. She was scared and unsure of what to do. "Hi, David," she greeted him. "How's Marie?"

"She's good, Moira," said David. "How are you?"

"She's fine," Skip interjected. "See?"

Moira tried her best to smile. "I'm okay, boys. Really, no need for the fuss," she said, noticeably holding back tears.

Greg looked at David who looked at Skip. "Sullivan," Skip said, nearly pleading. "This is the last time. *I promise.*"

David sighed and nodded. "We'll mark it down as a crank call," he said. Skip thanked them and they left.

"How many times has this happened?" Greg asked as they drove away from the house.

"This is the second time I have been called here. First was by Moira herself. Then she insisted I leave once I got there," David told him. "Women like that... What are you supposed to do? If they won't leave..."

Greg shrugged. "Skip likes to drink, huh?"

"No less than you," David teased. "Doubt he likes coke as much as you, though," he laughed.

"That reminds me," said Greg. "Tell Ellis I need some more. I'm not buying it off one of his street peddlers like some common junkie."

"You can tell him yourself when we have our meet tomorrow," David said. "Don't do too much of that shit, bro. It will get ahold of you."

"Don't worry about it," Greg scoffed. "I'm fine." David raised his eyebrows skeptically and lit a smoke. "Didn't Skip tell you to stop smoking in here?" he asked.

"I don't think Skip is going to be saying much to us about anything from here on out," David replied with a smokey grin.

30

THE LAMP SHATTERED against the wall. Marie jumped back in fear. Her face was flushed and wet with tears. "This is not okay!" she yelled. "You can't just break shit and throw shit around to get your way!"

David snarled. "Oh, now *I'm* the asshole! You push me and push me, Marie! I tell you to stop. I try to walk away, *but no!*"

"Because I'm worried about you!" she cried. "Because you disappeared in the middle of dinner last night. You come back, your clothes are covered in blood, and you won't tell me what happened!"

David paced furiously around the living room. "I told you, Marie! I can't talk about it! It's work, and honestly, you wouldn't want to fucking know." He was incensed. She had been riding him all day. He had told her to stop—to leave him be, but she just kept on. *And that look she had given him!* Like he was some kind of monster! She was so scared of a little blood. Such a typical woman—too fragile to comprehend the things men had to do. "I honestly don't know what you want from me," he protested. "This is who I am! I'm an angry person who's been kicked down by life time and time again. I'm tired of getting kicked, and I sure as shit don't want to talk about how it makes me *feel!* But you judge me for that!"

"No!" Marie sobbed. "I've never judged you! You judge yourself and pretend it's coming from me, David!" She shook her head and tried to calm herself. "It's you! You believe all the awful things about yourself that you think I believe."

Her words burrowed into his chest and left a lump in his throat. The next thing he knew he was in his office, the door slammed shut behind him. His hand trembled in pain. He looked at it, swollen, bloody, and red. Vague recollections of putting his fist through a door fluttered through his mind. Which door had it been? Was it the bathroom door? Wait, was it the door to Sean's room? No, it couldn't have been... *Was it?* Was that why the boy had looked at him with such fear? Or had the boy's look provoked his punching the door? Was it Sean's door he had punched? Everything was a blur.

When the rage took hold, it was as if his anger was behind the wheel. Rationality flew out the window. It felt like he was a hostage to his impulses, watching them play out and being unable to stop them. The rage clouded his memories, too. It wasn't that he was unable to recall what had happened, but as if the memory were fuzzy and disordered.

Still furious but wanting to calm down, David grabbed a joint and a lighter from his desk drawer and stormed out of his office for the bathroom. Marie was in the hall, assessing the damage to the bathroom door. "Move," he said gruffly, somewhat relieved to see it hadn't been Sean's door he'd struck.

She jumped out of his way like a squirrel dodging traffic. He slammed the bathroom door behind him, then stuffed a towel through the hole his fist had left to ensure his privacy.

No waiting for the tub to fill this time—he stripped down immediately and climbed in, sitting on the linoleum as the cold water filled in around him. He lit the joint and let the cold slowly wash over him. In his mind, he pictured his anger causing the water to boil.

Inhale. Exhale. David coughed. His hand trembled as the adrenaline wore off and the pain made its presence known. "Fucking dirtbag," he called himself, examining his hand. Marie was right about that much—he did believe the worst about himself.

The stress was getting to him, too. While everything with Ellis had been worked out, there was still a matter of Andrea and that fed who was snooping around. Could he trust her? What if she found out about his relationship with Ellis? David smoked his joint and tried to calm down, but the weed only increased his paranoia.

After his bath, he went out to the backyard with a beer and listened to the cicadas sing. He thought about his life and the person he'd become. He thought about all the shitty and awful things he'd ever done. Then, for some reason, he thought about his mother. Though he tried not to, he often wondered where she was. Wherever it was, she didn't want to see him.

He sat there for some time, thinking it all over, holding his beer, his revolver sitting on his lap. It had but one bullet inside. If it had not been for the fact that he feared what his boy and others may have thought of him, David may just have eaten that bullet. He didn't want people to remember him as weak, though.

Pizza is standard fuel for late-night work sessions. Daren opened the box and examined the last piece of pepperoni and sausage. "You want it?" he asked Andrea.

"It's all you," she replied, shaking her head, her focus trained on his laptop screen.

They'd been taking turns reading through pages of hateful comments while the other looked up the commenter's social media pages and personal information. It was a long, tedious, and thus far unproductive task. Around 11 pm, they'd ordered pizza and Daren had gone out to grab some beer. Now, shortly after midnight, the pizza was gone and the twelve pack of beer was quickly headed in the same direction.

"Yeah, I think I'm actually full," Daren said, shutting the pizza box. He sat on the edge of the bed where Andrea was working and examined the stack of papers she had brought over from Pastor Mosley.

"Well, get back to it, then," she said. "We got a ton of comments to go through still."

Daren sighed. "Can we pick up on this tomorrow?"

Andrea shot him a sympathetic look. "Burnt out?"

"Honestly, yes," he confessed. "I'm having a hard time seeing how close some of these comments are to things I used to think or even say myself. Not the explicitly racist stuff, but this attitude that Black people must be somehow responsible for their problems. Just *'Get a job!'* or *'Get a better job!'* People wondering, *'Why is there so much crime in Black communities?'* instead of looking at the country and asking what we did to create these situations."

Andrea nodded. "If I'm being honest, this crisis you're having is a little infuriating."

"Really?" he asked, surprised. "How is my realizing these things infuriating for you?"

"Because you represent so many Americans who just don't fucking get it," she said. "It's plain as day, written in large, bold print. Yet y'all don't see it. But now that the blood from that system is on your hands, *now* you've been forced to see it for what it is. I get it, I do," she added. "It's like I said, we're all products of our experiences. Yours was sheltered. So, I am happy for you, Daren. I'm happy you see things clearer now, but you're all up in my ear telling me the sky's blue and wanting me to what—praise you for it?"

"Yeah, I guess I could see how that might seem patronizing."

"It *is* patronizing," she corrected him with a smile.

"I'm sorry." Daren leaned over, opened the minifridge, and retrieved another beer. "Guess I'm just realizing how wrong I've been about a lot of things," he said.

"Humility, my friend," Andrea said warmly. "It will prevent you from dismissing other people's experiences *and* from patronizing them about it after you've figured out you're an ass."

Daren chuckled. "Is that all I need?"

"Mm-hm."

"So, what do you say? Want to call it a night?" he asked, lying back on the bed.

"Yeah, probably a good idea," she muttered. But when she punched a few keys on the laptop, her eyes widened. "Wait—" she said. "Hold on." She punched a few more keys. "Oh, shit."

"You got something?" Daren asked, sitting up.

"I think so. Look at this," she replied, scooching closer so he could see the screen. "One of the pages that left a few hateful comments last year has a group—The European Heritage Association."

"Sounds familiar," Daren noted.

"Check out their group logo," she said, pointing to the screen.

The logo was the life rune—the same symbol that Josh Dylan's similarly named group had used. The same symbol that had been carved into the tree where Devon Grey was hanged.

"Well, now that is certainly interesting," said Daren.

"There's more," she told him. "The group's administrator is listed as none other than Joshua Dylan."

"Motherfucker…"

"Which backs up what Avery said about his son and their intentions," Andrea concluded. "Maybe he's right, and Josh Dylan is the man we're after."

"But Josh Dylan was in North Carolina the night Devon Grey was killed," Daren argued. "Multiple eyewitnesses confirm as much."

"Yes, but there are other eight other members in this group," Andrea noted.

"Who are they? Can you see?" he asked.

"Not unless I'm a member of the group," she explained.

Daren took out his phone and made a call.

"Who are you calling?" Andrea asked. "It's after midnight."

"I'm calling the Bureau to get a warrant expedited, so we can force this website to give us those group members' names and info." Daren held out his finger, telling her to wait a moment. "Yes, this special agent Daren Renard," he said into the phone. "I need a warrant expedited immediately… Yes, I'll hold." Daren muted his phone, turned on the speaker, and placed it on the counter.

"What if Avery is right about this group wanting to start a race war? And what if you're right about the pigs? What if this group is connected to both, and they're planning some sort of attack?" Andrea thought out loud.

Chills ran through Daren's body. "I want that theory to be wrong," he said. "But I'm afraid that there's a chance you may be right."

"There's huge right-wing rally downtown tomorrow," Andrea noted. "That might just bring our persons of interest to us. Seems like their kind of event."

"We need to be down there," Daren agreed. "We need to get the names of these groups members and get their pictures to every law enforcement officer downtown. Any of them show up at the rally, we pull them in for questioning."

Andrea nodded. "You think they hung Devon?"

"Their signature is on the crime," Daren replied. "They're our only suspects right now." Andrea rose to her feet and grabbed her keys off the counter. "Where you going?" he asked.

"To get some coffee. It's going to be a long night."

Police officers have a distinct knock—three knocks with a pause after the first was common. But even when the pattern was different, the knock was distinct. It announced itself with the authority of someone who was coming in whether you wanted them to or not. When able, they would often ring the bell too. This was always a telltale sign the police were at your door. No casual visitor or even a nosey solicitor would first ring and then immediately knock—it was pure entitlement. David knew this well; it's how he knocked on doors at work. It was about establishing authority and control of the situation. The interaction was on the lawman's terms from the moment it was initiated.

That's why when David heard their doorbell ring, followed immediately by a distinctively authoritative knock, he leapt from the tub with urgency and peered out the bathroom window to the driveway. There he saw a Mount Pleasant police cruiser parked with its headlights on and the engine running. He could see two officers at their front door. That's when, to his horror, he heard Marie answer the door.

"*Shit!*" he exclaimed under his breath, grabbing a towel and wrapping it around his waist as he bolted from the bathroom. He crept to the edge of the stairs that led from the hall down to the front door, pressed his back against the wall, and tried to hear what was happening.

"Ma'am, we got a call about a domestic disturbance," David heard one of the officers tell Marie.

"No, sir, it's nothing like that," Marie politely insisted. "My husband was watching the game and… Well, you know how men get," she said with a forced laugh.

"Ma'am," the officer replied. "Are you okay? You're trembling?"

"I guess I feel like I'm getting pulled over," Marie said, forcing another laugh. "Makes me nervous!"

"Is your husband home, ma'am?" the other officer asked her.

"He is in the shower, actually," said Marie.

"What game was he watching?" the first officer asked.

"Oh, I don't know… It's all the same to me…"

"Ma'am," the officer replied. "What happened to your arm?" David furrowed his brow, unsure what the officer was talking about. "Nothing," Marie insisted. "I just bumped it."

"Looks like fingerprints," the second officer remarked.

"Ma'am, we're going to need to come inside," the first officer insisted.

"*Shit!*" David cursed to himself as he darted down the hall into the bedroom to retrieve his pants and badge. Then he hustled back to the door where his wife was doing her best to keep the two officers out.

"My son is asleep, y'all. Is this really necessary? I told you, everything is fine," said Marie, her voice panicked.

David came down the steps and put his hand on his wife's shoulder. "Honey, I'll take care of this," he told her. "Go on upstairs." Then he whispered, *"Call Skip,"* into her ear. Reluctantly, she headed upstairs. "It's okay, baby," David reassured her. Then, turning to the officers, he said, "Gentlemen, can I help you?"

"Good evening, sir. We got a call about a domestic disturbance. Caller said that you were out of control," the officer told him. "Anything going on you want to tell me about?"

"No, I was—uh—I just got angry about the game," David laughed. "Kind of embarrassing, honestly."

"What game was that, sir?" the officer asked.

David flashed his badge. "Listen, boys. I appreciate you coming out, but this is all a misunderstanding."

The first officer inspected David's badge. "Sure, sergeant. Mind if we come in and look around, just to make sure."

"You already talked to my wife," David objected. "What more could you want?"

"Alright, listen," the officer said. He stepped closer to the door and lowered his voice. "We're obviously not supposed to tell you this, but your boy was the one who called us."

David shook his head. "You must be mistaken."

"Any chance, when you got angry about the game, that you scared him?" the other officer asked.

"I mean—if he called—then yeah, that's what must've happened. But I don't think—" David stammered, in shock.

"Sergeant Sullivan," the officer replied firmly. "Your son called us. I'm sorry, but we're going to have to come in and make sure he's okay."

"Sir, is that marijuana I smell?" the second officer asked.

"I'm sorry?" David asked indignantly. "What did you just ask me?"

"Sir, please step aside," the first officer ordered him, his hand hovering over his taser. David sighed and stepped back to let them in, his mind racing.

Just then the second officer's cell phone rang. He looked at the screen and nudged the first office. "It's the chief…" he said in disbelief.

"Why is the chief calling you?" the first officer asked the second. "At this hour?" But the second officer just shook his head and shrugged. "Well, g'on then! Answer it!" the first officer barked.

"Hello?" the second officer said into his phone. "Hey, chief… Yes, sir… Yeah, we are…" He looked at David. "Uh-huh… Okay… Alright, then…. Yes, sir… Thank you, sir… You betcha." The officer tucked the phone into his pocket, looked at his partner, and shook his head. "Chief says Sergeant Sullivan here is an upstanding member of our community, and we needn't bother him any further."

The first officer nearly did a double take. "Oh, well, I do apologize, Sergeant," he said, obviously embarrassed and maybe afraid for his job. "We didn't know—we have to come when we get a call."

"Hey, that's okay," David said, flashing a warm smile. "I really do appreciate you coming here. Especially if you thought my family was in trouble." He shook both their hands. "Thank you for coming out," he added. "Sorry to take you away from more important things."

David shut the door and looked up the stairs at Marie. Her eyes were puffy and red from crying. "You called Skip?" he asked.

"Yeah," she replied meekly. "He said he would take care of it."

David was relieved but also suddenly ashamed. He sank to the floor and slumped against the door. Marie came down the stairs and sat beside him, placing her hand on his leg to console him. He looked at her with pain in his eyes and shook his head. Then he saw her arm. "I did that?" he asked.

She rubbed her arm and looked down at the floor. "It's nothing," she said.

Vague memories of grabbing her by the arm came back to him. He had only wanted to get by her, never to harm her.

David took Marie's hand and kissed it softly. Tears trailed from his eyes and onto her hand, and she too began to cry. "I'm so sorry," he sobbed. "I'm a monster…"

"You're not a monster," she told him adamantly. She took his head into her hands and wiped the tears from his cheek with her fingers.

"You don't know, Marie. You don't understand what I'm capable of," he confessed.

"I don't know you?" she asked, pulling his head onto her breast. She held him and caressed him, running her fingers through his hair as he cried. "You're my husband," she said. "I know you."

He wanted to let her love him and comfort him, but he knew he didn't deserve it. He pulled away and shook his head. "No, Marie. You wouldn't say that if you knew me. I've killed people. That blood on my clothes yesterday…" he stopped, trying to find the words. "I'm so angry all the time."

Marie blinked a few times to process what she had heard. "Did you do it to protect yourself or someone else?" she asked. David nodded. "Then you're not a monster," she concluded.

"It's not that simple," he argued. "Look at this house. Look at your arm. Our own son thinks I'm dangerous. He called the police on me, Marie." Had he become his old man? He couldn't help but think his family would be better off if he were dead.

"David, you need help, baby," Marie pleaded. "Ever since Gregory—"

"Don't," he interrupted, anger emerging from the grief. "Don't start."

"I'm just saying, you've been worse lately, baby. You need to talk to someone."

"About what, Marie?" he asked, sitting up and pulling away from her.

"Anything and everything," she exclaimed. "Whatever is bothering you."

"I'm supposed to talk about how my father would tie me outside to the porch in the cold when he was angry? How he would threaten to give me away? How we would tie me down and beat me with his belt? Or how my mother left him and never bothered to call or write me?"

"Yes."

"And that's going to what?" David scoffed. "Make it all better? Fix it, somehow?"

"I don't know, honestly," she replied. "But you gotta do something. David, please…" He lowered his head into her lap and cried. He felt so powerless, empty, and broken.

31

IT WAS BEFORE dawn when the sky gives its first hints of the coming day. Daren peered out his hotel window and over the rooftops of nearby buildings to the ocean beyond. He and Andrea had been up all night running down leads, making phone calls, waking up judges, and getting warrants. After several hours of tense phone calls, they were able to get the list of individuals who were in the European Heritage Association's social media group.

Andrea had been downstairs in the hotel's business center printing pages of background information and rap sheets on most of the men on the list. She came back into the room holding a large stack of paper, shaking her head in disbelief. "You're never going to guess what I just found," she said.

"Is it free continental breakfast?" Daren quipped. "Because I heard it's good. What does that mean, anyway—*continental* breakfast?"

Andrea raised her eyebrow wryly. It was too early for such poor humor. "Look," she said, handing him two pages from the stack. "Roger and Thomas Mayfield. Both did stints in county lock-up where they joined up with the Aryan Nation."

"Why is it always the ugly ones preaching about the so-called white master race?" Daren asked, grimacing at that their photos.

"Ain't their looks I'm concerned with," Andrea remarked. "Look at their employer."

"McHale Farms?"

"A pig farm in the Pee Dee."

"The what now?"

"The Pee Dee—it's what we call the northeast corner of the state."

"I'm not going to ask," Daren said with a shake of his head. "So, did we call these boys' employer?"

"I just did, and they were fired on Monday—"

"For stealing pigs," Daren said, connecting the dots.

"You guessed it!" she exclaimed. "Owner said he never liked them because they were cruel to the animals."

"Feds and local law enforcement here and in North Carolina have tracked down and accounted for every name on that list except Spencer Lawrence and the Mayfields," he informed her. "The Bureau will comb through every one of their homes, vehicles, workplaces, and anywhere they might keep stuff. Primarily, they'll be looking to see if there is evidence of any sort of plot, but if there is any evidence of what happened to Devon Grey, they'll find it."

"We should get down to local PD," Andrea suggested. "If Lawrence or the Mayfields show up for the rally today, we can scoop them up."

Daren nodded. "Alright then. Let's go."

"Unless you wanted to catch some rest," Andrea offered. "I can go."

"I'm fine," Daren said, brushing off her concern.

"You look a little rough, Renard."

"I haven't slept well in days," he confessed. "But now's not the time."

Daren didn't want to cause panic, but he had an increasing sense of anxiety concerning these Mayfield brothers. He wanted to find them as soon as possible before they had the chance to hurt anyone.

Cannons filled with concrete—now mere monuments to the wars in which they killed—were arranged pointing out over the water. Located at the base of the peninsula, the battery was one of Charleston's most popular parks. There, American colonists had defended South Carolina from his Majesty's Royal Navy during the War for Independence. Then, less than a century later, it was used to defend the city from the Union in a war fought to keep people enslaved. Now monuments to both wars and their seemingly opposing ideals stood side by side on the battery. It was here that the neo-confederates would gather to wave their Confederate flags and agitate locals and tourists alike every weekend. At first, there had been only a few but slowly, it grew. New groups began to gather together to defend the statues and their supposed heritage. When the counter-protests began, things started to get heated.

So, when Black activists found out that a large, well-funded right-wing gathering dubbed the "Save Our Heritage Rally" was being held at nearby Marion Square, they immediately planned a counter-protest at battery park—or White Point Garden, as the folks at city hall called it. From there, they would march as close to Marion Square as the city police would allow. Andrea already knew she would find Mikayla there among the counter-protesters.

Daren dropped her off near the battery. "I'll go swing by the rally and check in with the chief of police," he told her. "Call me if you see anything," he added.

She agreed and headed off towards the crowd. There were at least a few hundred people gathered there, holding signs and banners. To her surprise, the crowd was quite diverse. Black activists stood with allies of all colors. Their signs displayed messages like *Black Lives Matter* and *No Monuments to Hate!*

Andrea was dressed to blend with the crowd, wearing a plain red t-shirt, long enough to hide her sidearm, a blue baseball cap, and sunglasses. She spotted Mikayla and made her way to her.

"Hey, sista!" Mikayla greeted her with surprise. "Whatcha doing? Come to join the protest?" she asked as they hugged.

"Nah, girl. I'm working," Andrea replied. She took off her cap, adjusted her ponytail, and pulled it back on.

"What's North Charleston PD doing working a protest in downtown Charleston?" inquired Mikayla. "Y'all know these folks have a First Amendment, right?"

"I'm not here with North Charleston PD."

"Oh, that other thing?" Mikayla was surprised but intrigued.

Andrea nodded. "That other thing."

"I don't follow, baby. What's up?" Mikayla asked.

"We think a couple of suspects might show up at the rally." Andrea scanned the crowd. Until that moment, she hadn't considered the possible threat to these people.

"Then why aren't you over at Marion Square?" her sister asked.

Andrea was about to answer when a man on a bicycle with a green backpack whizzed by, catching her attention. The face looked familiar to her. The man stopped on the other side of the park, got off his bike, and started taking pictures of the crowd with his phone.

"I have to go check on something," said Andrea. "Just do me a favor," she added, grabbing Mikayla's hand and clasping both of hers around it.

"Sure, what?" asked Mikayla, noticeably concerned.

"If things start to get out of hand here, or if you feel unsafe for any reason, get these people out of here." She wanted to explain more, but the man was about to get back on his bike.

"Why would we be unsafe?" Mikayla asked.

"I'll be right back—just keep an eye out, please!" Andrea called over her shoulder as she took off running across the park. *"Hey!"* she yelled. *"You with the bike! Stop!"* She held up her badge. "Stay right there!" she yelled.

The man hesitated for a moment, weighing his options, then mounted his bike and took off peddling up the road. Andrea darted after him, pulling out her phone as she ran and dialing Daren. "In pursuit of a suspect!" she yelled into the phone as she rounded the corner. "He's headed up Murray!"

Around the corner, Andrea stopped and frantically looked around. The suspect was nowhere to be seen. She came to the entrance of the luxurious Apartments at the Battery, where she saw what she believed to be the suspect's bike leaning against the wall near the entrance to the parking garage. She looked around to see if Daren was nearby, then headed inside.

She emerged onto the first level of the parking garage and heard the sound of hurried footsteps up ahead. Andrea drew her weapon and carefully advanced down the row of parked cars and concrete pillars. As she reached the end of the first row of cars, the suspect emerged from behind a Subaru Legacy and bolted toward the stairs.

Andrea took off after him. He burst through the nearest doorway and down a flight of stairs, followed seconds later by Andrea. Panicked, he looked back as he was attempting to navigate the steps, tripped, and fell hard down the last few steps, landing on his back on the landing below. He grimaced in pain.

Andrea was upon him in a second, her gun trained on his torso. "Freeze, motherfucker!" Now that she was closer, she was able to identify him as Spencer Lawrence. "Got you, motherfucker." She kicked him over onto his stomach and ordered him to put his hands flat on the ground while she searched him for weapons. Finding nothing, she ordered him to stay put while she opened his book bag and looked inside. "Oh, Jesus, no…" Andrea gasped, covering her mouth with her hand in shock. The bag contained what appeared to be six pipe bombs. "What were you fixin' to do?!"

"You're too late," Spencer said with a mocking laugh.

Andrea took out her handcuffs, placed her knee on Spencer's back, and cuffed his left hand. She then yanked his arm up and cuffed the other end to the steel railing.

"*Ow! Fucking bitch!*" Spencer cried.

"Too late for what?" she demanded. Spencer just smiled and flashed her a rotten smile. Andrea cursed under her breath and began patting him down again.

"This is assault!" he protested.

Andrea retrieved his phone from his back pocket and grabbed his cuffed hand. "Oh yeah? Then what's this?" she asked, prying and twisting his index finger, and forcing it onto the phone's touchpad to unlock it.

"That's illegal!" Spencer cried. When Andrea ignored him, he let out a string of racial epithets and hateful slurs.

The pictures Spencer had taken were of the crowd and the two the police officers posted nearby. He had been sent the photos to two contacts named Roger and Tom—*the Mayfields*.

"Oh, Jesus… What have you done…" Andrea muttered?

Spencer laughed and shook his head. "I told ya. You're too late." Andrea bolted out of the stairwell and headed for the exit. *"You can't just leave me here like this!"* Spencer called after her. *"Fucking bitch!"*

The sight was enough to make any decent person sick. Confederate flags, neo-Nazi symbols, and hateful banners carried by angry crowds chanting chilling words. The rally to defend their alleged Southern heritage was really just a white supremacist rally. That much didn't surprise Daren—after all, who else was going to defend statues of men who led a rebellion to defend slavery? What did surprise him, however, was how openly groups that maintained they weren't racist were associating and marching alongside groups that proudly declared their hatred. The veil was so thin it was almost non-existent.

The rally-goers were gathered around a small stage set up near the large statue of John C. Calhoun standing upon an obelisk. Calhoun had been a prominent figure in South Carolina during the lead-up to the Civil War. Often credited as the man who caused the war, Calhoun articulated and popularized the very ideas the South used to defend slavery, and in the modern day, the arguments used to defend the Confederacy.

"We didn't expect this," a city councilman explained to Daren as they walked. "These groups have their rallies, beat their chests. We have to give them permits—First Amendment and all. But we never expected *this*. The right-wing media showed that damn freeway protest so much, they got every zealot from three states-over all worked up to come here." There must've been two-thousand or more protesters.

The chief of police shook his head. "We barely have the manpower to keep this crowd contained and the protesters at a safe distance. I'm sorry Agent Renard, but helping you locate these persons of interest just doesn't rank on my priority list."

"Chief, with due respect," Daren argued, walking fast to keep up with the two men as they headed down King Street and away from the rally. "I told you we believe these men to be a security threat. It's absolutely imperative that we locate them."

The chief stop, and waved his finger in Daren's face. "And I told you, my men have been shown their photos and if we come across one of them, we will detain them. But it's simply not our priority right now."

"But chief—" Daren started to say before he felt his cell phone vibrate in his pocket. He pulled it out and saw it was Andrea. "One monument, sir, please," he said to the chief before turning to answer the call.

Andrea was frantic and out of breath. "In pursuit of a suspect!" she yelled. Then she said something else, but Daren couldn't make out over the noise around him.

"Shit!" he exclaimed. "How do I get back to the counter-protest from here?" he asked the chief.

"About four blocks south," the chief replied, pointing to his left. "Why?" he asked, but Daren was already gone, sprinting down the street—he wasn't going to waste time explaining to the man who had already dismissed him.

Daren ran as fast as he could, knocking into a couple that was trying to take a selfie along the way. Up ahead, he could see the park green and the water beyond. He ran harder, concerned for Andrea.

Finally, he made it to the green, stopped, and nearly keeled over trying to catch his breath. He grimaced and looked around, anxious for any sight of Andrea. Not seeing her, he took out his phone and tried to call her, but it went directly to voice mail.

He walked along the sidewalk on the north side of the green, past a group of young children playing on stacks of cannonballs. In the distance, he noticed a tan pick-up truck parking along the east side of the green. It seemed to have some sort of metal container in the bed. Daren inspected it curiously as he walked closer. Something about seemed off. As he got closer, he could see that it wasn't a container at all but a single sheet of metal with a horizontal slat that ran the length of the sheet near the top. *What the hell was that?*

His phone rang again, and he answered it immediately. "Watts!" he said with relief. "Where are you? I'm at the battery."

"Daren! I apprehended Lawrence. He had a bag full of pipe bombs."

"Holy shit…"

"He sent pictures of the crowd to the Mayfields—I think they're going to attack the protest!" Andrea warned, her voice gripped in fear.

Daren zeroed back in on the truck with suspicion. He could see one adult male in the driver's seat. "I'm at the battery now," he replied to Andrea. *"Find the nearest officer! We need to clear the area now!"*

"On it," she replied. "I'm by the apartments, meet me on the north end of the park."

Daren ended the call and stuck his phone into his belt bag. Inside the pouch, he palmed the handle of his Glock and made his way across the street. He cautiously approached the tan pickup from the rear. He was only two cars away from the truck, when suddenly, shots rang out behind him, followed by several screams.

Andrea darted around the corner, the bag of pipe bombs in hand. There she found a uniformed officer in a safety vest directing foot traffic. She ran up to him, flashed her badge, and handed him the bag.

"Officer, I'm Detective Watts with the North Charleston PD, here as part of an interdepartmental FBI operation," she explained in as professional of manner as she could manage. Her heart felt like it was about to leap from her chest. "We have an emergency situation. I just detained a man with what appears to be pipe bombs," she said, opening the bag in the officer's hands.

"Holy shit!" he exclaimed, examining the contents of the bag.

"Listen to me!" she pleaded, grabbing his arm. "He's not alone! We're all in danger! Everyone here is—we need to evacuate—" Before she could finish her warning, several shots rang out from across the park. Screams and commotion followed as the crowd of protesters fled from the shots, toward the east end of the park. Andrea drew her firearm and ran toward the chaos, leaving the officer, who was frantically calling into his radio, with the bag of explosives.

Daren spun around and drew his weapon. A burst of shots had been followed by a single round. Daren scanned across the street and saw what appeared to be two bodies lying in the road. One of them, a police officer, was still moving, but she was badly hurt.

Daren rushed to aid the officer. She was struggling to move in a pool of blood. Daren knelt beside her and could see she had been shot several times, at least once in the abdomen and again in her right thigh. Lying about ten fight to her right was a heavyset man with only half a skull—the assailant she'd taken out.

"He came up behind me and shot me," she winced. "He thought I was dead, and went to open fire on the crowd. I drew on him—put him down as soon as he turned."

"We'll get you some help," Daren told her. "You saved a lot of lives." He thought about ways to tourniquet her wound, but before he could do anything, the horrific sound of a high-powered rifle rang out across the battery. *Pop. Pop-pop-pop. Pop-pop. Pop.* "Stay down!" Daren shouted to her. He knew exactly what was happening before he even looked up. The other Mayfield brother—the one whose brains weren't baking on the pavement—had climbed onto the back of that suspicious pickup truck and was now firing indiscriminately at the crowd through the slat in the metal sheet. He ran toward the source of death and carnage, his heart racing.

Pop-pop-pop. Pop. Pop. Pop-pop-pop.

Daren bolted to the nearest car parked along the north sidewalk of the park, a Black Lexus. He leaned over its hood, and fired two shots, shattering the truck's driver-side window. This got Mayfield's attention, and he turned his fire on Daren's location, just as Daren had hoped he would. The barrage of shots tore into the Lexus. Glass shattered over Daren's head as he crouched low.

Andrea was in the thick of the crowd when the barrage began. She dove to the ground with those around her, gunfire echoing around them. Several rounds hit the ground near here, displacing chunks of topsoil and dirt. "Get to the statue!" she screamed to all who could hear. She rose to her feet and helped a woman to her right onto her feet. The two then sprinted for the large confederate statue at the end of the battery. A group of a half dozen or so followed them safely to cover.

The group huddled together behind the statue as more shots rang out. Two little girls cried to their mother that their sister wasn't there. Andrea looked back at where they had run from and saw her, a scared little girl in a plaid jumper, curled up in a ball and trembling on the ground.

The girl's mother saw her at the same time and shrieked in horror. She then instinctively stood to run to her daughter, but Andrea grabbed her and held her back. *"Stay here!"* she ordered the mother.

Pop-pop-pop. Pop. Pop-pop-pop. The shots had started again, but all Andrea could think of was that poor baby girl, trembling with fear. She ran across the grass at full speed, hoping the bullets wouldn't find her. She passed men and women who'd been shot. Some were already gone; others were quickly bleeding out.

Andrea reached the girl and slid down beside her like she was sliding into home plate. She wrapped her arms around the girl. "I'm going to take you to your family!" she told her. The girl looked at her with tears streaming down her face and nodded emphatically. Andrea stood up, lifted the girl into her arms, and sprinted back to the statue. When she got there, the girl's mother took her from Andrea's arms.

"Thank you! Thank you!" the mother cried, squeezing her baby girl tight. The girl's sister joined the embrace.

Daren returned fire at the truck but knew he couldn't hit the shooter at that angle. His rounds buried themselves harmless into the truck body, or worse, ricocheted off the armor plating Mayfield had rigged to the bed.

Mayfield changed clips and was soon firing towards Daren again. Daren felt his heart racing and his breath shortening. The panic coursed through him and he felt frozen for a moment. Then he remembered what Andrea had told him at Carson's—to use the anxious energy. *Focus it.*

He leaned over the hood again, firing three shots before dodging back behind the car. But this time he didn't wait. Instead, he frantically crawled and his hands and knees to the next car, and then toward the end of the block, hoping the shooter hadn't seen him reposition. When he got to the end of the block, he slowly peeked around the corner from behind the bumper of an SUV. From there, on the east sidewalk of the park, he could see the front end and passenger side of Mayfield's truck.

The shooter fired at the Lexus Daren had been hiding behind again, confirming to Daren that his movements had not been detected. He took a deep breath and swiftly made his way toward the truck, both hands around his gun.

Pop-pop. Pop-pop. Mayfield fired at the Lexus again. Then, just as he was about to start firing at the fleeing protesters again, Daren came up behind him, pointed his Glock at the back of Mayfield's head, and fired once, killing him instantly. Mayfield never saw it coming.

A lone pistol shot seemed to end the gun fire. Andrea emerged from behind the statue cautiously and scanned the park. People cried in pain as others shouted for help. Shooting victims lay in the grass and the street; some dead, others bleeding to death. It had all been over in just a few minutes, yet so much damage had been done.

She knelt down to check the nearest victim, a middle-aged man who'd been shot in the back. He was breathing, but barely, and unconscious. Sirens echoed across the peninsula and seemed to be approaching from all directions.

The next victim she found was a young woman with red hair who'd been shot in the calf. Andrea ripped a piece of fabric from her t-shirt and used it as a tourniquet on the woman's leg. Andrea tried to talk to her, but the poor thing was in shock. She just sat there shaking, repeating over and over again: "My fiancé… My fiancé…"

Andrea looked around to see if she could flag a medic over to the woman. That's when she saw Mikayla, slumped against the pavilion steps, holding her stomach.

"No, no, no!" Andrea cried, running to her sister. There was so much blood on the steps around her, Andrea knew that it was bad. "Let me see," she said, carefully moving Mikayla's hands away from the wound.

"Somehow, I don't think looking at it is going to help," Mikayla said—always the smartass, even at a time like this.

At first, Andrea was confused. The wound was tiny and barely bleeding. Then she felt around to the back of Mikayla's abdomen and gasped. The exit wound was the size of a baseball. Mikayla slumped down, her eyes rolling into the back of her head. Having a sports bra on underneath, Andrea took off her torn t-shirt, wadded it up, and pressed it firmly against the exit wound.

"Hold on!" Andrea cried. "Hold on, baby girl. They comin'—they'll be here any minute." She looked over her shoulder and screamed, "*I need a medic!!*"

"Pray with me," Mikayla winced.

"No need for that, baby girl," Andrea insisted. "Just hold on." Tears streamed down her face. "*I need a fucking medic over here! Now!*" she cried.

"No," Mikayla groaned. She opened her bloody hand and revealed a silver crucifix, which Andrea immediately recognized. It had been their mother's. "Pray... Please, pray with me," she pleaded.

Andrea took a deep breath and took her sister's hand, clenching it in her own, the crucifix pressing between their palms. "I—I don't know what to say," she sobbed.

"It doesn't matter," said Mikayla. "Just pray," she urged her.

"Lord," Andrea started, doing her best to choke back the tears so she could speak. "Lord—I don't know why your world is full of so much pain, and hate, and suffering. None of us can ever know, I guess. But we come to you and we ask, in our hardest moments, to deliver us salvation. We come to you when the pain gets to be too much... When we don't know what else to do," she sobbed. "And we come to you, to ask for your grace... when it's time for us to come home." Mikayla's hand fell limp. Andrea took the crucifix from her sister's hand, held it to her lips, and cried.

32

DAREN HAD BEEN awake for nearly 48 hours when CPD dropped him at his hotel early the next morning. Black ribbons adorned the light posts outside the hotel. Flags flew at half-mast. The city was already mourning.

· Inside, his elevator ride was excruciatingly long; horrific images from the prior day flooded his mind as he waited for his floor. People in the hall looked at him with concern—probably because of the blood on his shirt. It wasn't his blood; it was Carol Leeds's—the beat cop who took out Thomas Mayfield before he could harm anyone else. Thanks to her heroism, the crowd had a safe direction to flee when Thomas's brother Roger opened fire from the back of his pickup. Now, Carol Leeds was in an ICU, fighting for her life.

Daren shut the door to his room tightly behind him and made sure it was locked. Finally, he was alone. He stripped on his way to the bathroom, started the shower, and hopped in before the water had a chance to warm. His hands trembled as he tried to wash. Thinking he must be cold, Daren turned the faucet, making the water as hot as he could. But no matter how hot the water got, he could not stop shaking.

He tried to dry himself afterward, but it seemed like too much work. Exhausted, he collapsed onto the bed, still sopping wet, and wrapped the blankets around him. In his mind, he saw Carol Leeds covered in blood, and heard the horrific sound of an assault rifle firing. He remembered shooting Roger Mayfield in the back of the head, and Bill Carson floating in the creek, and then, for some reason, that damn cockroach again, kicking its legs and waiting for death.

Daren began to cry and was soon sobbing loudly, cocooned in his blankets. He wasn't sure what he was crying about specifically—it was all just too much to bear. For nearly twenty-four hours straight, he'd shut off his emotions. He helped the wounded, coordinated with local detectives, and walked through the incident with the Bureau when they'd arrived. Then he had worked to coordinate the federal response with local efforts, and the entire time, he had held his feelings back. Now they were bursting out.

All of the remaining members of Josh Dylan's group had been rounded up in North Carolina, and Josh Dylan himself had been taken into federal custody attempting to board a plane for Mexico in Charlotte. The nightmare seemed to be over for now.

Daren wanted to call Andrea to see how she was doing, but he couldn't bring himself to move. Instead, he drifted to sleep.

Some hours later, Daren awoke to hear his phone ringing from somewhere in the room. He crawled out of bed and across the floor until he reached his pants, which were still lying on the ground by the door. Inside the pocket, he found his phone. "Hello?" he grumbled.

"Special Agent Renard?" asked the voice. Daren took a moment to realize it was his boss.

"Yes, sir," he replied, sitting up on the floor and clearing his throat. "Sorry, sir. It's been a rough twenty-four hours. I'm sure you know."

"You're damn right I do, and we couldn't be prouder of you," said Travers.

"I'm sorry, sir?" Daren asked, confused.

"Let me be clear: this is an awful tragedy. The country mourns with the people of Charleston. But thanks to our *hero agent*, the attack was thwarted, and countless lives were saved."

"I wouldn't say that exactly, sir—"

"Nonsense! I've read all the reports coming out of there. You shot the shooter, correct?"

"Yes, sir."

"And your deputized agent apprehended one of the suspects and prevented him from using explosive devices, correct?" asked Travers.

"Yes, sir, but—"

"Listen, we wanted a win," Travers reminded him. "Now we have one! And thanks to you two, we have brought down a homegrown domestic terrorism cell. That's fine work, Agent. Fine work."

"Thank you, sir. I appreciate that," Daren muttered. "It's just that, well, sir," he added, clearing his throat and searching for courage. "Fifteen people are dead, and ten others were shot. It doesn't feel like a time to pat ourselves on the back."

The line was silent for a moment. "I understand. You've been through a lot," said Travers. "Let's get you home, and we'll see to it that you are honored properly."

"Sir, I don't want any commendations," Daren objected. "All this bloodshed down here—it's all just another page in a long fucking book of institutional racism, and our hands are covered in it. It doesn't matter if it's ballistics reports or lynched children—we turn our eyes away because it makes us uncomfortable. Then we lie to uphold and defend a broken system." Daren spoke plainly, and honestly

"Book your flight, Agent Renard, and get some rest," Travers replied without regard to a word he'd just said.

"What about Devon Grey, sir?" Daren inquired.

"We just killed or arrested the entire cell. Their symbol was carved into the tree the boy was hanged from, right?"

"Yes, sir."

"Case closed," Travers concluded. "Our teams are combing through everything they own. We will interrogate them thoroughly, and I promise you, we will close this case."

Daren ended the call and sighed. He felt a sense of despair and futility. Everyone was saying he was a hero—that by engaging the shooter, Daren had forced him to focus his fire on him rather than the people who were fleeing for safety. All that was true, but Daren thought of Anthony Castile and didn't feel like much of a hero. Besides, the real heroes were Andrea and Carol Leeds. They were the ones who each realized what was happening, and together they neutralized two of the three attackers.

Daren didn't want medals or media praise. He felt like shit. Twice in one week he'd escaped death and watched others die. What made him so damn lucky? Why did he deserve to live? Perhaps this was his punishment: to witness this horror he'd helped set into motion.

She rarely smiled in photographs. There were pictures with family and some with friends, photos from school, and a ton from rallies and protests. But Mikayla had rarely smiled in any of them. In her childhood pictures, she looked stern and angry. In her adult photos, she always seemed determined and serious.

"She never liked taking photos," Andrea remarked fondly. "She hated being told to smile."

"Your sister always showed whatever she was feeling. It was the only way she knew how to be," Gram replied. She sifted through all the photos Andrea had printed, sorting them out on their kitchen table as she went. One pile was for the memorial services, the other were those that didn't make her cut. "Here's a good one," she said, handing Andrea a photo.

Andrea took the photo and sighed. The grief felt like a golf ball in her throat. The picture was of her and Mikayla on the pier at Folly Beach. It was taken on the Fourth of July by a mutual friend more than a decade earlier. She and her sister were embracing, their faces turned to the side and pressed together, both smiling brightly. Fireworks illuminated the sky behind them. "It's beautiful," Andrea said, tears in her eyes. "But she hated celebrating the Fourth," she added with a grin.

"But she loved you," Gram said. "And that's why she's smiling."

"Okay, this is the one we'll put by the door," Andrea replied affirmatively. "Thank you, Grammy." She leaned over and kissed her grandmother gently on her cheek.

"And to think," Gram said, shaking her head. "I always thought *you* were on the dangerous path in life."

"Yeah, me too," Andrea sighed.

"You saved a lot of lives yesterday," said Gram. "God put you where you needed to—"

"Don't," Andrea interrupted softly, pleading with her not to go there.

"I'm sorry but it's true."

"No," Andrea insisted. "God didn't do anything. I refuse to believe in a God that can control things like where I am, but who lets my sister die like that. I refuse to believe in a God that would allow such pain and suffering and hatred." She was crying again. "Oh, *I don't know!*" she bawled. "Maybe there is a God, Gram. *I want there to be.* I really do. But if there is, he's not in control. Maybe he's more like a compass, or a beacon—like a guide. It's up to us to get there on our own."

Gram dabbed her eyes with a cloth and fought back tears. "Maybe you're right, sweetheart. Maybe you're right."

The knock at their door startled them both. "At this hour?" Gram asked indignantly.

"I have no idea," Andrea said. She got up from her seat, walked to the door, undid the chain, and opened it to find Daren. "Oh, hey," she said. She hadn't expected to see him. "Just a minute," she told him. "My kid's in bed. I'll come out." She walked back to the kitchen, kissed her grandmother, and then retrieved her smokes from the bathroom.

"I thought you were quitting?" Gram asked.

"I quit quitting for now," Andrea smirked. Outside, she found Daren leaning against his rental car.

"How you doing?" he asked her.

"Okay, I guess," she said. "I don't know." She lit up a smoke and took a seat on the back of his car. "Too much grief and bullshit to unpack. Bad week to start facing my feelings, I guess."

"I saw a vigil downtown when I was heading here. A lot of people were there. I saw a picture of Mikayla."

"Yeah, I saw it on TV."

"Surprised you weren't there," said Daren.

"I don't know," Andrea demurred. "It's like this city only wants to come together like this *after* tragedies happen. Nothing that happened yesterday is new. It's the same goddamn problem we've had for as long as this country has existed. But people online and on the news don't even want to call it terrorism. I guess we reserve that word for people of color."

"If there's one thing I've learned, it's that I sure as hell don't know the answer, Watts." Daren sighed. "I'm not sure what I know anymore, to be honest. I don't even know if I want to be an FBI agent anymore."

"I find myself feeling that way about law enforcement," she confessed. "I wonder if I can actually do any good. Like... am I changing the system, or is the system changing me?"

"Well, the Bureau is pretty sure that the Mayfields or Dylan, or someone from their group lynched Devon Grey," he informed her. "They're going to dig in and press them about it."

"Why Charleston, though?" Andrea asked.

"What do you mean?"

"I get why they targeted the rally: the counter protest, the media attention. It was a big event. But most of these guys live in North Carolina or up in the Pee Dee. Why come to Charleston to hang some random Black kid?"

"Charleston's a unique city with quite a history. Who knows? Maybe they wanted to play on that, or maybe Dylan wanted to piss his daddy off," Daren suggested.

"I suppose only they know for sure," she replied.

"They'll sing," he said assuredly. "They got a lot of years hanging over their heads."

"So, that's it then?" Andrea asked. "Are we done?"

"Yeah, I guess so. I mean, if you want, we could keep running down our leads, see if anything traces back to Dylan," Daren offered. "I'm not flying home till Sunday evening."

Andrea shook her head. "I have to bury my sister. I'm not wasting time gathering crumbs of evidence for a case that the entire US government is focused on. Y'all don't need me."

Daren nodded and sighed regretfully. "Guess I just wanted to hang out a little more before I left," he admitted with a laugh.

Andrea smiled and put her arms out. "Take care of yourself, Daren," she said as they hugged.

"Thank you, again, for saving my life," he said as he pulled away.

"It was me who put it in danger," Andrea reminded him. "But you're welcome."

He smiled. "I'm so sorry about your sister."

"Thank you. I am too."

"I still can't help but feel partly responsible for all this."

"Well," Andrea said, pausing to find the right words. "It's okay for you to feel that."

"Oh…" Daren replied, noticeably stunned.

"I'm sorry, Daren, but I'm not going to assuage your guilt. I'm not the ambassador of Black people here to absolve your sins," she explained. "You were complicit in covering up systemic racism and violence. You have to live with that. It can't be undone. But if it hadn't been you, they'd have used someone else for the same results. And because it was you, that meant that it was you who came here, and I am thankful you were here."

"I guess that's something," he remarked.

"It's a place to start," Andrea replied. "Where you go from here is up to you."

33

THE FORWARD PASSED the ball, and Sean received it perfectly. With careful precision he dribbled the ball from foot to foot, maneuvering around his defender, then kicking it with all his might. The ball flew past the opposition's goalie and into the net, causing the referee to blow his whistle and the crowd to cheer.

"That's my boy!" David yelled, pounding his chest with pride.

"Go, Sean!" Marie cheered by his side.

Sean ran up the fence where David and Marie stood watching, eager for praise. "Did you see that?!" he asked, excitedly.

"You bet we did!" David replied enthusiastically.

"We're so proud!" Marie beamed.

"That's my son!" David shouted, pointing to the boy with pride.

"Go get back out there!" his mother urged him.

The boy smiled, turned, and ran back to the field. That's when David heard a familiar voice saying, "You guys are doing great, baby! Go back out there and keep it up." David tried to follow the voice, but the crowd by the fence was too dense. He saw the Black boy from Sean's team run from the fence line with glee. David furrowed his brow. *It couldn't be...*

David stepped away from the fence line, muttering to his wife that he'd be right back. He made his way through the crowd until he confirmed what he thought he had heard. Andrea was there, leaning over the fence, cheering for his son's team. "Dre?" he asked in confusion.

She turned around and smiled. "Hey, David! What are you doing here?"

"What *am I* doing here?" David asked with a laugh. "What are *you* doing here?"

"My son Marcus is on the team," she replied. "Wait," she said with a laugh. "Are you telling me, all this time, our kids have been going to the same school and playing soccer together? Wow, that makes me feel like a great mother." She shook her head and laughed, but David was unamused.

"Uh—I'm not sure I understand," David replied with a nervous laugh. "You don't live in Mount Pleasant, Dre..."

"Yeah, my cousin let's use their address," Andrea said quietly with a wink. "So, keep that between us." David was stunned. "Anyway, I've got Mikayla's wake on Monday. Maybe we could meet up after," she suggested. "God knows I will need a friend."

David shook his head. "I'm sorry, I guess I'm stuck on the part where you're breaking the law to send your kid to my kid's school."

Andrea took a step back and furrowed her brow. "Are you seriously upset about this?"

"Yeah, Dre. It's theft. I worked damn hard to get my family to a place where they can be safe, and my son can have a good education—"

"And what?" Andrea snapped back. "I don't work hard? I don't deserve those things?"

"I'm not saying that," David countered. His anger was rising. "I'm saying that it's not fair. If you want your kid to go to this school, you should live here and contribute to the taxes."

"Well, my cousin does, and she ain't got no kids," Andrea shrugged. "So, we're taking her spot."

"That's not the same. It's just not fair."

"No, I'll tell you what's not fair," she said, waving her finger at him like a dog that needed correcting. "My son was born poor and Black, so according to folks like you, he doesn't deserve the same opportunities. When my son says, 'Mommy, I want to play soccer,' I find a way to make it happen. Because I'll be damned if that's the first lesson he learns about ambition in this world—that if you're white, you have options, but if you're Black…" She shook her head again. "You know what, never mind about Monday night."

David fumed. "Go find some other dick to ride then!" he shouted, loudly enough for other parents in the crowd to take notice. Andrea put her head down and hurried away, embarrassed. David shook his head with anger and then turned to find his wife. To his surprise, Marie had been standing right behind him. The look of shock frozen on her face told him she'd heard everything. She stormed away toward the truck. "Marie!" he called after her. *"It's not what it sounds like!"*

A conflicted man wants nothing more than to not be alone with his thoughts. That's what brought Daren back to the stack of hate messages and comments that Pastor Mosley had given them. He read through them, disgusted by many, and ashamed of the more innocuous ones that reminded him too much of things he had once believed. But he read them all, sorting through thousands of hateful and awful messages, looking for any that may have come from Josh Dylan, the Mayhew brothers, or any other members of their group.

After about two hours, he took a break to grab some food and beer, then returned to his room, and resumed his task. After another hour of reading vile messages littered with misspellings and grammatical errors, Daren was ready to quit. That's when something stood out to him.

The pastor had circled all the offending comments in red. Just as he thought he could not read another, a circled comment jumped out. He grabbed his laptop and opened up his web browser. Punching a few keys, he was soon on the same social media site where the comment had been left. With a few more clicks he found what he was looking for.

"Son of bitch…" he muttered in disbelief.

Andrea exited the pizza shop in a huff and answered her phone. "What, you want to call me a thief again?" she asked with an attitude sharp enough to cut glass.

"Dre, I'm so sorry," David said on the other end of the call. "I'm a total asshole. I guess I never considered it from your perspective."

Andrea sighed. "You *are* an asshole! I can't believe you said that stuff. And you embarrassed me, David."

"I know," he admitted. "I really fucked up. I embarrassed myself, too… And Marie."

"She heard, huh?"

"Yeah, I guess the cat's out of the bag."

"I'm sorry, but… you know, I'm not sorry." She looked through the pizza shop window and saw Gram and Marcus eating pizza. She smiled and waved at Marcus.

"I get it. I deserve it," David replied. "I'm at the boat. I'll probably be here for a day or two until she calms down." Andrea couldn't help but grin. She had some dirty and wonderful memories of that boat. "Maybe, if you don't fucking hate me, you could come keep this lonely guy company later?"

"Maybe," Andrea said, her voice still stern. Then she lightened her tone and added, "If you're lucky."

"Okay, baby. Well, I'll be waiting and hoping that I am."

"We'll see," Andrea replied. "I'll talk to you later. I have to celebrate our victory with a hungry boy." She hung up and went inside. "Holy cow, how many pieces have you eaten, child?!" she teased as she sat down beside her son.

"Only two!" Marcus answered, laughing. Andrea tickled him lightly and he laughed some more. She didn't feel much like laughing and celebrating, but he deserved it. And besides, it felt good to be with her family.

'Well, you eat as many as you want. You played a great game today," she told him.

He smiled at her while sipping his soda. She noticed Gram was smiling at her too. Andrea smiled back and tilted her head slightly sideways as if to ask Gram what had her so happy. But Gram just raised her eyebrows and smiled wider. They both knew why she was smiling. Andrea blew her a kiss and grabbed herself a slice of pizza.

After several minutes of knocking, the door finally opened, but Daren was disappointed with who answered.

"Hi, I'm sorry to bother you," he said. "Is Andrea home?"

"No," Gram replied. "She took the car to see a friend."

"Shit," Daren replied. "I tried calling her. I think her phone is off."

"She's probably busy with her friend," said Gram, unamused by his urgency. "You the same man who came here last night unannounced?" she asked.

"Uh, yes, ma'am," he admitted. "Sorry about that."

"Even in my day that was considered rude," she scolded him. "And y'all got text messaging now. I don't understand it."

"Ma'am, I do apologize, but I need to find Andrea," Daren emphasized. "It's very important."

"I'm sorry, but I don't know where she is or how to find her," the woman replied.

Back in his car, Daren cursed. He picked up his phone and tried yet again to call Watts, but again, the call went straight to voice mail. "Watts, it's Daren. Listen I need to talk to you immediately. Call me. It's very important. Okay? Call me as soon as you get this. It's about the Grey case."

The cabin was quite charming, despite the boat's rough exterior. Inside the woodwork had all been carefully restored. A working mini fridge and a soft mattress were all it needed to create the ideal love shack. Andrea often teased David about how the boat would never float, but he didn't care. It was a place where he could get away. A place of his own.

Andrea was still pretending to be mad at him when she arrived. David apologized again and asked for her forgiveness. In truth, he was still angry with her over the whole thing, but it wasn't worth jeopardizing their relationship—especially now that he was on the outs with Marie. He smiled and batted his eyes at Andrea playfully.

She finally gave in and kissed him. He offered to make them some drinks.

She smiled. "That'd be nice," she said, pulling out her cigarettes.

"Better take that out to the deck," David advised. "I just put a fresh coat of varnish on the other day. Still smells." Andrea nodded and waited for him, but he urged her to go ahead. "Go on out. I'll mix us a couple drinks, and be right there," he said with a wink.

Andrea made her way out of the cabin, while David grabbed a couple of glasses out of the cupboard, and proceeded to wipe them out with his t-shirt. He grabbed the whiskey and two cans of Sprite from the fridge and was still pouring the drinks when Andrea called down from the deck. "Something just came up at work! *I gotta go!*" she yelled. "I'll call you!"

David put the whiskey down and darted out of the cabin. Andrea was already off the boat and climbing into her car. "Wait!" he called. "*What's up?!*"

"*Work!*" Andrea called back. She slammed her car door shut, started the engine, and punched the gas so hard the tires spun and kicked up gravel the car sped out of the parking lot.

"What the fuck?" David muttered to himself. "Guess I'll take a raincheck then…"

34

WEST ASHLEY - 8 MONTHS EARLIER

"**SO, I TOLD** her to shut her cock garage and walk away, or I would charge her skank-ass too!" Sergeant Gregory Noonan bellowed.

David nearly spat his coffee out. "Don't make me laugh like that while I'm drinking," he cried. He was laughing so hard he could feel his stomach cramping and his eyes watering.

"It was a shame, really," Greg added. "Because she had talent, bro. I mean, you could bounce a quarter off that ass of hers."

"Look while you can," David advised. "You'll be a married man soon."

Greg stuffed the last bit of a cruller into his mouth and brushed the crumbs from his uniform. "You're so full of shit," he replied, sipping his coffee.

"Oh?" David asked, feigning indignation. "How's that?"

"I know, I know," Greg muttered sarcastically. "You're husband of the goddamn year."

David adjusted the steering wheel, which he'd raised to allow him room to eat. The wheel back in place, he started the engine of the CCSO-issued SUV. "That's right, I am," he said with a smirk.

"Yeah, how's Detective Watts doing? Just asking," Greg teased.

"What can I say?" David cackled. "I like chocolate." They both laughed. This was how they started almost every shift. Their ritual of coffee and donuts over, David and Greg headed out for patrol. It wasn't long until they had a call.

The boy was small, and the bike he was peddling was too big for him to manage. He had a weedwhacker and electric hedge clippers precariously tied to his handlebars. As he steered, the bike teetered and swayed. He nearly crashed when the police SUV pulled up behind him and sounded its siren.

"How's it going?" David asked the boy as he approached.

"Alright," the boy replied sheepishly.

"Got any ID on you?" David asked as Greg inspected the lawn equipment.

"No… I'm only thirteen."

"Little late in the season for yard work," Greg remarked.

"Lots of people getting ready for spring," said the boy.

"In February?" Greg scoffed.

"Yeah, I got a few takers," the boy insisted.

"Whatcha doing with these tools, boy?" David asked.

"Yard work, man. Whatchu think I'm doin'?"

"You doing work for pay?" David asked.

"You got a work permit?" Greg inquired.

The boy looked at each of them, unsure of what to say.

"Look," David said with a smile. "We aren't gonna bust your ass about a work permit or nothin' like that. Okay?" The boy nodded. "What's your name?" David asked.

"Jerome."

"Okay, Jerome. Now, where were you working? Because my concern right now isn't work permits. You know what I'm worried about?" Jerome said nothing and stared at the ground. "See we got a call from one of these neighbors, saying they seen a boy who doesn't live around here, making his way down the road with expensive yard equipment. We've had a lot of break-ins and theft in these parts, you see?" David explained. "So, I'm thinking, was this boy doing work, or is he stealing tools from somebody's garage?"

"Where'd you get the tools?" Greg demanded.

"I bought them," Jerome defiantly asserted.

"Boy, when an officer of the law is addressing you, you look him in the eye," Greg said sternly. "I don't think you quite understand. You could be in serious trouble here."

"They're my tools, officer, I swear!" Jerome replied, looking Greg and then David squarely in the eyes as he began to cry. "I was working on Shadowmoss and Willow Terrace! I swear!"

"Alright, alright, stay right here for a moment," David said, motioning for Greg to follow him back to the truck. "Well, we can see what happened here," he told Greg as he leaned across the hood.

"Black kid working in a white neighborhood," Greg nodded affirmatively.

"Probably just some asshole neighbor," David agreed. "Wasting our time."

"Now it's our fucking problem to deal with. What if we take his word for it, and it turns out he just jacked that shit from somebody's house?"

"We could go check out the addresses. Ask if he was doing work for them," David suggested.

"Yeah, waste more of our fucking time on bullshit," Greg scoffed. "Should we cut him loose?"

"I don't know," Greg pondered. "I don't like the attitude he gave us."

David nodded. "Okay, we'll teach him a lesson then." They then returned to Jerome, who was noticeably frightened and anxious. "Listen," David said to him. "When I was a kid, my father moved me into a neighborhood where people looked more like you than me. You know what I'm saying?" Jerome nodded hesitantly. "I used to get my ass kicked all the time," David explained. He chuckled and put his hand on Jerome's shoulder. "I used to get so mad at those kids. But one day it occurred to me that I was an outsider in a place I didn't belong. Those boys were just looking out for what was theirs. Only I didn't have a choice where I lived. Jerome. You *do* have a choice: you don't have to work in neighborhoods where you don't belong. Places where nobody looks like you do. Do you understand what I'm saying?" he asked.

Jerome wiped the tears from his cheeks and nodded. "Yes, sir," he quietly uttered.

"I know it sounds shitty," said David. "But when people around here see someone like you, who they know doesn't live here, they get scared. They've had their homes broken into, and all sorts of things lifted from their cars. Everyone is on edge. You come around here knocking on doors, asking for work, and people get scared. Then they call us, and that wastes our time."

"But I put a flyer up at Walmart, and these the people who call me," Marcus protested. "I need to make money to help my mom!"

"Well, now you've been accused of stealing equipment," David explained. "And as an officer of the law, I am supposed to make you prove that you legally purchased these tools. Now, I don't suppose you can do that?"

The boy looked crushed. "No, sir."

"You didn't keep the receipts?" Greg asked with false concern.

"I—I didn't think I had to," Marcus stammered.

"Well, we're going to have to take the equipment, then, until you can provide proof or witnesses," David concluded, reaching for the weedwhacker.

"No, please!" Marcus pleaded. "I need it to make money!"

David stopped, and looked at Greg as if he were considering leniency. "Well, alright, then," he said sternly. "I wouldn't want to discourage you from working. But I gotta tell you, Jerome, if anyone calls us on you again, we will take the equipment and at that point, we will probably have no choice but to arrest you as well, for working without a permit. Do you understand?"

The boy nodded emphatically, desperate to keep his tools. "Yes, sir. Thank you, sir," he said.

"Go on, now. Get outta here," David instructed. Jerome peddled away quickly, and David and Greg got back into their SUV.

"Little fuck was pretty scared," Greg remarked as they drove away.

"Yeah, it's the natural reaction his kind has to law enforcement. It's like a hyena seeing a lion in the brush," David joked. They both laughed.

"He'll be doing B-and-E's before he's old enough to drive, anyway," Greg surmised.

"Probably," David nodded.

"Nearly shit myself when you told him to stay where he belonged," Greg cackled. "Not exactly P.C., Sergeant Sullivan," he teased.

"Yeah, well," David said, searching for the right words as he maneuvered through traffic. "The world would be a better place if everyone knew that simple truth: Stick with your own. Stay where you belong."

"Ain't gotta tell me twice," Greg affirmed. "Build the fucking wall."

"I'm not racist, either," David clarified. "It's just a simple truth."

"Ain't gotta tell me *that* twice, either."

"Everybody wants to be the same these days," David jeered. "But they're not. World's full of weak and strong, big and small. Ain't nobody equal to nothing."

"You're preaching to the choir, brother," Greg chuckled. "Except I am kind of racist," he laughed.

"People have always and will always distrust other groups of people. It's nature. The real problem," he expounded, "is that everyone thinks they're a goddamn victim these days."

"Got that right," said Greg. "Hell, that junior banger we just stopped is probably on the phone with the ACLU right now."

"Don't fucking joke like that," David replied with a laugh. He then let out a long, low whistle. "Boy, the last thing you want these days is to be a cop in a viral news story."

"I hear that cop who shot that monkey in Michigan is going into witness protection," said Greg. "He beat the investigation, but he and his family have been receiving death threats and shit. They had protesters, like, living on their front lawns."

"That's fucked up," said David.

"Imagine having to uproot your entire life because one stop went bad." Greg shook his head.

The rest of their shift was fairly uneventful. They busted some speeders, patrolled the local shopping centers a little, and stopped at Chick-Fil-A for dinner.

It was after dark when David pulled the SUV into the Ashley River apartments complex. "Just making sure these thugs are where we told them to be," he said, looking around.

"I thought Ellis's people wanted the Pit Stop and bowling alley?" Greg asked.

"Yeah, but these little fucks like to meet people down the street. That's too close to Ellis's territory. So, I told them to keep their asses in here. They didn't like it, but…"

"Tough shit, right?" Greg cackled.

"Lucky all they're selling is weed," David noted. "Ellis tends to get a bit more aggressive when it comes to other things."

"Like those white supremacist fuckheads we busted selling meth."

"Yeah, exactly. Ellis doesn't even sell meth either. He just didn't like them all that much, I suppose."

"I wonder why?" Greg asked sarcastically.

David drove through several parking lots until he spotted the group of kids he was checking on. "Right where they're supposed to be," he said with satisfaction. "Good boys."

The crew grilled them as they drove by. "Maybe there's a tax for looking at us like that?" Greg suggested.

"Maybe there is," David agreed, pulling the truck back around to the group of kids. "Hey!" David shouted from his window, extending his hand and motioning for the kids to come closer. "Don't just stare at me, get the fuck over here. Yeah, you, all of you. Come here!" A group of six kids reluctantly approached the police SUV. "Where's Malik?" David asked, scanning the group. "Where's the boss man?"

"Went to meet his cousin or some shit," one of the boys replied.

"He's sellin' to him? On Ashley River Road?" David asked. "He better not be…"

The boys looked away, and the one who spoke up hung his head in shame, knowing he shouldn't have said anything. David shook his head and quickly sped off. "Little fuckers don't know what's good for them."

"We going to bust him? Beat his ass?" Greg asked eagerly.

"Can't earn if we bust him," David replied. "But we can bust this cousin of his." The SUV tore out of the apartment complex and onto the main road. David punched the gas. "There's Malik," David remarked, pointing at the lone figure walking back toward the apartments. "Bet you that's his cousin right down there," he added, pointing down the road at another man heading in the other direction.

"Well, he looks suspicious to me," Greg added with a laugh.

David drove past Malik and down the road towards a Black adolescent male in a black hooded sweatshirt. When he was close, he flipped a switch on the dash, and the blue and red lights on top of the SUV came to life. He then hit the spotlight mounted to his side mirror and shined it on the boy. He grabbed the receiver to the radio and flipped on the external speaker. "Charleston County Sheriff's Office," he barked into the receiver. "Put your hands in the air and get down on your knees, now!"

Slowly, the suspect started to raise his hands. But then, without warning, he darted into the trees.

"Oh, no you don't!" David yelled, punching the accelerator, and cutting into traffic haphazardly.

"Go around to the back of the shopping center!" Greg exclaimed. "That's where he'll come out!"

David was already on it, flashing his lights and siren to clear traffic, blasting through an intersection, and then steering quickly into the parking lot of the shopping center. He turned off the emergency lights and killed the headlights, and then slowly pulled around to the back where the parking lot met the woods.

David scanned the woods with the spotlight, but Greg nudged him and motioned to the dumpster behind the building. There he could see the shadow of a man cast onto the wall of the building. David nodded, quietly opened his door, and exited the vehicle.

"Come on out now!" David ordered. He unclipped his holster and rested his hand on the butt of his gun. He carefully approached the dumpster. "Hands in the air and walk out slowly!" he ordered.

The suspect wisely raised his hands high into the air and slowly emerged from behind the dumpster. "I ain't holdin' shit," he told them.

"Yeah, you probably ditched it in the woods," David replied as he approached the suspect. "That's okay, I've got something in the truck we can say was yours," he added. He took out his handcuffs and prepared to apprehend the suspect.

Greg stood about five yards back, his hand resting readily on the butt of his gun.

"Y'all gonna do me dirty?" the kid asked. "That ain't fair."

"Fair?" David laughed. "Turn around, put your hands behind your back. Can't believe you grew up Black in the South, and you're still bitching about what's fair." David grabbed the suspect by the wrist and spun him around to cuff him.

"Fuckin' pigs," the suspect muttered.

"*What was that?!*" David barked, twisting the suspect's arm behind his back.

"*Ow! Fuckin' pigs!!*" the suspect shouted.

David saw red. He tightened his grip and wrenched the suspect's arm some more. "What is it with you people and not respecting the law?" he barked as the suspect writhed.

The suspect jabbed his elbow sharply into David's gut, catching him off guard. David felt the wind leave his lungs and gasped for air. The suspect tried to pull away, but David squeezed his arm tighter. *"Fucking animal!"* David shouted. He yanked the suspect closer and wrapped his right arm around his neck.

"Let me go, you fuckin' Nazi-pig-fuck!" the suspect cried.

Infuriated, David brought his other arm up to complete the headlock. "You want to fuck with me?!" he shouted. "What if I just choked you the fuck out?" he spat into the suspect's ear. "What's the matter?" he taunted as the suspect gasped for air. "Can't breathe? Don't fight it, just go to sleep."

"Careful," Greg warned, but David could barely hear him.

The suspect elbowed David again, further enraging him. He squeezed harder, and the suspect fought even harder. David squeezed his arms together as hard as he could and waited for the suspect to pass out.

It might have ended there, with the suspect passed out in his arms, if it had not been for a piece of broken concrete sitting on the ground near the dumpster. When the suspect pushed back against him, David tripped over the piece of concrete and fell backward, taking the suspect to the ground with him, his arm locked tightly around his neck.

As he fell hard onto the pavement, he felt something pop inside the boy's neck. Suddenly there was no more fight. The boy's body went completely limp. "Oh shit," David muttered.

"Is he alright?" Greg asked concernedly. "Did you knock him out?"

David pushed the boy off of him and checked him for a pulse. *"Fuck, man!"* he exclaimed, placing his head on the boy's chest to be sure. "I broke his fucking neck, man!"

"Oh, fuck!" Greg gasped.

David rubbed his eyes, then cupped his mouth in disbelief. He looked at his partner who was frozen in shock. After several moments of stunned silence passed, David stood up. "Help me get him into the car," he said, sitting the boy's body up.

"What? Why the fuck would we want to do that?!" Greg asked.

"We can't just leave him here!" David insisted. "What if someone saw us chasing him?"

"Let's just call it in, man. I'll say he attacked you. You were just defending yourself."

David scoffed. "Are you fucking kidding me right now? How does he end up with a broken neck that way?" he asked. "You want a grand jury investigation into us? Even if they don't find out about Ellis and all that shit—even if they don't find out that you're a goddamn coke head—we will still be in national-fucking-news, man. Do you want to end up like that cop in Michigan? Because I sure as fuck don't! I'm not giving up my life because of some fucking jigaboo punk who ran off during a police stop."

Greg seemed hesitant and unsure.

"Come on, bro," David urged. "You're getting married next year, for fuck's sake! You don't want to deal with all this shit. And I've got a family, bro. I could go to prison for this shit!"

Greg sighed and reluctantly grabbed the boy's feet. "What are we going to do with him?"

"We'll think of something," David assured him as they carried the body toward the SUV. "We'll make it look good."

Greg nodded, but David could tell he was still unsure. "Everything is going to be fine," he reassured him. "As long as we stick together, we'll be fine." They loaded the body into the back seat, checked to make sure there were no security cameras nearby, then got into the SUV and drove away.

35

THE TIRES SQUEALED as Andrea cut the wheel, sending the Focus bounding across two lanes of traffic and into the parking lot of a Waffle House. She hastily pulled into the nearest spot and brought the car to a sudden halt. Her heart felt as if it was going to leap out of her chest. The world around her was a blur. She tried to breathe and could feel her lungs doing what they were told, but the air didn't seem to be getting in. She breathed harder but still couldn't seem to catch her breath.

Andrea was well versed in dealing with anxiety and panic, but this felt different for some reason. A million thoughts and conclusions of inescapable dread flooded her mind all at once. This wasn't a threat she could shoot or run from. It was a realization she desperately wanted to be untrue. The more she fought against it, the more anxiety she felt.

She *had* to be wrong. There must've been something wrong with her brain. The conclusions it kept jumping to just couldn't be.

Use it, she told herself. *Let the emotions come.*

Once she stopped fighting her feelings, her heart began to slow, and her breathing steadied. She realized that more than anything else, she was afraid. Afraid that the man she had been sleeping with for years was a vicious murderer. That was the thought she had been trying to avoid—that she suspected something so awful of someone she trusted.

She took a deep breath, closed her eyes, and imagined how the pieces fit with David as the suspect. The pieces seemed to fit, but there was no way to prove it. Unless…

Andrea gasped. She had an idea. One that could prove whether or not she was losing her mind. She pulled out her phone and turned it back on—she always turned it off whenever she saw David. When the phone booted up, she had several text messages and a voice mail waiting for her from Daren telling her to call him immediately.

Andrea tried to call him but just got his voice mail. "Daren!" she exclaimed. "I'm heading to the National Express Business Center near the mall in West Ashley. Meet me there as soon as you get this!"

Clouds gathered on the horizon and the wind promised rain. Daren sat at the counter of the Early Bird Diner and tried yet again to reach Andrea to no avail. The man behind the counter poured fresh, hot coffee into his mug. "Thank you," Daren replied, pushing the plate with the remains of his lunch forward. "I'm all set with this, thank you."

"No problem," said the man, taking Daren's plate and depositing it into a wash bin behind the counter. "Anything else I can do for ya?"

"No, that'll be all, thank you," Daren said. He watched the wind whip through the palm trees across the street. "We got some weather coming in?" he asked.

"Oh, I would say so," the man replied. "Couple bad systems coming through. Heavy rain. Hail. High winds. Whole county is under a tornado watch."

"Fantastic," Daren remarked dryly. He decided to try Andrea one last time before leaving and noticed he had a message. He was relieved to hear it was from her. She must have called at the same time he was trying to reach her. She requested that he meet her at the National Express Business Center. It sounded urgent.

Daren tossed a $20 down on the counter and quickly made his way to the Dodge. As he drove away the first drops of rain began to fall.

Something about the way Andrea had left wasn't sitting right. It wasn't like her to leave in such a rush. Even if she had an urgent matter or a work emergency, she would have told him. To just take off like that...

David paced around his cabin, sipping his drink. He tried to call her but received no answer. He started to worry. All this had been trouble from the start. That fed snooping around, recruiting Andrea of all people. Why her? Had he been a complete fool? Had this entire thing been about him all along?

No, there was no way she could know. There was absolutely zero reason for her to even suspect him, and there was nothing to link him to the crime. It was probably just his guilt eating at him, turning in his subconscious, and making him paranoid. The only other person in the world who knew what had happened that night was Greg. No, she didn't know. She couldn't. He was safe.

He walked out of the cabin and onto the deck, sipped his drink, and took a deep breath to calm himself. The air was moist and cool. A storm was on its way. He sipped his drink, and examined the boat—it needed a lot of work. He looked at the paint, sealant, and rope he had bought in hopes of getting her into the water soon, and couldn't help but laugh at himself. He hadn't used any of it. Well, except for the rope…

The rope! He looked at the spindle of blue nylon rope, his mind racing. Had she seen the rope? Surely that wouldn't have been enough… She had run out of there awfully quick, though. As much as David wanted to deny it, his gut was telling him something wasn't right. He retrieved his gun from inside the cabin, tucked it into the back of his jeans, and pondered his next move.

The wind was getting quite strong by the time Daren arrived. He parked the Dodge next to Andrea's Focus and hurried through the rain into the National Express building. Inside, he found Andrea standing behind the counter with another woman, huddled over a computer.

"Finally," Andrea remarked without taking her eyes off the computer screen.

"Hey, I've been trying to reach you all day," Daren retorted defensively. "So, what's up?"

"Okay, here's the log from that day," the woman said to Andrea.

"Daren, this is Nicolette," said Andrea. "She runs the place."

"Nice to meet you, baby," Nicolette greeted Daren. She punched a few more keys and then tapped her long, red fingernail against the screen. "Mm-hm, you right, baby girl. There it is. Right when you said it would be."

"10:53 PM," Andrea said, tracing something on the screen with her finger. "This IP number right here is not one of your employees?"

"No, sugar. That's not one of theirs. And no one would be logging on at that time. That had to be an officer," Nicolette replied.

"What are you on to?" Daren asked, hardly able to control himself from jumping to conclusions.

"Hold on," Andrea said emphatically. She pulled out her phone and jabbed at the screen with her thumbs. She read her screen for a moment, then shook her head in disbelief. "Holy shit!"

"What?!" Daren asked, almost certain what she'd found.

"Look," Andrea said, pulling him around the counter and showing him the screen. "See this IP address? That's our tipster. 10:53 PM, February tenth. His phone logged onto the WIFI network here when he entered the building."

"Holy shit," said Daren.

"So, whoever it was had to have already have had our WIFI password," Nicolette added.

"And get ready for this," Andrea braced him. "The only people who have it other than employees are cops."

"How did you figure that out?" he asked, excited by the revelation.

"Last time I was here," she explained. "I noticed they give their WIFI password out to law enforcement officers."

"They like to take breaks in our parking lot," Nicolette confirmed. "Figure I might as well play nice with them."

"I know this sounds crazy, Renard, but I think the killer is David," said Andrea.

"Well, I might have thought you were losing your mind," Daren said flatly, pulling several folded-up pieces of paper from his back pocket. "But I have something to add to your theory."

"Are those the comments and messages the pastor gave us?" Andrea asked nonplussed.

"Look!" Daren said, handing the pages to Andrea.

Andrea read the comments Daren had circled and gasped. They were comments made on social media by David. In one, David had complained about the church using the tragedy to advance a political agenda. Another simply read: *"Tired of hearing about white on black crime. I'm a cop and I tell you it's black on black crime we need to worry about."*

"So, I did a little snooping on David's social media," Daren explained, showing Andrea another page. "Turns out he's quite the NIMBY."

"I know," Andrea confirmed. "He's always been anti-development. In fact, now I remember him bashing Grant Newton," she recalled.

"Check out the comments on those last couple pages," Daren suggested.

Andrea flipped to the last two pages. There she saw comments David had left under news articles about Grant Newton and the legal battles surrounding his new development in Mount Pleasant. *"Grant Newton is a snake that deserves to be whacked,"* one read.

"I'm also fairly sure he's working for a local gangster," Andrea added. "Which puts him into conflict with the crew Devon was buying weed from."

"Damn, that's a pretty solid circumstantial case. We got anything else?" Daren asked.

"Yeah, he's got the rope he used to hang Grey on the deck of his fucking boat."

"Wait, what's a NIMBY?" asked Nicolette.

"Nicolette, baby, please," Andrea chided. "Could you just give us one moment?" Nicolette was noticeably offended, but nodded, and walked about five feet down the counter, where she pretended not to be listening.

"Wait—you saw the rope?!" Daren asked.

"I was just at his boat," Andrea explained. "It's sitting right there. The same exact rope."

"Let's go pay him a visit," Daren suggested. "Have a little chat."

They thanked Nicolette for her help and were soon speeding through the thundering rain in Daren's Charger. "He might know that I am on to him," Andrea considered. "The way I ran outta there. He's probably suspicious."

Daren looked at her then back at the road. "I bet you were fine."

Andrea stared ahead and watched the wipers struggle to keep up with the heavy rain. Some thirty-five minutes later, they arrived at their destination. "His truck is gone," Andrea remarked as Daren pulled his car into the lot where David's stored his boat.

"Should we check the boat anyway?" Daren suggested.

Andrea had an uneasy feeling. "Let me call him and see if he answers," she suggested.

36

"HELLO," DAVID ANSWERED gruffly.

Andrea was surprised he did. "David," she said, feeling suddenly at a loss for words. She waited for a reply, but receiving none, she said, "David... *what have you done?*" Her voice trembled. "David, are you there?"

"Yeah."

"David, talk to me," Andrea pled.

"There's nothing to say, is there?" he said.

"*What did you do, David?*"

"What I had to." His voice sounded detached and flat. There was no anger. No defensiveness. Just acceptance, and maybe hopelessness.

"You killed a child. You—" She choked back tears. "You lynched him. David, how could you?" He said nothing. "David, you owe me an explanation here," she said.

"Why, so you can play the recording of this for your lover boy, the fed? You sold me out, Dre. You've been working me this whole time."

"I don't know what you're talking about, but if I'm right and you lynched that poor boy," Andrea said, her anger rising. "You better pray someone else finds you."

"It was an accident, Dre!" David cried defensively. "Greg and I made a deal with Ellis Bartley. We helped enforce his boundaries, and in return, he promised to keep violence down and bodies low. I know what you must think, but it worked, Dre. It worked. *I Saved lives!*"

Andrea shook her head in disbelief. "G'on then," she said. "Tell me what happened."

"We were riding around near Ashley Hall, making sure the crew stayed in their territories. We saw a deal go down where it wasn't supposed. So Greg and I figure, we'll shake them down, take the weed or whatever and let 'em go with a warning. Only this motherfucker ran, Dre. I caught up with him on the other side of the woods, and…"

"And what?"

"He resisted—he came at me, and there was a scuffle… I don't know what happened, but I ended up putting him in a headlock. The kid was strong, Dre—I was just trying to subdue him. I—I—I don't know, I tripped over this piece of curb and.—"

"You broke his neck," she concluded.

"Yeah…"

"So, then you stripped that child naked, and hanged him by his throat?!" she yelled, tears filling her eyes. *"What the hell is wrong is you?!"*

"Because I knew exactly what would have happened to me and my family, to Greg and his family—*I knew what they would do!*" he cried. "So, I staged a scene, and I pinned it on those racist fucks I busted cooking meth. I knew they were up to no good anyway."

"You're unbelievable," Andrea scoffed. "You really think you're the victim here, don't you?"

"Go ahead and judge me all you want. That's all anybody would have done, either way."

"But that's not all, is it David?" She waited for his reply but he said nothing, so she continued. "Was Greg running his mouth? Was he growing a conscience? Did you have him killed to shut him up, or were you just being precautious?

David was crying now. "That son of a bitch wouldn't listen to me, Dre," he sobbed. "He kept going on about it, said it was eating at him. He wanted to confess and kept telling me it wouldn't be that bad. Wouldn't be that bad—*they'd fucking lock me up!* Maybe it wouldn't have been bad for him…"

"So, you had Ellis kill your partner and best friend."

"At least he died a hero," David countered. "Better than living as a villain. That's all that would've happened if he had his way."

"Where are you?" she asked him.

"Doesn't matter. Nothing matters now. It will all be over soon."

"David, don't you do anything stupid." She shot Daren a concerned look.

"It's too late for that," David muttered. "Everything is ruined now."

"Turn yourself in, and end this," she urged him. "Please."

"I am ending this," he stated plainly.

"David, think about your family—"

"I am," he insisted. "They shouldn't have to bear this, either. It's my burden, but they will have to carry it, even if I'm gone. That's not fair to them."

"David—"

"I know what I have to do—to spare us all," he said. "Goodbye, Dre."

"David!" Andrea cried, but the call had ended. She turned to Daren, panic in her eyes. *"We need to get to David's house, immediately."*

The sleeping pills wouldn't dissolve well in ice cream.

As such, David was forced to crush up some allergy pills. A little chocolate sauce to help hide any taste. It worked like a charm. Sean was passed out in front of the TV by the time David got off the phone with Andrea.

He had to hurry; Marie would be home from shopping with her friends soon. Everything had to be in place before then.

David scooped Sean up into his arms and carefully carried him to the garage. There he gently laid the boy down across the backseat of his truck, and softly shut the door. He hurriedly grabbed a garden hose and duct tape from the shelf in the garage and began taping the hose to the end of his truck's tail pipe. Once that was secure, he carefully climbed behind the wheel, started the engine, and cracked the back window.

He paused for a moment, examining the face of the man he saw in the rearview. He didn't want to be a monster, but this was without question a monstrous act. He hated himself for it. The only thing he hated more was the thought of his son knowing what he had done. No, he didn't deserve that. David would spare him of that pain. Sean hadn't chosen his father, but his life would be ruined by him one way or another. This was the best thing for them all. David would spare them the pain of knowing.

He inspected his revolver. All that was left was to seal up the truck and wait for Marie. He would make it quick—he didn't want her to suffer, either. She had stuck by him through everything and deserved peace. Ideally, she wouldn't even see it coming. Just here one minute, gone the next. Then she would never have to know. David had the hardest role in what was about to happen, but that was his duty as the man of the house. He would carry that pain for them. It would all be over soon anyway.

The rain pounded furiously and the wind pushed forcefully against the car. Daren tried his best to keep the car at 60 mph as they navigated across the Ravenel to Mount Pleasant. It was raining so hard, that he couldn't go any faster while maintaining visibility.

"Mount Pleasant police said they'd send a car when they can," Andrea reported, sliding her phone into her pocket. "The bastards aren't taking me seriously."

"You're sure he's a threat to his family?"

"I know what he said," Andrea reaffirmed. "We need to get there faster," she concluded.

"I can't go any faster," Daren explained, exacerbated. "It's not going to help very much if we wreck."

David was affixing the hose to the back window of his truck when the door to the house opened from inside.

"You out here, David—" Marie started the trailed off. "What the hell are you doing?" she asked, seeing her son in the back seat and the hose David had rigged to the exhaust. *"Oh, my God, what are you doing?!"*

"Marie, baby, it's not what it looks like," David said with a disarming laugh.

Marie saw the gun tucked into his pants, just as he started to reach for it. Instinctively, she grabbed the nearest object she could find, an empty beer bottle from the stack of recyclables near the door, and chucked it at him as hard as she could. The bottle struck David hard in the head.

David keeled over, grabbed his wound, and groaned in pain. *"Fucking bitch!"* he cried, blood pouring from the gash above his right eye. He grabbed his gun and rose to his feet, but she had already come around behind him. Before he could orient himself, she struck him in the back of the head with a tire iron. David cried out in pain and toppled over, his gun skidding across the concrete floor.

Marie then struck the tire iron against the back window of the truck, shattering it to ensure his plan could not go on. She tried to flee, but David grabbed her by the back of her hair. He pulled her back, then wrapped both hands around her neck. He slammed her against the wall and squeezed her throat as hard as he could.

"Sorry, baby," he growled through grimaced teeth. "This isn't how I planned this, but leave it to you to ruin the day! Don't worry," he said as she gasped for air. "It'll be over soon."

David didn't realize that by pushing her against the wall of the garage, he had put his tool bench within her reach—a mistake he soon realized when Marie jabbed a six-inch screw driver into his shoulder. He screamed in agony and released her from his grasp. Marie kneeled him square in the crotch and took off running into the house.

David dropped down in pain and screamed as he pulled the screwdriver from his shoulder. Frantic and furious, he reached under the tool bench for the gun. He could hear Marie on the phone with the police, frantically telling them their address. He grabbed the gun and hurried inside to confront her, leaving Sean sleeping in the cab of the truck.

Daren cursed as he brought the car to a sliding halt. Just up ahead of the Dodge, the road was completely flooded. "That's impassable," Daren said. "Is there another way?"

"*There's no time!*" Andrea emphasized.

"It's too deep, the car will stall," Daren argued.

Andrea shook her head, racked a round into the chamber of her firearm, and then opened the car door. "*There's no time!*" she shouted, exiting the car into the pouring rain.

"Wait!" Daren called after her. By the time he was out of the car, she was already running full speed through the yard of the nearest home.

"Come on!" she cried before bounding over the property wall into the neighboring yard.

Daren shook his head and ran after her, leaving the car running in the road. The wind was whipping the rain so hard, that it hurt against his skin. He made it to the wall, climbed over, and immediately fell into the mud on the other side. Andrea was already running down the street on the other side of the yard.

Marie had locked herself in the bathroom. Unfortunately for her, David had already punched a hole in that door just days before. He pulled out the towel he had wedged into the hole and peered inside. Marie was attempting to crawl out the bathroom window. David angrily punched and kicked through the door, forcing his way into the bathroom. He lunged for Marie, but just before he could grab her, she slid out the window, falling to the ground nearly twenty feet below.

She let out a whimpered cry when she hit the ground. David peered out the window and saw her. Marie had injured herself in the fall. She tried to stand up to run, but her leg could not hold her weight. She fell, face first, onto the wet ground, the rain beating down around her.

David shook his head, angry at her for making this harder than it had to be, and then went outside to shoot his bitch wife.

By the time he made it out to the backyard, Marie had managed to get up, and was limping across the lawn toward the neighbors, crying out, *"HELP ME!"*

David sighed, and aimed his weapon at Marie's back. But before he could fire, he felt something strike his back. Confused, he looked down and noticed blood coming from his belly.

David turned around to see Andrea advancing towards him across his lawn, gun drawn. He raised his gun, and she fired hers twice more. The wet ground cradled him now, his blood pooling around him. David laid on his back, his leg twitching as he tried to move, but everything around him was fading away. He saw Daren standing over him, watching him die, as Andrea ran to aide Marie. He closed his eyes and thought of his mother. He could almost hear her laughter, and then, he was gone.

37

THE PIER WAS full of life; bustling with families and friends, tourists and locals alike. They smiled and laughed, holding drinks and ice cream cones, and stopping to take selfies with the beach in the background. It was like a Main Street fair over the water. A low-flying, noisy flock of seagulls glided overhead before continuing down the shoreline, over volleyballers, swimmers, surfers, and couples casually strolling hand-in-hand.

Fishermen lined the sides of the pier, which was equipped with deep sinks for cleaning their catches. The signs said that anyone could rent a pole and buy some bait, no license required. It was, however, strictly forbidden to purposely catch sharks. Daren wondered how one could *purposely* make a shark bite its line.

He made his way to the end of the pier, where he found Andrea seated on a bench wearing a Charleston River Dogs cap and sunglasses. Daren took a seat beside her and followed her gaze over the water. He didn't say anything—he simply sat there beside her for several moments, just listening to the sounds of the ocean, and feeling the warm breeze.

"Mikayla and I always wanted to come here when we were kids," Andrea said, breaking the silence. "Gram never wanted to come here, though."

"Why is that?" he asked. He had heard of Folly Beach even before his visit to Charleston. Seeing it in person, he understood why. It was one of the prettiest beaches he'd ever seen. Far nicer than what passed for a beach in Connecticut.

"She still remembers when Black folks weren't allowed here," Andrea replied.

Daren shook his head and looked around. "It really is beautiful, though."

"Spent the whole week showing you the worst this place has to offer. Figured I might as well bring you somewhere nice before you go." Andrea spoke softly while she stared out over the water, then took a deep breath. "I guess I wanted to come here, too. Something about the water calms me. It reminds me how small we are."

"This city has a lot of beauty," said Daren. "It's almost a shame."

"How do you mean?"

"I don't know... It's like you can almost see what it could be, but it can't let go of what it was. Like the city has one foot stuck in the past."

"I keep thinking about David's boy," said Andrea. "This therapist I go to talks about intergenerational trauma. It's like—horrible shit doesn't just affect the people it happens to. There are ripple effects because trauma changes folks. Makes them parent differently. So, they pass on that trauma to their children one way or another. But the children don't understand the pain they're carrying, and each generation is loaded with more trauma, and each following generation has to carry all that pain."

"Poor kid," Daren replied.

"And I think of my son," Andrea continued. "I think of what David did, and I—I could never even imagine doing that." She wiped the tears from her eyes. "But I have passed on my pain to him," she admitted. "In my own way, that pain has changed me and it caused me to put a wall between me and anyone I cared about. I think I thought that by keeping myself distant, I was giving him a chance—a chance to not inherit my bullshit. But all I really did was withhold my love from my son."

Daren didn't say anything. He just looked out over the water and thought about what she was saying.

"You can't avoid or outrun trauma," she added, shaking her head. "You can try, but until that trauma is acknowledged and addressed, it will keep being passed on, generation after generation. I keep thinking about that and thinking about this city and even this country. I think there's something there."

"I think you're right," Daren replied.

"I'm sorry," Andrea said with a sigh. "I've been spending a lot of time in my head today."

"I can understand that, you've been through hell," he remarked.

"Yeah, but I'm used to it," she said. "How you doing?"

"I can't sleep at night," Daren admitted. "I guess I've had trouble since Carson's, but after these past few days... It's been really rough."

"I'd like to tell you that you'll be alright, but it isn't that simple. I don't think anyone comes out of what we just saw okay."

"At first, I think I had trouble processing that I nearly died, but somehow now, having killed that man, I feel even worse."

"There's no easy way to process any of that," she told him. "Being on both sides of that equation doesn't make it any better."

"Yeah, I guess," he said. "The other part of it is that I still feel partly responsible for all this."

Andrea shook her head. "You can't change who you were or what you did," she told him. "You can't change the things you used to think. All any of us can do is take what we start with and try to grow. Try to learn."

"It's a lot to think about—to try and process."

"You should talk to someone," she urged. "Don't do what I did. Don't try to ignore it or run from it. It will catch up to you one way or another. Get professional help, Daren."

"Yeah…" He knew she was right, but the idea didn't sit well.

"I read your report," Andrea said.

"What did you think?" he asked, happy to change the subject.

"It's what happened, that's for sure," she replied after a moment. "You think that's what they want to hear?"

"Probably not," he admitted.

"It's admirable, but you know how it works. Nobody will see that report. At least, not all of it."

"Yeah," Daren conceded, waiting a moment to build suspense. "That's why I also sent copies to the Courier Post, the Times, and CNN."

Andrea grinned and shook her head. "So, you're leaving the FBI."

"Turned in my resignation letter this morning via email along with my report," Daren confirmed. "You should apply for my job, though."

"Damn, you must've damaged your brain when you were being held under water," she joked. "Why would I ever want to do that?"

"Because you were brave enough to join a police department in the South, and fight what needs to be done, and I think you could make a difference."

Andrea shook her head. "I don't even know if I made a difference here. I don't know that one person can."

"I think you know that isn't true," he countered. "It's just not as neat and simple as it ought to be. Change is hard."

"I don't know if the country can change, honestly," she replied, sadly.

"A country is just a bunch of people, right? So, if people can grow…"

"Maybe," she admitted. "But as far as taking your job, I'm going to stay where I am for now."

"That's good," he said. "I know you were having doubts, but I think they need you."

"I can make a hundred arguments why being a police officer is complicity to injustice," Andrea said. "But I can make a hundred more about the value of having representation in law enforcement, and how we need that to reform the system. Wherever power is making decisions that affect people's lives, people of color need to be in those rooms."

"That's admirable," he said.

"When a woman needs help, it will be me that shows up," she pledged. "When a Black person has been victimized, they'll see me, and they'll know I'm there to help." She looked down the pier at the families enjoying the summer day. "But for now, I'm going to spend some time with my family and grieve."

Daren nodded and checked his phone. "Well, I suppose I have a flight to catch. Gotta get home and find a job." He rose from his seat and extended his hand.

"Good luck, Daren." Andrea stood to shake his hand, then she hugged him. "I'm glad it was you," she said as they embraced. "No matter what path brought you here. I'm glad it was you."

"Thanks," he said with a sigh. "Good luck to you as well." He wanted to say more but couldn't find the words. He wanted to tell her that he would always remember her, and even more, he wanted to say something about the world they lived in—about how unfair it was.

But he realized she was already well aware. Then, with the acceptance that nothing he could say would be adequate, nor ease her pain or provide her with any semblance of closure, he walked away.

About the Author

KEITH FARRELL was born in Torrington, Connecticut, where he was raised by his single, working-class mother. An only child, Keith spent a lot of time daydreaming elaborate stories with his toy action figures. His storytelling soon progressed to writing. Often disinterested in class, Keith would disappear into his stories, pretending to take notes as he scribbled out pages of plot. He graduated from the University of Connecticut in 2013 with a B.A. in Urban Sociology and American Studies with an emphasis in law. In 2016, he moved to Charleston, South Carolina, where he lived with his wife for six years before returning to Connecticut. Keith has worked as a think tank researcher, substitute teacher, nonprofit founder, ghostwriter, and publisher. His first book, *The Line*, was published in 2018. He is currently writing a fictionalized memoir entitled, *This Will End in Tragedy*, and *The Toll*, a sequel to *The Line*.

CPSIA information can be obtained
at www.ICGtesting.com
Printed in the USA
BVHW082238250922
647977BV00017B/409

9 798985 287929